MIDNIGHT
AT SPANISH GARDENS

BY ALMA ALEXANDER

A riel said nothing, merely smiled, and held out a folded piece of paper. Simon instinctively reached out and took it.

"What is this?" Simon said.

"Instructions," said Ariel. "Should you choose to follow them."

There were only a few lines, in copperplate handwriting looking rather as though the entire thing had been penned by an old-fashioned nib pen. His eyebrows rose as he read.

Your life is filled with crossroads and you are free to choose one road or another at any time. Stepping through this door narrows your choices to only two - the choice to live a different life, or the choice to return to this one.

You make your first choice when you pass through the portal. Once you do, you will not remember the life you have left behind... until one single moment, when all memory will return.In that moment you must choose if you wish to return to your previous existence... or renounce it forever.

Remember this before you decide. Here, you change the world around you; there, you have to change to fit the world. Both are harder than you think. Choose wisely.

"Choose wisely," Simon said dryly. What is this...?" But when he looked up again, Ariel had gone.

Even as he looked away again, the writer part of Simon's brain was turning the idea over and over, dissecting it from different angles. You could choose? You could – in a manner of speaking – unchoose? Life was there to be sifted through and you could pick the bits you wanted, erase the things you would rather had never existed? It glittered before him like a jewel, the temptation, the chance to start again, to be young again...

OVERTURE

Thursday, 20 December 2012

Olivia could not believe how little had changed on the street where she stood. Twenty years had slipped by since she had last seen this place; twenty years, crumbling away with each step, days falling like leaves from autumnal branches and swirling around her feet. In an era where everything hurtled forward at a breakneck pace, where entire neighborhoods were swept away at a whim to create new malls or parking lots or great gleaming edifices of steel and glass with forlorn 'For Lease: Office Space' signs growing old and faded in empty windows, this particular street seemed to have remained alarmingly faithful to Olivia's memory of it—back in the days when she was young, at the top of the world, invincible, immortal.

In fact, it was a little disconcerting to allow herself to realize that the single thing that had changed the most from the way things used to be twenty years ago was... herself.

Well, but that's as it should be, she thought, allowing herself a little philosophical shrug.

But it was also... wrong. Wrong that everything else should be so changeless and immutable while she alone was the flotsam on the river of life, being carried hither and yon as the currents willed it, being allowed to tarry nowhere, only to find herself apparently cast back on the same shores she thought she'd left a long time ago.

The short winter twilight had passed while she lingered in the oddly empty street, wasting time, peering at shop windows and trying to recall if they were in fact identical to those she remembered being there before, or if she was just painting a mental landscape with the things that she knew ought to be there. There ought to have been a notebook in her bag—there always was, she carried one by what was part instinct and part ritual, but when she rooted around for it this time, at the moment when she really needed it, the thing seemed to have disappeared.

No matter. Her mind's eye would do She would transcribe later; it might not be the same, it might not be as good as it came in the instant when she was standing here resting her eyes on the scenery, but enough would remain. In the meantime, she rolled up her mental sleeves and sat down in front of a blank screen in the back of her mind, her hands poised over a keyboard that wasn't there.

A cursor blinked momentarily as she did a slow, apprising circle, raking the street up and down with a writer's recording stare.

Evening You walk down a shuttered street; there are "Closed" signs in shop windows and on doors as you stroll past Illuminated displays of things. This is not Rodeo Drive; you're likely to see cheap, ordinary shoes. Maybe tools. Printed T-shirts. A bicycle shop.

Olivia's footsteps seemed loud on the empty pavement. Things looked wet—as though it had recently rained, but not rained hard; not nearly enough water for puddles, just barely wet enough to reflect back the glow of street lights in a strange and oddly magical manner—as though it was not so much reflection that she was seeing but that the asphalt had turned transparent, revealing glimpses of an upside-down world beneath her feet.

She reached a gap between buildings—a narrow alley which someone who did not know that it was there would have probably missed completely, or dismissed as an insignificant cul-de-sac—and paused, glancing up and down the street again, and then down the short alleyway. The mind-screen woke again; words appeared in the wake of the blinking cursor.

A narrow alley opens between two buildings. There are no signs, nothing to indicate that it leads anywhere at all. But you turn.

The alley was lit dimly at the street end by a fluorescent sign hanging from the shop front facing the street on the corner, and at the far end by an old-fashioned collared street light with a large yellow bulb, barely pooling enough light at its foot to show that the alley was paved with irregular cobbles. Ordinarily this was the kind of place that might have been regarded with wariness, even suspicion—a mugger's lair where a single female should never venture alone—but that sense of vague danger was window-dressing, camouflage, and the far end of the alley was barely a dozen steps away. At the other end it opened up…

Olivia closed her eyes briefly, conjuring up the lay of the land in the courtyard at the far end. The words on her mind's eye-screen helpfully spilled into the space she had left for them.

The passageway between a couple of blank brick walls widens abruptly into a courtyard. There is a doorway, dark now, with some sort of gilt writing on the glass. An accountant, maybe, or a dentist—I forget what it was, and maybe it even changed once or twice during my time here. And across the courtyard, dimly lit, a coy sign above the door, there it is, Spanish Gardens.

It does not look very Spanish. It certainly doesn't look anything like a garden.

And then she was there, under the far light, and she opened her eyes…and smiled to herself, a little grimly. She might have stepped back in time, so much alike was it to what she remembered.

She paused for the longest time, staring at that door, at that sign.

The outside of that side of the courtyard was utilitarian. So ordinary, in fact, so far from being special, that Olivia wondered just by what kind of alchemy it had lingered in her memory with the kind of etched precision that it did. The door itself was a perfectly mundane metal frame, spare to the point of being almost industrial, with somewhat dusty glass, inscribed with the hours of opening (late afternoon, night; to this kind of place daylight was never kind). Next to it, a large shop window, with one of those half-curtains like one would expect to see in cafés or neat suburban kitchens, leaving the top part of the window open. Through the glass, it was just possible to glimpse the top of the till—not precisely antique, but not computerized, either— still obstinately analog, old-fashioned.

The glass door opened to a view of a narrow room, one side almost entirely taken up with a glass-fronted display cabinet such as one would expect to find in an old-fashioned neighborhood deli or a pastry shop, and the other side, against the wall, crammed with a couple of small tables covered with red and white checked tablecloths and flanked by pairs of old-fashioned wooden chairs, no two of them alike.

Olivia stepped closer and was somehow not surprised to see that over at the far end of the glass display case, beside a crimson-curtained doorway above which hung signs pointing the way to the restrooms, sat a tall bar stool surrounded by a mike and an amplifier and a couple of speakers. It was currently unoccupied, but she remembered all too clearly the young, long-haired troubadours of twenty years ago perched on that very stool, or one just like it, strumming guitars and crooning songs like "Starry Starry Night" and songs by John Lennon.

At first glance through that door, the interior of the place was cramped to the point of claustrophobia, once you factored in a coat rack and a line of hooks on the wall waiting to receive coats and jackets. But next to the table furthest from the entrance, there was an arched opening to another room. It had a further cluster of red-check-tableclothed tables and mismatched wooden chairs. A large blackboard adorned most of the far wall, festooned with graffiti from previous patrons, an ever-changing display. One couldn't see it from the vantage point of the entrance, but Olivia knew that just above the archway, facing into the second room, hung the only other piece of art in the place—a framed print of a bullfight, with a charging black bull and a matador resplendent in gold with a red cape flourished jauntily. The only nod to Spain in the place, if one didn't count the presence of the occasional guitar.

She pushed the door open. It gave after a slight resistance The oil lanterns on the tables had been lit, and the flames behind glass globes, grayed by years of smoke, flickered sturdily, leaving soft edgeless shadows pooling on the tables and the walls. If that had been the only available light, the place would have been cave-dark, but there were other lights strategically fastened to available walls—muted, to be sure, covered in dusty shades that made the light a mellow reddish orange-gold. Perhaps it was that permanent half-light that changed the place, metamorphosing it from shabby to enchanted. One entire wall of it, facing into the courtyard, was no more than a couple of huge plate glass windows—but it was impossible to tell that from the inside, where the harshness of that enormous expanse of cold glass was softened by an almost theatrical floor-to-ceiling red-plush curtain. In a more garish light it might have looked cheap and contrived; in what light there was, it looked mysterious, warm, inviting, intriguing—as though one was on the stage, on the wrong side of the curtain, waiting with a sense of rising excitement for the curtain to go up and show you the audience beyond.

Olivia stepped inside and allowed her eyes to fall sideways at the glass deli cabinet. There were things on display here, pies and pastries. The laminated menus in metal holders on the individual tables also offered burgers and fries, pasta, toasted sandwiches, and soup. The food was always plain but substantial here—because this was a student place, had always been, knowledge of it passed like arcane secrets from senior to freshman through time-honored underground channels, advertised nowhere except by word of mouth. A scattering of the usual clientele occupied the main room, girls with pony tails and fresh faces, young men with long hair and intense eyes, leaning across the tables toward one another, fingers intertwined between them on the tabletop.

Oh, dear God.

Olivia closed her eyes briefly. The cursor on the screen in her mind's eyes blinked briefly, words falling after it in another burst of memory.

This was a place of celebrations—you would come here for your graduations, your anniversaries. Young women with long lanky hair and bold eyes were given wine-red roses at these utilitarian, almost dingy, tables, and their memory of it is glamoured in a romantic spell. You bring your girlfriend here to propose…

Four times. Four times she had been asked that question in this place. She could remember each occasion quite vividly—twice it had happened almost by accident, meant more as a joke than anything else; the third time, over at the table in the far corner right underneath the blackboard, the potential groom-to-be had been broken quite recently by a rejection of a similar proposal made to another girl, the love of his life, a friend of Olivia's. Initially he had brought Olivia there to pour out his misery to her. The proposal came out of nowhere, had been slipped into his tale of woe born out of sheer desperation. The evening had ended badly—because Olivia had come out with the young man as a friend, because she could listen and commiserate, and had been entirely blindsided by the sudden switch in his focus. Rejecting him was the only thing to do, but she remembered feeling like dirt, stammering, groping blindly for words that would not slice like flensing knives and yet would not come out resembling anything remotely like an intention to even seriously consider the question. They both knew the proposal for what it was—and yet there was a thread of seriousness there, and if she had uttered anything close to a yes he would have taken it as a promise. He had finally gone very white, very quiet, and they had left early, knowing that they would never see each other again—after that night, it would have been entirely too excruciating to endure one another's company.

The fourth time it had been Sam, and she had accepted, flushed and flustered; there had been a ring and the resident troubadour on the bar stool had smiled and had sung… something appropriate…

"Oh I can't have possibly forgotten," Olivia muttered to herself, aggrieved, astonished that she could remember every nuance of the scene except the soundtrack. But it was no use, the song was gone, vanished—and the only memory that remained was that she had broken the engagement less than a month later, and fled the city, and had not come back for years.

"Forgotten?" asked a cheerful, pleasant male voice to her left.

She turned her head slightly, eyebrow slightly raised, and met a pair of friendly smoke-gray eyes of a young man vigorously drying some glassware with a clean cloth behind the deli counter. Olivia's first thought was that she could have sworn there had been nobody there a moment ago. Her second was that he looked uncannily familiar. It's as though he and the counter, he and the whole place, were part of a seamless whole—as though he must have been standing there just like this when Olivia had walked out of the place in stiff silence with the young man whose rebound proposal she had just fumbled in turning down—or even when she had floated out on a cloud of short-lived euphoria when she had left with the one whose proposal she had accepted It was odd, how she almost… recognized him. And yet he was nondescript, almost calculated to be erased from memory—average height, average build, hair that was neither blond nor brown, his only outstanding features those astonishing eyes and possibly the long-fingered hands working the cloth in the glass.

Olivia shook her head, her lips twitching up into a slight smile.

"Ah," she said, with a self-deprecating little shrug "I forget a lot of things these days."

"That's what some people come here for," he said. "To forget stuff."

Olivia's eyebrows came together in a puzzled frown. "What do you mean?"

"Unless they come here to remember stuff," the young man said enigmatically.

"It looks just the same," Olivia said, almost reflexively, glancing around as she began to unbutton her coat.

"That's the point," he said, putting the glass down.

"The point of what…?"

"It looks the same. It looked the same twenty years ago, or ten, or two, or last month, or last week. The world ends tomorrow, according to some, and it still looks the same on the eve of that. There is nothing that will change this place. Ever."

Olivia stared at him. "I'm sorry, do I know you? You look awfully familiar…"

"I don't think so," he said cheerfully.

"So you changed?" Olivia asked. "This place never changes… but you're new?"

"Perhaps," he said cryptically. "I'm Ariel."

"Get out of here."

"Pardon?"

"Sorry," she said, looking embarrassed. "It isn't…a common name. Last time I saw it, I think I was reading Shakespeare."

Ariel had the grace to laugh. "It could be worse," he said cheerfully. "Can I be of assistance?"

"I'm meeting a bunch of people here tonight—I don't suppose any of them are here yet…?" Olivia said.

"Nobody who said they were meeting a bunch of people," Ariel said. "But the big table over in the corner—the one with the bench—you can go grab that, if you like. I'm sure your friends will be here soon."

"Thanks."

As she turned away, Spanish Gardens reached for her and swallowed her whole. Whether she was one of those who came to remember or to forget, she didn't know—but the place was redolent with memory anyway. The cursor in her mind's eye blinked at her, and more words spilled out on the waiting screen.

You come here in a rowdy crowd after the pomp and circumstance of the graduation ceremony, and you order Irish Coffees ("Keep 'em coming!") and you get beautifully, headily, cathartically tipsy while some crooner weaves his way through "House of the Rising Sun" on his high chair and you bellow the lyrics with him when you can actually remember them. You came here to laugh, and to cry, and to share, and to grow, and to guzzle cream pies and to linger over coffee after some sad movie show, and to be able to tell some newcomer, somewhere, sometime, "Ah, yes I know the Spanish Gardens".

Irish Coffees. *That*, she remembered. The cheap and plentiful food was not the real reason that this place was a legend with generations of students It was the Irish Coffees—this place made the best Irish Coffees on the planet, bar none.

Olivia's mouth curved into a wider smile.

"You guys still do Irish Coffees?" she flung at Ariel over her shoulder, reaching to hang up her coat on a free hook on the wall.

"Sure do," he said.

"Send one over to the big table with the bench," Olivia said.

"Make that two."

The new voice made Olivia turn so fast that she nearly dropped the coat in a heap on the floor Just inside the narrow entrance, a man stood looking at her, one eyebrow lifted in inquiry.

"John...?" Olivia said carefully.

"I've changed *that* much?" John asked, sounding a little plaintive.

"Hardly at all, actually, if you disregard the gray on the temples and a little, um, *broader* than you used to be," Olivia said. "There was a time you could practically disappear if you turned sideways..." She bit off the rest of the sentence, flushing. This was the kind of banter that she used to be able to have with John; it suddenly seemed presumptuous to assume that she could just pick it up where she left off, with both of them twenty years older.

"Yeah, well," John said with a grin, apparently unconcerned by Olivia's misgivings. "Aside from the fact that your hair was *never* that color and that you have the tiniest touch of laugh lines where there weren't any before...I'd have known you anywhere."

"Old friends?" Ariel asked, with a knowing smile. "Two Irish Coffees, coming right up."

Olivia dropped her gaze, suddenly awkward; her hands tightened around her coat. She suddenly wanted to *hide* it, to bundle it out of sight—the bright red coat with its fetching cowl that could be raised as a hood, the coat she had loved, the coat that she had walked out of her home in when she had walked out on her marriage carrying only an overnight duffel bag, a laptop case, and a battered teddy bear under one arm. The coat that had matched the Olivia whom John remembered—the girl with hair the color of French-roasted coffee or of bitter chocolate, not the dark auburn that she wore now and that suddenly and hopelessly clashed with the bright red of the coat, something Olivia had not noticed until now, had not cared.

The coat that had her initials—her initials—*then*—monogrammed onto its lapel in elegant cursive: OHB, Olivia Halloran Boyes. Irrationally, helplessly, she would have given the world right now for that B to be erased, for John never to have to see it, for her never to have to answer questions about it, or to defend it, or to *explain*.

But John showed no indication that he had noticed. He had shrugged out of his own jacket, generic yellow-and-black Goretex, and draped it untidily over the nearest coat hook. When he did reach for Olivia's coat, it was just a gentlemanly gesture.

"Let me help you with that," he said. "Let's go sit. The rest of them should be along shortly."

"Why did I ever think that coming back here would be a good idea?" Olivia muttered under her breath as she turned away from the coat racks and led the way to the big table in the corner where she had been told to go.

She slipped onto the bench, on the edge of it, leaving John the choice of coming around the far side to slide down the length of the table, if he wanted to sit beside her, or to take one of the chairs on the opposite side. He did the latter, smiling a small crooked smile; Olivia kept her eyes down on the shadows dancing on the tablecloth. One of her hands, flat against the side of the bench, rubbed experimentally against the material upholstering the seat.

"Can you call this Naugahide?" she said, apparently apropos of nothing. "I've often wondered what a Nauga looked like, or if they were killed humanely in order for their hides to be sat upon..."

John rolled his eyes a little. "And this, *before* you've had your first Irish Coffee...Simon phoned me earlier, he said he and Ellen are going to be running just a little late—he said to go ahead and order something to nibble before they get here if we're starving."

"Ellen's late, eh," Olivia said, looking up with a smile. "Oh, *God*, this brings back memories. Ellen was *always* late. She never wore a watch, and she behaved as though time itself was the Devil's construct made just to annoy her. I remember her falling into lectures ten minutes after they started, tripping over people's bags, causing complete havoc and bringing everything to a standstill until she was settled, the center of attention, waving to everyone like a queen..."

"I always thought that was the point, rather," John said.

"What?"

"The being late. The being the center of attention. Hey, don't knock it, it worked. I did think that having kids might have beaten it out of her, though. Children have regimented lives— the first time she tried being 'late' to a 2 AM feed she would have been disabused of the notion of using the lateness quirk to hog the spotlight. The screaming kid gets the spotlight. Every time."

"Speaking from experience?" Olivia asked, lifting an eyebrow.

John shook his head "No No kids. Never married. I heard you did, though—"

Olivia made a small sharp gesture with her hand. "Lasted only long enough to cure me."

"Cure you? Of what?"

"Being a romantic. Remember what Simon said to me, twenty years ago, in this very room...?"

"Should I?" John asked, sounding startled.

"He was passing down his oracular pronouncements on everyone's future, that time we came here after graduation, remember? He told you that you were the person who would damn well prove that hard work and dedication really could be enough because you'd get whatever you went after..."

"That didn't turn out too well," John said. "Sometimes life *is* just a crap shoot. But what was it that he told you?"

"He said..." Olivia began.

"He said, 'You? You are just misguided'," a new voice said, from the archway separating the two rooms.

Olivia turned, and John pushed back his chair, getting to his feet, his face cracking into a broad grin.

"Quincey! Q! You look great! It's so good to see you!"

"All right, all right, down," said Quincey, making warding-off gestures—but her face was wreathed in a matching grin as she ran one hand through close-cropped blonde hair. "Let me get rid of this coat..."

"Two Irish Coffees," a girl wearing a small black apron over tight pants and a short-sleeved white peasant top said, setting two tall glasses on the table between Olivia and John.

"Hey," Quincey said, "you can bring another of those, next time you swing by."

"Sure," the girl said, spinning on her heel in an almost balletic motion and skipping back behind a curtain that separated the café from the kitchen area.

"I was never that young," Olivia groaned, watching her go.

"Yeah, you were. But you left it all in a heap right here in this room and they feed on it. It's the picture of Dorian Grey, all over again. We age, and they never do, the people who work in this place. They never get a day older than eighteen," said Quincey. "Budge up. You're taking up the whole bench."

"Well, that's depressing," Olivia said, shifting up a space so that Quincey could slip sideways onto the edge-of-the-bench seat she had claimed earlier.

"Is Simon here yet, or are we just talking about him behind his back?" Quincey asked, settling back against the wall.

"Late," John said.

"Figures, if Ellen's in the picture. Even the end of the world doesn't make the gears grind faster," Quincey said, glancing at her watch. "I meant to have something to eat *before* I got here but time got away from me. Can we order a basket of garlic bread, at least? I've waited on Ellen often enough to know that I'll be ready to eat *her* by the time she gets here."

Olivia glanced sideways at Quincey's long, lanky body, lean and tight, not an ounce of extra weight anywhere on her. When she had first spoken, she had been leaning against the archway—a woman in her forties who might have been poured into her jeans, her long-fingered, slender hands bare of ornamentation except for one silver and turquoise ring, a close-fitting long-sleeved t-shirt outlining her small breasts, a loose man's shirt that she wore over the top of it, flat-bellied, long-legged, slim.

"How do you do it?" Olivia asked, smiling, but serious. "How do you stay looking like that? Someone with an appetite big enough to devour Ellen shouldn't have your hips, damn it all. All I have to do is *think* about a box of chocolates and the pounds appear on my backside just like magic."

"Stress," Quincey said.

"If you could sell that as a diet you would make a mint," Olivia said.

"Your coffee," said the girl with the pony tail, setting another glass before Quincey.

John leaned his elbow on the table beside his own coffee, pillowing his face in his hand, staring at Olivia with frank curiosity.

"What?" she said, a touch defensively.

"You really did drop out of the world," John said. "After we all sailed off in different directions, we all...somehow kept in touch with each other's lives All except you. You know nothing about any of us, and I have no real idea what you've done with yourself since you walked off the stage with your diploma."

"She's got something deep dark and terrible to hide," Quincey said, grinning.

"So do we all," John said.

"I know all about everyone's lives I knew it before everyone else knew it, sometimes. I knew about Simon's book long before it was a book," Olivia said, suddenly feeling as though she was supposed to defend her life and her attitudes. "I read it when it was an embryo of a draft. I know more about the origins of it than you all..." She broke off, took a deep breath. "I read Ellen's books when they came out. Ellen and Simon got married. Quincey got married, divorced and married."

"Only because you were invited to the weddings. But you didn't come."

"I kept track. I know who's had kids."

"Only because we're here today because Ellen and Simon's Abby turned 21 yesterday. And that's odd too—you don't come for their wedding, but it's okay to come to a reunion of the old crowd, in *this* place, on the flimsy excuse that Simon and Ellen's daughter is turning 21 and you weren't even going to the party?"

"I got her a present," Olivia said.

John raised an eyebrow but said nothing, sipping his coffee. Olivia suddenly shivered, looking around at the dimly lit room.

"I can't believe this place is still here," she said in a low voice, as though she was trying to prevent the café from overhearing. "I was fully expecting it to be gone by now, probably gone for a good few years—the whole shebang, the red curtains, the checked tablecloths, the secret recipe for Irish Coffee, the guitars, even that wretched picture of the bullfight, *everything*. I thought it was a memory, only living on in my head. And yet my feet brought me here by themselves, apparently without any conscious effort on my part, and it's all still here, exactly like I remember it. I could almost swear that the same guy was behind the counter when we first came here. And you don't think that's weird?"

The door to the café opened and closed again. Quincey swiveled around in her seat, Irish Coffee precariously tilted, to peer through the arch and back into the entrance hallway And then swiveled back, placing her glass on the table with slow deliberation.

"It's Ellen," she said. "No sign of Simon."

"He may be parking the car," John said. "I had to park a couple of blocks away—circled this one twenty times before I gave up on finding anything closer."

But that wasn't what Quincey had meant.

"Livy," she said quickly, turning to Olivia, "you *really* haven't seen Ellen since college?"

"I've seen the author photograph," Olivia said. "I know she's turned rather gray, that she doesn't dye it, and that she's cut her hair. I also know that she's not...."

"I wasn't asking if you would recognize Ellen in the street. Have you actually spoken to her at all since...?"

Olivia shook her head mutely, and Quincey was out of her seat in one fluid motion, apparently wrapping herself at right-angles around the corner to head off Ellen at the pass.

"Ellen! You made it! We've a basket of garlic bread on order, but for once you arrived before the emergency provisions..."

Quincey's voice was bright and chatty, but Olivia's face was white and pinched, and John, his eyes snapping from Quincey's back as she retreated around the corner to Olivia's expression, frowned slightly.

"I have a feeling I am missing something," he said.

Olivia managed a wan smile. "I daresay you won't be, by the time this night is over. You may want to watch for sudden ice in your coffee...depending on how Ellen plays this..."

The voices from beyond the archway had dropped into near-silence, but now they lifted again, into a more normal range. Quincey stepped back out into the main room wearing an odd, slightly fixed smile.

"Is it safe?" she mouthed at Olivia.

Olivia's reply, a slight toss of her head, was ambiguous in the extreme—but they were out of time, and Quincey was followed into the room by another woman, shorter than Quincey by a head even in reasonably high heels, her silver-gray hair falling about her face in carefully styled waves. She wore a shade of lipstick that was perhaps a little too garish for the circumstances, leaning rather too far into scarlet to sit comfortably on any face other than something from a publicity poster for a Hollywood starlet of an era where they still showed lovers smoking in bed after the fade-to-black scene—it was as though she had tried to cast about for a way to recapture a lost youth, and missed. But her eyes were the same eyes that Olivia remembered—an unusual shade, a warm golden brown, what Olivia had once called cat-amber. The scarlet mouth was curved into a slight smile, but it had not yet reached those eyes—the eyes were a little wide, wary, sweeping swiftly around the room and then homing in on Olivia's own gaze, which they met and held.

Some part of Olivia was aware of her surroundings—aware of the way that Quincey's breath was suddenly held for a little too long, of the way that John's expression deepened in puzzlement—but mostly she saw only Ellen's face, curiously superimposed on the face from her own memory of an Ellen two decades younger, and trying to recapture something of what the two of them had shared back then.

The smile she had painted on her face for John widened a small, painful notch.

So did Ellen's.

"It's been a while," Olivia said at last, because somebody had to say something.

Quincey let her breath out slowly.

"Yes," Ellen said faintly. "Hasn't it."

"Scootch up, Livy," Quincey said with sudden determination. "I'll squish in next to you and Ellen can perch on the end."

Olivia obeyed meekly, shifting even further along the Naugahide bench, reaching out to pull her Irish Coffee after her along the countertop. Quincey, who seemed to think that it was a good idea to keep a warm body between Olivia and Ellen, at least for the first part of the evening, slid in after her and Ellen obediently sat down on the same outside corner which Olivia herself had started out at, trying to get John to choose the chair rather than the bench.

There was a slightly awkward silence, and then Ellen smiled.

"I'd forgotten about the Irish Coffees," she said. "Are they still as good?"

"Better," John said. "I've had twenty years to wait for one. The anticipation kind of adds to the spice."

Ellen caught the eye of one of the passing waitresses, and then pointed to Quincey's glass. "Another," she said.

Olivia drained hers, and put the empty glass with its foam-smeared side back on the table rather too hard. "Make that two."

"My God," Ellen said, placing her hands on the table before her and lacing her fingers tightly together before finally giving the room a closer appraisal, "it's like a time machine…"

Quincey coughed slightly over a mouthful of coffee, and

Olivia looked away, into her empty glass.

"Hasn't changed," she said. "We have."

Ellen appeared to gather together whatever shreds she could of dignity and civility and grown-up politeness—but also a veneer of cautious coolness in her face—and turned to Olivia across the barrier of Quincey's rangy body.

"We may as well get it over with," she said. "You didn't stick around long enough, before. But for what it's worth, I'm sorry. For the circumstances, possibly not for the event itself, given the outcome—which was, after all, Abby, who is now improbably enough 21 years old and is the reason we're all here in the first place. Possibly it was rash and misguided—but we were both so young…"

"Simon wasn't," Olivia said.

"Simon was misguided," Ellen snapped.

And then, somehow, they both managed a real grin, in unison. This was going to be one of those nights. Simon's words had come full circle—he had called Olivia the same thing once, in this very place, and now Ellen was turning the tables.

Ellen leaned over and stuck out a hand across Quincey.

"Truce?" she asked. "Please? If you want to, we can have a catfight outside later. But for now—when Simon comes back in after finding a parking spot hopefully within the same zip code as this place—truce?"

"Truce," Olivia said, reaching back to slip her hand into Ellen's briefly—very briefly, without squeezing, it was a truce after all and not a peace accord.

"Oh, thank God," Ellen said, sitting back. "I was actually *dreading* tonight. Just a little. At some point, I can probably explain—but until then, let's not talk about it."

"About *what*?" John muttered under his breath.

Olivia favored him with one stern glance that made him subside in his chair, looking rebellious and suddenly very much younger, as though he really did belong with the young bodies which had begun to cluster around the tables surrounding theirs.

When Olivia turned back to Ellen, it was to a deeply understanding smile which, this time, reached into cat-amber eyes. Ellen had noticed the exchange.

"So, tell me," Olivia said. "How are the books doing?"

"Mine or his?" Ellen asked.

"The family oeuvre," Quincey said, happy to nudge the conversation into less fraught channels.

"His...critically acclaimed, and up for two major prizes this year. Mine... selling like hot cakes, thankfully, but being rather sniffily reviewed, if they are reviewed at all. The latest one I let get under my skin spoke of the wife of the acclaimed novelist who has published a few—what did they call them—'slight' volumes of children's stories on her own behalf. As though I've ridden Simon's coat-tails all the way into this. As though it is possible to ride *those* coat-tails and get to the place that I am at—which is on a different planet from him, really. We are so not writing the same..."

"Whoa," John said, laughing, flinging up both hands in a defensive gesture. "Feels like someone kicked over a wasp nest."

Ellen shut her mouth with a snap, flushing a little. "Sorry," she said. "Sometimes it just bugs me. And it isn't often I get a chance to let it out when Simon isn't over there in the corner, listening in. It feels rather too much like sour grapes when he's listening. And it's not—it's *not.* It's just that it's all so different and all anyone ever sees is..." She stopped again, closed her eyes for a moment as though she were centering herself, and then turned to Olivia again.

"Seems everything's unsteady ground," she said, with a lopsided grin. "Well, there's mine, in all its boggy grandeur. Your turn?"

"Nothing much," Olivia said. "This and that. Never quite got around to using the actual degree. Floated on the surface of the stream, waited to see where I'd wash up."

Ellen glanced at Olivia's hands. The ring finger was bare, but she wore rings on other fingers and the bareness suddenly seemed to stand out in stark relief; Olivia surreptitiously folded her left hand under her right, hiding the evidence.

"I thought I read in the society pages that you *did* get married," Ellen murmured, and then bit her lip.

"Oh-ho?" John said. "The society pages?"

"She married a Vanderbilt," Quincey said, with just a touch of acid, but the look she turned on Olivia was sympathetic—*You might as well get it over with,* it said.

"A *Vanderbilt*?" John said, sitting up. "I thought they were extinct."

"They're a family, not a clutch of Velociraptors," Quincey said, a little sharply. "Of course they aren't extinct. But even so, it was meant as a metaphor."

"Boyes," Olivia said faintly. Her voice was very soft, but every one of the others turned toward her instantly, as though she had shouted the name out loud "His name was Brandon Boyes, all right? And yes, he's a 'Vanderbilt', if you want to use that as a qualifier—his family's got money, and we moved into an apartment in New York, Upper West Side, and all that jazz."

John blinked. "And?"

"And what?"

"Well, you're here. And there's no point in sitting on your hands, we all noticed there's no ring. You don't have to tell us anything, Olivia, but we used to be friends."

Olivia flushed darkly, staring down into her lap. And then, looking up, met the eyes of everyone at the table for a moment.

"Fine," she said, and she felt as though she was trying to talk through a mouthful of molasses. "If you *have* to know. The whole thing was a cliché, really. I met Brand because he collided with me in a coffee shop and poured scalding coffee down my arm—luckily I was wearing a padded jacket and it didn't actually burn me but the thing was dripping wet with hot coffee and it *did* drip down onto my hand and it was still hot, and I dropped the book I was holding and then just stood there and looked shell-shocked while he fussed around and apologized fourteen times in the space of the next five minutes… and after that I found myself having dinner in posh places which were so exclusive there were no signs outside the building that indicated there was a restaurant there at all…"

"Kind of like this place," John murmured.

Quincey cut him down with a look, and he subsided.

"The courtship lasted four months, and then he asked me to marry him and I said yes because he turned my head," Olivia said. "It took the next *six* months to mollify his mother, and I suppose that should have been the clue I needed—I kind of went home in tears several times, but Brand said not to take it personally, that she was a bitch to everybody—well, he didn't say *that*, he would never say a bad word about momma, but that was the gist of all the paraphrasing that he did—and that all I needed to was to learn to ignore her. Just like he did. Or so he said."

"What happened?" Quincey asked gently.

Olivia shrugged. "We got married, eventually. That was the society pages, Ellen. I wore a designer gown, and the flowers I was carrying cost more than a dinner for four in the Village. There were pictures. Everyone said I looked very happy. Everyone said that mother-in-law *tried* to look happy. I learned very quickly, after, that she really was the power behind the throne. There was no decision in our household that didn't need to be vetted by Mother, and if Mother said no then that was that. And she said no rather a lot, especially if she thought that the idea she was vetting had originated from me. *Particularly* then. And when I was married for less than half a year she began planting the seeds—that I was still not pregnant, that the only reason her precious boy had married me was because he wanted a kid, and when was I going to, um, so to speak, deliver? And the thing is, it didn't really matter to us—not then, not in the beginning, if the children came they would come. But then Brand started getting obsessed with the idea, and the more he did the less I wanted it—because it had started to feel a lot like I had been bought and paid for, and only to be used for the purpose or creating the next generation to inherit it...."

Quincey said nothing, only reached out and covered Olivia's hand with her own.

"Well," Olivia said, taking a deep breath. "To cut a long story short. It came to a head. Hurtful things were said...and *meant*. Brand didn't exactly raise his hand to me, not right then, but the look in his eyes told me that it could come to that... if his precious Mama told him to do it. And if I did have a child in this toxic atmosphere, it would be taken from me at birth and indoctrinated with the proper attitude, until I was no more important than the wallpaper in the nursery. That was the end of it. I felt like I'd just woken up from a nice pleasant dream—but that nothing in that dream was mine. I walked out of the apartment while he slept, at two in the morning, and I took what would fit into an overnight bag, and my computer, and the bear my mother gave me when I was two years old because the poor thing might have been stuffed and inanimate but I couldn't even think about leaving him behind in that apartment. He was mine, I took him there, and it was up to me to take him out. That, as they say, is that. From there… to now."

"So what have you been doing since you walked out?"

"This and that. Made do. I've had what people like to refer to as an interesting life. It did seem to consist of jumping from ice floe to ice floe on a dark river while the ice was breaking up under my feet and trying to keep my balance. My father had a Mencken quote stuck above his desk for years—I don't remember it precisely, but what it boiled down to was that truth and error are not opposite, that the opposite of an error may simply be another error, sometimes worse than the first…"

"I kind of remember it," John said. "Something along the lines of, 'The world makes the assumption that the exposure of an error is identical with the discovery of truth, that truth and error are simply opposite. They are nothing of the sort.' And that when the world is cured of one error it usually turns to another, probably worse than the first…"

"So you think you made a mistake, leaving?"

Olivia shook her head. "Some romantic remnant in me sometimes thinks so. But that particular ice floe disintegrated long ago. All right, we've done me. Can we change the subject now? Or, rather, you guys do. Excuse me for a sec I think I need to go visit the restroom and give myself a bit of a pep talk in the mirror."

She had begun sidling out of the bench before she finished talking, and slipped free as she finished, grabbing her handbag by its long handles as though she were strangling it by the neck and making her escape through the archway before any of the others could react at all.

"Wow," Ellen said, after a beat. "I had no idea I'd break *that* dam. Serves me right, trying to deflect fire from my own petty concerns."

"Is she going to be all right?" John said anxiously, trying to peer after Olivia through the archway.

"I think she'd rather a moment of being alone right now," Quincey murmured.

But Olivia, who had paused by the coat racks to lean unsteadily on the wall with one hand and try and catch her breath, was not allowed any such luxury. In her hurry to leave, with no real destination in mind other than to be momentarily free of others' eyes, she had forgotten they were expecting another companion, and had turned her back to the door.

When the voice came from behind her, familiar and barely changed by the twenty years that had passed, she froze for a moment, like a hunted hare.

"Olivia...?"

She turned on her heel, sharply, her arms not so much crossed as grasping one another, her fingers and knuckles white with pressure where they gripped the complementary elbow.

Simon's hair had also turned gray, but he had kept all of it, and almost kept the old style he used to wear it in—slightly longer than a respected novelist and a University professor ought by rights to wear it and be considered respectable, waving back from his forehead just like it had used to do when he was still her brother's best friend, and her own heart's desire.

Her mouth curved in what might, in other circumstances, have been described as a smile but there was something in her eyes that made Simon actually take a step back as if he had been struck. It might have been a smile, once. Right now, it was a slash of pain.

"For God's sake, what did I *do*?" Simon demanded, his eyebrows coming together in a bewildered frown.

"You remind me," Olivia said savagely, skipping small talk entirely.

"Of what?"

"Of all the things you were. Of all the things that David could have been."

"David...?" Simon sounded thrown. That was a name from

the past, and not, for better or worse, one he had come here armed to deal with. He made a valiant effort to regroup. "David made his own choices. I was hardly his conscience."

"You were his friend."

Simon shut his mouth with a snap. "Not his keeper," he said finally, tightly leashed, his control of the words that left his mouth almost visible. "But I don't think David is really the matter."

"He was the origin."

"Of what?"

"Of my own life. Of the things that I went on to do once David chose what he chose—and then you weighed in—everything went bad, after that."

"Let's see If I remember correctly, David enlisted and went to the Gulf. Your family shredded into political streamers and your mother is still not talking to your father who is not really speaking to you—well, that *was* the situation, and I think it's still pretty much current, knowing what I do about your father. And you, once upon a time, talked to me about it…"

"I told you all the things that David told me. I showed you the letters. You were his friend."

"Yes…and then I wrote a book about it," Simon said "That's one of the flashpoints, isn't it?"

"You used him," Olivia whispered.

"*Used* him? Liv, I wrote about the horrors of it I wrote what *you* thought. Not what David wrote about. He was proud of what he was; I don't think you will find much of that in the book that I wrote. I was against the damned war. Same as you."

"You were against it for all the wrong reasons." Olivia said.

"Which are? Does it really *matter*?"

"It mattered then," Olivia said "It mattered enough, back then, to make for a nice bonfire, anyway. One I burned a lot of things on."

Simon crossed his own arms, leaning back a little. "You built it," he said. "The bonfire."

"You betrayed my confidence, and your friend," Olivia said. "And then, when I called you on it, when you showed me the first draft of the book…"

"I remember it well," Simon said. "I've never seen you that furious, or that inarticulate. You *shrieked.*"

"I never shriek."

"You did then My neighbors came around after you stormed out to ask who won World War Three. You don't even remember it."

Olivia tilted her head a little. "It's a little... hazy."

"Incandescent rage will do that," Simon said dryly.

"And then you slept with my best friend," Olivia said, her voice suddenly flat and level, icy. The best friend in question was currently only the thickness of a brick wall away—Simon's wife, now, mother of his children. "Was that payback?"

"I thought you had just broken up with me," Simon said.

"But...*Ellen,*" Olivia said helplessly, unable to articulate the burden of all the hurt and betrayal that she had carried with her through the years, and yet managing to stuff it all into a single word, that name. It had all the impossible weight of a black hole and, like one, was sucking in the light and air that was between the two of them in that hallway.

"She was there," Simon said, after a short, painful pause. "And she said yes."

"But you asked."

"It takes two to make that decision. Olivia, what do you want from me?"

Olivia turned away, bowing her head, letting her hair fall over her face like a concealing curtain. "I have no idea," she said dully. "I just wish...if all of us had made different choices, I might have had a different life." After a moment she glanced up again, her lips twisting into another small bitter smile. "You were a lousy teacher."

"That's not true," Simon said, stung.

"Oh, but it is. You were of the 'it's never going to be good enough' school, and you passed that on, more than you knew." She paused. "You called me misguided once, right here in this place, the night after graduation, remember?"

"Yes," Simon said warily. "I said that."

"I took it at face value, back then I never asked. I'm asking now. Why?"

"Because you had just walked away with a degree that would never make you happy," Simon said. "The diploma was still hot off the presses, and you were making plans about where to go from here, and already the regrets hung about you like a shroud."

"I was happy," Olivia said. "If you were right... I ought to have been miserable. So how come nobody else noticed but you?"

"Because I knew you," Simon said gently. "Your passions were always words, not numbers. If you were to have anything to do with science, it was going to be writing poetry about the gas nebulae or visions about what it meant to be human as they unraveled the human genome."

"You think I wasn't capable of doing the *actual* science behind those things?"

"Who said you weren't capable?" Simon asked. "Don't put words in my mouth. But the capability itself wasn't going to make you happy. You could have probably designed a star drive—but what you really wanted to do was be on that rocket ship when it left this planet and send back poetry about the strange new worlds it would land on. A scientist, Olivia, cares about the *how* of things—you always cared more about the *why*, or the *who*. Dissecting a flower or a frog or a human being might have made you enlightened, but it would never have made you happy."

"Damn you," she said, after a pause.

"What does that mean? Do you forgive me?" Simon asked, and then tossed his head in a frustrated movement, spreading his hands. "Will you tell me what it is that you forgive me *for*?"

Olivia made a small sound that was halfway between a sob and a giggle. "If you don't get it, Simon, there's little point in it. Excuse me, I need to pop into the restroom and stick something cold on my eyes before the others start asking questions back at the table."

She turned away without another word and the door of one of the two bathrooms swung closed behind her. Simon stood speechless, staring after her.

"If you want to use the other one, that's okay," Ariel said.

He had slipped from behind the counter somehow without Simon noticing, and now stood beside Simon, his expression pleasant but somehow alert as if he was expecting Simon to offer some sort of secret password which he knew he had to be on the look-out for.

Simon stared at him. "It says 'Out of Order' on the door," he said.

"Oh, that. It's only there to keep out the uninvited."

"You have to be *invited* into the restroom?" Simon asked, furrowing his brow. "That's a new one. Come to think of it, you've *always* had a bathroom out of commission. Ever since I can remember, and I've been coming here for years. For *decades.*"

Ariel said nothing, merely smiled, and held out a folded piece of paper. Simon instinctively reached out and took it.

"What is this?" Simon said.

"Instructions," said Ariel. "Should you choose to follow them."

Simon unfolded the paper and glanced at it. There were only a few lines, in copperplate handwriting looking rather as though the entire thing had been penned by an old-fashioned nib pen, the kind you had to dip into an inkwell—the language, oddly old-fashioned and portentous, had the same feel of a weight of age on it. And yet the paper looked rather like it had been torn from a mass-produced notebook available in any stationery store for a few bucks, and the ink looked barely dry.

His eyebrows rose as he read.

Your life is filled with crossroads and you are free to choose one road or another at any time. Stepping through this door narrows your choices to only two—the choice to live a different life, or the choice to return to this one.

You make your first choice when you pass through the portal. Once you do, you will not remember the life you have left behind... until one single moment, when all memory will return. In that moment you must choose if you wish to return to your previous existence...or renounce it forever.

Remember this before you decide. Here, you change the world

*around you; there, you have to change to fit the world. Both are harder
than you think. Choose wisely.*

"Choose wisely," Simon said dryly as he finished scanning
the paper. "Take a step into a bathroom and flush a life down a
toilet. Some choice...?"

But when he looked up again, Ariel had gone. The counter
was deserted, too, but the café had started to fill up, like it always
did as the evening wore on, and there was an ever-louder buzz
of conversation as voices rose to be heard above the background
noise. It was not the weekend, but it *was* technically the Eve of
the End of the World, which was a sort of special occasion—and
there was even a young man clutching a guitar by the throat,
fussing with the connections of mike and amp by the high stool
of the musician. He gave Simon a half smile as their eyes met
and held briefly.

Even as he looked away again, the writer part of Simon's
brain was turning the idea over and over, dissecting it from
different angles. You could choose? You could—in a manner of
speaking—unchoose? Life was there to be sifted through and
you could pick the bits you wanted, erase the things you would
rather had never existed? That couldn't be right—it wasn't fair—
you couldn't unwrite something that had been written, simply
unremember something that you wished to forget. But still—it
glittered before him like a jewel, the temptation, the chance to
start again, to be *young* again and to have the world unfolding
in front of him before he narrowed it down by the things that
he thought, that he believed, that he had allowed to happen to
him and to twist him...

Simon pursed his lips, folding the paper and pushing it into
his pocket.

"What the hell," he muttered. "The world ends tomorrow
morning anyway."

He hesitated briefly at the door to the second bathroom,
with the tattered 'Out of Order' sign that hung on the doorknob,
but nobody called out to tell him that he was an idiot and
couldn't he read the sign. His hand landed on the knob, at first
very lightly, and then it tightened and he turned it with rather

too much pressure, as though he was expecting it to be locked and unyielding—but the door swung open at a mere touch and hung ajar, showing only darkness beyond.

Simon shook his head.

"That's it," he said to himself firmly. "I've finally, officially lost it."

And then he pushed the door open all the way, and stepped through.

The door closed behind him. The sign swung lightly on its doorknob once or twice, and was still.

SIMON

SUMMER, 1970

Simon didn't know what woke him, or precisely what time it was—but it was almost as though the sound of crashing glass, distant but clear, had invaded his dreams and then thrown him out of them. His eyes flew open and he lay in his bed for a long, quiet minute or so, holding his breath, searching out the familiar shadowy shapes of the furniture in the bedroom. Nothing seemed to be out of place, but it felt *late*, really late, so far into the middle of the night that daylight was either a memory or a dream and hours of darkness still lay between Simon and the sun.

He became vaguely aware of one small difference—for the lateness of the hour, which he sensed in his bones, there was a thin and unexpected sliver of light at the bottom of his bedroom door. There were lights on in the house. In the middle of the night.

After that, as though things were filtering in slowly, one at a time, he heard the whispers and the footsteps. Someone walking carefully but quickly past his door, outside in the corridor. Something that might have sounded like a stifled cry. Then a rising and falling susurrus of voices, coming closer to his door and drifting away, footsteps on the stairs (he knew the creaky second stair from the top, recognized its sound), more whispers.

After a while his eyes drifted closed again; the whispering frightened him, on some level, but it was also lulling, and he began to drift back into sleep. At first it was the sort of light surface slumber where some part of him remained alert and aware and conscious of a strong feeling that his world had just

somehow shifted on its axis but unable to put a finger on why—
and then he let go of it, and went deeper, into dreams. The
dreams were roiling and strange, just this side of nightmare,
but he slept, and when he woke again the sun was well up, and
the light outside was that of late morning.

He allowed that thought to percolate through his mind for a
moment before it connected with something else. It was *too* late
in the morning. It was as though the world had stopped and he
had slept too long and now something terrible was waiting for
him outside.

He swung his legs out of bed, knuckling at his eyes and
yawning, and then padded in bare feet to his bedroom door.
When he opened it a crack and peered out, the corridor was
empty—but the light, the one at the top of the stairs which was
the last one that Grandma Cecy switched off at night before
going to bed, was still on. As though it had not been switched
off at all the previous night.

Simon opened the door a little wider and stepped out of the
room. He took it all in, a sweeping glance of recognition, the
pale cream walls and the dark floral carpet in the corridor and
the doors leading off into the three bedrooms and the upstairs
bathroom, all closed. His mind's eye pictured the downstairs
with the same fond familiarity—the kitchen with the cabinets
Grandma Cecy had been swearing she would refurbish or
replace for several years now but never did, the coffee-maker
on the counter making burping noises in the mornings when
Simon came down for breakfast, the framed tapestry above the
fireplace which Simon's mother, Grandma Cecy's only daughter,
had done when she was still a girl living here in her mother's
house, the comfortable chintz sofas in the sitting room...

It was familiar and comfortable and he had an affection for
this house and for Grandma Cecy, but it was not home. This was
not where his mother and father lived. They had gone away, on
a trip, and that's why Simon was staying here—but this was
not home, not *real* home, the familiar place of sanctuary, his
own room strewn with his own books and discarded inside-out
sweatshirts and kicked-off sneakers with their laces still snarled
tied.

Except it suddenly, somehow…was. As though some aura had got transferred. As though he had been cast adrift in a strange sea, and this place, Grandma Cecy's house, was the only lifeboat that there was.

He had not realized that he had crossed the corridor and stood hovering on the top of the stairs—or that he had taken the first hesitant steps down. Not until the creak of that telltale second step stopped him in his tracks…and alerted Grandma Cecy, who must have been just inside the arched opening from the hallway into the living room, and now stuck her head out from underneath the arch, peering up the stairs.

"Are you awake?" she asked, her voice warm and comforting but oddly afraid. "There's breakfast, if you're hungry—I've made waffle mix, and it will only take a few moments to be ready."

"Okay," Simon said carefully.

"Come on down," Grandma Cecy said, and then, just as Simon began to obey, she ducked back out of sight into the sitting room and he heard her talking to someone in a low voice.

Simon froze on the stairs Someone else was here.

Someone he suddenly had a very strong feeling that he did not wish to meet.

Grandma Cecy peered out again. "You coming?"

Simon didn't know what he was braced for but the expression on the face of the man in a police officer's uniform who was perched on one of Grandma Cecy's chintz sofas stopped his heart for a moment as he walked uncertainly into the sitting room. He knew even before Grandma Cecy's arm slipped around his shoulders for support and comfort that it could only be bad news.

"Honey…" Grandma Cecy began, and then smiled, a little too brightly, and squeezed his shoulder with her fingers. "Well, but come on. Breakfast first, eh?"

The police officer sat with a peaked cap in his hands, loosely dangling between his knees.

"I'll be going, then," he announced suddenly, getting to his feet, giving every impression of a man who devoutly wished to be somewhere else, anywhere else, right then.

"Yes," Grandma Cecy said. "Thank you. Go into the kitchen,

Simon, I'll be right there—I'll just see the gentleman out."

There were more murmurs at the front door, too low for Simon to catch, but he thought he heard the unmistakable sibilant syllables of *I'm sorry.*

The eyes that met his grandmother's as she came back into the sitting room and then on into the kitchen where he waited were huge and afraid.

"Just tell me," he said. "Something has happened."

To her credit, Grandma Cecy hesitated only a little—and appeared to come to a decision not to sugarcoat, or lie, or promise things she could never deliver.

"Your Mom and Dad... they were in a bad accident last night," she said to the boy. "It seems...the driver of a big truck must have fallen asleep at the wheel. He managed to drift off the road, jack-knifed the semi, and they...didn't have a chance to stop in time. Your Mom is in hospital, right now, but she is... bad. Very bad."

"Dad...?"

"Your Dad is gone, honey. He was driving."

Simon blinked, looking puzzled; the information made no sense, as though he had asked what time of day it was and got a response that it was Wednesday. It was not something he could process right then. The weight of the words threatened to crush him. He pushed it aside, grasping at any possibility of good news.

"But Mom's going to be okay...?"

"We're hoping, sweetie. The hospital said they'd call if there's news."

"Where is she? Can I go see her?"

"She's in a hospital a little over a hundred miles from here. I've talked to the doctors—they don't know if it's all right for her to have visitors yet. They said they would call. Now come on, please eat something. You'll need to be strong today."

Simon's throat closed at the thought of food. He shook his head. "I'm not hungry," he said.

Grandma Cecy straightened, smiling at him in a slow, sad way. "Well, you know best," she said. "I'll make sandwiches, they'll be in the fridge if you get hungry later—and do promise me you'll eat something in a little while."

"Okay," he said faintly. "Can I go back up to my room now?"

"Sure," she said, releasing him.

There was another flurry of activity, a few hours later, when Simon heard the phone ring downstairs—he crept out of his room and crouched at the top of the stairs, listening. Nothing he heard made much sense. He thought he heard Grandma Cecy say goodbye to whoever had called, then dial another number herself, talk quietly for a little bit longer, and apparently put the phone down. It promptly rang again. And it kept on ringing, through most of the early afternoon—short choppy sharp rings, calls answered on the first or at the most the second ring, often lasting less than a minute.

Simon retreated back into his room where he didn't do much of anything—he sat in the bedroom's window seat, built into the dormer window, and stared at the puffy white clouds scudding across the summer-blue sky. Ordinarily he might have found shapes and pictures in them—he was forever finding clouds shaped like fighter planes, or ducks, or dragons—but on this day they seemed to be empty of meaning, just blank white silhouettes against the blue.

Grandma Cecy's bedroom door was ajar when Simon poked his head out into the corridor again, a couple of hours later, but he didn't go in despite the unspoken invitation. He hadn't heard the phone ring for a while. Out in the corridor, he suddenly remembered the sandwiches that his grandmother said that she would make, and his stomach grumbled at the thought; making an abrupt decision, he padded down the stairs into the kitchen, found a plate of sandwiches (ham and cheese, his favorite) on a plate in the refrigerator, and calmly ate two of them. Then he returned the rest to the fridge, climbed back upstairs, and knocked on Grandma Cecy's door.

He heard her get up off her bed, and then she was at the door, opening it wider, giving him a small sad smile.

"Yes, sweetie?"

"I want to go and see her," Simon said. "Mom. Can we go?"

Grandma Cecy hesitated only for the briefest of moments, and then nodded firmly. "Of course we can. If that's what you

want to do. I'll get dressed and you go comb your hair. I'll meet
you out in the driveway in five minutes."

The drive up passed mostly in silence, with Simon staring
out of the passenger window, his hand resting on the plastic
sill. Grandma Cecy took a wrong turning twice on the way to
the hospital, and had to ask for directions the second time, but
eventually they found the place and she drove into the parking
lot, found an empty spot, and turned the key in the ignition.

Simon sat unmoving.

"Honey?" Grandma Cecy said quietly.

"How... bad?" Simon asked at last, after a long pause.

"Pretty bad," Grandma Cecy said. "They told me she was on
a respirator. A machine that actually breathes for her."

"How long is she going to be on that?"

"They don't know." Grandma Cecy paused. "What do you
want to do?"

"We didn't bring flowers," Simon said. "You should bring
flowers when you visit somebody in a hospital."

"We can get some inside," Grandma Cecy said. "I'm sure
we can."

"Okay."

They walked from the car toward the hospital entrance,
very close but not touching. Simon's heart felt heavy, like a
stone in his chest; they had got here just before sunset, in that
hour when the sunlight turns heavy and shades into amber and
gold and then deeper into blood orange, and the white hospital
building was almost rust-colored in the light, like dried blood.
Simon noticed everything at once, as if his mind was taking
a photograph—the lights that were starting to twinkle in the
windows but were not yet strong enough to compete with the
power of the dark-as-gold sunlight, the warble of some bird close
by in the ornamental shrubbery somewhere, the clean lines of
the ambulance parked a little to the side of the main entrance
with its mirror-writing on the front, the merest whisper of a
breeze against his cheek and ruffling his hair as though with a
mother's gentle hand, the faint smell of medicine and antiseptic
and air freshener as they walked in through the door and into
the air-conditioned lobby. There was a gift shop off to one side

of the hallway, and it had a small wire display stand in front of it with four small bouquets.

Grandma Cecy looked around the entrance hall, but could not immediately see anybody at what looked like a reception desk facing the main doors. She touched Simon gently on the shoulder as she saw a nurse hurry by, glancing at her watch.

"Here," Grandma Cecy said, fishing out a twenty dollar bill out of her handbag and folding Simon's hand over it, "why don't you go and get some of those flowers. I'll find out where she is."

Simon hesitated for the longest time before the flower stand, staring at the offerings. At least one of them looked oddly wilted, as though it had been sitting dry and forgotten for hours; the others passed muster in terms of freshness but none of them spoke his mother's name to Simon. They were too bland, too generic, nameless pretty flowers bound together with no intent or meaning—it was just like the clouds, empty, formless. For a boy to whom the world always managed to speak through the language of imagination, nothing was imaginable on this day. It was as though his mind had gone dark.

He finally reached out and grabbed a bouquet completely at random; the girl at the till took his money, yawning, and gave him change; he turned back to look for his grandmother...and found her standing a few steps away. For a moment he could not interpret her expression, but then he thought he saw...fear.

Which didn't make sense.

Unless...

His hand with the bouquet dropped reflexively, until he was holding the flowers upside down, only barely not sweeping the floor with them.

"Your Mom..." Grandma Cecy began, and then her hands closed spasmodically around the handle of her handbag.

She didn't say anything else She didn't need to.

It was over.

Simon sank down very slowly on the cold, clean marble floor of the hospital, gathering up the flowers into his arms and hugging them to his face. A single tear, huge and heavy with grief he did not yet know how to understand, rolled out of the corner of his eye and down his cheek, and onto the red petal of a flower which he held against his face—and hung there like dew.

"Can we go home now?' he whispered, into the flowers.

A man in a white coat was hurrying over to them. "Mrs Milligan? Cecilia Milligan? I'm Doctor White, I just wanted to say…"

Grandma Cecy lifted her eyes from her grandson with an effort, with main force of will.

"We're going home now," she said. "You heard Simon."

"But the arrangements…"

"I will be back," she said, "tomorrow, to make the arrangements I am taking my grandson home now." She reached out and gently disengaged the bouquet from Simon's grip, asking a question with her eyes and receiving the faintest of nods in return as he gave up the flowers Grandma Cecy handed them to the doctor, meeting his eyes with a steadfast gaze which nevertheless glittered brilliantly with unshed tears. "In the meantime," she said, "Simon brought some flowers for his mother. Would you see that she gets them, please?"

The doctor accepted the bouquet, looking a little nonplussed. Without another word, Grandma Cecy reached out her hand to Simon. He took it, and managed to get back on his feet without wobbling too badly. Holding his hand tightly in hers, her head held high, she turned her back on the hospital and walked out of the same door through which they had entered scant minutes ago.

She was taking Simon home.

Simon was twelve years old when he became an orphan. He was vaguely aware that he was the subject of a legal wrangle when it came to custody of him after his parents' death, but somehow it never occurred to him to doubt that Grandma Cecy would win whatever war she had to engage in to keep her grandson by her side.

In the beginning, it was awkward; he had to change schools, and the teachers thought it would help if his classmates knew a little about him as he started there. But the tragedy hung about him like an infectious disease and few of the kids in his class found anything to say to him—perhaps it was just a matter of not finding the right words to offer to someone whose parents had just been taken from him in such a shocking and sudden way. But Simon didn't really care so much about that, and was perfectly content to muddle through on his own. It was the adults whom he had no defense against—people oscillated from an embarrassed sort of sympathy, as though it was somehow uncouth to mention the accident which had claimed his parents' lives in his hearing because he was entirely too fragile to bear it, to a sort of condescending and somehow accusatory indictment, leaving him uncertain as to whether the fact that he had been home in bed and asleep when the accident happened should leave him guilty of some misdemeanor of which he was not aware. He didn't know which he resented more.

There was only one sanctuary from this that Simon knew—his grandmother's house. Here, he was neither 'that poor boy' nor the one who should have known better than to survive his entire family. Grandma Cecy hid her own broken heart at the unexpected loss of her only daughter and took on the rearing of her grandson with a sort of pragmatic grace that left him the breathing room to rest and heal and grow, all the while letting him know in a hundred little ways that she was, and always would be, the sturdy pillar of support which held up his world. She would never make any decisions for him—had never done it right from the start, but she would throw her weight behind any choices that he did make; she would let him fail, if he reached too far, but she would be there to help him up so that he could try again. She was a safety net, not a crutch.

"You know best," she would say—her iconic phrase. She was quite willing to be his sounding board, listening quietly while he argued out his decisions with himself, playing devil's advocate merely by being present and silent until she heard a choice harden in his debate, a decision being made, and then she would offer no more than a nod a smile and those three words *You know best.*

Simon was left to map out his own life, sometimes on a hit-and-miss basis, before he turned thirteen.

In some ways that, and his isolation from his classmates at school, made him precociously self-reliant and capable, and frighteningly observant. In other ways, it locked him away inside himself. He was used to sharing his life with nobody, to making his choices to suit himself, to being the loner whose best friends were books rather than people. But he never gave an impression of that being a hardship, or something that made him suffer—instead of being an object of pity amongst his more social peers he became something of a mystery, an enigma, someone a little apart and aloof whose solitary habits and the customary book that was always in his hand commanded a reluctant respect rather than mockery and derision. By the time he was fifteen, and beginning to grow out of his rangy adolescent body and acquire the angles of the face he would wear as a mature adult, people would occasionally cross the line he had drawn around himself and extend invitations to parties or gatherings; he would even, occasionally, accept one.

But he was not an ordinary teenager, and the demands on his time were many and varied—which sometimes left the social life by the wayside. Grandma Cecy never said anything to him about financial matters, but he was not unaware that by taking him on she had stretched her resources a little thin—and he had quickly decided that he needed to make a contribution to the household in whatever way he can. He started out with a paper route but that lasted only long enough for him to realize that he hated getting up early, that the monotony of the job bored him, and that his bicycle was an older model which required a fair amount of work on the hills near his grandmother's house and getting a newer one to make the job easier would pretty much eat up all the money he was actually making, and then some. But he was still a little too young for some of the better-paying jobs out there, so he had to take what he could get. He put out flyers in his neighborhood, and people paid him to run their errands, rake their leaves and mow their lawns, wax their cars.

A friend of Grandma Cecy's who ran a local café took him on as a busboy when he was fifteen—and Simon did his duties without grumbling or complaining, only wincing occasionally at some of the greasier messes that people left behind for him to clean up. He quickly developed his own system, though, and although it might have looked to an outside observer that he was drifting and daydreaming through the work it all got done somehow, and in a manner more efficient than anyone else could manage.

His immediate supervisor, a youth only a few years older than himself with skin still pitted with teenage acne, chose to resent Simon's methods, perhaps because they somehow forced him to work twice as hard as he wanted to in order for the junior employee not to show him up spectacularly. His response to Simon was to micromanage everything to as great an extent as he could, down to criticizing the way that Simon would stack the dishwasher in the kitchen and once or twice even rearrange things to his own satisfaction. Simon hid his flashes of irritation but would not compromise his own standards for his resentful, meddling, sarcastic supervisor.

He never complained about it to Grandma Cecy—the café was owned by a friend and the job itself was obtained through that connection—but on the day that he quit he did bring his reasons back to her.

"He thinks he knows better just because he's a rung above me," Simon said. "Both of us work for Mr. Landon but he actually thinks I work for him, and it's kind of starting to bug me. It isn't as though I'm serving tables and getting tips—for what the wages are the job isn't worth it."

"You got your patience from your mother," Grandma Cecy said, smiling a little. "Which is to say, you have it in limited quantities, but when you lose it it's lost for good and that's that. But it's okay, Simon. Indentured servitude is not required."

"I'll find something else," Simon said.

"I've no doubt," Grandma Cecy said.

Simon's first babysitting gig was accidental. He happened to be home, by himself, when Grandma Cecy's neighbor ran in asking if she'd keep an eye on her toddler for an hour or so while she rushed off to deal with an unexpected emergency.

"She's not here," Simon said. "She had to pop into town herself, she only left about half an hour ago."

The neighbor shook her head in frustration. "I can't take Missy with me..."

"I could baby-sit," Simon said.

She looked at him. "Ever done it before?"

"Nope," Simon said. "But how hard can it be?"

The mother could not help a wry grin at that. "I'm almost inclined to let you try it without any hints whatsoever," she said. "Just for saying that. But it's only for an hour, and you're Cecy's blood, and if you're anything like her, you'll know how to deal with the unexpected. You'll get Missy and a few scribbled instructions. I do want her back in one piece, but other than that you're on your own."

"Yes, ma'am," Simon said, ducking his head and tugging at an imaginary forelock. "Missy and I will get on fine."

Missy was three years old, and was certainly no slouch at tantrums and pure stubborn obstinacy—but Simon would find out about those particular attributes later, on subsequent occasions. On this first trial run Missy seemed to have decided that it was her duty to provide Simon with a sort of babysitting reference, and behaved beautifully, being clean, contented, and in good spirits when her mother came to collect her. She gracefully allowed Simon to claim the credit. Her mother was pleased with Simon's services, and returned to tap him for babysitting services even when Grandma Cecy was available— word spread, and soon Simon had more babysitting work than he could handle, or even want

It was paying work, it paid quite well compared to some of the things that he had done, and he had no argument with that at all—and it had the extra advantage, as far as he was concerned, that it was unnecessary to pursue activities which bored him by their repetitiveness or which necessitated getting filthy through sheer hard physical labor of whatever description. But he did occasionally find some of his younger charges a little trying on that less-than-perfect patience which Grandma Cecy had once called his mother's legacy. Perhaps it was this that guided an instinctive shift, as he himself grew a little older, to an increasingly older set of children he was entrusted with— and with whom he had an increasingly better connection.

One of his favorite charges was Kim, a fiercely precocious twelve-year-old who resented utterly the fact that her parents still thought it was necessary for her to have a 'minder' in the house when they were out, particularly given that the minder in question was less than five years older than herself. Kim's older half-sister from her father's first marriage, Lizzie, an independent-minded sixteen-year-old, did not live with her father full-time and only spent the occasional weekend there— but Kim treasured those weekends, and thought that Lizzie was amazing. She tended to follow in her footsteps, watching the things that Lizzie watched on TV (sometimes clandestinely, if she had to, when her parents thought a show was 'too old' for her), played the games that Lizzie played, read the books that Lizzie read. She didn't seem to make much distinction between the books that Lizzie chose to read and those she had read for school. Simon wasn't completely certain how it had come about that Kim got immersed in *Romeo and Juliet*, except that it had been handed down from Lizzie, and was thus treated as obligatory.

Kim wasn't above voicing her own opinions of the play.

"I don't *get* it," she complained to Simon, sitting at the breakfast bar in her parents' kitchen as Simon was throwing together a sandwich for her. She kicked her heels against the footrest of the high stool on which she was perched, as if to punctuate her remarks. "They talk funny, and they're all a bunch of idiots."

"Juliet was only a couple of years older than you are now," Simon pointed out.

"I know, she's supposed to be fourteen or something."

"And you don't think you're going to be smitten with somebody, just like that, in two years' time or so?" Simon asked.

Kim threw a crumpled paper napkin at him. "Yuck."

"You have to remember," Simon said, finishing off the sandwich and cutting the large piece of brown bread into two halves for Kim, "that she lived in very different times. Back then, when she was fourteen, it would be like you were, oh, at least in your twenties today, probably. Or at the very least Lizzie's age."

"Doesn't matter I still think they're a bunch of idiots." Kim wrapped both hands around the sandwich and took a large bite out of it. "I mean, everyone insists that they hate everyone else, and it's all supposed to be tragic, but I don't get it—what's their problem? I can't tell the families apart—"

"Ah," Simon said, laughing, "a rose by any other name..."

Kim swallowed a large mouthful of sandwich. "What?"

"One of Juliet's little speeches, remember? Telling Romeo to forswear his name."

"What's he got to swear about?"

"*Forswear.* It means to deny, to give up, to renounce. What she's telling him to do is stop being a Montague and everything would be just dandy."

Kim shrugged. "Like I said."

"But they weren't to blame for their families," Simon said. "And they fell in love, and they weren't supposed to even meet each other. And it was different, in those days It mattered."

"Don't *get* it."

Simon laughed out loud "All right, then. We can do this the modern way. Let's see... who's the queen bitch in your school?"

"Emma Tennant," Kim answered without a pause.

"Tell me."

"She's got hair streaked green and purple although the school doesn't allow it and nobody says anything," Kim said. "She can do whatever she wants, and everyone just smiles and nods."

"She'll do. Now, who's the Alpha Male? You know, the guy who gets picked first for every team? No—actually—the guy who gets to *pick* the teams...?"

Kim thought for a moment. "Mark," she said at length, having considered the matter. "Mark Collins. Everyone says he'll go and get rich playing basketball or something when he's left school."

"So, they both like to be the center of attention, right?"

Kim stared at him "Well, *duh.*"

"Now imagine that they had to fight for it. For that attention. Only one of them could have it, and the other would have to— you know—just be like everyone else. So what happens is that they start a feud over it; Montague versus Capulet. What was it...Tennant...? Tennant versus Collins."

"Yes, but they aren't..." Kim began, wrinkling her nose in a puzzled frown.

Simon held out a hand. "Yes, but it doesn't end there. Let's say Madame Tennant grows up and has a son, let's call him Julian, and Master Collins grows up and produces a daughter, let's call her Romy. And they wind up in the same school together And—given who their parents were—let's say that the memory of glory lives on. So people remember The Tennant, and The Collins. And now here they are, the next generation And they're supposed to take their parents' line, and hate the other's guts, right? So what do you think happens if they decide to ignore everything and kind of fall for each other instead?"

"*Oh*," Kim said, putting what was left of her sandwich down on her plate, a dawning understanding on her face.

Kim's father stopped Simon in the street on the following Saturday.

"I had a talk with Kim," he said, "about Romeo and Juliet. Seems you re-told that little tale beautifully."

Simon allowed himself to roll his eyes a little, with a self-conscious grin spreading on his face. "Context," he said.

"Indeed," Kim's father agreed, laughing. "I teach high school English, you know. Maybe I should hire you to come in and explain some of the stuff my own students are getting bogged down in."

"Alas," Simon murmured, "poor Shakespeare. I knew him well…Who needs Romeo and Juliet and high medieval tragedy when you have the corridors of the average reasonably affluent American middle school?"

"Seriously. I mean, Kim's a little… unusual… but there are plenty of kids getting stuck on plenty of things out there, and you seem to have the knack for explaining it in their terms. Interested in a tutoring job? I could set you up—and it pays better than babysitting does."

"Sure," Simon said immediately, before the other man had a chance to finish the sentence. "I'll do it."

It started small, and within a week Simon had a brace of students whom he would meet in the library, or in their own homes, or at Grandma Cecy's dining room table. When the sessions were at his grandmother's house, she played hostess—offering the student being tutored a soda, or tea, or a plate of home-baked chocolate chip cookies—and then she would retire upstairs to her bedroom, leaving Simon and his charge the run of the downstairs and their privacy. She listened when Simon told her of his students, and heard far more than he thought he was telling her—it was her house, after all, and she wasn't completely unaware of what was going on downstairs. When it was Simon's turn to think about his future, she did not steer or prod or otherwise seek to influence—but, in her own inimitable way, she had her say.

"I'd say you had a gift for it," she told him. "For getting ideas into people's noggins. Some people can understand a subject perfectly, but are utterly unable to convey the first thing about it to somebody who doesn't already know what they are talking about. You, you have a knack for making someone grasp a difficult concept. Once you understand something, you can make others understand it. You ought to think about teaching—you know, as a career."

"I don't know if I could hack it," Simon said frankly. "It's one-on-one, what I do, mostly. They pick a tough subject, and I shine a flashlight on it, and once they've figured out what's real and what's shadow, the rest is self-explanatory. In a classroom full of kids some of whom will *never* figure out what the shadows are...? I'd lose it."

"Children," Grandma Cecy said, "aren't the only ones who need teaching."

"Gramma, you told me yourself that when God was giving out patience I was standing in a different line," Simon said. "I was thinking something else, something different, something I can, you know, keep my own company doing."

"Like?" she asked.

"Oh, I don't know I was thinking astronomy. Or anthropology. Or architecture. Or aeronautics."

"Got past the first letter of the alphabet yet?"

He grinned. "Nope, but I'm running out of subjects to study. Maybe I should just go straight into theoretical physics and learn how to build atomic bombs. But then, it's a messy job, killing people, even if you're that far removed from it. On the whole I prefer reading about my wars, preferably in fiction."

"Well, you know best," Grandma Cecy said. "Let me know if I can help."

The trouble was, Simon didn't really know at all. He had spent the first year after his parents' death simply coasting through school on autopilot, and with a sufficient amount of native intelligence and an ability to think on his feet managed to survive tolerably well in terms of academic achievement. Afterwards, as things shook down, it was somehow always assumed that Simon would one day go to college—Grandma Cecy quietly but firmly took that part of it as read, as her duty to her daughter who did not live to see the day—but what he would major in, what the focus of his life would be, had never really been discussed. He didn't appear to have a major vocation or something specific that called him, and he was moderately good in most academic disciplines, if not acutely brilliant in any.

He had his share of career-planning sessions with the advisor at his school, but these were frustrating for both of them. The advisor tried to focus Simon's interests; Simon obstinately persisted in viewing his world through a wider lens than he was being forced to look through.

"What do you want to *do* with yourself for the rest of your life?" the advisor asked helplessly, throwing his arms out in a gesture of exasperated resignation.

"Live it," Simon said.

"Something's got to pay the bills of living it."

"Something will."

"Simon, you should be applying to colleges if you want to go to one. You need to figure out what you want to be applying *for*."

"I've thought about law, eventually," Simon said. "But that's a long way down the line."

"Well, it's a start. What kind of law? That might help a pre-law course of study. You might want to weigh in on the physical sciences or biology, if you are interested in environmental law. Economics?"

"Or political science," Simon said. "I could go into politics."

"We could explore…"

"Except that nobody ever went to school to learn to become

a politician. They're probably born obnoxious. Knowing human psychology—"

"There's a major."

"Which—politics, psychology, or being obnoxious?" Simon asked, keeping a commendably straight face. And then shrugged. "I haven't a clue. Really. I'll figure it out as I go along."

In the end it was none of the subjects beginning with the letter A that finally got him into college. His final choice was governed by a couple of moderately unrelated things. Some were merely parts of his personality—a combination of fastidiousness and a disinclination to get his hands dirty, a preference to stand on the sidelines and use his keen powers of observation to chronicle events rather than take a direct part in them himself, an unexpected ability to both use and understand the kind of academic language which is so essential in all communication in the halls of higher learning. Others were more esoteric— serendipity, coincidence, habit.

He added English Literature to his curriculum in college almost by accident—because one of the last conversations he had before he went to sign up for classes had been with Kim's father, and that had reminded him of his early Shakespearean re-interpretations—adding the English class had been pure whimsy.

Perhaps he should have been less surprised than he was when that particular class turned out to hold the greatest interest for him—and that it triggered something that he had never even thought about. He began to carry a notebook around, to keep a journal of first his days and then his thoughts and ideas, and then, eventually, in a different notebook, to experiment with fiction of his own.

He was a student of literature—and his first efforts, predictably, were pastiche. His words were brittle, brilliant in terms of craft, and utterly empty of meaning except inasmuch they were copies of someone else's search for it. He never kept a piece of writing for longer than a week before becoming acidly disillusioned with it, balling it up into a crumpled sphere of rejection and tossing it into the nearest waste paper basket; he certainly never breathed a word to anybody about having produced it at all. He was not alone in this particular pursuit—plenty of his peers were experimenting with writing, and some were far less shy about admitting it than Simon was. Simon found himself in demand as editor and critiquer, because he could look at a piece and analyze it with a shrewd and often brutal honesty—but it was, perhaps, his inability to turn this particular quality off when it came to his own efforts that stymied his early forays into the craft.

He didn't tell anyone when he tried something new, either—a story which was not based on grand ideas snatched from the ether, but something far more personal and closer to his own experience. It was a struggle, because writing something like that required that he not only turn off the inner editor but also turn his back on the solitude and isolation he had cultivated so successfully since he had been twelve years old—for, in a way, it was his own story he was telling. That meant, by default, that he was erasing the lines that had been drawn between him and the world.

It was still not at all certain whether he would ever allow anybody to actually read the new thing. But he was *writing* it. His first reader was already there, even if it was only himself.

In a lot of ways college was very different from school, and Simon was a different person when he stepped into that world. He was enjoying himself, acquitting himself reasonably well in the academic sphere and actually, for the first time in his life, finding himself the subject of social demand as he discovered himself to be unexpectedly popular with the opposite sex. He got caught up in it all, his head spinning and his schedule full. He had chosen the college in his own home town because that meant he could stay with Grandma Cecy, but he found himself with barely enough time to occasionally eat supper together, regaling her with stories of college life when he had the opportunity and could snatch the time.

"You've lost weight," he told her once, after almost a week of hardly seeing her at all. He had come upon her washing dishes in the sink, and it had struck him with a sharp jolt—it suddenly seemed to him as though the strings of her apron were far too long, that there was far too much of them left hanging after she had tied it around her waist.

"About time I did," Grandma Cecy said, turning her head slightly and giving him a small smile. "Been trying to for years."

"You okay?"

"Fine. Let me just finish up with this lot, I want to soak the pot before it sets, but supper's ready—you can take it out of the oven and dish out if you like. Don't give me too much—you *always* give me too much when you dish it out. Keep in mind that I'm an old lady and you're still a growing boy."

Simon snorted. He stood a couple of inches over six feet now, and towered over his diminutive grandmother. "If I grow any more you may have to raise the ceilings."

He had left it at that. He had left it at that the next time that he had made a comment on her appearance—that she looked tired, and pale—and again she had deflected him, and he'd backed off.

The third time, he thought he heard noises in the bathroom late one evening—the door was ajar and the light was on, and he knocked gently.

"Gramma? Are you all right?"

"Fine," she said, but her voice was odd, breathy, as though she had to force it out through clenched teeth.

"Gramma?…" Simon said, suddenly concerned. "I'm coming in."

"No," she said, "I don't…"

But he was already opening the door, and then he had crossed the rest of the distance with one stride, sinking down to one knee beside her as she sat on the edge of the bathtub with one hand holding onto the sink and the other folded across her middle as though in pain.

"Are you all right…?"

"My pills," she said. "Medicine cabinet. On the left."

He jumped up to get the bottle of pills, opened it up, shook out a few into his palm.

"How many?"

"Two. I need two."

He poured the pills back into the bottle, all but the two in his palm, snatched up a glass from the vanity next to the sink and splashed water into it, and handed her both; she took the pills with a hand that was shaking, lifted the glass of water to her lips and took a few slow, painful swallows.

"I'm calling Dr. Maxwell," Simon said.

"Don't bother the man, it's late," Grandma Cecy said, a shade more firmly. "I'll be fine."

"If I don't call him now, you're going in to see him tomorrow," Simon said. "And I mean that."

"All right, then. I will," she said, without meeting his eyes.

It was in that moment that Simon became truly afraid.

Grandma Cecy had never believed in doctors—not for herself, anyway. By the time she could no longer hide her pain, by the time Simon realized that something was wrong... something was *very* wrong, too wrong to deal with. When her own doctor sent her straight to the hospital after the few preliminary tests, Simon knew that the situation was already beyond human help—and further tests proved him right.

Grandma Cecy had cancer, and it had spread into the lymphatic system, and she was told that it was only a matter of time.

"I should have known," Simon said, sitting perched on the side of her hospital bed, holding one of her hands in both his own. "I should have trussed you up like a Christmas turkey and taken you off to see a doctor years ago."

"Wouldn't have helped," she said. With her white hair pulled back tightly against her skull and her face a chalky white, dressed in a pale lavender hospital gown, she was practically invisible against the starched linens of the hospital bed. "We all have to die of something, honey. Otherwise there would be no room in this world for those who come after us. It's my time, that's all. There's no need to fret about it."

Simon's eyes filled with tears, and she saw, and raised her other hand in a gesture of admonishment.

"Now, none of that," she said. "If you want to be of help, read me something—my eyes get tired so quickly these days and it's been trying just lying in this bed doing nothing. No, not that book—I've finished that, or as much of it as I care to read. Have you got anything new with you?"

Simon hesitated, but only briefly. "I've started a book of my own," he said.

Grandma Cecy looked at him with her head tilted a little, her eyes bright. "Oh?" she said.

"It's about…Mom and Dad, and me when I was young, I guess," Simon said.

"About time you let that go," Grandma Cecy murmured, her eyes softening. "How much have you done so far?"

"Barely begun," Simon said.

"I would love to see it," she said, her voice rising a little in inflection as though she were asking a question rather than making a request.

"It's way raw," Simon said. "It's…I'd never have mentioned it, yet, until…"

"Well, you're right, I don't have that much time left," Grandma Cecy said. "And it doesn't matter if it isn't perfect. Nothing in this life is. But I would still love to see it. Did you say you have it with you?"

"It's just scribbles in a notebook, right now," said Simon, glancing at the small knapsack resting against the back leg of Grandma Cecy's hospital bed. "But I always carry the notebook."

"Read it to me," she said. "Please."

Simon fished out the writing notebook, a ratty-looking spiral-bound thing that looked thinner than it ought to be, as though it had had too many pages torn out of it, with a cheap ballpoint pen advertising a bank clipped onto the cover.

"I changed it around," he said, hefting the book in one hand, hesitating. "Quite a bit. It isn't the way it really happened."

"It isn't supposed to be, if you're writing it as fiction," Grandma Cecy said, settling back against her pillow and closing her eyes.

"Well… this isn't really chapter one, but it's somewhere close to the beginning… I haven't figured out yet where the real beginning…"

"Honey," she murmured, her voice very soft, "I know it isn't finished. But I'd like to hear what you *started*."

She had asked for very little from him, over the years. She had simply stood by him all the days of his life, and that was, in her eyes, the way that things should have been—she had expected nothing in return. She was asking now, and Simon found himself torn between being appalled that he had made her do it at all—surely he could have figured out that she might have wanted to know about this project of his, and had every right to wish to see it—and recoiling from showing this woman, of all people, something that wasn't worthy of her, that wasn't perfect, or as perfect as he knew how to make it. He had every intention of showing her his work—eventually. But they had run out of eventually, and turned the corner into the place of raw truth. There was some small part of Simon that was still a child, a child who thought that forever really existed, and that you had forever with the people you loved. He, of all people, ought to have known better than that—the knowledge that everything comes to an end should have been part of his armor—but now he was finding that something in him had wanted to believe that Grandma Cecy would never leave him. And reading her his words almost meant... that he was giving up, that he was acquiescing to her dying, that somehow he was giving her permission to go. An irrational thought that he might keep her alive and by his side if he refused to ever see his writing did cross his mind—but he knew it as irrational, and pushed it aside.

She was asking. For something that he could give. There was nothing beyond that. Not now.

"Okay," he said, faintly, flipping the notebook open. "Okay, then."

The sequence of events surrounding his parents' accident was different in Simon's novel fragment—in this version, one of them had died on impact and the other had survived the accident, living on in the pain of its consequences, until the protagonist of the book, the character who would have been Simon, was in his late teens. It was only then that he had introduced the character who was the equivalent of his grandmother.

He had started stammering a little when he got to that point—the truth was, he didn't have a lot on this section of his book, but he found it even more difficult than he thought it would be to read this part to the living model for the character who inhabited his pages.

He paused twice, looking up, seeing his grandmother lying back against the pillows and looking like she was asleep. But she would lift a hand and reach out to unerringly touch his own, a light brush of her fingers to indicate that she was still listening and was merely keeping her eyes closed, and he would continue. When he finally came to the end of what he had written and sank into a longer silence, she lay without any reaction at all for a moment, and then opened her eyes to look at him as a slow smile spread across her face.

"You're writing a fairy tale," she said simply.

"Actually, it feels very real," Simon said, closing his notebook. "As though some part of me actually did live *that* version of events, as though I'm kind of remembering it rather than making it all up."

"Anything is possible," Grandma Cecy said. "But I meant, about me, that character whom you've cast as me. I was never that good."

Simon leaned over to kiss her on the cheek. "Better," he said. "If anything, I don't do you justice."

"Thank you for reading it to me," she said. "I think I could sleep a little, now. Maybe you'll have more for me next time."

"A little bit at a time," Simon said. "Until I'm done. But I wish I could have shown it to you when it was finished, after I had a chance to polish it up and smooth out the rough edges—when it was perfect…"

"Nothing is ever perfect," Grandma Cecy said faintly. "Not in the way you mean. You might make it better, but it will be a different kind of perfect then. It was perfect just as it was, right now. There are times you just need to know when to let go." She squeezed his hand, her pressure very light, as though she did not have strength for more. "Good night, honey."

Simon turned at the door of the ward, glancing back at her bed—her eyes were still open, but the eyelids were drooping, as though she had to fight to keep them so. He raised a hand, gave her a half-wave and a smile, and she lifted her own hand from where it rested on her abdomen in a response that was equal parts farewell and blessing. The eyes were already closing before the hand came back down again, before Simon fully turned away, a fragile old woman drifting off into the shallow sleep of old age.

When Simon came to see her the following afternoon, they told him that it had been a sleep from which she had never woken again. Grandma Cecy was gone.

For Simon, it felt like someone had driven a fist into his solar plexus without warning. There was, for days, no air, no heartbeat; it was that terrible day all over again, the day when he woke up and found himself orphaned, lost, a child without parents. With Grandma Cecy it hadn't been an accident or even unlooked for—but it was sudden, and sharp, and it hurt with a kind of pain that Simon could not believe he could carry and yet call himself alive. As a coping mechanism and a suit of armor, his tendency to isolate himself from the rest of the world had worked for him before—but that was when he had still had Grandma Cecy at his back, standing on the edge of that circle of defense, the bridge between him and humanity. But she was gone now, and the circle closed, and Simon was alone in its center.

Grandma Cecy had showed him a blue enamel box once—just once—and told him that if anything happened to her he would find everything he needed in that box. Simon made the necessary arrangements with the hospital and the funeral home, and then took the time to go through the contents of the blue box. They were neither numerous nor complex—they consisted of a checkbook, a safety-deposit box key, and a letter addressed to Simon. He might have hesitated to open it, wary of its contents and their potential to derail the fragile calmness with which he was approaching this task, but it seemed necessary in order to put the rest of it in context.

He needn't have worried about it. Grandma Cecy had never been one to indulge in extended sentimental farewells—what had been between her and her grandson, they had known about, while she had still been around. There was no need to go over it again. The letter was short, and very simple.

Dear Simon, I haven't dated this letter because somehow it seemed to be tempting fate—but whatever today's date is, you and I both knew it had to come someday. The key in this box is to the safety deposit box at my bank. It contains all the necessary documents that you will need to dot the i's and cross the t's of my life, as well as the details of a small savings account, which is already in your name. You'll also find a copy of a will, and the phone number of the attorney who holds the original—it's quite simple, and there should be no trouble with it. It shouldn't surprise you to learn that everything I have to leave I have left to you. I will leave no detailed instructions as to what should be done with me, you do as you think best, but I don't think I would care for a headstone in a graveyard. If you decide to keep the house and not sell it, perhaps you could just scatter my ashes in the garden—but please do remember that I need no physical token to be always near you. Whatever you make of your life, I know that you will find a way to be happy.

My blessing on you and on all your days.

That, aside from her signature at the bottom, was all.

She had been right—there had been no trouble with any of it. Simon had taken no more than two days off from his studies; he even handed in on time a paper that had been due less than a week after his grandmother's death. His professor received it with mild astonishment.

"I expected you to ask for an extension on this one," he said.

"Having to think about that, rather than about everything else, actually helped," Simon said. He was calm, almost icy, brittle but hard; there was something in his face, in his demeanor, that made the professor decide not to pursue the matter.

"Thank you," he said, tucking the paper away into a folder on his desk. And then hesitated, after all. "If there is anything that I can do, Simon…"

Simon's mouth twitched. "I just need… to keep busy."

He meant that. He loaded his next couple of semesters at college with extra classes, and kept his head down and his mind occupied, and it almost worked—he could almost pretend that the worlds he kept inside his head were the only ones that existed, or certainly the only ones that mattered.

But the real world was not ready to relinquish him completely, and creatures of flesh and blood rather than those of ideas still had power over him that he could not completely ignore.

"You want to grab something to eat?" one of his classmates asked at the conclusion of one of the late afternoon lectures they shared.

Her name was Amanda; she and Simon had been part of the same group on several outings, and if they had not exactly dated, that did not mean that she was unaware of him in that potential context. She knew about Simon's recent bereavement, and she, like everyone else, had been content to respect his apparent vow of solitude for a while. But she had apparently finally made a decision that Simon needed a helping hand back to the land of the living, as it were, and that she herself would be the perfect person to extend one. She had long, lank dark hair, and bold eyes, and the kind of single-minded determination to be a force for change that had cost her a number of relationships in her life so far. She had something of a reputation in that she was always on the look-out for a project, and Simon had just become a challenge—he carried around a large neon sign that flashed *Danger—do not touch*, a sign invisible to any but Amanda's kind, and to her it was not a warning but an invitation.

Simon glanced up at her, at first genuinely bewildered. "Pardon?"

"You do eat, don't you? It's kind of necessary, every so often. I just thought, if you were on your way to eat something, do you want a bit of company?"

"I, uh, no, I was going to…"

"Spanish Gardens," she said. "Come on. You need a couple of hours away from a desk, here or back home. I'll buy you an Irish Coffee if you buy the next round."

He had wanted to say no. He had meant to. But something in the smile that curved her lips into the dimples in her cheeks, something in her eyes, suddenly made him smile back. The smile was difficult, if only because he was a little out of practice, but it was real, and he found himself enjoying the fact that he had been betrayed into one.

"Okay," he said. "Okay, then."

He had actually laughed at things she said, long before

they got to Spanish Gardens, laughed without guilt or second thoughts or the sudden cold touch of the memory of things he had lost. She had flung open the windows of his tightly shuttered mind, and he found himself gulping at the fresh air, greedily, with an appetite he hadn't realized was there.

It was Amanda who suggested sharing a plate of spaghetti and meatballs.

"You *have* seen 'Lady and the Tramp', haven't you?" she said coyly.

"A long time ago," he laughed.

But he remembered the scene she was talking about, and he found himself willing to play along. The plate of pasta was shared messily and increasingly intimately. The first long piece of spaghetti that Amanda picked out, putting one end of it in her own mouth and the other, her fingers lingering just a little too long, between Simon's lips, broke soggily in half between them when they tried to re-enact the Disney scene, splattering spaghetti sauce on them; Amanda giggled as she picked bits of it off Simon's shirt, dipping a piece of her paper napkin into her glass of water and rubbing at the greasy spot to try and stop the greasy spot from setting—and then tilted her head up obligingly to allow him to return the favor, his fingers flaking off the spatter that had landed on her collarbone. The second attempt at eating a single string of spaghetti worked spectacularly well, and ended in a long, deep kiss, with Simon's hand coming up to the nape of Amanda's neck, the two of them straining toward one another across the table.

The spaghetti was never quite finished, but they had another Irish Coffee or two apiece, Simon's hand covering Amanda's on the table, her foot sliding against his under the table, her hair tickling his neck where she had laid her head against his shoulder. Spanish Gardens had served its purpose; they were there only long enough for certain things to be asked and then answered, without wasting unnecessary words. The road out of here inevitably led to Simon's own little house, another bottle of red wine, and Simon's bed.

"Hey," he had asked her sleepily, after, tangled in her hair and the long limbs twined with his own, "will you marry me?"

"Of course not," Amanda said, turning to kiss him on the cheek—the only part of him that she could reach while being pinned in position with his arm across a swathe of hair. "But ask me again sometime."

He did not ask her again. In fact, they spent only about three weeks together as a couple before they split up. But when they parted company it was as friends, and Amanda was followed by others—Patty, Vivian, Jill, Sara, Jayne, and more. The relationships stretched anything from a couple of weeks to several months, but they always ended, and someone new would find her way into Simon's life and his bed. He did not keep count—they were not trophies, or notches on his bedpost. They were merely birds of passage. If he was meant to settle down with any one of them, he failed to read the signs.

Simon had friends, and he had lovers—but they remained on the periphery. There was no center to his life, no human being to whom he opened up completely—it was as though when his circle closed, when the bridge that Grandma Cecy had once been vanished from under his feet, there remained no way back in to where he had hidden away his soul.

One of his lovers had called him on it once, when they had reached the end of their road together.

"You go through life watching it through the windows of a train," she told him. "You never step off the train. Now and again you allow somebody else to step on, share a compartment for a little while, and then they get put off at the next station and you go on—sitting by the window, looking out at the scenery, knowing always and precisely where you are and what lies around you but never staying long enough to get to know any of it, or to truly love it. Simon, doesn't it get lonely?"

He had considered that, and then smiled, a little sadly. "Sometimes," he said. "But it's safe."

Nothing could ever die for him again... because everything would be transient, seen and touched and perhaps loved but only in passing. If things withered in his wake he would never know, because he would already have walked away from them.

It was ideas that took the place of people. Simon immersed himself in words, in books, in work. In his final year as an undergraduate he was already working as a part-time teaching assistant to one of his professors, who persuaded him to stay on after graduation and pursue a postgraduate degree—complete with a full Teaching Assistantship stipend to help with the tuition fees. He was appointed a junior lecturer while he was still working on his PhD dissertation, and he was both young enough and brilliant enough to accumulate a circle of devoted fans, younger students with whom he socialized outside working hours and who formed the nucleus of what was to quickly become something of an institution at the department— Simon Alderwood's Writing Group.

It had never been an actual class—not for academic credit, anyway. But it had taken on a life of its own after a small but critical mass of young writers swirled around Simon and coalesced into a permanent group, an open secret passed down from one generation of students down to the next much like favorite student meeting places, like Spanish Gardens, were handed down the line as every year's influx of new freshmen flooded into the department. In the beginning it was only a handful of them—the most intense handful. The ones in whom dedication almost blurred into obsession, the ones in whom other people's words had woken their own, early, and in whom words had become a passion. Simon had begun using the initial writing group as a teaching tool, turning the students' own words into examples, sending them out to read other books by other writers who had already done—for better or worse— the things that the student writers themselves were trying to accomplish. He would make them articulate what they had learned from their reading when they returned to the group, and then take away both their own writing and the things that they had learned from their reading and combine the two into something new, and bigger, and better.

The first handful of students who were to form the nucleus of the group began to meet in his office, but word spread quickly and Simon's tiny office rapidly became too small to contain the gathering—and somehow the weekly meetings of the group ended up not in a bigger seminar room somewhere in the department but in Simon's own living room. It wasn't, after all, a formal class; it required a different atmosphere than that of a lecture hall in order to fulfill its function, and every Friday night Simon's sitting room would be graced by anything from half a dozen to almost twenty eager young writers lounging on his sofa, or perched uncomfortably on the edge of a dining room chair, or sitting cross-legged on the floor with their notepads in their laps. Simon held court sitting in his leather armchair, occasionally leaping up to pace up and down if there was room or going off to one of the many bookshelves in the room to pluck out a volume and toss it at whichever student happened to be in the spotlight at that moment, illustrating some point that he was making.

"It's *tame*," he said to a girl who had been trying very hard to write a dark and passionate scene of doomed love. "And what's worse, you know that. It's a snapshot—a beautiful photograph—but it's *bloodless*, soul-less. Put away the camera, show us what you're taking a picture of, and make us understand why you thought it was worth taking. Look at the words you are using—the language itself is getting away from you—you can't create the madness you want in there with words alone. You need to show us. Use your *characters* to show us. Don't give us a lecture, give us deeds. Kazantzakis had it—that madness—here—" And he would toss her a copy of "Zorba the Greek" from his bookshelves. "Read that and try it again."

He had no patience with excuses.

"Shakespeare," Simon said, when students attempted to defend some lackluster piece of writing which had aimed high but failed to measure up to his exacting standards by claiming that they were too young to have had the life experience required to do justice to the subject matter, "did not, to my knowledge, have a father murdered, nor ever talked to his father's ghost. He was certainly never a Prince of Denmark. He wasn't remotely ever a woman, or insane. He was never a jealous monster, or destroyed by one. Yet he created the characters of Hamlet and Ophelia, and Othello and Iago and Desdemona, and hundreds of years later actors who interpret his lines on stage find things in those characters with which they present the audience, and it rings *true*. Here—" He hauled out copies of "Hamlet" and

"Othello" from his shelves, and handed them out to reaching hands. "Read that. No, better—Shakespeare was a playwright, he was meant to be heard, not read in silence. Here, take this scene—pick a part—read it out loud. Right here, right now. Listen with your heart."

In the second year of the group's existence, Simon had gone to the department head with a handful of stories.

"There used to be a journal that was run by the department," Simon said. "I know there did, I came across copies of it in the library. It kind of… quit, though. What happened to it?"

"Staff cutbacks at the time. The person who ran it disappeared, and then it fell through the cracks for a while. It got revived about five years back or so, but it got nowhere much."

"Well, I want to revive it again," Simon said. He laid his hand over the small pile of stories he had laid on the professor's desk. "These deserve it. I'm not saying everyone from this department who's ever set pen to paper is an undiscovered genius—and yes, those with the potential to succeed at this will no doubt send their stuff elsewhere and get it published…but I know I've got some amazing people here, and it would not be at all bad if their own department was the one that recognized them first. We would get noticed, too."

"You want to take it on?" the professor said. "There's very little budget for it—we couldn't offer much in the way of payment…"

"I'll put in a request in next year's budget," Simon said. "And trust me, I can get plenty of volunteers to help run this thing."

"Your baby," the professor said, shrugging his acquiescence.

And Simon had thrown himself into the project. He took himself out of the actual process, appointing himself a "Departmental Advisor" in the masthead and contenting himself with arranging the practical aspects of the new journal—striking a deal with a local print shop, arranging distribution in local bookstores, paying for national advertising out of his own pocket. The students in his group chose acquiring editors for different departments—fiction, poetry, essays, literary criticism—from amongst themselves, and it wasn't too long before they began receiving contributions from outside the University itself, from people in different cities or even states than themselves, several times from different countries. It was a small publication, but somehow it turned up at the right place and time to gather an enormous amount of academic prestige.

The journal staff and Simon's writing group were overlapping but not wholly identical circles of people—there were those who were interested in the writing part of it who attended the writing group seminars but who were not interested in running a literary journal.

One of the journal's young student editors, Olivia Halloran, who was not herself a regular member of the writing circle but who attended the gatherings occasionally, who asked Simon if she could bring a friend along.

"She's awfully shy about it but I've seen some of her stuff and she could be really good if she gave herself a chance," Olivia said earnestly. "She would *never* just turn up—but if I brought her along with me, she'll come. She may not say much, probably won't in fact, at least not in the beginning, but I think it would do her the world of good just to sit there and *listen*. Okay if I just drag her in by the scruff of her neck?"

"By all means," Simon said equably. "Whether she stays is her own province, but she's more than welcome to see if it suits her."

So Maura Simmons joined Simon's circle, drifting in at Olivia's side, barely opening her mouth for long enough to give people her name when she was introduced to them. Maura was an intense young woman who—as Olivia had predicted—initially had very little to say in the seminars. She admitted to writing poetry, but rarely shared any—and when she was finally coaxed into doing so by the group, the few occasions that she did so were less than comfortable for those who were put in a position to listen. Maura wrote about deeply personal things and used words like a scalpel to slice open the places that ached until she drew blood—and even though she was not writing about other people's darkest and most closely held secrets, because she did not know them, it felt as though she was, her writing large enough to encompass multitudes, her insights often devastating.

She proved to be unexpectedly and unnervingly good at this, and that made people wary of her—because she would use what she was given, and she did not differentiate between what was offered freely and what sometimes slipped out by accident. If she had been dark-haired and dark-eyed and given to wearing black, she might have been described as Goth—but on the face of it she was oddly disarming, a small-boned pixie of a girl with wispy blonde hair and washed-out pale blue eyes often framed by too much make-up. She was someone who, on the face of it, looked pallid and shallow, unlikely to bother even looking underneath the surface of things, never mind having any ability to actually perceive and understand the things she might encounter there if she did delve deeper by accident. But Simon had quickly revised that initial dismissive opinion, because it was her words that made him judge the kind of person that she was, not her misleading looks.

She had attended his group for just over four months, and then she stopped coming. Simon had asked, but Olivia had simply shrugged her shoulders and said that Maura was unpredictable. Simon would still see Maura drifting through the corridors on her way to lectures, and knew she hadn't dropped out of school—but she seemed to have decided that she was just as uncomfortable with the group as the group had been with her. Simon found himself regretting this—some part of him, the teacher core now honed by years of experience, recognized that she had something that was extraordinary, unique. But the group was self-regulating, no registration, no obligation, no commitment beyond free choice, and he had to respect hers.

Until the day that there was a knock on the door to his office, and when he called out permission to enter it was Maura's dandelion-haired head that was revealed as she peered around the edge of the door.

"Do you have a moment?" she asked diffidently, obviously ready to bolt as soon as he mentioned the fact she was here at a time which definitely wasn't covered by the office hours posted on the outside of the door.

"Sure," he said instead, confounding her. "Come on in."

She slunk in almost unwillingly—almost as though she

had been banking on him turning her away, and then stood awkwardly a couple of steps into the office, clutching the small knapsack that served as her book bag. Simon waved her further in, indicating one of the visitor chairs that sat across the desk from him.

"Come in, take a seat," he said. "Missed you in group. What have you been up to?"

"Writing," she said. She edged in, sidled up to the chair, subsided onto it and perched right on the edge, knapsack balanced on her knees.

"Your poetry was always…"

"Not poetry," she said, and then looked vaguely appalled that she had interrupted him.

Simon sat up, leaning his elbows on his desk, his interest piqued now. "Oh?"

"I've got a story," Maura said. "Maybe a novel."

"*Maybe* a novel?"

"It wants to be one. But it's running off with me. I don't know where it's going. Olivia said you could help."

"You want to come back to the group?" Simon asked. "Perhaps the others can help to focus the thing."

Maura shook her head once, sharply. "No," she said. "I can't let them see it, not yet. It's not good enough. But I thought…I wanted to ask *you*…"

She hesitated, and then abruptly unzipped the top of the knapsack and flung it open, reaching inside and extracting a blue unmarked folder.

"This is all I've got so far," she said. "It's not quite done, but…"

She was holding the folder very tightly—but she was also holding it out toward Simon, in a gesture that matched her earlier entrance into the office. She wanted him to take a look at her work, but she was waiting for, and looked as if she might be rather relieved at, a refusal.

Simon reached for the folder—he had to tug at it for her to release it, but he didn't have to tug twice.

"All right," he said. "I'll take a look. But it will be a couple of weeks, I've all those term papers to grade…"

"That's fine," she said quickly, looking down and veiling her eyes with pale lashes.

"Come by after the seventeenth," Simon said.

But it didn't take him that long. What she gave him was raw, to be sure, but it made the hair on his arms stand up as he read it and knew that he held something special in his hands. It had all the searing, incisive insight of her poetry—but it had been channeled now, into something more accessible, into *story*. What emerged was a weapon of words no less potent than the poetry had once been, but Maura had learned to wield it with a savagery that was all new—the kind of savagery that left a wound which the recipient would not have noticed they even received until it started to leak out heart's-blood.

Three days after she left the folder with him, Simon stopped Maura in the corridor.

"Come see me," he said. "I finished it."

She flushed again, and just nodded, without speaking.

Her nerve failed her, for two days—and then she was finally there, on the third day, her knock almost too quiet to be heard. But Simon had been expecting her, and he motioned her inside. When he handed her back the folder, she cracked it open a little way, enough to see that there were marks on the manuscript and comments written in the margins, and closed it again abruptly, keeping her eyes down.

"That shouldn't scare you," Simon said, having noticed her response. "What should scare you is a manuscript that came back to you pristine. That would mean it had not gone far enough to have touched anything at all. This…this needs work, but Maura, it's terrific. Are you sure you won't come back to the group with this? There are a dozen things that you could teach them all just by sharing the first five pages of that."

She shook her head. "I showed some of it to Olivia, but not the rest—not now. Not yet. Not until I am happy with it. And *you* weren't, or you wouldn't have edited it…"

Simon grinned. "Why don't you take a closer look at some of those edits?"

She gave him a wary sideways glance, but opened up the folder and began to pore over the things that he had written down. Her cheeks alternated between a hectic blush and a waxen pallor, and Simon could see her fingers trembling where she held the folder open. But after a while she became engrossed in the matter, and slowly lost the stiffness in her shoulders, the tightness in her back. She asked a question, without looking up; then another, lifting her eyes a little; then a third.

Simon ended the session, a little regretfully, almost an hour into the discussion.

"All right," he said, "no group. But there's plenty to talk about there; and it would be a privilege to help you knock this one into shape. Do you want to come back tomorrow and pick up where we left off?"

"Are you sure?" she said, putting the folder down on her knees and finally lifting her eyes to meet his own squarely. "What you've done already…it's more than I had hoped for…"

"I look forward to it," he said firmly.

She flushed again, murmured something that might have been a thank you, and almost fell over her own feet getting out of his office.

The collaboration was uneven, and intermittent—every so often the two of them would get to some point which was somehow viscerally important enough to Maura to make her back off and pull away, and then Simon had to wait for her to get over the stage fright and come knocking on his door again, sometimes unrepentant about the things that they had discussed and refusing to change them, sometimes with a sheaf of new pages which she had re-drafted to address the issues that he had raised from the original version.

Maura wasn't given to flowery turns of phrase, and her already honed writing style was nurtured and sharpened in the sessions in Simon's office until the manuscript began to turn into something darkly beautiful, spare and deadly.

She remained insistent that it was not good enough, that it was not what she had really wanted, that it was not perfect— and for a while Simon went along with it. But at some point in the process, in the midst of one of Maura's attempts to pick apart and re-knit a particular scene for what must have been the tenth time, he finally sat back and crossed his arms.

"Maura," he said. "It is *done.*"

She looked at him wide-eyed, almost terrified. "No, it isn't nearly finished! There are so many things that I could still fix..."

Grandma Cecy's voice came drifting back into Simon's mind—*Nothing is ever perfect. You might make it better, but it will be a different kind of perfect then. There are times you just need to know when to let go.* He himself had never quite taken that advice to heart, not when it came to his own work—but he knew enough to realize the wisdom of it, and he could certainly recognize the time when letting go of the thing that one held onto so fiercely became the only thing that one could do if that thing was in any way cherished or loved; the time when hanging on was only hurting its chances.

He gazed at Maura now, and knew with an unshakeable certainty that she was there, at that point. This was the only thing he had left to teach her.

"It will never," Simon said slowly, "be as good as you think it can be. As it *should* be. But there comes a time...when it's the best that you can make it. When it is good enough."

She stared at him, and then slowly, very slowly, closed the folder over the manuscript within. "What do I do now?" she asked, very quietly—but it was a question posed with serenity, without any of her usual self-doubt or blushing insecurity.

"Let me put out a few feelers," Simon said.

His own novel, the one he had started so long ago, the one whose first halting version he had read to Grandma Cecy on the day she died, had undergone a couple of revisions, and gone so far as to have the first couple of chapters reach the second or third typed-up iteration—but they had been shown to a publishing professional only once, almost in passing, and had received no more than an encouraging noise or two and a pat on the back. He had never really pursued it, leaving that particular ambition behind him, sinking instead into the teaching and the academic work at the University. The novel fragment had languished at the back of a filing cabinet, gathering dust for years. But he had kept up a contact or two from the days when he had entertained the notion that the book might go further—and now he reached out again, not with his own novel but with Maura's.

His acquaintances included an editor who was no longer in the business, but who asked to read the manuscript anyway—and then, once he had done so, wrote back to Simon that he still knew people in publishing circles and almost begging for the opportunity, if Maura agreed, to pass the manuscript along into their hands.

Simon turned the matter over to Maura at that point, and stepped away.

She smiled at him in the corridors if they happened to cross paths, but said nothing more of the book—he asked, once, because there was an odd needling need to know, but she merely said that she had heard nothing back.

So he stopped asking, and tried to make himself forget the matter.

Until the day—almost a year later—that there was a knock on his door and Maura all but fell into his office, radiating excitement.

"I had a letter," she said, without preamble.

Simon didn't need to ask what the letter had said.

"Congratulations," he said, and he was genuinely happy that someone else out there had seen the potential in Maura's novel. What he had not been prepared for was a stab of completely unlooked-for and acidly burning jealousy that sank into his spirit like a hot needle. He mastered it, controlled it, invited her in and sat her down, had her show him the letter of acceptance, talked it over with her, congratulated her once again... and came close to coming completely undone when she turned at the door to the office, about to step out.

"I couldn't have done it without you," she said, earnest, sincere, with a grateful glow in her eyes. "Olivia was right—she sent me to you—and you taught me so much. You're the best teacher I've ever had."

He managed a smile.

"Thank you," he said.

He did not have the strength for more, but she didn't need it. She gave him one last vivid smile, and danced out into the corridor.

Simon sat unmoving for some time. He had no teaching

commitment for that afternoon and it was just as well, because he couldn't seem to find a way to marshal his thoughts into a single coherent sentence—they fluttered around inside his skull like a flock of birds disturbed from a resting perch and unable to settle to rest again.

He had worked for this, with Maura—he had helped, and shaped, and shared his instincts and the insights gained from years of reading and teaching and knowing how to recognize excellence. He had dreamed her dreams right alongside her. And yet, in the end, he could not stand in the spotlight with her. Maura might have meant every word of what she had said—she would probably, when her book was published, make sure that his name was in the acknowledgments—but in the end it was her achievement, and not his.

For the first time in a very long time Simon found himself restless in that train in which one of his long-gone girlfriends had told him he lived his life—found himself peering out of a dirty window at some station just passed, wondering if that had been his own destination, now forever left behind.

Some part of him wanted desperately to dig out his own novel, or what there was of it, and start poking at it again.

Another part of him, aware of the quality of Maura's work, recoiled from the very idea of that—lest he find his own words irredeemably lacking in merit.

If he never looked at that old novel again, he might return to writing, some day. If he did crack that manuscript open, he might never write another original word again.

But Maura was young, and the world was ahead of her. Simon suddenly felt older than Methuselah, lost in the world of young dreams and young talent, feeling as though he had missed a turning somehow, somewhere along the way. He had become… something different than what he had once thought that he might. His chance at being something unique, someone with a unique contribution that nobody else but him could make, had gone; what he had become, by definition, was a teacher, someone whose role in life was to shape others into being those things while he himself remained in the background.

He had thought—he had firmly believed—that this had been

enough, that it would have been enough. Now, on the brink of watching one of his students step out onto that stage in front of an adoring audience, he was uncomfortably aware that there had been a time—a time which was apparently not yet past—at which he might have wanted to claim that stage and all that it meant for himself.

He had a good life. He'd found his niche in the academic life. He might have been a no more than adequate administrator, but without any false modesty he knew himself to have become an excellent teacher—his department valued his contribution, and his students loved him. And he didn't like the feelings stirring inside of him, the sense that it had all been wasted, somehow, because he had wanted something different all along.

He waited until the corridors grew quiet, with students dispersing to their final afternoon lectures and seminars, and then slowly stood, pushing his chair back and stepping away from his desk, leaving everything on it exactly as it was and making no effort to tidy anything away at the end of the day as he usually did. It took him only a couple of minutes to lock up his office and walk down the empty, echoing corridors, full of a flat gray winter light, to the front door of the faculty building.

It was barely after three in the afternoon, but the lights were already on in the main avenue of the campus. Simon paused for a moment as he stepped outside, tilting his head a little to look up at the heavy sky as he adjusted a scarf around his neck. Even as he lifted his eyes to the low clouds, the first wet flakes of snow began to fall, drifting down slowly and gently, touching the woolen sleeve of his winter coat and the stone lions guarding the entrance to the building, melting as they made contact with both and then becoming a part of their shape and texture. It wasn't sticking, not yet, but it would soon. The world would be white and silent by midnight.

Simon's gloved hands lifted the collar of his coat against the back of his neck, and he walked out into the snowfall, hatless, the flakes catching on his dark hair. He did not feel like going home; the whole world seemed empty except for him and the snow right now, and back in his small house he would be shutting even the snow out. At the same time, he didn't particularly feel like seeking the company of anyone in particular. He wanted the sound of human voices around him, to be able to see human faces, but on the whole he would prefer them to be those of strangers. He didn't want to be a friend to anyone, not tonight. He merely wanted to blend seamlessly, invisibly, into the continued existence of his species, knowing that there were others of his kind out there but not feeling the necessity to make a closer acquaintance with any of them.

He got into his car, shuffling the possibilities in his mind. He could go to a movie, and while a few hours away in front of other people's dramas and problems. He could indulge his occasional craving for a good dinner at a restaurant of good repute, the kind where he would occasionally wince inwardly as he paid the bill. Or he could go to where the memories were, to the places which held his past, trying to peer back through the years and recapture things that, perhaps, were better left unhunted.

The decision didn't seem entirely up to him, in the end, and he found himself a little astonished to be parking the car underneath a streetlight already muffled by falling snow—in a street near a place with which he had had a long acquaintance but which he had not visited in some time, and had not even consciously included as a possible destination when he had first given thought to where he wanted to go. It was, in fact, according to memories which now surfaced, a little odd to be able to find a parking spot so close to where he wanted to be— parking was usually at a premium around here, and he had often had to park several blocks away when he had come here in the past. But perhaps it was just that he had arrived relatively early, on a week-night, and on an evening on which weather was already becoming an issue.

Spanish Gardens was almost empty—Simon had expected as much, but he still looked around expectantly, as though he had come here to meet someone. He caught himself at it, shook his head in self-deprecating chagrin, and walked purposefully toward one of the smaller tables in the corner by the plush curtain which concealed the giant plate-glass window frontage that gave into the courtyard beyond. Right now, with the curtains drawn against the snowy evening outside, the effect was one of softness and warmth; something inside Simon, long frozen, cracked open and began to thaw.

"Sir?" One of the young waitresses had paused by his table, menu in hand.

Simon waved it away. "Nothing to eat. Not yet, anyway. Bring me an Irish Coffee."

"Coming up," she said, and walked away with the bouncy energetic step of youth.

The Irish Coffee materialized on his table fairly quickly— but it was not brought by the girl who had taken his order.

"Something to drown your sorrows in?" a male voice inquired as the glass was placed in front of him.

Simon glanced up. The coffee-bearer was of an indeterminate age—he might have been anything from twenty to a youthful middle-age, of average build, his hair nondescript and falling to barely brush his shoulders, the hand which unfolded from the handle of the coffee glass long-fingered and pale. The smoke-gray eyes gazing down at Simon were friendly, and oddly knowing.

"I'm sorry," Simon said, frowning a little, "I have an odd feeling I should know who you are, but I can't remember..."

"Ariel," the young man said helpfully. "I'm Ariel. I work here. We've met. And it's time to remember."

Simon's frown deepened a notch. "Pardon?"

"May I?" Ariel said, and pulled out a chair at Simon's table. "You want to talk about it?"

Simon, who was so fiercely private and protective of his own space, somehow completely failed to take issue with the liberty. Instead, he took a thoughtful sip of the Irish Coffee, and then stared down at it, the glass cradled between his hands, with a distant and unfocused gaze.

"I never expected... envy," he said slowly. "Not quite that. Not in the way that it came at me."

"Maura?" Ariel asked.

Simon's eyes flickered up to Ariel's face. "You know her?"

"It's my business to know everyone," Ariel said.

"But..." Simon's eyebrows knit in a frown again. "She

only just found out—she only just told me—how could you possibly—"

"Everyone, and everything," Ariel said. He pulled out a photograph from the back pocket of his jeans. "You mean this?"

Simon turned the photo so that it faced him, and stared at it for a long moment. It showed Maura—a different Maura, he couldn't quite put his finger on it at first, but it was subtle enough, her hair a little longer, her expression not quite the hunted self-conscious one he had grown to recognize on her features. She was standing next to a red-haired woman, beside a table piled high with books.

Books with Maura's name on them.

The book she had just come into his office to tell him had been accepted for publication.

Simon looked up.

"This hasn't happened yet," he said.

"I took a short cut," Ariel said. "It's going to. *You* helped it happen. Well, Olivia brought her to you, but in the end it was you, yourself, who helped her find her voice. And—look—" He fished out another pair of photographs, flicked them onto the table on top of the first. One showed Simon's hand being shaken by a young black man with square-rimmed spectacles and a huge grin. Simon recognized him—Anthony Bates, one of his postgraduate students, a year into his MA. The other photo showed a couple of people he didn't know, two young women who might have been in their twenties, with an arm draped around one another's shoulders; one of them was giving a thumbs-up gesture with her free hand, and the other held a book out toward the camera.

"Who are those two?" Simon asked.

"You haven't met them yet, but they're on their way. And so is that book. And you're already glimpsing Anthony's. And you've just heard about Maura's. Olivia might have brought you Maura, but she was only the first—all of these are yours—your hand on the future of all these people. Your name on their lips. You were the muse. The mentor. The teacher. The inspiration. Without you, nothing. You were the catalyst for it all."

"There was a time," Simon said, "that I thought—that I

knew—that I was the actual reaction, the primary reagent, not the catalyst. I myself had something to say."

"You did," Ariel said gently.

And there was a book on the table. Simon wasn't quite certain where it had come from—it was hardcover, too large to have been in a back pocket, and Ariel's hands had been free of anything but the coffee he had brought to the table when he had arrived—but it was there, solid, unmistakable, a book...with his own name on the cover. He picked it up and there was a strange energy running through his fingers, as though the book was electric. On the back of the cover, a quote from a New York Times review, and a blurb by another writer, well-known, with the kind of household name that sent a shock of recognition through Simon.

And this, too, was Olivia's doing. For this book, she had not brought him a young genius to nurture—she had shared something of her own personal life, brought the letters her brother had written from the wars to show him, to inspire him. This was the book that had lost him Olivia, in a different lifetime, a different world...

"I wrote this," Simon said, knowing he spoke the truth, knowing that he was saying something impossible, remembering with a sudden and desperate clarity two different lives, two different pasts.

He cradled the spine of the book in one hand, let it fan open before him. A photograph fell out from in between the pages, somewhere in the middle of the book—a snapshot of a family picnic, someone who was obviously himself standing with his arms around a teenage boy with a woman and a slightly older teenage girl sitting on a blanket spread out on grass, a picnic basket between them.

"Ellen," Simon said. "Abby. Josh. They're... this is my *family*,"

"Look in your pocket," Ariel said gently.

Without relinquishing his hold on the photograph, Simon put down the book and fished in his pocket with the free hand. He came up with a folded piece of paper—and stared at it with another shock of recognition, suddenly remembering the circumstances in which he had first received it, from... from...

He looked up again. "You gave me this," he said. "It was here, right here in Spanish Gardens. There was a... there are people waiting for me in here..." He looked around the still relatively empty café, found no face he recognized, but his mind's eye now supplied what he needed. "Ellen," he said. "My wife's in here. And Quincey, and John, old friends, and... Olivia...I just argued with Olivia..."

"Read it," Ariel said. "Remember it all."

The words on the slip of paper pulsed at Simon.

Your life is filled with crossroads, and you are free to choose one road or another at any time. Stepping through this door narrows your choices to only two-the choice to live a different life, or the choice to return to this one.

You make your first choice when you step through the portal.

Once you do, you will not remember the life you have left behind... until one single moment, when all memory will return. In that moment you must choose if you wish to return to your previous existence...or renounce it forever.

Remember this before you decide. Here, you change the world around you; there, you have to change to fit the world. Both are harder than you think. Choose wisely.

"It isn't just envy, it's the stirring of that memory—the memory of the life you've already lived," Ariel said. "You *had* the life you sat in your office thinking that you wanted. It was you who received the letter about the book."

"That wasn't the book I started to write," Simon said. "I began a story that was about...about *me*."

"It wasn't a story," Ariel said. "It was the other reality. Here are the things you need to consider. *Here*, you're a teacher. You're revered. You'll become more so as the years go on; you will retire from teaching with your name long remembered... but not for what *you* did, for what you helped others do. You will die alone, however—here, you never settle down for long enough to start a family. You don't have a wife. You don't have children, except the ones that you mould in your classes, year after year. Here, you were principled, idealistic. There, in that other life, the life that's connected to that book you're holding - your mother survived the accident, you had her with you for longer, but she was in chronic pain all the rest of her life—and Grandma Cecy died earlier, died younger. *There*...you have a wife who is a sort of a rival, which you often resent. You have two children, but one of them was born because of a sort of betrayal—and the book you wrote was not the story of your own life but the story of someone else's, a story given to you by a woman who didn't expect you to do what you did with it, who didn't expect you to turn to her friend when you broke with her. A very different Olivia than the one you knew. That might have been another crossroads—another life to choose— but that's no longer the choice. The choice is between the *here*, and the *other*. What do you want, in the end? What do you want to be remembered for?"

"What happens...to Maura...to the others..."

"You mean if you choose to go back to the life where the books are your own?"

Simon nodded.

Ariel laced his fingers together, shaking his head. "Not your problem," he said, with maddening serenity. "Not your responsibility. They are living their own lives. They are responsible for their own choices. You are only responsible for your own."

Simon buried his face in his hands. "God. *God!* Why me? Why did you pick me?"

"I...? I pick nobody—I'm just the messenger," Ariel said. "If I turn up, it's because I was needed—all I ever do is listen out for when the call comes in. Besides, whatever makes you think that you are the only one who has been offered this kind of choice? In fact, if that will make you feel better, I can tell you that before this night is over at least four people whom you personally know will be faced with the same choice you are wrestling with right now."

"And that means that *their* choices will affect me," Simon said.

"Possibly. There are an infinite number of bridges that

can be crossed. And once you choose one of the possibilities that becomes the only firm ground—all the rest is smoke and dreams."

"I don't know if I can do this. Who am I to choose…? And all those others—you go to them, too? Like this—like now, with me?"

"Some manage to choose all by themselves, without any assistance," Ariel said. "Those are the ones who choose with the heart, with feelings, with instinct—they hesitate, sometimes, at a crossroads and then they simply start walking again, and it's the only road, and it's like the crossroads never were. For them, anyway. For you—you analyze. You think. You might get a glimpse of the crossroads, and then you'll stand there and worry at that idea until night falls, and you get lost in the darkness. Sometimes, I need to be there."

"Like a guardian angel," Simon said, his eyebrow climbing into his hairline.

Ariel laughed. "If you insist," he said. "Or you might think of me as a manual of sorts. Something to consult when you need to write the final version of an academic thesis."

"It feels selfish," Simon said. "To want to have had my own voice. To have walked the world out in the sunlight, rather than in the shadows."

"Nothing is ever selfish," Ariel said. "At least, nothing that you can possibly do in this moment."

"I will remember, and regret," Simon murmured.

"Read the instructions again. You will remember nothing— nothing specific, nothing to have regrets over. You yourself may or may not emerge changed by this choice, this experience—but memory will have nothing to do with it. You might never have met Maura in your other life. You might pass her in the street and never recognize her, or she you. You either choose to have had a hand in her life, or not. She may or may not *ever* show anyone that brilliant book of hers. But what becomes of her if you choose the latter…you will never know. That's the price you pay."

"How do I put a value on something like this?" Simon demanded, his fingers going restlessly to the book on the table, tapping on the title embossed on the jacket. And then he reached out for the photographs—the sheaf that Ariel had brought, of the students who had found success because he had been there to guide them to it, of the family at the Sunday afternoon picnic. "How do I put a value on *this*? What is the measure of contentment?"

"Only you can know," Ariel said.

"Stepping off the train," Simon said, staring at the picture of the family. "This means stepping off the train."

"Something like that," Ariel said. He stood, pausing for a moment to allow his eyes to go to the back of the café, making sure Simon's eyes followed his gaze. "Over there," he said. "Back there, where the restrooms are. The 'Out of Order' sign, remember? Take as long as you need to—but make a choice. Here. Now. Tonight. And when you're ready…go back through that door. It will take you where you need to go. You will remember what you need to remember, and forget the rest." He turned back to Simon for a moment, and the gray eyes were full of an odd compassion. "I'll leave you to think about it," he said softly. "Remember. Choose wisely. You may never remember the details of the things that you choose to give up—but if you choose wrongly now, there might come a time when you turn around after a shadow and think you might have seen it before, somewhere, sometime, in a dream, and feel—if only for a little while—strangely lost, and bereft. You will never know why."

"That seems oddly unfair," Simon said, with a lopsided grin.

"I never promised *fair*," Ariel said, pushing himself off the chair. "There's no rush—finish your coffee. Good luck."

Left to himself, Simon sat staring at the photographs spilled on the table before him, trying to come to terms with a rush of complex and unexpected emotions. His mind was at once empty, and overfull with two overlapping sets of memories; he was literally faced with weighing the lessons and gifts and griefs of one lifetime against those of another, both owned, both his to claim, both his to lose.

When he finally looked up, his face pale but determined, it was to realize with a start that the place had filled up around him. He took a few moments to let his eyes roam around the room, taking it all in, as though he was still hesitating, still undecided, waiting for this place to give him the final push one way or another. But the pause was misleading; he had already made up his mind. Reaching out to take a single photograph from the table with one hand, the slip of paper bearing Ariel's instructions in the other, he pushed the chair back with his knees and stood; if he paused at all it was only momentary, long enough for the last choice to fall into place and lock into position.

Then he walked resolutely toward the back of the room, pushing past a newly-arrived crowd of young people who were laughing and shaking fresh snow off their coats and their hair, and pushed open the door to the second restroom, the one with the 'Out of Order' sign swinging from the doorknob. He passed inside without looking back. The door swung closed behind him.

INTERMEZZO 1

Thursday, 20 December 2012

"Oh, hey, Simon," John said, glancing up as Simon rounded the curve of the archway and stepped into the main room. "We were beginning to lose hope. Find parking?"

"Found my spot," Simon said faintly.

Ellen looked up sharply. "What's the matter? You look like you've seen a ghost."

"I have," Simon said.

Ellen and Quincey exchanged a long look.

"You ran into Olivia, didn't you," Quincey said.

"Um. I didn't expect her," Simon said. But he was already coming back to himself, looking a little less shell-shocked, as he slipped into the empty seat on the bench which Olivia had lately vacated.

John stared at him. "You knew she was going to be here. *You* invited us all."

"I know. I was just hoping…for a little warning," Simon said.

"What did you say to her?" Quincey demanded.

"Nothing," Olivia said, herself coming into the room just in time to hear those words and to be aware of the glare of daggers that Quincey had pointed at Simon. "It's all right, really. Can we all just agree that twenty years ago was twenty years ago? And would everyone please stop looking at me as though I was made out of Dresden China?"

John had already risen from his chair as she had entered, and now pulled out the second chair for her sit on. "Right after this," he said, grinning.

"Twenty years," Quincey said. "I don't know which is worse—feeling like no time has passed at all, or feeling like it's been more like a century. I know I've managed to stuff a lot of unhappiness into those two decades."

"I heard about Martin," Olivia said, looking down at the table. "I did write to you, back then."

"I appreciated that," Quincey said softly. "You just never know, do you? Thirty five years old, and he dies because of a bad heart. Neither of us saw it coming."

Olivia reached out a hand across the table and laid it over one of Quincey's. "I'm so sorry," she said.

"But you remarried, didn't you?" Ellen murmured. "A Senator or something, was it? I seem to remember that you went to Washington…"

"Congressman. Al. Yes. I married that bastard. Six years of my life that I just know I am going to want to have back one day."

Ellen's eyes went round with surprise. "Gosh," she said, astonished at the vehemence of the reply. "I'm sorry. I didn't mean to stir anything nasty up."

Quincey waved her hand in a gesture of dismissal. "Nasty? I guess. It was more just par for the course, as it were. I mean, I was in my mid-thirties when Al and I got married, but that was three years before he made the jump from city councilman to Congressman, and really, Congress ruined him."

"Politics will do that," John said, with a smirk. "You can't say you didn't see *that* one coming…" And then his face changed a little, as Quincey's words of only a few moments ago echoed in his subconscious. *We didn't see that coming.* Her first husband's death.

John winced.

"Sorry," he said.

Quincey bestowed a look of absolution on him. "Hey," she said. "It's okay. I brought it up."

"What happened, with Al?" Ellen asked, leaning forward, her elbow on the table, chin cupped in her hand.

"Sure you want to know? Everything else we've spilled so far seems to have blown up in our faces…" Olivia murmured.

"Oh, it's no great secret. The usual, you know," Quincey said, shrugging her shoulders. "It actually stopped *hurting* a long time ago. Al... well... he knew all along that I was not a trophy wife—I came with a toddler, for God's sake, he knew I wasn't young and nubile any more. And as far as personality goes, he moved in with me and Sam almost a year before we got married, he ought to have known exactly what he was getting. But somehow...once he set foot into the House...all of that seemed to come as an unwelcome surprise to him. He suddenly seemed to become something completely different, to want something completely different. I guess I can't blame him. There aren't that many black Congresscritters, even now, and I suppose he had something to prove..."

"I'm guessing he proved entirely the wrong thing," John said.

"Well, since we're playing catch-up—we kept it out of the media, but yes, there was a girl. One of his office interns. Nineteen years old, blonde, and so very eager to make the Congressman happy. I kind of...walked in on the moment."

Ellen covered her mouth with her hand. "Oh, *Quincey*."

Quincey's lip curled. "You know what he did? He just kind of... looked up... and said, 'Hi, Quince'—I kind of decided right then and there that I had always hated him calling me Quince. I was not a fruit."

Olivia actually giggled, and Quincey's own mouth twitched into an answering grin.

"Yeah," she said. "I guess it was funny, at that. Under the circumstances, it probably wouldn't have been the first thought you might have expected to enter my head."

"What did you *do*?" Ellen asked.

Quincey shrugged. "Turned around. Walked out. Went home. Changed the locks."

"You could change the locks?...On a Congressman...?"

"Well, no," Quincey said. "At least, I didn't change the locks *yet*. Not that time. And he did come home and kind of raged and wept at me. Swore it would never happen again. But 'never' comes around far more often for some people than for others, apparently. He did the same thing, with a different intern, the following year. I *did* change the locks then—I moved out, to a place to which only I had the keys. I mean, the kids were pretty young, but I'd coped alone with a toddler before—and this time Sam was old enough to help out..."

"How old were they?" Ellen said sympathetically.

"Chuck and Jessi...? They were four when I walked out. Al gave me a divorce very meekly when I said that I'd go public if he didn't—and he didn't want a scandal, not one beyond a divorce, anyway. I was perfectly happy to let him paint me as the harpy who left *him*, back with his Capitol Hill buddies, it was no skin off my nose, but if I went to the press and told them the real reason I left he'd be left with a nice political omelet on his face. All I wanted was the kids, no questions asked. And he seemed happy to oblige." She snorted. "He's been circling lately, actually. They're ten now, the twins, and they're starting to be photogenic—and his next wife, the one he married after me..."

"Not the intern, I take it," Ellen said.

Quincey gave her a limpid look. "You were *expecting* him to marry that little slut?"

"*She* probably was, at the time," John said.

Quincey shook her head. "I have no doubt she was. But no, he needed a more savvy political wife. Trouble is, the one he did come up with is far too perfect to mess up her life with kids—and he's a politician, and the kids that he's already got are becoming a good photo op. And seeing as he got the no-fault divorce with nary a breath of scandal attached, he thinks he can now come and pick up those two when he needs them for the cameras. Well, it don't work that way."

"They have no contact with their father?" Simon said. "For all his sins, that might have been hard on the kids."

"Oh, they have contact," Quincey said. "He gets them one weekend a month, and he can pick if he wants them for their birthday or for Christmas. I have no problem with him pouring out some of that political money on them—they go to a good school, and they have their gizmos and gadgets. But Jessi, at least, can't be bought by that. She likes her father, but she knows exactly what those gifts are for. Chuck..."

She paused, and Ellen, glancing at Simon, nodded. "Boys," she said. "Abby loves her dad, and they have plenty in common—books and stuff—but Josh *adores* him. I was just Mom. Simon is his *father*."

"Fathers," John said curtly, "can be overrated."

Olivia reached out abruptly for the pile of menus someone had left balanced precariously on the edge of the table. "Do we want to eat?"

The presence of the menus seemed to come as a surprise to everyone, and they were passed around. Quincey sniffed.

"You know, with kids, it's exactly the sort of stuff that I *always* find on menus anywhere I go. Why couldn't you have picked a nice up-scale French restaurant instead, Simon? You know, the kind where the entrée comes in impenetrable colors and is squarely in the middle of an otherwise fascinatingly empty plate and leaves you hungrier when you finish it than when you started?"

"You've spent too much time in Washington," John said. "You aren't allowed to talk any more. I'll pick something for you to eat."

"You'll pick something my son would pick," Quincey said.

"Yeah, and...?"

"He's *ten*," Quincey said, looking at him over the rim of the menu, her eyebrow raised. But the menu had been lifted to cover her face because she could not help grinning, and Ellen, who glanced over and could see behind the menu, responded with an answering grin of motherly understanding. After a moment, it became too contagious to resist; they all laughed.

"Part of being grown up enough to be able to choose those restaurants, Quincey, is that you can choose *not* to go there," Simon said. "I've been to enough of them. I've kind of learned the hard way not to eat anything I can't pronounce properly."

"You speak French," Ellen reminded him tranquilly, without lifting her eyes from her own menu.

"Did they have that much pasta when we used to come here...?" John asked, glancing down the menu. "I certainly don't seem to remember *ever* seeing a salad on this menu before..."

"No pasta," Simon said, faintly but firmly. And then, when his words fell into a pool of puzzled silence, looked up to see four pairs of eyes regarding him in surprise over the tops of their menus, gathered his brows into a frown. "What?"

"What is it about you and European food tonight?" Ellen asked.

Simon blinked, trying to clear his head—there was something that felt oddly cobwebby trying to fight its way into the light, a memory of *this place* and *pasta* that blended in ways he did not recall as being true...and yet were absolutely true...as things in dreams were true, sometimes, when they inadvertently lodged into real memories.

"I'm sorry," he said, "I seem to remember an occasion where young folk shared pasta plates and ate spaghetti Disney-fashion, single string from both ends until they'd kind of meet in the middle, and it suddenly triggered an awful sense of déjà vu..."

Quincey snorted. "Even my twins are older than that," she said. "I thought your kids were over the Disney phase years ago."

Ellen shrugged her shoulders, a little self-consciously. "Hey, *I* am not over the Disney phase. I think I own that movie on DVD."

"You do, hon," Simon said. "Which is probably where I got this silly idea in the first place. The scary thing is that I seem to remember it sitting on the shelf between *Schindler's List* and *Breakfast at Tiffany's*—which is, now that I start to think about it, scrambling my brain considerably. We have to organize that movie collection someday."

"Someday," Ellen said. "I rather like eclecticism. Mess is creative. Just look at my desk."

Simon arched an eyebrow. "*My* desk is always tidy."

"You were an academic for too long, Simon," Quincey said.

"And what's *your* desk like?"

"I'll tell you when I find it. When my kids grow up and move out and take their crap out with them," Quincey said.

Olivia giggled.

"I swear—you guys, you've got two of your own, didn't *your* kids have piles of dirty laundry that lay around on every available surface and reproduced like amoebas?" Quincey asked, turning to Ellen and Simon. "You'd think that the phrase

Clean your room was some form of child abuse, the way they pout and whine and moan when it's addressed to them—and their idea of 'clean' never quite comes close to what I had in mind when I said it..."

Ellen gave her a pitying look. "Did you say they were ten?... You haven't even hit the teen years yet..."

"Yes I have, thank you very much—Sam is only barely getting out of them. But I've just *trained* her—she's finally leveled up enough to start picking her own wet towels off the floor after her shower. And guess what? She'll be out in an apartment of her own next year, sharing with a couple of friends who are probably barely tidy-trained themselves, and I have serious fears of ever being able to set foot in that place without riding in on a broom which I would then immediately use to start sweeping up six-month-old Dorito crumbs from under the sofa."

"Their sofa," Olivia said. "Their Doritos. When they pile up high enough to make the sofa uncomfortable to slouch in, they'll clean up."

"Olivia," Quincey said levelly, turning to point a quasi-accusing finger at Olivia, "you don't know what a pile of Dorito crumbs *looks* like."

"I do, if you mean that I've had to clean up my own crud," Olivia said. "Not Doritos, to be sure, I don't like them much. But let me tell you, chocolate chip cookie crumbs—particularly when they're the actual chocolate chips themselves and get melted into upholstery and harden into scabs—it's just as bad."

John managed to look amused and pained at the same time. "Ladies," he said. "Please. We are about to have dinner. I am not sure I want to go there discussing food items that have spent the last year of their lives being stepped on, sat on, crudding up in other various nefarious ways, or have passed in any shape or form from being edible to being detritus..."

"I love a man who can use the word 'detritus' in a working sentence," Simon said, looking up with a grin. "Hell, I love a man who actually knows how to pronounce that word."

"He used to bait Josh with vocabulary," Ellen said, laughing. "Our boy learned the long words at the breakfast table. He was polysyllabic before he could ride a bike without training wheels.

It was torture, but it was done by his own loving father for all the best of reasons…possibly to ensure that Josh would be able to read his book someday…"

"He enjoyed it," Simon said, looking a little stung.

"Oh, so did I," Ellen said, deliberately sidestepping the issue of whether Simon had actually meant that Josh had enjoyed his book rather than the breakfast vocabulary lessons. "I should have kept notes. I don't remember if 'detritus' was one of the words you flung at him, but if it was he would probably start out by pronouncing it something like 'de-trots', or worse. There were times I had to actually leave the kitchen if I didn't want the poor boy to think that everyone was laughing at him…"

"Ready to order?" One of the pony-tailed young waitresses had come to hover at John's elbow, pen poised above a pad, favoring everyone at the table with a bright grin.

"Salad," Quincey said. "Just put the dressing on the side. I don't care what kind."

"Well, I'll have the pasta," Ellen said, glancing at Simon. "The spaghetti Bolognaise, I think."

"Same," Olivia said.

"Burger," Simon said, pointing. "Hold the pickles, and extra fries."

"Reuben, with coleslaw," John said. "Did we ever order that garlic bread?"

"I'll check in the kitchen," the waitress said.

"Fine—and if we haven't, then add it to the list and bring it out now, while we're waiting for the rest."

"Sure thing. Won't be long."

She bounced away, threading a path through the increasingly crowded room and managing to insouciantly breeze straight past at least two hopeless signals for attention which did not fail to catch the attention of the five at the corner table.

"Lost a bit off the tip, right there," John murmured.

"By the time it comes to that, she'll come round with the bill, smile, lean forward a bit to let that T-shirt come into its own, and it'll all be back in the tip kitty," Quincey said.

"Speaking from experience?"

"Eh. The serried ranks of interns that passed through the

office of the Congressman weren't much older than that, and they used their business suits in much the same way," Quincey said laconically.

"Is Sam in college? What does she want to do? She's had a bit of a glimpse into politics, living with her step-dad—you think she'll follow him to Washington? Seems like it's the right time for the bright young thing…" John said.

"Over my dead body," Quincey said. "And besides, it's all irrelevant. It's the end of the world tonight. She's home free…"

Ellen suddenly looked thoughtful. "I wonder, if I were Abby's age, or your Sam's, if I would be quite so glib about that."

Quincey turned on her. "Oh, nobody actually *believes* that. We aren't all going to go up in flames at the stroke of midnight tonight. Good grades will still matter in the morning. So will long-dead Doritos under the sofa. The end of the world is going to be remarkably anticlimactic…"

The noise level had been steadily rising, and now a burst of loud laughter from the table next to them interrupted Quincey mid-sentence. They all turned to glance at the group at the other table, and were in time to hear a loud and fairly slurred young male voice declare loudly that, with a bit of luck, he wouldn't have to marry 'the bitch' next week after all if the world cooperated in the rumors of its impending demise.

"Odd thing to celebrate," Quincey said, looking a little pained.

"To the end of the world," Simon said, hoisting up his Irish Coffee glass. It came up rather too fast; he glanced inside. "Time for another of these, maybe."

"You do, and I want the car keys," Ellen said, "I'm driving home."

"The world only ends once," Simon said, lifting a professorial forefinger to make his point.

"The world ends every day," Olivia said softly. "Pipe down, Simon. We aren't them anymore."

"Them?"

"Them, the rest of them, out there, in here. Abby, and Sam, and *these*." She waved a hand to indicate the youthful clientele of Spanish Gardens. "We were *them* a long time ago."

"Well, that sure lifted the mood," John said.

"Things might be looking up," Quincey said, glancing at a young man with a guitar case who squirmed past their table on his way to another where a group of friends awaited him. "That one was pretty damned useless. Is there someone else up at the mic? Can't see from here."

John peered through the archway into the next room. "A girl," he said. "No, wait, three girls. One of them has a fiddle and the other one some sort of banjo..."

"That's it, no more Irish Coffee for you," Simon said, laughing. "You can't even count to three anymore.

"Number three doesn't have anything, thank you," John retorted. "Looks like she's just the pipes. They're setting up now, looks like they'll be a while..."

Their waitress returned with a large wicker basket which had seen better days, beginning to unravel at the sides, with a red-check napkin wrapped around the contents.

"Your garlic bread," she said. "We're working on the rest.... Another Irish Coffee?" she asked as Simon waggled his empty glass at her. "Coming right up!"

"It's going to be a while, for the rest, judging by the crowd they've got in here," John said, reaching to unwrap the napkin and breaking off a piece of baguette slathered in garlic butter. "Dig in."

None of them had thought that they were particularly hungry, but the smell of the garlic bread suddenly made everyone realize that they were starving. Ellen slapped away three other reaching hands, snaked the basket in front of her, and began passing out pieces to the others. The basket looked seriously depleted by the end of the first round, and John looked up, trying to rake the room for their waitress.

"She'd better bring another one of these, this one isn't going to last very long," he said. "There she is—hey—*heyy*—"

But the singer had started singing something, quietly, except that somehow she managed to make herself heard over the hubbub. The tables closer to the mic fell silent as she began to weave a simple folk melody, initially *a capella*, but then the fiddle picked up and provided a haunting harmony and finally the banjo or the mandolin or whatever the instrument was that the third girl played came in and provided the baseline, the ground in which the ethereal tune could take root and grow and flower.

They ended the melody on a high quivering note, to applause, and they smiled and started something else, something more folksy and less haunting, and John, who had been craning his neck to watch the three girls perform at the mic, settled back into his chair.

"They're good," he said.

"They *are*," said Ellen. "They're wasted here, right now. They ought to be someplace where people are actually paying attention...Quincey, is that your butt that's ringing?"

Quincey abruptly reached for her pocket. "Uh. Sorry." She fished out a slim cell phone out of her pocket, glanced at the caller ID on the screen, and then looked up apologetically at the others. "*Fuck*," she muttered. "Talk about the devil—you guys must have invoked them, talking about them earlier. It's my kids. Excuse me, Ellen, I'll go take this out in the hall..."

Ellen slipped out of the booth to allow Quincey to exit; Quincey had the phone at her ear as she eeled out, nodding her thanks, her attention already elsewhere.

"Chuck? That you? I *told* you not to call me tonight unless your sister was on fire. What's the matter? Where's Sam?"

"She went out," Chuck said helpfully. "And I can't find my favorite mug anywhere. And Jessi wants to know if she's allowed to watch the late movie..."

"What do you mean, Sam went out? Went out where?"

"She went to the store, Mom, don't freak out," another voice chimed in—Jessi, Chuck's twin. "I'm not on fire, Chuck is being a baby, and Sam went out to get a quart of milk because we were out and Chuck whined that he wanted hot chocolate with milk, waaah. Sam should be back in five minutes and really, Mom, we can survive alone for that long. And... about the movie... Sam just said that she wasn't sure that I should..."

Quincey made a sharp noise much like a hissing cat, and Jessi's voice abruptly cut off.

"If Sam isn't sure, then the answer is probably no. And if that mug isn't buried under the tons of crap I told you to clean out of your room last week, I don't know what happened to it—and I can certainly not unearth it for you from here. Here being one of the rare, the *very* rare, evenings I've had with, you know, grown-up company since before you two were born. When Sam gets back, enjoy your hot chocolate…and then start thinking about bed. Yes, *both* of you. If the movie is on that late it probably isn't aimed at you, Jessi. You'll live. One day you'll be all grown up and you'll be able to figure these things out for yourself. Right now…Sam is your authority. She's *me*. You'd better believe it. If you don't do exactly as she tells you, she's to call me to lay down the law… and if you do that I will be very unhappy and the law will not be pleasant."

"I thought you said we shouldn't call you," Jessi said.

"You shouldn't, unless it's a dire emergency. But from now on Sam decides what the real emergencies are—you two obviously think a missing mug is one. I'll be home tomorrow morning. Suck it up."

"Okay," Jessi said faintly. And then added, her voice hopeful, "Love you, Mom."

Quincey grimaced. "Love you too," she said, her voice softening a little but managing to retain the edge of sternness in her tone. "Now go *away*."

The phone went dead, and Quincey toggled hers off with a sigh, shaking her head.

"How old?"

She looked up, startled, and met the sympathetic smiling eyes of Ariel behind the glass counter. He nodded at the phone, his mouth curved in a slight and very understanding grin.

"I gather it's kids," he said. "On their own?"

"They're ten," Quincey said. "I left Sam in charge—she's their oldest sister—half-sister—she's nineteen and she can usually be trusted. It's only for overnight—I left home this morning, and I should be back there tomorrow, and really, they're pretty good ten-year-olds as far as that goes. But sometimes I think that Chuck will never get to be older than five, always yanking at my sleeve with 'Mooooommy'—I know that he's the youngest, but he's Jessi's twin and *she* manages to act Sam's age sometimes. Boys."

"Sounds like he may feel outnumbered," Ariel said, laughing out loud now. "Mom, one older sister, one bossy twin sister. He can either become thoroughly obnoxious, just to keep his place in the pecking order, or he can go juvenile and hope that everyone will just take pity on him…"

Quincy stared at him, but one corner of her own mouth had curved up in a smile. "Thanks for the analysis," she said, "I'll keep it in mind. Speaking from experience?"

"I have lots of siblings," he said. "We tend to get left to fend for ourselves unless we screw up really badly and need help from someone higher up on the responsibility scale."

Quincey glanced down, weighing the phone in her hand, shaking her head a little. "Telling them not to call me, it's more than a little self-preservation. I hear their voices, I start missing them. It's that simple. *God,* I could use a cigarette."

"Filthy habit," Ariel said.

"Can't disagree," Quincey said. "Which is why I quit. Still doesn't mean I can't think about wanting one every so often." She glanced around, at the now busy and very loud café. "Good God, when did it get this full? Feels like New Year's Eve came early…"

"Well, maybe it did, in theory—but in either event it's the New World's Eve, and the real New Year's Eve might not even come. I guess they're celebrating early."

Quincey shook her head. "Hogwash," she said. "They're all going to get a rather nasty surprise when they discover that the new world in the morning starts with the mother of all hangovers." She glanced toward the back, where the restrooms were. There was, somewhat miraculously, no queue there. It suddenly seemed like a good idea to take advantage of the situation.

Ariel's voice followed her as she turned away toward the restroom on the left.

"That one's occupied—and you dropped something."

Quincey nodded her thanks as she bent over to retrieve a folded piece of paper from the floor next to her foot—it must have fallen out as she stuffed her phone back in her pocket, but she didn't recognize it, didn't remember putting it in there. She unfolded the paper, glanced at the contents, frowned slightly.

"What *is* this…?" she murmured.

"Instructions. For the other one."

She looked up to see Ariel indicating the other restroom with a toss of his head.

"But the sign…"

"Hence the instructions. You *can* go into that one, if you are careful to follow the instructions."

"What, go into a broken-down restroom and find a new life…? That's…funny. If there's anything worse than a hangover in the morning, it's actual crap right now."

Ariel's smile did not slip. "The sign…is only really there to make sure that only the right people go in there tonight," he said.

Both Quincey's eyebrows rose all the way into her hairline. "You're a restroom usher?"

"Well, when you put it that way," Ariel said. "I know, doesn't sound very glamorous. But we use what's given to us. Today, here… it's an 'Out of Order' sign on what seems to be a perfectly ordinary restroom door. But that new world in the morning that you spoke of…? That can start right here. Right now." He nodded at the paper in her hand. "Instructions. If you choose to follow them. Excuse me, I'm wanted in the back."

He gave her a small bow, putting down his cloth on the shelf behind the glass counter, and slipped away into the crowded room without a backward glance.

Quincey stared after him, her expression puzzled—but now she was in earnest about stopping by the facilities before she went back to the others at the table. She tried the left-hand side door first, but Ariel had been right—it was locked, and a muffled voice from within shouted something unintelligible which only served to prove that there was indeed someone still using the place.

She glanced once again at the sheet of paper in her hand, and finally reached out to try the other door, turning the knob which had the 'Out of Order' sign hanging on it; she looked over her shoulder once to see if anyone was behind her about to ask her snidely if she could read—but she seemed to be completely on her own, unnoticed by the throng inside the café proper. She might as well have been invisible, or a passing ghost.

She could see nothing but darkness as the door began to swing open, and a caress of cool air coming out of that darkness gently touched her cheek, stirred her hair.

There was a moment in which she hesitated, frozen, one foot stopped mid-motion as she began a step forward and then stopped—but then she was swept with a strange certainty that if she did not complete that one step the rest of her life would be spent regretting that choice, wondering what might have happened.

So she squared her jaw, the fingers of the hand holding the piece of paper allowing the page to fall back into the lines along which it had been folded before and reaching to stuff it back into her pocket even as she completed that first step into the unknown and let go of the door, allowing it to close gently behind her as she passed through.

Behind her, the trio of girl singers had begun another song. The lyrics drifted in behind Quincey, increasingly muffled by the slowly closing door... something about the circle never ending, and about all the roads leading home.

QUINCEY

Fall 1989

The day had been oddly warm, almost a throwback to summer, but as it waned and the sun hurried to what suddenly seemed a very early set, the gathering twilight brought in a bite of fall, a sharp coolness that nipped at exposed skin and reminded Quincey that she was in fact closer to October than she was to August. When she had been getting ready for the concert, she had dithered for a while between a light wrap and a full jacket—and although the wrap might have looked better with her dress, she was just as grateful that she had chosen the jacket as she slammed the door of her car and shivered as a draft of cool air swept through the parking garage from the great open concrete arches which surrounded the parking area on three sides.

The low wedge heels on her only real pair of dress shoes made a hollow, echoing clicking sound as she made her way to the elevators. The garage was nearly full—she had been lucky to find a space—but it seemed to be devoid of life except for herself. She wasn't afraid, not precisely, but she could not dismiss the feeling of relief when she finally stepped into the elevator and the doors closed behind her. When it released her a few moments later, into the marble lobby of the theatre complex, she joined the stream of people flowing toward the main auditorium, joyful anticipation stirring in her as she fished around in her small evening purse for her ticket.

The poster outside the auditorium door bore a large and artistic black-and-white photograph of an enigmatically smiling man in a snappy Thirties-era pin-striped suit and a scrolling headline across the top of the poster which announced 'S

Marvellous! Happy Birthday, George Gershwin! Concert goers slowed their steps as they passed it, to look at it, to smile—it was a good crowd, for a Tuesday night—and for once Quincey felt a sense of actually belonging somewhere, that all of these people who had made the effort to come here mid-week were somehow *like* her, adrift and displaced in the overwhelming majority of their lives but able to find, here in this place and awaiting an evening of Gershwin music, a place where they belonged and were welcome.

The usher, a young man with black curly hair and a ready smile, pointed Quincey to her seat. Her row was already almost full and she minced her way apologetically to her mid-row seat trying to avoid other people's feet, exchanging apologetic nods and smiles with people already seated, finally falling gracelessly into her own seat trying to juggle purse and program and the jacket which she had taken off as she had come into the hot and crowded theatre lobby and finally managing to balance them all on her lap and crack the program open to see what was to be presented.

The first half of the evening was to be wholly instrumental—iconic pieces like "Rhapsody in Blue" and "An American in Paris"—but the second half was billed as a Gershwin Surprise, promising a "wide selection of songs from the Gershwin songbook, as chosen by the performers" and giving away no more than a list of names of the singers who would be on stage that night. There were arguably some instantly recognizable names on that list, mixed in with some which were thoroughly unfamiliar. Quincey sighed in frustration. It didn't dim her anticipation, but she would have liked at least a list of potential songs which were expected to be performed. She had her favorites. She might have liked to know that she had even a chance of hearing one that night, or if other songs had trumped it.

A woman scrambled into the empty seat next to Quincey, murmuring an apology as she bumped into the program which Quincey was reading.

"It's okay," Quincey said, glancing up reflexively to see who had nudged her and then dropping her eyes back onto the program—only to snap back in a double take as she took in her neighbor.

She saw appreciative smiles on other faces, on the periphery of her vision. The woman next to her had outdone herself—she was wearing a vintage Thirties dress, properly accessorized with what looked like period stockings, shoes with diamanté clasps, a pearl choker, white gloves, and a fox fur stole around her shoulders. Her dark hair was slicked back into a smooth glossy wave away from her high forehead and gathered into a tight chignon at the nape of her neck; her eyebrows were plucked and pencil-drawn into smooth arches; her mouth was a perfect scarlet Cupid's bow. She had a small, round mole on the left side of her chin, just below her lip—with the rest of it, it was hard to tell if the mole was real or if it was another period piece, the finishing touch.

"Wow," Quincey said.

The woman glanced over and smiled, her teeth white and even, the smile at once genuinely delighted and archly coy—two layers, perfectly balanced, of the real woman and the role she had chosen to play that night.

"Thank you," she said, and her voice was warm and deep, golden like honey, ever so slightly accented. "I so rarely get a chance to play dress-up any more. When a perfect opportunity like this comes up, it's a shame to let it go by without at least trying. I've always loved Gershwin, and that whole glam era—so I thought I would just throw together something of the look for the man's birthday party..."

"You just threw that together?" Quincey said. "I'm even more impressed now."

"I used to be in theatre," the woman said. "And the stuff from those days that I liked, I kept—the dress, for instance. The rest, well, you just don't know what you can find in thrift stores these days."

"Now you make me regret that I didn't make more of an effort," Quincey said.

"Next time," her neighbor said, and stuck out a hand. "Hi. Dorotea Rochas."

Quincey shook the proffered hand. "Quincey. Quincey Thorne."

"Nice to meet you, Quincey Quincey Thorne," Dorotea said. "Mind if I look at your program book? Somehow I seem to have got this far without one."

"Be my guest," Quincey said, handing over the glossy brochure she was cradling on her lap with her free hand. "The part after the intermission looks like it'll be interesting."

Dorotea glanced over to that section of the program, and pursed her lips a little. "Oh dear. I hope they pick my song."

Quincey grinned. "My thoughts exactly," she said. "Which one's yours?"

Dorotea gave her a flirtatious look through lashes heavy with mascara, drawing off her gloves very slowly. "If they sing it, I'll let you know."

The long, elegant fingers with their nails painted a vibrant scarlet might have been perfectly comfortable with some sort of antique ivory cigarette holder dangling languidly from them—but they were equally at home beating out the driving jazz rhythms of the symphonic half of the Gershwin concert on Dorotea's lap. Quincey's own feet were tapping, but Dorotea looked as though she were playing the piano parts of "Rhapsody in Blue" on her thighs, as though she knew how, and if there had been a keyboard under her fingertips instead of the silky material of her dress she might well have produced the real thing. Quincey found herself riveted by those hands, her eyes straying to the lap concerto whenever they slipped off the orchestra on the stage; Dorotea's own gaze never left the stage, her back straight against the back of her chair, her profile clean and perfect—high forehead, aristocratic nose, slightly parted lips, strong chin, flowing into a long, slender neck and elegantly sloping shoulders. Quincey herself, although she had taken the trouble to put on a pretty dress and the only pair of heeled shoes that she owned, felt distinctly underdressed next to this vision—and yet somehow it didn't make her feel annoyed or upset, merely admiring. It was obvious that Dorotea had not done it to upstage anybody, but merely to please herself.

Dorotea stood as the first half of the concert finished and the house lights came on for the intermission, unhooking her fox fur wrap and draping it across the back of her seat. Straightening from that, she glanced down at Quincey, still sitting in her seat, her pile of possessions piled neatly on her lap.

"Are you coming out for a drink?" Dorotea asked.

"It gets a little crowded out there," Quincey said.

"It's Gershwin's birthday. It's worth a glass of champagne. Come on, I'll treat you—we're both here on our own, I can use the company."

"Oh, no, I don't think..." Quincey began, but Dorotea's smile widened a little, and became irresistible.

"Oh, but I insist," she said. "Please, it would be my pleasure."

Quincey hesitated, but then rose from her seat, leaving her jacket and the program book stuffed into the folding chair as it came up, and followed Dorotea down the row until they could join the chattering masses that were flowing along the aisle into the lobby where the bar was. Dorotea made a kind of magical progress through the crowd, a hot knife through butter, with people parting to let her through—of course Quincey had no such free pass and had to fight to keep up with her. The same effect became evident at the bar itself where the young man behind the counter skipped over three other patrons already there waving money to serve Dorotea with her two flutes of champagne. She smiled her thanks, turned away in one smooth motion offering one of the glasses to Quincey, and somehow that small gesture seemed to be enough to pass on some of Dorotea's own magical powers or else the crowds were given a signal that Quincey was to be included in Dorotea's entourage. They were not separated by pushing people again, and even managed to find a space to stand and sip their champagne without being jostled or pressed too closely into other bodies—Dorotea seemed to be an expert at this, finding a spot a couple of steps up on the lobby staircase, leaning her back against the balustrade, a perfect place to watch the people and be seen doing so. Quincey knew that she could not pull off that insouciance, so she didn't try, standing beside Dorotea with both hands wrapped around the stem of her glass.

"Good crowd," Dorotea remarked.

"Yes, I was thinking that earlier. Funny, I didn't think there would be that many people coming to the birthday party—it's not even a jubilee of any kind."

"But it's a fun date anagram," Dorotea said. "A date-a-gram. He was born in 1898, and it's 1989—it's like it's his real birthday, and some dyslexic birth certificate scribe made a mistake on the year...It's like we *are* celebrating his birth, kind of. Literally."

"So," Quincey said after a pause, "what *is* your favorite Gershwin song?"

"I'll tell you mine if you tell me yours," Dorotea said.

"They often skip mine," Quincey said.

"They occasionally skip mine, too. But although I love hearing it sung—I love hearing it sung well. And sometimes they'll take it too fast, or too slow, or it'll be the wrong voice for it altogether, and I appreciate the gesture, as it were, but I'd much rather they left it alone..."

"Which one?" Quincey asked, now honestly intrigued.

Dorotea hesitated, but apparently it was not shyness— because once she seemed to come to a decision she did not so much say the name of the song in reply as sing a stanza from it, with apparently no self-consciousness whatever. Her voice was a strong, smoky alto, the perfect voice for the song, the perfect tempo, enough to make a couple of the nearest knots of people sipping their champagne actually turn around with a smile and take notice.

"Wow," Quincey said again, for the second time in an hour, taken aback at the power of the performance. "You certainly got them watching you."

"Ah, but watching *over* me is different, and none of them are volunteering to do that," Dorotea murmured, spinning her flute gently between her fingers. She suddenly looked strangely uncomfortable, as though she had broken some unspoken rule which Quincey had not been aware of and was now having second thoughts about it all. But she recovered quickly, and lifted her eyes from the rim of the champagne flute to meet Quincey's again. "Now, fair's fair," she said. "What's yours?"

Quincey didn't know she had it in her, the little streak of exhibitionism, standing there head and shoulders above everyone else as though on a podium or a stage, but she responded in kind—her own high, sweet soprano just as perfect for the song she chose for herself as Dorotea's had been for hers, drawing out a gentle air of summertime, the quiet lullaby of a summer evening. She actually sang the entire first verse of the song, she thought quietly enough, but apparently enough people heard that there was actually a smattering of applause close by when she was done. She flushed, dropping her eyes, suddenly acutely conscious of where she was and who she was with and the weight of people's eyes on her.

"That was quite beautiful," Dorotea said, and her voice had changed a little, her tone admiring and astonished.

"Are you ladies part of the concert?" one older gentleman standing at the foot of the stair asked, glancing up at them. "Because if you aren't you ought to be."

Quincey shook her head mutely, but Dorotea smiled. "Thank you," she said. "No, we're not professional—we just both love Gershwin's music."

They returned to their seats when the bell rang for the end of the intermission; Quincey's champagne flute was still half-full when she left it balanced on one of the already overflowing round tables in the foyer, but she rather felt as though she had consumed at least three full glasses of bubbly on an empty stomach—she felt oddly dizzy, and her stomach was full of butterflies. Dorotea showed no side effects, gliding her royal glide down the aisle and getting the crowds to let her through, even managing to waft sideways along their row and avoid stepping on the toes of those already seated (which Quincey, following apologetically in Dorotea's wake, emphatically made up for).

They were both a little disappointed in the second half of the concert—Dorotea's pursed lips and a tiny disapproving shake of her head after her own song had been performed gave the impression that she had heard it done better, and Quincey's song was never sung at all. At the end of the concert Quincey fumbled her purse, managing to spill half its contents on the floor by her feet; she heard Dorotea say that it had been nice to meet her, and looked up to try and respond, but already there was nothing there but the memory of scarlet lips and dark hair, and a dissipating cloud of spicy perfume.

Quincey did look around for her, as much as that was possible, when the crowd carried her out into the lobby—but it was too hard to pick out any one single person in the mass of theatre patrons streaming out of the auditorium. Quincey had to wait for the fourth elevator car in order to get one which she could find a spot in, and rode it up to the third floor of the parking garage where she had left her car.

This time the parking garage was not empty—it was full of distant and incomprehensible conversations and laughter, a syncopated echo of many feet, the occasional bleep of a car alarm being deactivated or a remote entry pad being pressed. Her own keys dangling from her fingertips, Quincey made her way toward the spot where she had parked.

A vehicle in the row across from her own caught her eye, its hood up in a manner that suggested engine trouble. Quincey glanced that way, mildly interested, and then looked again as she realized that the recognized the long fingers with their scarlet fingernails folded around the edge of the hood.

"Do you need help?" Quincey asked softly.

Dorotea popped her head around to look out from behind the hood. "Oh, it's you," she said. "Funny how my favorite Gershwin song seems to come true all the time. I do need constant surveillance, it seems."

"What's the matter?"

"Battery, I think." Dorotea stared into the innards of her car, a tiny frown creasing her features. "I seem to remember that Heinlein once said that a human being should be able to do any number of amazing things—"

"Change a diaper, design a building, set a bone, program a computer, solve equations, fight efficiently, die gallantly, I forget the rest," Quincey said. "Lazarus Long." She paused, thinking, and then opened her mouth to speak, at the same time as Dorotea did.

" 'Specialization is for insects'," they both said at the same time, completing the quote, and laughed.

"He never said anything about knowing how to fix a car," Dorotea said morosely.

"Do you need a jump start? I have leads in my car—it's that

one, just over there. I don't know if they're long enough—I can probably noodle my car close enough to try it—or we can wait for whoever owns this one to get here and either volunteer their own services or move so I can park closer," Quincey said.

Dorotea gave her a long look. "You know how to do that?"

"Enough," Quincey said.

"I knew there was a good reason I met you in there," Dorotea said, giving Quincey a flirty look through the Thirties-heavy black lashes. "Thank God you're here."

The couple who owned the sedan parked on Dorotea's left turned up only a few moments later, however, and the gallant older gentleman proved to be both willing and able to provide the necessary services to help re-start Dorotea's car, rendering Quincey's offer irrelevant. Oddly disappointed, she backed away, giving Dorotea a diffident wave.

"Well, you'll be okay now," she said. "I'd better be going."

"Thank you—wait—do you want to…"

But Quincey had already crossed to her own row and slipped into her own car, and Dorotea was effectively trapped by her own troubles. Quincey raised a hand in a small gesture of farewell as she backed out of her bay and drove away, and Dorotea echoed it, somewhat helplessly. Quincey drove toward the exit ramp, and into the night, annoyed at herself, wondering what she had not let Dorotea finish, wondering what kind of fluke sat that exotic angel next to her that night, resigned to the fact that she would probably never cross paths with her again.

But she did, not three weeks later, stopping off at a coffee bar for a late coffee one evening after work. The voice that came at her from a table across the café was warm and deep and totally unexpected.

"Quincey Quincey Thorne? Summertime girl from Gershwin's birthday bash?"

Quincey turned, halfway through extracting money from her purse to pay for her coffee. Across the room, Dorotea raised a mug of something hot and steaming to her.

"I *thought* it was you," Dorotea said, her lips parting in a smile that was pure contentment; if she'd been a cat, she would have purred loudly. She indicated the empty chair at her table with a nod. "Join me?"

Quincey hesitated—her coffee had been to-go, and there was an open notebook in front of Dorotea which indicated that she had perhaps been doing something other than just taking a break with a cup of coffee—but it was momentary, and quickly quashed.

"Sure," she said. "Thanks."

By the time she had her coffee in hand and made her way over, Dorotea had cleared away her papers and now sat sideways to the table, one elbow laid on the edge and the other arm draped across long legs crossed in a manner that managed to be both demure and provocative at the same time. There was little left of the Thirties glamour girl from the Gershwin concert. The woman in the café was all elegant, contemporary casual chic. She wore her hair loose and softly framing her face—it was shorter than Quincey had thought, falling to barely below her shoulders, and it was the color of bitter chocolate. She wore a sweater whose folds spoke of high-end yarn, alpaca or cashmere; her skirt was hip-hugging corduroy and ended just above the knee, revealing shapely calves which disappeared into black ankle-length boots. A dark leather jacket was draped over the back of her chair.

"Hi," she said, as Quincey sat down in the chair across from her. "Nice to see you. I wanted to stop you, back at the theatre, get your phone number at least—I tried looking you up, there can't be that many of you—I mean, Q Thorne? But you don't seem to be listed…"

"I share an apartment with a friend," Quincey said. "Peter Shaw. The phone's in his name."

Dorotea's eyebrow lifted a minute amount. "Oh? Boyfriend?"

"No, just friend. He doesn't seem to be capable of keeping a girlfriend long enough for one to move in, and my share of the rent helps him stay in his apartment, so it works out for everyone—and I can practically walk to work from there, so it's convenient."

"Where do you work?"

"In a medical lab, just up the road there." She took a sip

of her coffee. "I'm a biochemist—I thought I'd end up curing cancer or something but instead I do blood tests for a battery of MD's who work in a collective in that building. Who knew. What about you?"

"I own Herstory," Dorotea said. "It's a little feminist bookstore a couple of blocks from here, with a sideline in art books, and a bit of history, and some travel, and a section on fantasy and science fiction. I try to keep up on stuff that interests me. You should come by sometime."

"Sounds fabulous," Quincey said, genuinely envious for a moment. "You live in the city too?"

"Above the store, as it happens," Dorotea said. "My family owned the building, and I inherited it when they passed— opened the bookstore on the bottom floor, and rent out the apartment on the second floor. It's currently tenantless, and I'm looking—if your friend does come up with a girlfriend who sticks, you can always give me a call if you need a berth. I live on the top floor. You might say, the penthouse. Me, and as many books as will fit. I have a bit of rooftop, and I grow a couple of pots of wilting kitchen herbs up there."

"I'm running out of room to *put* books," Quincey said ruefully.

Dorotea chuckled. "Having a bookstore makes it both better and worse," she said. "It's probably easier when you don't know how many books are out there that you *want* to have. I've just got a whole new batch of stuff in, and the flavor of the month seems to be Japan—travelogues from Kyoto, histories of the Shogunate, photo books on geishas, that sort of thing. It all looks quite beautiful—I haven't really had time to pick it over yet, but some day soon I'll go and take a look for myself."

"They're having a visiting exhibit on Japanese swords up at the museum, I saw something in the paper the other day, it's coming in for a limited run sometime in November, I think," Quincey said. "Maybe they're bringing a bit of it over here for you."

"Oh? I should go take a look at that," Dorotea said. "Japanese swords are works of art."

"I read about them," Quincey said.

"Would you like to go?"

"Pardon?"

"With me. To the exhibition. When it comes."

"Er... Well, yes, I would love to see it..."

"Give me that unlisted phone number," Dorotea said. She reached out for her purse and fished around in it, coming up with an ivory business card—it bore only her name, the name of her shop, an email address and a phone number. Dorotea held it out across the table. "Here's mine. Call me when the thing gets here—or I'll call you—and we can make a plan."

"Okay," Quincey said. "Sure. Sounds like fun."

She scribbled her own number on a piece of paper torn from a notepad in her pocketbook, and tucked Dorotea's neat card away into her purse.

They chatted about other things for another quarter of an hour or so, and then Dorotea glanced at her watch and exclaimed that she had to go. She rose to her feet, shrugged into her jacket, gathered up her belongings, and held out a hand to Quincey.

"I'm really glad I ran into you again," she said. "I drop into this place quite often—maybe I'll see you again before then, but if not then I look forward to exploring the cutting edge with you next month."

Quincey was very aware of the light pressure of Dorotea's fingers around her own as her grip tightened for a moment and then gently released. She looked up, and managed a smile. "So do I," she said.

Quincey avoided the coffee shop for a week after that. She could not have told anybody exactly why, had they asked her—it was a strange unease, an unsettled feeling in the pit of her stomach as she thought about Dorotea in her penthouse and her books and the wilting herbs on her rooftop. All of it was like a soft scabbard, a camouflage, and there was—as Dorotea had said herself—a cutting edge hidden in there somewhere which had nothing at all to do with the art of making Japanese swords.

But when the travelling Japanese exhibition did arrive in the city as scheduled, Quincey suddenly could think about nothing else but Dorotea. She hauled out the elegant ivory card several times, twice when she was actually near a phone, but didn't call, couldn't quite make herself do it, had no idea what she would actually say if she did call and Dorotea answered. In the end, defeated, she went walking down the side street where the Herstory Bookstore was situated.

Just to take a look, she told herself.

But once she was there, in the street, and saw the front of the store with its neat and inviting window display which spoke eloquently of Dorotea's own touch, Quincey found herself drawn into the shop, as helpless as a paperclip before a powerful magnet.

A slender, heavy-lidded girl sitting behind a counter made out of some blond wood looked up as Quincey entered. She wore a nose stud in her left nostril, and her fair hair was streaked with green and purple—but somehow, in this place, none of that seemed remotely odd. It was perfectly natural and not at all unexpected that Dorotea's employees should themselves not be run-of-the-mill.

"Hi!" the girl said cheerfully, with a smile. "Let me know if I can help you find anything."

"Actually," Quincey said, before she completely lost her nerve, "I was looking for…"

A curtain across an arched opening on the far side of the shop lifted theatrically, and Dorotea stepped out from behind.

"Hey," she said. "It's you."

"I dropped in to see if you still wanted to go to see the swords," Quincey said faintly.

"Absolutely. Friday?"

"I work half days on Fridays," Quincey said.

"Perfect. Maybe we can grab some lunch, and then go see the exhibition. How does that sound?"

"Actually… perfect," Quincey said, smiling.

"There's a Japanese restaurant a couple of blocks from here," Dorotea said. "We could set the mood…?"

"Okay," Quincey said. "I could swing by here after work."

Dorotea nodded. "Sold. And now, since you're here, and if you've acquired any more room for books lately, look around…"

Quincey wound up buying a thin volume of antique Japanese art prints. Dorotea herself, not the purple-streaked minion, stepped up to the till to ring up her purchases—and on the way paused to snag a display copy of a collection of Sappho's poetry, bound in elegant pale blue.

"You might like that," Dorotea said. "Just a thought."

Quincey flipped through the book quickly, taking in the evocative but not explicit pen-and-ink drawings—and then, her cheeks flushed a little, added it to the Japanese book on the counter.

"Okay," she said faintly.

Dorotea offered nothing other than one of her trademark smiles that managed to be both sincere and enigmatic as she slipped both books into a paper bag with the Herstory logo on it. "Enjoy!" she said as she handed the books over. "And I'll see you Friday."

When she left work that Friday, on her way to meet Dorotea, Quincey found herself staring at her face in the mirror of the ladies' restroom at her place of employment, hauling out a tube of lipstick which she had barely used in the last year but which now seemed to be essential in order to touch up her mouth, realizing that she had put on eyeliner that morning but having no conscious memory of having done so, or even of having made the decision to do it. Her shoulder-length bob was pulled back into its usual workaday clip that kept it off her face in the lab, but now she took out the barrette and shook it loose around her face, examining the effect.

How she looked suddenly seemed to matter, for the first time in...she couldn't remember how long.

Dorotea herself looked effortlessly wonderful, as usual, dressed in dramatic scarlet and black. The Japanese restaurant she took Quincey to was quiet but with an air of shabby gentility which appealed to Quincey's sense of atmosphere— and afterward, at the museum, the exhibition of Japanese swords and the art of their making was endlessly fascinating. The conversation didn't feel as though it had run its course by the time Quincey had to leave, there were a lot of things left to say and they both knew it, and Dorotea suggested dinner over the weekend, to continue where they had left off. Quincey accepted without hesitation. They met at a cheap and cheerful

Italian restaurant on Saturday night, segued from ancient Japan to grand opera (they both liked them) and fondue (they both thought it was a fad, and a pretentious one at that) and cats (they discovered that Dorotea had two, and that Quincey's housemate had one fiercely territorial and going-on-geriatric cat which meant that Quincey could have none of her own in that apartment). The evening ran late, but dinner itself was middling to mediocre and Dorotea invited Quincey up to see the two cats which they had talked of, and the 'penthouse', the weekend after—on which occasion she herself promised to attempt a superior version of Spaghetti Bolognaise, with the possible addition of some of the wilting herbs from the pots in the rooftop garden.

Quincey went home, after, to a bed empty of pet or fellow human, and could not decide whether she felt like laughing or bursting into tears.

She deliberately downplayed her appearance for the visit to Dorotea's the following weekend—but at the last moment, not sure of her motivations, she booked an appointment at the hairdresser's for that Friday afternoon.

"Shampoo and blow-dry?" her stylist asked. This was a woman to whom Quincey had been going for her occasional trims for years, and the question had become routine.

The correct response would have been, "The usual, please." But this time Quincey hesitated, running her hands through her hair.

"No," she said at last. "Something new. I want something different. Shorter."

The stylist raised an eyebrow. "Okay, then," she said. "Let's see what we can do."

Quincey walked to Dorotea's shop with a knitted cloche hat over her cropped hair, lifting the collar of her jacket against the newly-bared back of her neck. At Dorotea's door, when Dorotea reached out for her coat, Quincey took off the hat in a gesture at once self-conscious and defiant, and Dorotea stopped mid-motion, giving her a long apprising look.

"I just thought…I wanted a change," Quincey said. "Too dramatic?"

Dorotea reached out with one hand to trace, with just her fingertips, the feathered blonde hair that framed Quincey's face, shaping her features into something new and immensely vulnerable. "No," she said. "I think I like it. It suits you. Come on in, let me show you around. The cats are hiding—they usually do when I have company—but they'll thaw soon enough."

The place was pure Dorotea, in many ways—it wasn't perfectly tidy, but it gave the air of everything being in precisely the place where Dorotea knew where to lay a hand on it if she wanted it. Bookshelves made out of aged and weathered wood lined several walls; framed photographs adorned others. The floor was hardwood, with scatter rugs where they seemed to be needed. The kitchen had a lot of stainless steel, and from it issued a heavenly aroma which made Quincey give an appreciative sniff in that direction.

"Something smells really good," she said.

"Secret recipe," Dorotea said. "I had to come up with something special for the third date."

Quincey looked around, startled. "Are we *dating*?"

"I rather thought we were," Dorotea said. "I hope so, anyway."

She leaned over and brushed Quincey's lips with hers, very lightly, very quickly, and then turned away with a comment about having to check on her sauce—Quincey was barely able to convince herself that the kiss had happened, that it had been a kiss at all, that it had been intended as one...and what all of that meant.

Her reaction was not at all what she might have guessed it would be if she had been asked what she would have thought or felt if another woman kissed her on the lips in the manner of a lover. She had never been attracted to her own sex, but in this moment, in Dorotea's warm and welcoming home and with the smell of home cooking coming from the kitchen and with the soft texture of Dorotea's lips still lingering on her own, all she could think of was that she had wanted this kiss. Had been expecting it. Hoping for it. Waiting for it with the same kind of fluttery butterflies in her stomach that she associated with being in love.

That she was, in fact, in love.

That her mind had already decided on this, and that her body was responding to that decision in ways that she was not expecting, with her heart beating faster and a warmth which she could only think of as breathless desire spreading through her body.

Dorotea stepped back into the room, realizing that Quincey had not moved.

"Are you all right?" she asked softly.

"I'm...I...I don't know how to do this," Quincey whispered.

"I can show you," Dorotea said, her own voice suddenly husky. "If you're sure."

Quincey had dithered for an hour over what she was going to wear to Dorotea's that night, and had finally settled on a pair of reasonably smart black jeans and an emerald-green cotton sweater which someone had once told her set off her eyes. Dorotea's hands, at the tiny nod which had been all the answer she had received to her not-quite-question, alighted like exotic butterflies on the exposed skin at Quincey's wrists and then slid up over the silky cotton weave to her shoulders where her thumbs found skin again and traced Quincey's collarbone down to the hollow of her throat. They slid up again, along the sides of Quincey's neck, to reach her face and hold it cradled between Dorotea's palms, gently, as if it was something unutterably precious. Their eyes held for a moment, and then Quincey closed hers, the eyes that her sweater was meant to set off. They were so beyond that right now, as she felt Dorotea's hair on her neck and her cheek, Dorotea's lips on her own, firmer now, open, leaving no further doubt as to the intent of the kiss.

Quincey made a small noise at the back of her throat, and lifted her own hands to grasp at Dorotea's elbows—but Dorotea whispered something soft and inarticulate against her mouth, sliding her own hands across Quincey's shoulders, playing her fingers down her spine into the hollow of her back, and then underneath the green sweater, lifting it away from skin and then upwards. Quincey lifted her arms to let the sweater be pulled over her head...and then, after a moment, when Dorotea's hands did not return, her eyes fluttered open, just in time to see

Dorotea shrugging out of her own long-sleeved t-shirt. In that precise moment it was halfway up, with Dorotea's arms lifted and the t-shirt effectively hiding her face...but revealing a lacy bra cupping a pair of full breasts, and a torso that tapered down to a slim waist and rounded hips still coyly veiled in a flowing skirt that covered her from waist to mid-calf. She really was all honey, from the tone and sweetness of her voice to the color of the skin on her breast and belly; Quincey only became aware that she was staring when Dorotea let out a smoky laugh, jolting her back into herself.

"You're beautiful," Quincey said.

Dorotea traced the inside of Quincey's arm with her forefinger. "Likewise," she said, and kissed her again.

Dorotea taught Quincey things about herself that she never knew that she knew—how a woman made love, and received it; the bewildering and astonishing sensations created by another woman's lips or fingers, by the brush of a woman's long hair on her hip or thigh; the heartbreaking sweetness of a woman's voice whispering endearments into the shell of an ear, the way her body responded to all of this with an agonizing and exquisite release of her own need, and the way Dorotea guided her, gently but firmly, how to return the sensations she was being given.

Quincey had never liked sharing her bed too closely with anyone, preferring to have her own space when she was sleeping—but that didn't seem to apply here, and she and Dorotea went to sleep in one another's arms, whispering to one another until they both drifted off. When Quincey woke in the morning it was to a bright square of blue sky in the skylight in the master bedroom, and unaccustomed autumn sunshine streaming pale and lovely through the picture window. Its angle told her that it was still early; Dorotea was sleeping peacefully beside her...and the two of them had company. Two cats—one a dainty tuxedo cat with an oddly supercilious expression imparted by the pattern of the color on its face and the other a large sprawling orange tabby with golden eyes and a disturbingly lion-like head—shared the bed with them; the orange cat had taken over the foot of the bed on Dorotea's side and the tux, when Quincey woke, was lying across Quincey's own feet, and when she opened her eyes and met the cat's it began to purr very softly.

"Hey," Quincey whispered, and lifted herself on one elbow so that she could reach out to scritch the cat behind its ears. It closed its eyes, its purr marginally increasing in volume, tilting its head so that she could have better access.

"It seems the cats approve," Dorotea's sleepy voice came from behind her. "Are you staying...? If you're looking for more room to put your books... there are a couple of bookshelves I can clear for you..."

Quincey was suddenly breathless, as though Dorotea's words had knocked all the air out of her. She stayed bent over, tickling the purring cat, her heart beating fast enough to feel as though it was going to leap from her throat any moment.

This was not who she was. Waking up in a strange bed, playing with cats whom she did not know, a lover's voice drifting from behind her from where last night's lover still reclined against pillows...a *woman*'s voice...

What have I done? The words were clear in her own mind, as though spoken out loud. But they could not have been. She could not have uttered them. Instead, she managed a faint, fake laugh, and spoke without turning to face Dorotea, aware that a fiery blush was spreading across her face and down her neck all the way beyond her collarbone and onto the tender skin above her breasts.

"Well, for a little while, at least," she said, in answer to Dorotea's languid invitation, leaving out the subject of the bookshelves entirely. And then, trying to change the subject, said brightly, "What happened to that sauce you were cooking up last night? I... kind of...it slipped my mind. I hope it didn't get ruined..."

"I set it to slow simmer," Dorotea said. "It'll be the better for having taken its time. We could have it for lunch, later, if you like. But if you don't want to fiddle with that right now, it'll keep—we can always order in Chinese. Ordinarily I don't like crumbs in the bed but under the circumstances it might be fun to crack open a couple of fortune cookies there..."

Quincey abruptly pushed the cat off her feet, gathered up the bed sheets around her for modesty as she swung her legs out of the bed.

"I...ah, I think I do have to go, actually," she murmured. "I promised...a friend... I'd help them move today..."

"Okay," Dorotea said, her voice tinged with chagrin—belatedly aware that she had perhaps pushed a little too far, too fast—and regret, resignation, acceptance.

She slipped out of bed, into the bathroom, closing the door behind her softly and allowing Quincey some privacy.

The orange cat gave Quincey a jaundiced look and leapt off the bed, stalking out of the bedroom. The tux stayed, still purring almost inaudibly, green eyes fixed on Quincey who suddenly felt like curling back up into the pillows and crying her eyes out. But those pillows—this bed—reminded her all too vividly of what had happened here the night before, of the fears that had been faced and calmed, of the curiosity that had been met and satisfied, of the unexpected heart-stopping joy of it all and of the yawning chasm of choices which had opened in its aftermath.

If she were to give way to tears, it could not be here, could not be now. She needed to be away from this place, from Dorotea—needed some quiet time, to process, to probe, to think.

It was awkward. Quincey didn't want it to be, but the more she smiled and tried to pretend that it was a Sunday morning like no other, the less ordinary a Sunday it became, and harder it was to find anything to say at all that didn't trigger things she didn't want triggered right then. In the end, hesitating at the door, flailing about for something innocuous to say in farewell which wouldn't sound like she was fleeing forever, Quincey found her eyes filling with the tears that she didn't want to shed—and it was these brilliant eyes that she turned to Dorotea, her fingers twisted from one hand into another, both hands held at her breast as though she was trying to hold something between them, something that, if allowed to escape, would run rampant and eat the world.

"I'm sorry," she said.

"I'm sorry I made you feel sorry," Dorotea said.

A few steps away from the door, Quincey turned her head—Dorotea was still standing in her doorway.

"I still have your number," Quincey said, stumbling over the words, not entirely certain herself what she had wanted them to convey.

But Dorotea seemed to understand anyway, and smiled. "I hope so," she said. And she raised her fingertips to her lips, kissed them lightly, and blew the kiss in Quincey's direction before she stepped back and quietly but firmly shut the door.

Quincey walked, for over an hour—aimlessly, without a destination in mind, just wandering the quiet streets of a Sunday morning. It was the smell of coffee wafting from a café as somebody came out and the door was briefly open that reminded her that she had kind of skipped dinner the night before and had not had breakfast that morning, and that she was hungry. She drifted into the café and sat down on an unsteady wooden chair which seemed to her suddenly to be an appropriate metaphor of her life, and ordered a cup of coffee and a bagel with cream cheese. The place was not packed, but it was hardly empty—and Quincey found herself watching the other patrons as she munched her bagel. There was one family—mother, father, two noisy toddlers—and a couple of people eating alone, like herself, but the rest of the clientele consisted of three or four couples who all seemed to be in the throes of first love, sitting close together with legs seamlessly joined from hip to knee or else with ankles tangled together under the table, holding hands, heads leaned toward one another so that their hair and their breath mingled and their eyes were filled with nothing but one another. It seemed as though there was a message here, but Quincey could not bring herself to parse it out. She finished her bagel quickly, downed her coffee, tossed what she owed onto the table, and left as fast as she was able.

It was still relatively early when she finally turned her key in her own door and stepped into the apartment she shared with Peter. He was in his bedroom, but not asleep—apparently at his computer if the noises coming out of that room, with its door ajar, were any indication—but it seemed as though whatever he was doing was holding less than his full attention. In the time it took Quincey to close the front door and take a couple of steps down the corridor toward her own room, Peter was peering out through the crack that his own door was open, and then pulled it open wider, all the way.

"Oh-ho," he said. "You're only coming in now? Let's see— you didn't come home after your dinner, but you *did* come back in time for breakfast, at least theoretically...so it was good enough to stay the night, but then he did or said something that made you run for your life...do you need tea and sympathy?"

"Had coffee," Quincey murmured. "And she didn't..."

She closed her mouth with a snap, but too late. Peter did a perceptible double take.

"*She?*" he echoed quietly.

"Oh, go back to your game," Quincey said, hanging her head and wishing that she still had the longer hair, so that she could hide behind it.

"Do you want to talk about it?"

Her head came up for long enough for her to meet his eyes, her own startled, even shocked—and then she looked down again, at the floor between her feet. "*Talk* about it?"

"It messes with your head," Peter said. "I did it once, after a party where I drank way too much. Woke up in a strange bed. Next to another guy."

"You never said—"

"No reason. It never came up."

"She...asked me to...she wanted me to..."

"And did you want to stay?"

Her head came up again, and she stared at him, wide-eyed, frightened, spooked.

"None of your business," she said faintly, and then turned away. "I'm going to my room."

He watched her go, and said no more. She heard his door close a moment before she closed her own.

But she really didn't want to be alone. The rest of Sunday stretched out before her, empty, endless; whatever she thought about in terms of how to spend the rest of the day, she found herself dismissing it before the idea had a chance to fully formulate itself. The simple truth, the truth that she wasn't ready to face, that she didn't want to face, was that she wanted nothing more than to be back with Dorotea in that rooftop apartment right now. Even the prospect of fortune cookie crumbles on the bed sheets seemed inviting. She kept on circling around to that, coming back to the center of the labyrinth, and then shying away violently as the realized where she was going, slamming the door against those wishes, those memories, every time they swam back into her consciousness. She picked up a book, trying to distract herself by reading, but the book on the top of the pile next to her bed happened to be Sappho's poetry, the book she had bought in Dorotea's bookstore not so long ago— and she threw it back down, on her bed, where it landed on her pillow and flipped itself open as if daring her to read what was revealed inside. There was another book beneath that, a novel, but somehow Quincey knew that she would make very little headway with that at this moment.

There was TV, but that would mean going out to the living room and possibly facing Peter again, which was something else she didn't want to do right then. She could go out again, but it was Sunday, and her options were relatively limited—she had nothing that she needed to go shopping for in stores which were open on a Sunday, she couldn't walk around in the streets all day, and she didn't feel like going to the movies alone.

Her skin felt too tight, as though she no longer fit into it properly. As though she, herself, the inner being, had somehow changed—grown new curves, or new angles—and the old skin chafed like an ill-fitting shoe.

She found herself missing, of all things, the presence of Dorotea's purring tuxedo cat—a living being that could keep her company but would not insist on talking, and would not judge and either condemn, or approve (at this point Quincey could not make up her mind which would be worse). She suddenly realized that she had very few people in her life whom she could call friends, certainly not close friends, anyone to whom she could talk freely about the thing that spun like a wheel of fire in her mind. Peter had offered to talk, to be sure, but she shied away from that. If they talked, and if he reacted in a certain way, then they would both have to live with that—and more importantly, with each other—in the aftermath, and it wasn't something she wanted to think about right then. She briefly thought of her family but dismissed them almost before she had finished the thought. This was not something she could discuss with any of them—especially not her own mother.

In the end she took out a pack of cards and laid out one furious and silent solitaire after another until she heard stirrings out in the corridor, and then Peter leaving the apartment. She raked through an unfinished solitaire at that point and wandered into the kitchen to make herself something to eat—and found herself haunted by the smell of Dorotea's pasta sauce even as she smeared peanut butter on a piece of two-day-old bread.

Monday could not come soon enough, and she was early for work, which didn't happen often. Unhappily, her boss was not around to notice it—and her lab-mate, Annie, was particularly late that day, so Quincey had her bench to herself for nearly an hour and a half, and worked at a furious pace. She had almost finished a full day's work by the time Annie arrived, and barely looked up to give her the time of day.

"What bit you?" Annie asked, slipping into her lab coat and coming to perch on her stool. She consulted the clipboard tied to the back of the bench, noted the crossed-out jobs which Quincey had already done or which were in progress, and glanced at her bench-mate again. "I might as well have taken the day off, you've already done all the work…"

"New batch of tests coming this afternoon," Quincey said, a little lamely. "I thought I'd try and clear the bench…"

"Well, you've damn near done it yourself. What do you want me to start on?"

Quincey pointed. "The Harris job. Haven't started that one yet."

"Don't want to talk this morning?" Annie said, with a grin. "Okay. I'll get on with the Harris job. But we're taking an early lunch today—out at the diner, not at the cafeteria—and you can tell me then what brought on this spurt of enthusiasm…"

"No, I don't think that we—"

Annie lifted an admonishing finger. "Tut-tut! I insist. I'm even buying, if that's what it takes. Now—Harris job, here I come."

Quincey didn't want to take time out for a gossipy lunch—would have worked steadily right through lunch-hour if she'd been given a chance—but Annie wasn't taking no for an answer, and Quincey found herself eating a green salad with dressing on the side in the diner down the street from their lab while Annie leaned in closer in a conspiratorial fashion.

"Now. Spill. New guy?"

"Sort of," Quincey said with a twisted grin.

"How long you been seeing him?"

"Um. Met tail end of September. Gershwin concert."

"Only a few weeks? And it's already had enough time to drive you to distraction?..." Annie said, grinning.

Quincey groaned. Annie was the closest thing she had to a friend, here at work—but this, this was...too much...

"Spent the night, Saturday," Quincey said at last.

"And?" Annie asked, agog. "Was it good? Wait—Saturday? What happened Sunday? Did he want you to stay and you didn't or did he kick you out and you wanted to stay?"

"Does it matter?"

"Oh yeah. A whole heap. It would explain you, today, in two totally different ways."

"Not he," Quincey said faintly, and looked almost ludicrously astonished to hear herself saying those words.

"What was that?"

Quincey looked up, folded her hands together, rested her chin on her interlaced fingers, and stared at Annie directly. "Not *he*," she said, more firmly, owning the words at last, challenging a reaction. "She. A woman."

Annie had unconsciously shifted gears, with the pronoun. "You stayed at a *friend's* on Saturday? What—did she have the problem? Is that what's distracting you? Oh, honey—tell her, there's more fish in the sea..."

"Annie...she *is* the fish. Her name is Dorotea, she's funny, she's smart, she's full of life and of passion, she can cook..."

"And you...she... you..."

Quincey nodded imperceptibly. Because she was watching for it, she saw it come—the wary sideways glance, the sudden hooding of Annie's eyes, the faintest gesture of withdrawal as she pulled her hand away from the middle of the table back toward her and away from Quincey.

"Oh," Annie said. And was then silent.

Quincey had not realized how much this stung—but also how enraged it was making her feel. She glanced at her wrist.

"We'd better get back to work," she said.

"Yeah," Annie said. "We'd better."

Annie must have put in a request for an immediate transfer almost as soon as they returned to the labs—it took a few days to come into effect but it was a new girl, Jennifer, who came to work beside Quincey on the following Monday.

"Where's Annie?" Quincey asked.

"Oh, she's transferred to the other city lab," Jennifer said brightly. "I'm your new bench mate."

"Nice to meet you," Quincey said automatically.

And then said very little else for the rest of the week.

It had not, perhaps, needed to be this way—but she quickly realized that she had made life unbearable for herself. She had opened her mouth about Dorotea to two people—Peter and Annie. Annie had fled at the mere mention of the possibility of such a relationship; Quincey's flat-mate seemed sympathetic, but the admission stood between them like a glass wall which had changed things between them to the point where the strain was taking its toll.

It took Quincey far longer than it should have done to remember Dorotea's words at the café, at their second meeting— about the apartment below hers, the apartment that she was renting, the apartment for which she was 'looking' for possible tenants. Or had been, then. It was entirely possible that she had already found somebody—and Quincey really didn't want to go back and see Dorotea just yet anyway, not while her own insides were in such a turmoil—but it suddenly seemed to be an obvious solution, to everything. The two of them might circle one another at leisure, more warily, and perhaps become... who knew...just good friends, after all. She'd be away from Peter and would have her own space.

When she phoned the number on Dorotea's little ivory card, finally, she could not believe that it had taken her that long to do it. But all she got was an answering machine, that time, and she lost her nerve and slammed the phone down without saying anything, wondering if Dorotea had caller ID on her phone and would know who had phoned anyway. Thinking about this for five minutes made her skin prickle with the shame of having copped out, and she dialed again, ready to leave a message.

But instead, Dorotea picked up.

"Hello," she said, a statement, not a question. She definitely knew who this was.

"I was thinking," Quincey said, without preamble. "That apartment below yours, above the shop. Is it still for rent?"

"Yours if you want it."

"I think I do," Quincey said, her voice sounding very faint to her own ears. "I think I *do* want it."

She was acutely aware that she might have been saying more than the mere words conveyed. And that Dorotea was just as aware of the same thing.

But Dorotea kept it calm, kept it level, kept it strictly business. "I can have the key to you by the end of the day."

"Done," Quincey said. She had not asked how much the rent would be. Whatever it was, she would pay it.

She left an extra month's rent with Peter, by way of apology for her disappearing act. Peter asked no questions about where she was moving, or why; he even offered to help her move her things, but she declined. It took her no more than two days to pack her belongings and move everything into the new place. After living in a single room in someone else's apartment for so long, her new digs felt ridiculously huge and empty; she drifted around the hollow and echoing rooms like a ghost for a while, trying to come to terms with the space. She unpacked slowly, living out of boxes for a couple of weeks, as though she was uncertain that she would stay. But every day after she came back from work she would find something waiting for her by the door—a potted plant, or a parrot-headed umbrella stand, or even just a couple of books left in a tidy pile next to her front door. And she'd take them in, and set them in place, and it was like a little bit of Dorotea came in with each of them and took root in her space, in her heart. Dorotea herself didn't intrude, although she didn't exactly go out of her way to avoid her new tenant either—but her greetings on the stairs, if they happened to meet there, were banked warmth. Nothing effusive, nothing deliberate, just a constant and consistent aura of always being glad to see Quincey—whatever the context or the circumstances.

After a little while of this, Quincey began to relax a little, sensed something unwinding inside of her, letting go. She did not speak to anybody else about the new arrangement and its roots—she merely told her work administration that she had moved and gave them notification of a change of address—and her outward face was still ice and steel; but inside the building where she now lived the atmosphere changed, slowly, subtly, without her even realizing that it was going on at first. In time, she found herself listening out for Dorotea on the stairs, or wondering if she were upstairs in her own apartment and what she was doing. A little further on it began to seem silly to keep a degree of separation. The conversations became longer. They began to end while one of the two of them was lingering in the open door of her own apartment. And a little later they began in the bookshop or in the stairwell and ended up over cups of coffee in one apartment or the other. They didn't talk about their having made love in Dorotea's bed, but, over the space of weeks and then months, they slowly began to talk about things that formed the bedrock of that.

Dorotea's cats had got used to Quincey's presence—once or twice Dorotea had even asked her to cat-sit while she was away at a bookseller's conference or a weekend off somewhere by herself—and would bother her for dinner if she happened to be in the apartment at the correct times, which occasionally resulted in them getting two dinners some days with both women being conned into providing food. When Quincey came across a quaint fridge magnet at a novelty shop one day—a black-and-white cat which had a dangling reversible button which said "The cat has been fed" on one side and "The cat has not been fed" on the other, she bought it for Dorotea, and brought it up to the apartment, her turn to bear gifts. Dorotea laughed, pronounced it one of the most useful things that she had ever been given since her life with cats began, and asked Quincey in for a cup of coffee.

It was raining outside, and cold, and the wind tumbled old newspapers down abandoned wet alleyways; inside Dorotea's apartment it was warm, and the walls radiated contentment and security. It felt...like home. It felt more like home than Quincey had ever felt anywhere, and unintended tears into her eyes as she stared into the distance, lost in thought, over the rim of the coffee cup which she held cradled against her lips with both hands wrapped around it.

"Penny for them," Dorotea said softly.

Quincey looked up. "I don't know how we happened," she said, without preamble, finally ready to cross a threshold. "You...when we...I got scared."

"I know," Dorotea said. "I'm sorry."

"It wasn't your fault. I just couldn't find myself, right then. I kind of lost all notion of who I was, of what I was. I had *never* looked at a woman...that way. I've never..." She glanced at Dorotea, then away, swallowed hard and put down her coffee cup. "I've never...fallen in love with a woman before. I don't know when I suddenly became... gay."

"Oh, honey. You don't *become* gay. It isn't like flipping a switch," Dorotea said. "There's a little bit in all of us that recognizes beauty—or that which we call beauty—in other people, be they male or female, and no matter what your own sex is. What's different is just when you slide the cursor along that line and suddenly realize that you are responding more to one side or another. But it isn't something you choose, or become. You *are*. You just—find out—and then you act on that, accept it, or you bury it deep and you never talk about it again. Ever. With anybody. And that night...I saw something. I thought I saw something. The way you looked at me...I'm sorry if I pushed it, or forced it. I didn't mean to do that."

"But it was kind of what I needed," Quincey said. "It was... it felt good, back then. So good it scared the living daylights out of me. This was so not me, not the person I thought I was...I think I am..."

Dorotea leaned in a little closer. "What are you trying to say, Quincey?"

"I guess... that it's lonely downstairs...."

Dorotea tilted her head a little, the beginnings of a smile tugging at the corner of her mouth.

"Would you mind if I took in a cat?" Quincey said, looking up, her expression earnest.

Dorotea's own expression changed, a little, and Quincey's eyes sparked at the realization.

"And would you mind terribly," she continued, "if I laid claim to one of yours?" She laid a hand on the head of the tux cat, who had curled up next to her on the arm rest of the armchair she sat on. "This one seems to like me around..."

"Are you telling me...?" Dorotea began, for once taken off guard.

"Those shelves you cleared for me," Quincey said faintly. "Are they still on offer...?"

Dorotea leaned over, finally breaking into that smile, and brushed her lips over Quincey's, lightly but firmly.

"Honey," she said huskily, "they've been standing empty for months, waiting for you to ask."

Quincey didn't bother packing boxes. She and Dorotea took a day to carry all of her stuff one floor up to the penthouse apartment, and by evening Quincey's clothes hung in her half of the closet in the master bedroom, and a couple of empty bookshelves were beginning to look lived in.

They ordered in Chinese on that night, and ate fortune cookies in bed.

Quincey's said, *Your life may be about to become very interesting.*

Quincey let her parents know of her change of address, but did not elaborate on the circumstances; she knew her mother well enough to anticipate her response to the situation, and shied away from that confrontation until it became necessary. There were times when it was difficult for Quincey herself to wrap her mind around the nature of her new life—that she was in fact making a statement, declaring her hand, having gone literally overnight from being a somewhat lonely and isolated but perfectly heterosexual young woman to someone whom her mother would inevitably, as soon as she became aware of her daughter's living arrangements, call 'flaunting' her sexual preferences and probably hysterically demand of herself where she had gone wrong in the raising of this child. She did not spell any of this out for Dorotea, not explicitly, but Dorotea did not pry; her own parents had been dead for years and she had been an only child and she had no family drama to contribute.

She did ask, when a year had somehow managed to slip by and the two of them were still together and a stronger couple than they had ever been before, if Quincey wanted to ask her family over for dinner one night. Quincey shook her head.

"Not yet."

"You're going to have to tell them sometime," Dorotea murmured.

Quincey shot her a desperate look. "Not yet."

"Okay," Dorotea said. "You know them best."

Quincey had every intention of telling her family about Dorotea. Every time she dropped them a note, or sent them an email, or talked to them on the phone, she would find herself scrambling for neutral ground. It was Dorotea herself, who initially went along with all of it, who took matters into her own hands one day—almost two years after Quincey had moved in—when she happened to be the one to pick up the phone when it rang.

There had been a pause after she said hello, and then a female voice unfamiliar to Dorotea said, "I'm, uh, could I speak to Quincey Thorne, please?"

"She's in the shower," Dorotea said pleasantly. "Can I take a message?"

"It's her mother. Uh, just tell her I called, could you, er...?"

There was an obvious fishing for identity, and Dorotea supplied it.

"I'll certainly tell her that her mother called," she said. Quincey stumbled in from the kitchen, her eyes panicked, and Dorotea met them levelly across the expanse of the living room. "This is Dorotea, her partner."

There was a moment of silence, and the phone went dead.

"I said I'd tell them!" Quincey said, flushing.

"There's only a few years left in this century," Dorotea said.

Quincey bit her lip. "I'd better phone her back."

Dorotea intercepted her as she made for the phone, her

fingers closing in an almost painful grip on Quincey's arm. "Are you ashamed of me?"

"What...? No!"

"Afraid of them." It was a statement, not a question.

Quincey closed her eyes, shook her head. "You don't know them."

"Well. Perhaps it's time I did." She let go of Quincey's arm, looked away without meeting her eyes. "Before we're all a hundred years older."

Quincey agreed, in principle. But the phone conversation that followed this exchange, and several phone conversations that followed, told her that she needed to let a little bit more time pass under this particular bridge. There was a tentative attempt to arrange a lunch with the family, but Quincey's mother developed one of her migraines on the day, and Dorotea set her lips and held her peace. After that, there was nothing, for a while.

And weeks turned into months. And months turned into years.

Quincey and Dorotea laughed a lot, together. They went to museums, play openings, movies, weekends away by the sea. They quarrelled—over money, over trivialities, over bad habits each had gained over the years and the other thought that she was too slow to shed. They lost the big orange tabby to cancer, and cried in each other's arms, and then acquired two other kittens, whom they named Gertrude and Alice.

Almost five years to the day after Quincey moved in, Dorotea began to get an itch for travel. Brochures about places like Patagonia and Macchu Picchu and Japan began to litter the living room, and Dorotea would plan wild itineraries around these destinations, often lasting up to six months or longer.

"I can't afford it," Quincey said, riffling through the brochures. "Either financially, or the time—I can't take a year's leave from my job, they'd just fire me."

"It isn't a matter of money, we're doing fine," Dorotea said. "Just the rent from the downstairs flat will finance most of it and Victor can take care of this flat and the cats while we're away, and Sandy can run the shop on her own for a bit, I've certainly taught her that well, and I could always hire her another assistant on a temporary basis. And if you're desperately worried about the job you can take over that one when we get back, not that you need to."

"What, be Sandy's assistant in the bookstore?"

"Well, Sandy might want to disappear herself. You can take over the store."

"What about you?"

"You can be *my* assistant."

Quincey sighed. "That isn't the *point*, Dorotea."

"Oh, you can be such a wet blanket," Dorotea said, throwing a glossy brochure about Andorra at her.

They played this like a tennis game, batting it back and forth, baiting one another with it, until Quincey realized that Dorotea had finally found something that she thought was more special than the rest, something that she really wanted to do.

It would take a while—but she wanted nothing less than to travel the old Silk Road across Asia, take lots of pictures, keep a diary, and perhaps write a book about it. She always had an enthusiasm that was contagious, and when she spoke about this plan she did so in terms that made Quincey see it all come to life before her eyes…and she flew right at Dorotea's side, buoyed by her eagerness and passion. But then they'd separate for a while and out of Dorotea's orbit Quincey's own enthusiasm for the project would cool in the face of practicalities.

Until Dorotea finally sat her down one cool rainy evening in early fall and stared into her eyes, holding both Quincey's hands in her own.

"I don't know why but you are still uncertain about this sometimes," she said. "About me. About us. And I think that committing to going on this trip…means far more to you than you realize. So let's make it real, for you. Let's… get married. Let's make this a honeymoon—the honeymoon we never had."

"Dorotea," Quincey said, taken completely by surprise, "we can't get *married*. Not legally, or within any kind of faith. Neither the law nor any kind of church I know of recognizes…"

Dorotea shrugged. "Pah. We need neither. Human law doesn't matter, and as far as dogma is concerned it's just the human interpretation of the word of God, and what do humans know? I was raised Catholic, and I know I am pretty much damned already according to the faith of my childhood—the stern old God to whom I raised my eyes at Mass when I was *this* high has long since closed his eyes to me, if I am to believe the catechism…which I haven't, for a long time now. But that doesn't *matter* anymore. This is between you, and me, and whatever God we choose to believe will hear us. There are those who will choose to see it as something lesser—although I don't know why anyone would denigrate anything that has been a called a 'ceremony of commitment'—God knows true commitment is rare enough for it to be precious when it's found. That's all a wedding is, a ceremony of commitment. I know a woman who can marry us, and will—rules and regulations be damned— and we can have the wedding right here. It doesn't matter what anyone else thinks of that—I think, I hope, that someday it will come, that it will be just as possible for you and I to get married as it would be for any Tom, Dick or Harry to marry any Mary, Sue, or Jane. But until then—it's between us. We can write our own vows. It will be wonderful. Will you marry me, Quincey Quincey Thorne?"

Quincey swallowed, her fingers tightening on Dorotea's, her eyes filling with tears even as her lips curved into a smile at the resurrection of the running gag of the double-barreled name.

"I already have, in my heart," she whispered.

"And will you come to Mongolia with me…?"

Quincey stared at her, and then threw her head back and laughed. "All right," she said. "You win."

Dorotea leaned in to kiss her, a deep, passionate kiss shared between lovers of long standing. "I'll give the Reverend Matilda a call," she said.

"Can I do something…?"

"Just write your vows," Dorotea said. "And this time… invite your family."

"They may not come," Quincey said, her fingers tightening on Dorotea's.

"That's their business. Yours is to ask them. It's time."

Quincey sighed, and bowed her head.

Dorotea took on the new project with her usual energy. Within a week they had a firm date less than two months away, an officiant, a folk singing group to provide the live music, a caterer, and an order in at the printer's for a hundred invitations. Most of those went to their friends, people whom they knew as a couple and who replied with enthusiastic acceptances. Two of them went, with misgivings, to Quincey's family—one to her parents, Joe and Addie Thorne, and one to her brother, Joe Junior, and his wife, Linda, and their two young sons. The responses took so long to come that Quincey almost hoped that they would all refuse; but finally they did come, the little postcards which had been enclosed with the invitations for the purpose of a reply.

They were coming. They were all coming.

"This is a bad idea," Quincey said, holding her brother's reply card between her thumb and forefinger as though it was something vaguely unclean.

"All they have to do is be civil," Dorotea said.

"I'm not sure they can."

Dorotea squeezed her fingers. "Nothing can spoil this."

The date of October 15, a Saturday, was circled in red on every calendar in the apartment—in the kitchen, on two different calendars on Dorotea's desk, in Quincey's weekly planner. The two of them smiled mysteriously at one another if they happened to catch one another's eye while in the process of scribbling down something to do with their vows, or pinning down another small detail of the party.

About a week away from the ceremony, Dorotea walked into the bedroom to find Quincey staring morosely into the closet, wearing an expression of doom.

"What's the matter?" Dorotea asked.

"I'm supposed to be getting married in a week."

"Yes, and?"

Quincey made a short choppy gesture toward the contents of the closet. "In what?"

"Well, there's your...there's..." Dorotea flipped through clothes hangers, giving Quincey's clothes short and dismissive apprising glances as she sorted through them, one by one. "You might be right," she said at last. "But come to think of it. you really should have something new and fabulous for the occasion. Leave it to me, I will make it a priority to find something for you to wear that will blow them all away when you walk into the room. Hmm, but it's a challenge—I don't have much time…"

"Hardly seems fair that you get to choose what I wear if I don't get to pick what *you* wear," Quincey said with a grin.

Dorotea's eyes sparkled. "Oh, *perfect*! I can't wait to see what you pick for my wedding outfit!"

"Whatever I pick?" Quincey asked.

"Whatever you pick. If you wear what I choose, I wear what *you* choose."

"Oh, *so* done," Quincey said. "I already have the perfect thing in mind…"

"Should I be afraid?"

"Would I do that to you on your wedding day?" Quincey asked. "But perhaps I should be…"

"Quincey…you do know this is a game. I'd be proud to stand up with you wearing anything from this closet—you could wear your lab coat and nothing else, or I could wrap you in a burlap sack and tie it on you with wire and you'd still look beautiful on Saturday," Dorotea said, her voice low and intense.

"You wouldn't," Quincey said, backing away in mock horror.

"Trust me," Dorotea said, laughing.

"I do," Quincey said, suddenly very serious. "With the rest of my life."

They exchanged the wedding outfits which they had chosen for one another—kept in secret places until then, and wrapped in brown paper for increased security against stray glances—on the Saturday morning, mere hours before their first guests were due to arrive. Dorotea opened hers first, at Quincey's insistence, and was, for once, rendered speechless at what she saw—a dress modeled along the lines of a Chinese *cheongsam*, fitted across bodice and hip, white silk shot with gold thread.

"How do you know this will fit?" Dorotea said, running her hand along the sumptuous silk laid out on their bed. "It looks so tailored—"

"I gave a seamstress your exact measurements—and also,

I invited her to the wedding, she's coming here first, well in advance of anybody else, so if any last-minute adjustments need to be made she'll do it. Try it on."

"No, open yours first," Dorotea said.

Quincey gasped when she first glimpsed what lay underneath the brown wrapping—a flash of rich jewel-red, ruby-colored silk. She ripped away the paper with eager fingers to reveal a V-necked sleeveless sheath which looked as though it ended just above the knee, simple and elegant, perfect for showing off Quincey's coloring and her slender figure.

"In India, red is the color of weddings," Dorotea said. "And you always did look spectacular in these richer, darker colors."

"I don't have a single pair of shoes which will do this justice," Quincey said.

Dorotea grinned. "Sure you do. Go look in that red box in the back of the closet."

The box, when unearthed, proved to contain a set of high-heeled open-toed pumps which matched the red dress perfectly. Quincey's eyes filled with tears, and Dorotea shook her head.

"No—oh, no, everyone else is allowed to cry today but you and I are not. Absolutely not. Deal?"

Quincey sniffed. "I will make you absolutely no promises on that score."

The *cheongsam* fitted well without the need for the seamstress's attentions, and Dorotea and Quincey paused to give one another loving, admiring glances in their bedroom when they were both ready for the festivities to begin—they had not wanted their guests to see them before they made a grand entrance, so they had co-opted Victor, the tenant from the downstairs apartment, to act as host and usher as people arrived giving the two of them the chance to prepare in a semi-leisurely fashion.

Quincey, who rarely wore make-up, even gave a nod to the occasion by submitting to Dorotea doing her face, and was astonished at the difference when she looked into the mirror and stared at two wide and beautiful eyes outlined by kohl and lashes darkened by mascara, a full mouth wearing lipstick which closely matched the shade of her dress, a touch of blush on her cheekbones. Dorotea was smugly triumphant at the success of her ministrations; she had done her own make-up, with the usual expertise, but the brilliance and sparkle in her eyes and the glow in her face owed very little to powders and paint. They stood and stared at themselves, standing side by side, the woman in white and the woman in red, and they knew a moment of perfect happiness. And then Dorotea caught Quincey's eye in the mirror, and smiled, holding out a hand.

"You ready?"

Quincey took the hand, laced her fingers through Dorotea's. "If you're coming with me."

Dorotea knocked on the door of the bedroom, and cranked it open just a notch; Sandy, the girl from the bookstore, stood guard outside, and glanced into the room as Dorotea gave a signal. Sandy stepped away from the door, caught the eye of the musicians and gave them a nod, and they wound up the piece they were currently playing, allowed a moment of silence to alert the now-crowded living room that something was about to happen, and then began to play the piece that Quincey and Dorotea had chosen for their entrance.

The two of them stepped out of the bedroom, still hand in hand, and there was an appreciative murmur from their friends in the room as they entered it. Quincey raked the room swiftly with her gaze, trying to find her family, but could not spot them quickly and then she was out of time—she and Dorotea were pacing solemnly behind Sandy, who walked before them parting the crowd in the living room and leaving them an open path to walk down to where the Reverend Matilda, a gray-haired woman with a seamed face and bright black eyes, waited for them clad in formal blue robes with sleeves that fell across her wrists and half covered her folded hands.

When they came to a halt in front of her, she smiled at them, and then lifted her eyes to gaze out at the audience.

"We are here today because these two people love one another," the Reverend Matilda said. "They have chosen to offer a vow, each to the other, taking one another in a lifelong partnership which is a true marriage of minds and hearts, and accept one another as spouses, partners, the two halves which, together, will make both of them whole. Dorotea, Quincey, you may state your vows."

Dorotea went first. She turned to Quincey and took both her hands into her own.

"My life is your life. My days are your days. I will walk with you in sunlight and under the moon, in shadows and in darkness, in both joy and fear—and I will know contentment, for the rest of my days, just knowing that you are near. I promise to help you, support you, trust you, honor you, and be on your side in all things. I will be your family, and your friend. I will always love you."

Quincey's eyes were full of tears, but Dorotea shook her head minutely. *No crying. You promised.*

"I never knew, before you walked into my life, what a soul mate truly meant," Quincey said, her own turn at saying her vows. "You make me happy. You make me complete. You make me... truly me, the person who I never thought I could be, and cannot be, without you at my side. I look down the years that are to come, and I know that for the rest of my life I need never be alone again, or afraid, with your strength and your passion by my side, my partner, and my friend."

Sandy stepped forward at a nod from the Reverend, and presented her with a small velvet bag. Reverend Matilda loosened the drawstring, and drew out two plain gold rings.

"Dorotea and Quincey have agreed to seal their vows with an exchange of rings," she said, holding them up for a moment for the audience to see, and then she laid them on one palm and held them out to the two who stood before her.

Dorotea took one of the bands, and slipped it onto the ring finger of Quincey's left hand. Quincey took the other, and placed it on Dorotea's hand with fingers that trembled so much that she nearly fumbled it—but managed a save, and the ring was safely bestowed before she had a chance to drop it.

Someone in the room behind her sniffed loudly, obviously crying, and Quincey nearly lost it—but then looked up and met Dorotea's eyes and, instead, broke into a brilliant smile.

The Reverend echoed it, beaming at the two of them.

"You may," she said benevolently, "kiss the brides."

Dorotea did, to cheers and applause from the room.

"Congratulations," the Reverend Matilda said. "I wish I could make it legal for you—but even if all I can do is bear witness, it's been a privilege. Go, enjoy your party."

They turned together, to face the room, and were instantly swamped by a crowd of well-wishers who wanted to hug them, or shake their hands, or just nod and smile with tears streaming down their faces—some of them were Dorotea's friends of some years standing, together for far longer than Dorotea and Quincey had been, for whom the moment was nothing less than miraculous. Sophie Lavelle, a large copper-skinned Creole woman originally from New Orleans who led the NotChickLit Women's Book Club at Dorotea's bookstore, and her partner Lili Grossman, both of them women in their early sixties who had been together for almost half their lifetimes, buried Dorotea and Quincey in a group hug; Sophie was crying, openly and messily, making no effort to wipe away the tears.

"I've wasted so much time," she hiccoughed into Dorotea's shoulder. "We should have done this, something like this, *decades* ago, Lili and I. And we will. We *will*."

"You haven't asked me yet," Lili said, laughing through her own tears.

"Hey, guys, congratulations!" The voice was young, male, and the women opened up to see who it was.

"Hey, Mike. Thanks."

Mike, who was a frequent customer at Herstory Books and had picked Dorotea's brain numerous times on several unlikely subjects he was studying at the local college, pumped Dorotea's hand vigorously.

"This was so *cool!*" he said, his face split wide open by a grin it seemed barely able to contain. "Thanks so much for inviting me!"

"Congratulations!" That came in an incongruously deep masculine voice, issuing forth from what looked to be like a very elegant woman with long blonde hair and a multi-tiered pearl choker with diamanté clasps around her neck.

"That was *amazing*—thank you for letting me be here!"

"All best!"

"It was lovely!"

The voices came at them from the people in the room, people who came thronging around them to smile, to touch, to hug, to share the joy. And Quincey was carried by this, allowing herself to be buoyed, seeing that hope burst like the sun spilling through clouds, laughing with the rest of them through the tears, watching in joy and sheer amazement as the flicker of a new gold band on her marriage finger caught her eye as she moved her hand.

And then she looked up, and through a gap in the happy throng she caught the frozen gaze of her mother.

She glanced at Dorotea, saw that she had seen.

"I need to..." Quincey began.

Dorotea nodded, squeezing the fingers of the hand she still held. "Yes. Go. Just remember, I have your back."

Quincey nodded, and looked away.

Her parents seemed rooted to the spot, letting the rest of the party swirl around them. Quincey's father smiled as she approached—and the smile was a little strained, but genuine.

"Hey, baby girl," he said. "I—uh—congratulations. You look great."

"At least you didn't wear white," Addie said.

"*Adeline*," Joe Thorne said, watching his daughter's face go white, then flush bright scarlet.

But Addie Thorne just shook her head a little.

"I'm sorry, but—I don't know—we didn't get you a present, we thought—"

"Aunt Cyn sent one," Quincey said. "A beautiful quilt."

"We didn't—"

"She's the only one, of the family," Quincey said. Her voice was level, preternaturally calm. She was keeping a tight rein on it. "Our friends did, but not family. Oh, it doesn't matter—we don't need anything. But a card might have been nice."

Addie looked down at her feet.

Quincey was about to say something else when she suddenly saw Joe Junior approaching, out of the corner of her eye. Her brother was not aging gracefully; he was a decade older than Quincey, to be sure, but he was still not quite forty yet, and already his hair was thinning on the top of his head in a most unflattering way and he carried the beginnings of a paunch. He held a plate, and was eating something from it as he walked, shoveling it from the plate to his mouth with the fork. Almost too fast for Quincey to see. Almost.

But she did see. And her face went white, bloodless, as she stared at him.

"Hey," her brother said. "Nice digs. Nice shindig. Nice cake."

"That is my *wedding cake*."

"Eh?..."

"We made a special request for the icing to be two rings. I know they were on the cake, I checked when they delivered it. I know I left a special knife on a saucer next to the platter. Dorotea and I were to cut it ourselves. That is my wedding cake, Joe."

"Steady on," he said, putting the plate down on a nearby table. "Hey—it didn't even *look* like a proper wedding cake. It was just, you know, a cake, and it was there—I didn't think you'd mind. The boys wanted some—and it's not as though it was even like, you know, a *real* wedding."

"You insensitive *idiot*," Joe Senior growled, scowling at his son.

Dorotea must have realized, even half a room away and separated by a crowd of people, that something had gone wrong—because she was suddenly there at Quincey's side, smiling, holding out a hand. The left one, the one with the ring on it.

"Hello," she said, her voice smooth, pleasant. "You must be Quincey's parents. I'm Dorotea. I'm glad to finally meet you."

"I'm Q's dad," Joe Senior said. "Likewise."

Addie raised a limp hand. "Hello."

"Hey," Joe Junior said, sidling up to Dorotea. "I'm the big bro. Do I get a hug, here?..." He slipped an arm around Dorotea's waist as he spoke, pulling her off balance and a step closer to him. "You know, it's such a waste—you should have tried a man of the family to give you a little bit of..."

Dorotea slapped him, calmly and quite dispassionately. Startled, he let go, lifting his hand to his smarting cheek.

"I just married your sister," Dorotea said. "I think you

should mind your manners."

"The cake... he..." Quincey began incoherently.

Joe Senior stepped forward, shoving his son to the side.

"Please forgive me for allowing this to happen. I should have kept a closer eye on my ill-bred son. But I should really like..." He turned his head, realized his wife was wearing a silk scarf tied loosely around her shoulders, and lifted it up over her head before she had a chance to react or object, working at the knot as he did so, shaking the square of silk out even as he spoke. "I would like to see you girls cut your cake. I brought a camera, and I would very much like to have a picture of that. And don't worry how it will look in the photograph. I'll drape this over the vandalized end, and it won't show. Shall we?"

He offered an arm to both women, and Dorotea, glancing at Quincey, slipped hers into the crook of his elbow first. Quincey stood frozen for another moment, and then did likewise. Joe Senior escorted them to the table with the cake, personally laid his wife's silk scarf over the end which had been cut into, and then motioned them in closer, taking a few steps away as they reached for the cake cutter with the red and white ribbon wrapped around the handle which lay on a saucer beside the cake, smeared with crumbs.

"Let's not use that," Quincey said. "Hold on a sec. Sandy, could you nip into the kitchen and get the big bread knife, please?"

"Sure," Sandy said immediately, turning away to obey.

"Addie," Joe Senior said, holding out his hand, without taking his eyes of his daughter's face. "My camera. Please. It's on the chair, right there next to your purse."

"Dad..." Joe Junior, who had followed them, began, but his father raised a hand briefly, index finger raised in admonishment.

"Not a word," he said. "Addie. Camera."

It was put into his hand just as Sandy returned with the bread knife and, as an afterthought, discreetly removed the cake cutter from the picture frame.

Joe Senior lifted the camera to his eye with one hand, making a courteous gesture with the other.

"Please," he said.

Dorotea laid her hand over Quincey's on the bread knife handle. They lifted the knife together, brought it to hover over the cake, plunged it into the icing, sliced. The crowd broke into applause; in the noise the soft sound of the shutter was almost lost—once, twice—and then they had slipped out the first slice of cake, cut it in half, and Dorotea playfully fed Quincey one half, her eyes smiling, waiting for Quincey to reciprocate. The shutter clicked one more time.

"I've got your back," Dorotea whispered into Quincey's ear. And then turned slightly. "Sandy, would you do the honors? Make sure everyone has a slice…"

Sandy marshaled the rest of the cake cutting, and Dorotea and Quincey stepped over to where Joe Senior waited for them, camera dangling at his side.

"Yes," he said, "I know. We'll be going now. But thank you for asking me, Quincey. You looked very happy, at least before Joe put his boot into it—and believe me, he'll not forget about this soon, I promise you that. Even if I say nothing at all Linda saw him get that slap and you can bet she knows why he deserved it. Dorotea… thank you for making my baby girl happy. That's all I could have ever asked for."

"Thank you, Daddy," Quincey managed.

Joe looked back to where Addie waited. "I'll talk to your mother," he said softly. "But right now…it's your party. I think it's best if she was someplace else. And I don't think you want Joe anywhere near you for a little while. Can't say as I blame you. I'll give you a ring, later, to find out if everything's okay. You enjoy your party. Your… your wedding day." He reached out to take one of Quincey's hands in his free hand, squeezed her fingers tightly, and then released her; glancing over at Dorotea, he gave her a small nod. "I'd give you a hug, but I don't suppose you want hugs from this family after what he pulled."

In answer, Dorotea stepped up and wrapped her arms around him, giving him a brief sharp hug and then letting him go.

"You're a good man," she said. "Thanks for the help."

He looked as though he might say something more, decided against it, merely lifted a hand in a gesture of farewell and turned away, gathering his family to him with a curt toss of his head. They all followed him meekly enough—Addie beside him, her shoulders bare of the silk scarf still gracing the wedding cake, and Joe Junior and his family, his kids' cheeks still bulging with food they were masticating, being herded in front of him like so many goats. Victor, Dorotea's tenant, opened the door to let them out, and then closed it behind them.

Quincey drew a long shaky breath.

"I told you," she said.

"Your father made up for the rest of them," Dorotea said. "Now come on. Let's nip into the bathroom and fix your make-up. Your mascara has started to run. I *told* you you weren't allowed to cry."

Quincey and Dorotea left for their Silk Road trip five days after their wedding party; Dorotea never did write the book she had thought she might get out of the experience, but they did bring back several leather-bound journals in which they had both written about their experience, and thousands of photographs. Some of them found their way to the walls of their apartment, others went downstairs to the bookshop where they were universally admired. Quincey's job had been kept open for her, or more to the point the lab where she had worked before the trip had a reasonably high personnel turnover and she quickly found her way back there. Dorotea seemed to have kicked the travel bug.

The two of them settled down to a quieter daily life, changed only by the fact that their wedding ceremony had given them higher visibility and put them on the radar of several gay and lesbian organizations in the city—and Dorotea got involved with at least one of them to the point that she was more or less running the show within a handful of years. It was through this channel that Dorotea was kept aware of the steadily gathering momentum of the attempts to make same-sex marriage legal and binding in the law of the land, with the full rank and privileges that it conferred—but it was Sophie Lavelle who brought the news home to Dorotea's apartment, climbing the stairs to the penthouse with slow and measured steps and lots of breaks to gather her breath with Lili, her partner, a step behind, hovering in case she needed assistance. It had been ten years since she had done it without a pause, to attend Quincey's and Dorotea's wedding, and those years had piled on the pounds; she was still a mainstay in the bookstore, but she hadn't been upstairs at the apartment in several years. Dorotea received her at the door with an admonition.

"You could have sent somebody up to get me. Those stairs can be hard on an old lady."

"Who you calling old?" Sophie retorted. "I may have passed seventy but that's just these old bones, girl. Inside, I'm not a day over sixty four."

Lili laughed. "She's feeling feisty today. Nothing doing but she had to come up and tell you in person."

"Tell me what?" Dorotea said, smiling at them both. She stepped away from the door, motioning them inside. "Come in, take a load off, can I get you something to drink?"

"*Cher*, no—I came to tell you—"

"We *brought* the drink," Lili said, and Quincey realized that she was carrying a bottle of champagne by the neck as she thrust it into Quincey's hand. "Can you open that?"

"Sure," Quincey said, retiring with the bottle. "I'll go in the kitchen in case it explodes…"

"What's going on, Sophie?" Dorotea asked, helping her to settle into an armchair.

For answer, Sophie held out her hand. Her left hand.

A gold ring glittered on her somewhat pudgy ring finger.

Dorotea, took up the hand, looked up at Lili, who held out her own left hand, bearing a matching ring.

"We did it," Lili said. "We heard they were actually issuing marriage licenses, in San Francisco. To people like us. *We could get married*, Dorotea. Legally. For real. So we just packed up and went—and we did it. We stood up in front of somebody in the City Hall who actually said the words, 'By the power vested in me', and then declared us married."

"After forty years, it's about time, don't you think, that we made honest women of one another?" Sophie said. "God knows I've had my share of miracles in my life, and perhaps it was foolish to try and snatch one last one before I die—I never really thought the day would come. This is lagniappe, God's gift—it seemed like we'd be turning our back on God's smile if we didn't go out and grab it. *Laissez le bon temps rouler!*"

The pop of a champagne cork punctuated that comment, and Quincey emerged from the kitchen with the bottle in one hand and four wine glasses dangling by their stems from the other.

"I heard," she said. "Congratulations!"

Dorotea rescued the glasses and held them out, and Quincey poured the champagne—they toasted each other, through laughter and tears.

"We did it properly, we thought we would mark the occasion in some way. So we've filed the paperwork—we've legally taken each other's name. I am now Sophie Grossman. Put *that* in your pipe and smoke it!"

Quincey giggled into her champagne. " Which makes you Lili Lavelle? It sounds like a stage name for Broadway, Lili, or some glamorous Thirties spy..."

"Eh, I'll get used to it," Lili said, grinning.

"She's got the starring role in the rest of her life," Dorotea said.

"And you can't beat that with a stick," Sophie said. "We just wanted you to be among the first to know, *cher*—and there was nothing quite like coming up here and showing you the rings. We'll probably have a party to celebrate properly, out at our place, maybe later in the summer."

But that summer was gilded glory, false promise, and it was only mid-August when Dorotea came home tight-lipped with a press release clutched in her hand.

"They declared it all illegal," she spat out, throwing the single sheet of paper at Quincey. "*All* of it. Thousands of marriages. Thousands of couples. They've all been reversed, the California weddings."

Quincey was on her feet, clutching the page she'd reflexively caught, her eyes on Dorotea. "Sophie..."

"Yes. This will devastate them."

"We'd better phone..."

"No. We'll go over there. They'll need a friend."

It was Lili who opened the door to the apartment when Dorotea and Quincey knocked, and let them in without a word.

"Are you all right?" Dorotea asked, laying a hand briefly on Lili's shoulder.

Lili squared her jaw. "I'm Lili Lavelle, legally, and there is nothing they can do about that," she said. "We know we've been married. The rest is politics."

"And Sophie?"

"It hit her hard," Lili said. "She's got a bad ticker, you know—it's been giving her grief for years now. She's in bed, she was there with some sort of summer flu—but she was well on her way to kicking it, until this broke. I actually tried keeping it from her, but someone brought her a newspaper, and that was *the* newspaper that she shouldn't have had. The news knocked her back good. I don't know if she's awake—she's been sleeping a lot lately—I'll go see, make yourself comfortable in there, I'll put some tea on in a minute."

"Did you know?" Quincey said in a low voice. "About the heart?"

"I knew she was finding stairs difficult, but I thought that was just the age and the weight catching up with her. I didn't realize..."

Lili stuck her head around the door.

"She's awake," Lili said. "She wants to say hi—come in here a sec, you two."

"Hey, Sophie," Quincey said, stepping into the room. She had meant to say something flippant, something light, something to make everyone smile, but her first glimpse of Sophie snatched the words from her mind. Sophie's face had fallen in, as though she had suddenly lost a lot of weight, and there were deep lines etched around her eyes. Quincey reached out and gathered up one of Sophie's hands from where it rested on the quilt, holding it between both of her own. "I'm sorry," she said, instead of everything else she had been planning.

Dorotea had gone around to the other side of the bed. "Sorry to hear you're feeling on the down low," she said. "Is there anything we can do?"

Sophie glanced from the one to the other of them, her eyes

still bright and black. "Eh," she said, "I have no regrets, *moi*. I've lived my life as I chose, for most of it, and I've had my last miracle."

"Sophie..."

"Yes, you can do something. The two of you." She took one of Dorotea's' hands with her own free hand and brought it down over Quincey's, holding it down. "You be happy, the two of you. Stay happy. You can do that for me. Dorotea... would you tell the book club I might miss another week or two? I don't think I feel up to it, right now."

"I'll let them know," Dorotea said.

Sophie's eyelids fluttered. Lili touched Quincey's shoulder. "Come on," she whispered. "She's... she should get her rest."

Quincey leaned over and kissed Sophie's leathery cheek. "Sweet dreams, *ma vieille*," she said, and carefully withdrew her hand from beneath Sophie's. Dorotea followed her out, and Lili quietly closed the bedroom door behind them all as they stepped outside.

"Lili," Dorotea said, "I'm no doctor, but..."

Lili shook her head. "Neither am I. Neither is she. And we both know. Hush, now. We've had a lifetime together, she and I, and we both knew it had to end sometime. I'll treasure her for as long as I've got her."

"Call us, if you need us," Quincey said.

"I need you now," Lili said with a small tired smile. "Come and have that tea. Tell me something good. Let the sunshine into the room, at least for a little while."

It didn't take long. Sophie just got more and more tired, and one day, two weeks after Dorotea and Quincey visited, she simply fell asleep and failed to wake up.

They buried Lili, too, less than six months later.

They had both made wills, and the attorney who had been left as executor phoned to ask Dorotea and Quincey to drop into his office, to pick up a small bequest. When they did so, they were handed an envelope which proved to contain nothing at all except a pair of wedding rings. The wedding rings Lili and Sophie had exchanged in California, when they had stood up to get married to one another.

There was no message. Sophie had already delivered that, from her bed, weeks before. *Just be happy, you two. Do that for me.*

"We should do something with these," Dorotea said as they left the lawyer's office, tucking the envelope with the rings into her purse. "In their memory."

"Yes," Quincey murmured. "We should."

But it took four years for that something to take shape.

"There's a book festival in Brooklyn in the first week of October," Dorotea said casually to Quincey one hot August night as the two of them were sitting, iced teas in hand, out on Dorotea's rooftop in the faint hope of catching whatever breezes might have wandered into the city.

"Mmhhm?" Quincey said, inflection rising into a question.

"How about it?'

Quincey turned her head. "How about what?'

"You want to come with me?…Fall, lots of pretty scenery and trees turning pretty colors…"

"In *Brooklyn*?"

"In Massachusetts," Dorotea said quietly, and sat up, setting her iced tea down on a scuffed plastic table. "Where the law says we can get married. Properly. Legally. Forever. How about it, Quincey Quincey Thorne? Will you marry me all over again?"

"Sophie's and Lili's rings," Quincey said.

"Yes. I think it's about time. I can start putting out feelers now—we can see what's available, if the season hasn't scooped up everything already, I have no idea how early one needs to book to get a place anywhere near there in the fall colors season."

"I have a friend, we went to college together, who lives out near Salem. I could give her a call," Quincey said, and then her mouth twisted into a small wry smile. "A couple hundred years ago they would have burned you and me in Salem as unnatural, you know."

"All the more reason to go now," Dorotea said. "It's time we took it back. But I was actually thinking somewhere on the North Shore—out by the ocean…we could…"

"Yes," Quincey interrupted. "Yes. Let's. Let's do that."

"I'll book the flights tomorrow," Dorotea said.

When Quincey phoned Olivia Halloran to tell her of

the plans being made, Olivia eagerly volunteered to be Johnny-on-the-spot.

"You guys, you just turn up," she said. "You both need to be here to get a marriage license. That's immutable. The rest...I can organize. I'll find you a minister, I'll find you a place to stay, trust me on this. Just tell me when you plan on getting here, and I'll sort out everything else."

"We're flying in to Boston," Quincey said. "October 6. That's a Monday. We thought we could get the license, in Boston—I think it takes about 3 days, as far as Dorotea could gather...? And then, if we can get that squared away, we can make our way down to New York for the book festival over the weekend, and then we could be back in Boston on Sunday night, or Monday— that's October 12 or 13—and take it from there."

"You'd have to pick a long weekend in early fall," Olivia grumbled. "All the pretty places will probably have been booked solid for months now. I'll do my best; you have my number, call me when you get back to Boston, and I'll give you directions from there."

Olivia met them at Logan Airport when they flew out to Boston, and accompanied them to the City Hall where they went to apply for the marriage license. She was with them when they picked it up, too, and hugged them and wept when they received the document, and hinted that she'd already arranged a great many things which were just waiting for them to come and claim them.

The book fair in Brooklyn was a business trip for Dorotea, and Quincey was left at something of a loose end for most of the day on the Friday and the Saturday—but Dorotea herself found it hard to concentrate on the matter at hand when she had other things on her mind, and in the end, although the festival ran for the full day on Sunday, they decided to cut it short and returned to Boston by Sunday night. They phoned Olivia from the train, telling her that they were due in at about half past seven that night.

"Great," Olivia said. "Here's what you do. Rent a car—you *have* to have a car, you'll want to drive around and see the place a *little* bit, it's gorgeous out here—and drive up Route 129 and follow the signs to Nahant or Swampscott—"

"*Swampscott?* That sounds pleasant," Quincey said.

"You're not going to Swampscott. I said follow the signs. When you get to the roundabout, go about three-quarters round—are you writing this down?—and keep going straight, just keep the ocean on your right, don't turn off to Nahant. You're going to go *through* Swampscott, and it isn't that bad, thank you, and eventually you'll hit Marblehead. You'll be on Atlantic Avenue. Stay on that until the second set of lights, turn left, and then turn left again at the next light. It's a lovely street called Pleasant Street. The place you're looking for is called Marble House Inn, on your left. They'll be expecting you. And tomorrow morning, eleven o'clock, I've got Reverend Nesbitt lined up for you. He's in his sixties, semi-retired, and very, very happy to be a part of this wedding. I'll come get you at the inn. Got all that, or do you want me to repeat the directions?"

"We'll get there," Quincey laughed. "Thank you, Olivia."

"You bet," Olivia said. "I can't wait to see you guys stand up before the Reverend. I'll see you tomorrow."

It was close to half past ten that night that they eventually rolled to a stop in front of Marble House Inn on Pleasant Street in Marblehead. Their room turned out to be a suite, with a sea view and a working fireplace; they were too tired, and it was too late, to start a fire in the fireplace that night, but Quincey beckoned Dorotea over to the window.

"Look," she said, "the moon is full, out over the sea. It's beautiful."

"I didn't plan a full moon, but I'm glad we got one," Dorotea said, slipping an arm around Quincey's waist as they stood at the window staring out at the silver orb in the night sky. "Moonlight becomes you..."

Quincey turned, smiling. "You *romantic.*"

"What? I'm getting married tomorrow!"

"Technically we should be in separate rooms tonight," Quincey said, teasing.

"As for that, we're *already* married," Dorotea grumbled. "Let's not go overboard. Come on, let's go to bed. There's a lot supposed to be going on tomorrow morning."

"Did you check the weather forecast?"

"Some clouds. No rain. We might luck out."

They slept well in the giant old four-poster bed and feather quilt, and descended down to the house's wood-paneled dining room at around half past eight for breakfast. It was a leisurely affair—buttermilk pancakes with maple syrup, fruit, hot coffee—but eventually they were done. Dorotea lifted her arms above her head, stretching, giving Quincey a flirtations look from under her elbow.

"We'd better start getting ready. Your Olivia might be by any time."

"We're getting married," Quincey said impulsively to the woman who came in to clear the debris off the table.

"Congratulations!" the woman said, with a smile of genuine delight. "My spouse and I tied the knot almost two years ago now, when the law changed. We've had quite a few folks like you, since that time—only a week ago we had a couple of gentlemen from Boston, architects both, who came up here for the weekend and got married in Marblehead. The other couple staying here that weekend—a straight couple, he was from England, Old England I mean, and she'd grown up somewhere near Salem, they were visiting her old haunts—threw them a party when they got back from the ceremony. Anything can happen here—and usually does..."

"How long have you been running this place?" Dorotea asked.

"It's quite lovely," Quincey added, sneaking some more coffee into her cup from the stainless steel coffee pot on the table.

"This was a going concern, a Bed and Breakfast place, when my husband and I bought it as a business, oh, ten or twelve years ago—back when I was still, um, *traditionally* married. Then I decided I didn't want to be married to him anymore, and the business was tanking anyway so he was happy to let me have this place—and nothing else—in the divorce settlement. And then Kathy came along, about five years ago now, and just moved in—and took to this like the proverbial duck to water. She inherited some decent money from a childless aunt who apparently squirreled away more than anybody realized and didn't seem to have anyone else to leave it to, so Kathy got it all—and sank every penny of it into refurbishing this place. It's pretty newly finished, all of it—we got done with the last bit of remodel and painting only this summer."

"It must be gorgeous here in the summer," Dorotea said.

"It's best right now—with all the trees. We're usually full-up in early fall, but your friend phoned as if by fate just as I had put down the phone on a guest who'd had to cancel for this weekend, and so here you two are... You picked a lovely time of year for a wedding. Do you want the fire lit in your room, for later?"

"That would be lovely," Dorotea said. "Thank you."

They wore the same colors that they had worn at their first wedding, back at Dorotea's apartment, but not the same dresses. Quincey wore a claret-red cashmere sweater and matching flared skirt, with soft tawny suede boots; Dorotea chose a cream knit dress with a cowl-neck, an oversized cream-and-brown paisley scarf knotted casually around her shoulders, and fawn-colored pumps with kitten heels. Quincey wore a cream-colored rose pinned to her sweater; Dorotea wore a crimson one in her hair.

They apprised one another in their room, when they were ready.

"You look even more beautiful than when I first married you," Dorotea said, reaching out to gently brush Quincey's cheek with her fingertips.

"You *always* look beautiful," Quincey said, smiling. "Have you got Sophie's rings?"

"Yes. Let's go get married."

Olivia picked them up from the lobby, exclaimed over their outfits, and then packed them both into her car and drove off in a mysterious direction. Dorotea and Quincey had been told nothing of the arrangements, and they now discovered that they were brought down to the sea, where a cherubic white-haired man waited to receive them.

"Reverend Nesbitt, the brides, Dorotea Rochas and Quincey Thorne. Ladies, Reverend Anthony Nesbitt, Unitarian minister.

Reverend, let's get these two hitched!"

"My pleasure, and privilege," Reverend Nesbitt said, smiling. "If you would come and stand before me here…"

Quincey and Dorotea, brought up in different Christian traditions, both knew the wedding service more or less by heart (with a few differences enshrined in the actual phraseology, given the different denominations). Reverend Nesbitt used his own words, instead. Dorotea and Quincey didn't write their own vows, not this time; the Reverend said all the things that needed to be said, about marriage being a sacred and solemn undertaking and not to be entered into lightly or thoughtlessly, and then asked them whether they took one another—in sickness and in health, for richer or poorer, till death do them part—and they both said, "I do".

Reverend Nesbitt paused when he came to the rings. "You are already wearing rings on your wedding fingers," he said.

Dorotea glanced at Olivia, to whom she had given the other set of rings for safekeeping. "We have these," she said. "If you would. They were bequeathed to us… by dear friends. We plan on wearing both sets."

"Ah. I understand." He took the rings that Sophie and Lili had vowed their lives to one another with, blessed them for the new union, and then asked them to repeat after him the time-hallowed words.

"With this ring, I thee wed…"

They slipped the rings on one another's fingers, outside of the ones they already wore. Reverend Nesbitt smiled, and closed his book.

"Whereas Dorotea and Quincey have consented to be joined together in matrimony, and have attested the same before God and this witness, by the powers vested in me by the laws of the Commonwealth of Massachusetts, I now pronounce you…spouse and spouse." He nodded at them, beaming. "Congratulations," he said. "It's okay to kiss now."

Olivia squealed like a little girl, clapping her hands together; when Quincey and Dorotea took their lips from one another's, tears glittering in their eyes, she came up and hugged them both, hard, also crying through her laughter. They untangled themselves for long enough to deal with the necessary paperwork, and then Olivia herded the newlyweds back into the car.

"I have a place to take you for lunch," she said. "And then, later, you have reservations for dinner—trust me, you'll want to go, this place is amazing, it isn't very far from where you're staying, and you have to *eat*..."

"Lead on," Dorotea said, her fingers laced lightly through Quincey's. "We'll follow."

Lunch was a sweet little diner with red checked tablecloths... which reminded Quincey of something, but she couldn't quite put her finger on what right then, and anyway there was lots else to talk about and laugh about and celebrate. Olivia took them back to their lodgings to get their rental car, pointed them at some particularly nice fall foliage, and then handed them a folder with their dinner reservations and the directions to the restaurant and left them alone, after another hug for each of them.

"The wedding certificate will be mailed to my address," she said. "I'll send it along as soon as it arrives. You look beautiful, and you look very happy, and thank you so much for letting me be a part of this with you..."

Alone together, Dorotea and Quincey stared at one another, smiling a little.

"Want to go back to the room...?" Dorotea asked. "Or do you want to risk stepping into Salem as a couple of newly-wed witches and see if anybody is waiting with torches and pitchforks?"

Quincey laughed. "As you said to Olivia, lead on, and I'll follow," she said. "We could take the camera and get some pictures for the wedding album."

"Yes, and then, as she pointed out, we gotta eat," Dorotea said.

They ran through a glory of autumn leaves underneath trees aflame with fall, took photos of one another and asked passers-by to take photos of the two of them together, and finally, as the light began to fade, followed directions they had been given to the restaurant Olivia had made reservations at.

It turned out to have a resident live band, including a singer, playing pleasant covers of well-known songs to which several couples danced on the small dance floor at the foot of the band stage. The food was astonishingly good—that, or they were in the kind of euphoric mood where they could have been eating cold pizza from three days before and still thought they were tasting the food of the Gods.

Quincey eventually laid down the teaspoon with which she had scraped the last of her Crème Brulee from its ramekin, and settled back with a contented sigh.

"It's been a perfect day," she said.

"It isn't over yet," Dorotea said, winking at her.

Quincey actually blushed. "Um. Excuse me for a sec. Need to visit the ladies room."

By the time wended her way back to the table from the rear of the restaurant where the restrooms were, Quincey could see that Dorotea was not there—it took her a moment before she realized where she was, up at the band podium, talking to the singer. And then she turned her head, saw Quincey watching, smiled, and stepped up to the podium, taking the mike from the singer, who backed away with a small bow.

"Having a good time?"

The voice came from Quincey's left, and she turned her head to look at the speaker. He—or she—the face was oddly androgynous in the restaurant's discreet lighting—was of a height with her, nondescript light-brown hair falling down to the shoulders, hands stuck into the pockets of a pair of trousers that looked far too casual to be accepted attire in this restaurant at this time of day. His (Quincey decided it was a he) eyes were extraordinary, huge and smoky gray, oddly luminous in the dim room.

"Do I know you?" Quincey murmured.

"It'll come to you," the young man said. He pointed his chin at the band podium. "Listen, though."

Dorotea had been saying something, but Quincey had been distracted—however, now their eyes met across the dance floor and Quincey knew what it must have been. And then the band struck up a tune she recognized, and she felt tears well up in her eyes all over again as Dorotea lifted the mike to her lips and sang it, low and sweet and at the perfect tempo, her favorite Gershwin song, the one she had sung in the foyer of the theatre at Gershwin's birthday concert.

She was still asking the world, asking God, for someone to watch over her. Only this time she sang the whole song, with the band playing backup, and she had changed the words— changed every "he" to a "she", and singing it directly to Quincey across the room, holding her eyes, sharing her soul.

When she was done, the room broke into applause as she took a small bow and handed the mike back to the group's own singer—and then made her way back across the dance floor to where Quincey waited, transfixed.

"Time to bring the perfect end to the perfect day?" Dorotea said.

"Oh, yes," Quincey said, suddenly breathless.

They left money on the table, far too much, an extravagant tip on top of the price of the meal, and walked out, arms around one another.

Their hostess had lit the fire in their room, as they had requested, and had been keeping it quietly banked until they returned. Dorotea now threw an extra log or two on the flames and by the light of that alone they undressed each other, taking off their wedding finery until only bare skin reflected back the firelight, and climbed into the four-poster bed and each other's arms, on their wedding night. They had celebrated another wedding, before, but they had been the ones to call it that. They had never not taken it as having been a true wedding— but this, this was different, and even after their years together and the previous wedding night which they had shared it felt solemn, and sacred, and enormous. They were married now. *Married*. And this was the first night that they had made love as a married couple, as "spouse and spouse", as the Reverend had dubbed them, and they gave it everything that it was due, lost in one another, exploring curves grown familiar over the years with new-born fingertips and rediscovering one another all over again. Quincey cried; Dorotea kissed away her tears, and then they both laughed, out of sheer joy, holding one another close and then even closer, twining limbs and souls and spirits together in the light, and the light was firelight and moonlight, the hot and the cool and brilliant, and they were only two sparks in a sky full of stars.

Dorotea fell asleep, afterwards. Quincey could not. She lay there in the light of the dying fire, watching Dorotea sleep beside her; she was turned away, her dark hair spilled over the pillow, facing the window, and the moonlight pouring in through the panes—they had not drawn the curtains—lay pale and gentle on her face and the full, parted lips. She slept on her belly, head turned sideways on the pillow, one arm under her pillow and the other hand curled on top of the pillow just before her face, curled protectively as though Dorotea was cupping something fragile and strange. The fire had warmed the room and the feather quilt was hot; Dorotea had flung one of her legs out from underneath it, from the knee down, and it lay at an oddly provocative angle, the golden chain around her ankle glinting slightly in the moonlight, the foot arched with a dancer's grace. She might have been said to have sprawled across the bed, taking more than her fair share of the space—but she sprawled gracefully, and Quincey was happy to cede the territory.

She could not seem to settle, was far too wound up, her mind still awake and milling with a thousand thoughts and emotions, and her body seemingly unable to lie still in the shared bed. Finally, after the second time Dorotea stirred and murmured something in her sleep as Quincey twitched beside her, Quincey decided that it would be best to let Dorotea sleep undisturbed for a while until she could get herself calmed down enough to go back to bed and try and sleep.

They had not packed robes—they had not even packed nightgowns—and now that the fire was dying down the temperature had dropped in the room. Quincey dragged on a sweater and a pair of knit pants she used to travel in, and, wrapping herself in the quilt from the bed, crept into the second room of the suite...where she was astonished and alarmed to realize that she was not alone.

The androgynous young man from the restaurant lounged on the over-stuffed sofa in the suite's sitting room, his eyes still gray and glowing strangely in the gloom.

"How did you…who are…I should call…"

"Shhhhh." He lifted a finger to his lips, as though she was a child. "It's all right. If you call anybody, I won't be here when they arrive, so I wouldn't do that, really. But it's time we had our talk, you and I."

"Who are you? Quincey asked sharply. "What talk? How did you get in here?"

He gestured toward the big bay window, flooded in moonlight and dark shadows. "I am air and darkness, in the end," he said. "I can go where light goes. Ariel. The name is Ariel, Quincey."

"Red checked tablecloths," Quincey said, apparently randomly.

Ariel nodded. "See? I told you it would come to you."

"What are you doing here?"

"Ah, a pertinent question at last," Ariel said. "Well, let's see. The last time we met. Do you remember now…?"

Things stirred in Quincey's mind. "I… red checked tablecloths. Spanish Gardens… a place called… Spanish Gardens… I have friends I'm meeting… A phone call. I just had a phone call. From… from…"

Ariel said nothing, just sitting and watching her in silence, waiting for her to grope her way into the place where he needed her to be.

And then he saw her remember, saw it go through her like a hot wire through butter, saw her double over as though in pain, as though someone had kicked her in the belly.

The belly that had once borne…

"My children," she said faintly. "A phone call from my children. I have kids. There—in that place—I have—I have kids…"

"Of all of them, you," Ariel said, and there was real compassion in his voice. "Do you remember what you were told, back in that hallway in Spanish Gardens? That you could taste another life—have another lifetime—that you would remember nothing of the one that you'd had, until one moment, and one moment only, and then you would have to choose…

forever. Of all who make that choice tonight…you. You, with your life's happiness right here, the other half of you asleep in the bedroom just through that door, and the flesh of your flesh and bone of your bone and blood of your blood waiting in that other world, the one you left behind. The children who annoy you, drive you crazy, worry you, anger you, exasperate you… and whom you love so very much… how could you not? You, of all of them. You, with two kinds of love. The love born from the heart and the mind, between friends and lovers and equals, and then the love that was born from your own womb, your own body, a part of you."

"What are you telling me?" Quincey whispered, tears trembling in her eyes, spilling and falling unheeded down her cheeks. "That if I choose one, I turn my back on the other? Forever…? Your timing *sucks*, Ariel. I just got married today." She turned her head, back toward the door of the bedroom, but she could not see the bed or its occupant from where she was standing.

"I know," Ariel said. "I'm sorry. I am not given the right to choose. *You* are. Only you are."

"What does it matter? Who gains by this?…"

"You," Ariel said. "I know it's hard to believe, but… *you*. There are things you will learn about yourself this night, whether you want to know them or not."

Quincey turned away, staring out through the window, out to where the ink-black sea was painted by pale moonlight. "Maybe I don't want to know," she said. "Maybe I never did."

"If that had been true you would not be here. You would never have chosen to step into this life at all."

"But… but I'll forget it all, you said," Quincey whispered, clutching the quilt closer about her shoulders, suddenly shivering with far more than just ordinary cold. "Whatever I choose. I will forget the other, whatever I choose."

"That's what I said," Ariel agreed. "And it's true, but not in the absolute way that you mean. You will take something from either life, back to the other—a feeling, no more. For instance, you were not happy, back there. Back where the children are. You were searching, always searching, but never finding what you sought—because you had turned your back on what you were truly seeking, because you would not, could not, ever admit to yourself that certain instincts existed within you. The instincts which led you to Dorotea—who was your heart's desire, and who was the one your soul was searching for all along."

"But I was… married," Quincey said. "To men. To the men who fathered my children."

"Were you ever happy when you were married, to those men, back there?" Ariel questioned softly.

"I was…" Quincey whipped her head around, to stare at him through narrowed eyes. "That is not fair. I was not wildly unhappy. My first marriage… ended by his death, not by choice. I was content, at least."

"And then you chose again, and married someone who might not have been worthy…"

"That's neither here nor there," she said sharply. "I am not responsible for them—for my husbands—for the men I married. They were who they were. And I didn't know, back then—I had no idea…"

Her voice trailed away, thoughtful.

"What would you choose now, now that you know?" Ariel asked.

"Does it *have* to be an either-or question?" Quincey said.

"Right now," Ariel said, and there it was again, that softness, that compassion, "right at this moment…yes."

There was a long silence, and then Quincey drew a long shuddering breath. "What would happen," she questioned softly, "if I stayed?"

"The other life would vanish," Ariel said.

"Vanish… how, vanish… all the people I've ever known…"

"They would have different lives. Ones that never crossed yours. Or crossed it in a different way. For instance, Olivia might never have lived in New England, just at the right time to arrange your wedding today."

"And my children…?"

"Will never have been born, Quincey Thorne," Ariel said softly. "Those children—those particular children—those *particular* lives—they are too intimately connected with your physical body. If you do not bear them, they do not bear your genes; they, or something like them, might have been born to some other mother. Or might not. But these children—*these*—they are gone. Vanished. They exist, because you existed, there, in a certain way, in a certain aspect. Without you...no them."

"All right," Quincey whispered, her voice muffled with pain. "All *right*. I get it. What of her? What of Dorotea?"

"Well, she wakes up tomorrow morning... in a different place, I guess," Ariel said. "For her, *you* have not existed. You and she never met, never mind got married, never mind got married *twice*."

"But is she happy...?"

"Why would that make a difference?" Ariel said. "She exists. Her existence is independent of you. You have nothing to do with her, should you choose not to stay here and wake beside her in that bed tomorrow morning."

"But I can't leave her—I can't just leave her—she is everything that I..." Quincey's voice broke, and she turned to take a few blind steps toward the window, staring through it, seeing nothing at all through a haze of her tears. "Is it too late... for *everything*?"

"It's never too late for anything, in my experience," Ariel said, maddeningly cryptic. "With this kind of thing—this is the instinct that you might take back with you, you know. The instinct that there is someone out there, for you. The instinct that makes you keep searching."

"And if I don't know that she's a woman, I sail past her, like two ships in the night, and neither of us knows any different—that's assuming we do meet at all. Which is not a given."

"Correct," Ariel said.

"But if I stay with her now... if I stay..."

"Only you can make this choice. But you must make it now, I am afraid. Look behind you."

Quincey turned her head, blinked away tears until she could make out things through the blur... and realized that there were two doors leading out of the sitting room now. Not one, like before, opening back into the bedroom where she had spent her wedding night. Two. *Two.*

"Go. Look."

Ariel's voice was hypnotic, gentle but firm. It had be obeyed. Quincey did not want to go and look—every part of her mind was screaming against this fork being forced upon her—but her body obeyed that voice, and she came to an abrupt stop at a point where she could see clearly into both bedrooms at once. In one, Dorotea still lay sleeping, just as Quincey had left her— beauty and love in the moonlight. In the other, two beds sat in the far corners of a small bedroom. Each of them had a child in it, asleep. A boy, a girl.

"Jessi," Quincey whispered, naming them. "Chuck." She turned back to Ariel. "But this is... wrong... they are older..."

"You currently stand in 2008," Ariel said. "That's what they looked like, four years ago.'

"Six," Quincey whispered. "They were almost six years old. Chuck lost his first baby tooth that year. They started school, the year after that. The math homework. The baseball practice. The dance class. Jessi coming to my bed to curl up against me one night, when I felt low, when I was crying—Jessi, with that impossible little-girl voice, telling me that everything was going to be all right, and I believed her. Chuck, who cannot tie his own shoelaces without falling over his feet. And Sam—where's Sam—there's another..."

"Quincey. The hour approaches."

"I can't," she said, broken, falling to her knees where she stood, staring first into the one bedroom, then the other. "I can't. I can't do this—I can't choose this—it's *inhuman*—you can't make me do it..."

"Those were the rules of the game," Ariel said. "The game that gave you Dorotea at *all*."

"Does she exist, in *that* world?"

"You asked that. She might. She might not exist...for *you* though."

"But she might...?"

"Quincey," Ariel said, "it is that simple. It's a game of ifs and maybes—up to a point. All human relationships are ifs and maybes. All, except that one. Those kids. You can choose to remember that you were happy with a woman, that you could be happy with a woman, and you can take that much back with you. But no more than that. And remember… if you do this thing, and it blossoms, you will have a complication in *that* life that you never had in this one. What your children will think of that choice."

Quincey stared into Dorotea's bedroom, for a long time, as though she was trying to remember every line of her, every curve, every shadow.

"You won't," Ariel said, apparently reading her mind. "You won't remember her… like that. It isn't allowed. You will remember the love. The idea of the love. The aura of glory, not the face of the person who stands in its heart."

"It's no choice at all, that you give me," Quincey whispered. "You split my soul in half when you make me think of turning my back on her. And my heart turns to stone, and my womb to slow poison, if I choose her. It isn't fair. It isn't *fair*…"

"*Now*, Quincey." The voice was finally that of an angel, full of power, full of pity. "Now."

Quincey staggered to her feet, her body heaving with sobs that shook her from shoulder to hip, loosing her hold on the quilt which fell from her and pooled around her feet.

"I can't…I can't…"

She felt a gentle hand on hers, thrusting something between her nerveless fingers. She curled her fingers around it instinctively.

"You did," Ariel's voice said next to her ear. "You already have. But because I can… that's your phone, in your hand. It has her number on it. A certain Dorotea Rochas… who lives, in your own reality, in Sedona, who may or may not be gay, and even if she is may or may not be free for you to love her. But there's a bookstore, and I do believe it carries Sappho's poetry. You may have to make the first move, over there, to start again—to start something new. But you've already chosen. Look, if you don't believe me."

The bedrooms were gone, both of them. Quincey stood trembling in the hallway of Spanish Gardens, her hand clutched convulsively around a cell phone, her cheeks streaked with tears, her mouth open and gasping for breath.

She flipped her phone on and speed-dialed, waiting breathlessly for a reply, feeling an odd sense of something that was both relief and a knife thrust into her heart when a familiar voice answered.

"Hello?" Sam said, her older daughter, who had caller ID on the home phone. "Mom? What is it?"

"Is everything… all right…?"

"Of course it is, why shouldn't it be? Are you okay?"

"Yes," Quincey whispered. "I'm fine. I'm fine. I'm sorry. Sorry if I woke them up. Tell them…tell them I will be home tomorrow. Good night, sweetie."

"Night, Mom. Take care."

The phone went dead.

Quincey wiped her eyes with the back of her hand, thrust her phone into her pocket, and stepped back into the café on the eve of the end of the world.

If the sun rose on schedule the next morning, there was a phone call she needed to make—the memory nagged at her, amorphous, something she was unable to pin down. She could not remember why she had to make the call, or what it was about—not really. All she could remember was that it involved a woman named Dorotea, who owned a bookstore, which sold poetry.

INTERMEZZO 2

Thursday, 20 December 2012

"You okay, Quincey? Are you *crying*? Is everything all right back home?"

Quincey shook her head. "Fine. Just fine. Chuck lost his favorite mug. Ask me if I am surprised. His room always looks like the aftermath of the Big Bang."

"You think that's how *this* universe started?" Ellen said with a grin. "Some godling's teenager let their room get out of control, and presto, there's a whole new slew of stars out there. All that stuff that was piled up into festering piles—life will find a way…"

"Chuck has an on-going war going on with the forces of gravity," Quincey said. "I honestly think that he believes any horizontal surface *whatsoever*—his bed, the floor, the desk, anything—is there only to break the direct line of power of that gravity, and only exists for the purpose of preventing that gravity from sucking anything he might have put on such a surface into some localised black hole only he can see. It doesn't particularly bother him, though, when gravity wins in the end and things end up in piles on the floor, like something the tide washed in, the flotsam and jetsam of a life. And he isn't even a *teenager* yet."

"You wait," Ellen said, smirking.

"Oy," John said, raising an eyebrow. "I will have you know that being a messy little pig is not something that is the absolute heritage of every boy on the planet, by virtue of his being young and male. I was obsessively tidy, myself."

"Yes, well, some of us are strange," Ellen said. "But then again, these are our flesh and blood, they are ours whatever their faults, and it's kind of hard to stay mad at them for long."

"Perhaps that's it," John said.

Ellen turned to look at him. "What is?"

"I did not, strictly speaking, belong to my family. Or I did, but not in the way you mean. I was kind of bought and paid for rather than, uh, progenitored."

"What do you mean?" Simon said. "Were you adopted? I never knew that."

"You never saw the woman who raised me, whom I called 'Mother' all my life," John said. "If you had, you'd have known. She was blonde, blue-eyed, and *round*—she would have had cheekbones if the full-moon cheeks hadn't kind of buried them. Me… look at me." Apparently some of the glances aimed in his direction were a little skeptical because he clicked his tongue against his teeth in a gesture of annoyance. "Well, *remember* me, then. I may have put on a few pounds since my student days. Olivia already pointed that out."

"Oops," Olivia said faintly. "Sorry…"

"Eh. It isn't as though you were wrong. But I don't make you think—I *never* made you think—of a blue-eyed blonde ancestor. I barely even looked like I warranted my own name. I never did tell any of you this, before, but it probably won't surprise you too much if I told you that the name on my original birth certificate was actually Juan, not John. My father…"

He stopped talking, his mouth suddenly thinning into an angry line.

"Hey," Olivia said, "it's all right—you aren't required to—"

"Seems to be the time for spilling the secrets, isn't it, though?" John said. He fished around in his pocket, came out with a wallet, and extracted a photograph from it, giving it into Quincey's hand. "That," he said, "was my mother. It's the only picture I have of her. If there were any others… my father destroyed them all. That was back when the plan was never to tell me the truth at all."

Quincey stared at the photograph, with Ellen craning her neck to peer at it over her shoulder. It showed a slightly blurry image of a young woman with long black hair parted severely in the middle, with large sad dark eyes and bronze skin, full lips, flat cheekbones, a broad nose. Her expression was wary, almost afraid.

"Her name is Rosalina," John said. "That's all I really know. Other than that she was about sixteen when my father bought her, and then brought her to his house to bear the child that his wife could not have."

"*Bought* her?" Ellen said, shocked. "How do you mean?"

"He had money. He needed a vessel for his seed. He was in the market, and there were people who could deliver," John said. "Margaret Atwood might have written *The Handmaid's Tale* twenty years after, but that's what it was—a handmaiden to bear the child of the patriarch. Atwood might have sat in at our house, for her research. My father wanted a son, his wife could not have a baby because she was rendered fat and diabetic and infertile because of some disease of the ovaries, and my father emphatically did not want to adopt some strange child about whose provenance he knew nothing. He wanted his *own* genes procreated, thank you, not some poor farmer's from China or India or Mexico. Hence this solution. He would bring in a girl, he would get her pregnant, and then they would take the child. And call it theirs."

"That's illegal," Simon said, frowning.

John shrugged. "Long done with. Who's left to sue? My adopted mother is in hospice care, my father died years ago, and as far as Rosalina goes…who knows? All I know is that she had enough gumption—even while she was being bought and sold like she was a piece of prize fillet steak—to take matters into her own hands and run, when she had the chance. She did, you know. They'd made her sign all sorts of papers—but being functionally illiterate in English and a minor to boot she had no idea that she was signing me away until someone told her that, just after she had me. Apparently she had the presence of mind to ask to see me, just once, and then took me and gave everyone the slip and vanished with me… for almost three years. That's how long it took my father to track her down. I think I remember that, actually, the night they came for me. We were living in a single room somewhere, she and I, and they came, with flashing lights, and noise, and they broke down the door, and they dragged her out, and she was screaming, and I was screaming too, and that was the last time I ever laid eyes on the living woman. That's all really—just pictures. It's all I probably could remember—I was very young, and I spoke absolutely no English at the time, anyway. Even if somebody had tried talking to me I would not have understood a word of it."

"That's... appalling," Olivia said, staring at him as though she had never seen him before.

"Where did you get the photograph?" Quincey asked. The photo had done the rounds and returned to her, and she now handed it back to John.

He took it, began to tuck it back into his wallet. "Stephanie gave it to me. My adopted mother. I stopped calling her Mom when she told me all this."

"She told you?"

"She and my father were getting a divorce. Even she could not stand the bastard any longer. But he had pulled strings—he knew people—and I was lost to her, and I was all that she had really wanted. So she took her revenge on *him* by practically destroying me. Although... I was grateful, eventually. For the truth. She gave me whatever she had—the original birth certificate, the photograph, the 'adoption' papers. The newspaper cuttings of the raid on the illegals that night, the raid that took my real mother away."

"What did they do with her?"

"I asked my father that, later. When he was dying. I asked him and he just shrugged and said he didn't know, they probably deported her."

"To where?"

"Guatemala. That's where she was originally from—somewhere in the highlands, apparently, from the looks of her. The very first words I ever spoke as a baby were in a Mayan language from the dawn of time. Perhaps it's more than just a little fitting that I should remember her here, tonight. It is her people's reckoning that tells us that the world ends tomorrow."

"Wait—you said you were what, three...?"

"Something like that, yeah."

"And you were born in 1964?"

"Yes. April."

"My God," Simon said. "That would mean she got back there a few years shy of 1970. When the civil war really started to..."

"Yes," John said levelly, holding Simon's eyes. "The bastard sent her straight to Hell."

"*Sent* her?" Quincey said, twisting her fingers together before her on the table. "I'd say he did a pretty good job of creating it for her in his own house, for some time. She might have been relieved to go back to a situation where people merely shot at her—at least she could duck bullets. Locked up in her room in that house, there was nowhere to hide when her lord and master came in every night..."

"How old were you?... When you learned all this?" Olivia asked, looking shaken.

"I was eleven when they divorced," John said. "Stephanie lost custody; he had a lawyer deep enough in his pocket to push through some cockamamie story about me being his biological child but not hers and therefore she had no real legal rights to me anyway. But she had been Mom for as long as I had been aware and conscious, and it hit me, hard. When she came to see me one day, at school, I was actually glad to see her—I *ran* to her, she was Mother, she was whatever love was—and we kind of set up a 'don't tell your Dad' kind of clandestine operation where I invented some activity I had to stay at school late for, once a week, and I'd meet up with Stephanie instead. That went on for almost six months before he found out, my father, and the scene which followed... was fit for a schmaltzy Hallmark movie. They both threatened to call the police. Neither of them did, of course, because doing so would have meant that they both took the fall—accomplices, and all that. But what it meant was that Stephanie realized that she was running out of time. She gave me her files the last time we met up, and just gave it to me, straight, the whole story. I was just shy of twelve years old."

"Oh, my God," Ellen said. "What did you do?"

"I read the papers," John said. "I went through rage, and then terror, and then denial, and then hyper-acceptance."

"Hyper-acceptance?" Simon echoed, puzzled.

"I spent the next couple of years steeped in that heritage which I hadn't even known was mine," John said. "It was partly to punish my father, who hated it. *Hated* it. But throughout high school I was the punk kid, the rebel, I wore my hair as long as I could get away with it and if it was forcibly shorn—that happened, a couple of times—I would just defiantly grow it again, and get it long, and black, and scraggly, and I would take pains to make myself look as dangerous and exotic and non-white-collar-American as I possibly could. It reflected on my father's social standing, naturally—yes, he had the son he wanted, but it was not the sort of preppy kid he could take into a country club or for dinner at a classy restaurant somewhere to show off the continuation of his genes. I used as crass and coarse a language as I knew, I got in with a bad crowd at school, I even had a jaguar tattooed on my shoulder at sixteen, which made my father threaten to put me under the knife…"

"To do *what*?" Ellen gasped.

"He was a plastic surgeon. It wasn't as though he didn't know how to remove a tattoo," John shrugged.

"Did he?" Ellen said. "Remove it, I mean?"

"It was a complex war," John said. "I'm not sure who won, really. I continued to live at his house, at his expense, and go to good schools—although I didn't do much to get anything spectacular out of the latter, to be sure. He wanted me to go on to medicine, to follow in his footsteps, in which case he would pay for college, too—but at some point I recoiled at that. It wasn't that long after I got the tattoo that I actually moved out—I was living out on my own by the time I was seventeen, sharing a crowded apartment with a bunch of other misfits, and we all pitched in and cobbled the rent together every month somehow. But that was kind of the end of the college dream—or the easy college dream, anyway. If I wanted it, I would have to provide it for myself."

"But you did," Simon said. "Fairly obviously. Because otherwise we'd never have met at all. I never knew any of this; I'm astonished, and appalled, and impressed all at once."

"Well, when I finally did get it through my head that school mattered it was almost too late—but I managed to pull a rabbit out of a hat in my senior year at high school," John said. "With those marks, and with Stephanie helping to subsidize the first year, I did manage to get into college. But not medicine. I kind of… walked away from that, for good, I would have done even if I had had all the grades in the world. It would have meant… becoming *him*, turning into my father, and it made me feel ill just to think about that. So I picked arbitrary subjects, in the beginning—just stuff across the board, humanities, you know, psychology, anthropology, social sciences, that sort of thing—and then I kind of narrowed down the focus, even without realizing I was doing it, and it all came to a head when that woman from UNESCO came out to speak on campus…"

"I remember that, I think," Quincey said. "I went to that talk. She was dry as dust, and boring, boring, boring… if it's the same person I'm thinking of. I don't even think I stayed to the end of the lecture. Apparently I must have missed something. What did she say to inspire you?"

"Not her. There was someone with her, a young post-graduate student who had travelled in with her as her assistant. We got talking, after, she and I—her name was Miranda, as I remember, and she was of mixed parentage, also, she had Asian blood in her, Korean I think, she was very pretty. Whatever, we hit it off. When she left, she gave me her contact details, and we kind of kept in touch. That's when I realized that I wanted to do that kind of thing. To be a voice for the silent. To be a shield for the vulnerable. To… to protect girls like my mother, from having someone like me. So I studied for that, to become that. And I did. It's what I do, these days. I travel to places where I am needed, I am the organizer, I put together teams to get clean food and water to people who don't have them, I haul bodies out of firing lines, I help abandoned kids find homes. Mostly I write reports and take photographs, actually, but I appear to be very, very good at that—and I seem to have the kind of organizational skills which are in demand."

"You should write a book," Ellen said.

"More than enough of us here are writing books," John said. "It isn't a story for me. It's all—it's far too real for me to write it down as a story."

"I don't mean fiction," Ellen said. "There's plenty of truth out there to keep you busy."

"Have you ever gone back to Guatemala?" Quincey asked quietly.

"I've been all over the place," John said. "But not there. It's odd, isn't it—I've been to Rumania, to Rwanda, to Bangladesh, to Indonesia. But I've never been south of the USA borders. Not even to Mexico. I've always... found other places to go, other projects to throw myself into, other people to help."

"Are you afraid you'll find your mother?" Olivia asked quietly.

"I don't know if I'm more afraid of finding her, or of never finding her," John said. "Or of finding far too many like her, who could have been her, who still might be her as soon as my back is turned. My father might be gone, but there are others out there just like him—moneyed, and entitled, and above the law so long as they take appropriate steps to ensure that they are never actually caught in any kind of act, as it were, that can be construed by a good lawyer to be illegal. And it would be... personal, there. Elsewhere I see a child in pain, and I can deal with that, try and find ways to make it better. In a place like Guatemala... those children would look... a lot like me. They might be my own brothers and sisters. It might unravel me. Fast."

"I can barely believe that all this lay buried beneath the surface, twenty years back," Simon murmured, shaking his head. "I remember you, back then—you might have had a little bit of the 'brooding young man' about you, but who didn't, and when you weren't off on that kick you were just as young and happy and full of *joie de vivre* as any other sophomore on campus."

"You make it sound as though it was a mask," John said, a little sharply. "As though I put that mask on in order to keep everyone in the dark about what I truly was—the kind of Dark Avenger, ticking away like a time bomb, waiting to blow up on whoever said the wrong word at the wrong time..."

"Hey," Olivia said, reaching out to lay a hand on his arm. "I never believed that."

He glanced at her, managed a small crooked smile. "And what did you believe?"

"It sounds awfully pat, now that I say it," Olivia said. "I didn't know about what you carried, and God knows I had baggage of my own—but I confess, what I was actually thinking a moment ago was, 'I believed you were just like me'."

"What, young and white and well-off and happy...?" John asked.

Olivia flushed. "I *said* it sounds trite, now."

"Oh, but I would have loved it if it had been true," John said. "Or even if you had *believed* it to be true, back then—true enough to matter. Did you even know I carried a torch for you for years? Back when we were both... that trite thing you mentioned."

Olivia's hand, which was still lying on his arm, trembled a little at that, as though her first impulse had been to snatch it away. But she controlled it, and her voice, and after a moment managed to say, sounding quite normal, "Did you...?"

"I didn't say anything," John said. "Naturally enough. I brought you a daisy once, one I'd found poking through a fence somewhere on the way to... somewhere... maybe even here... and I lopped it off and I brought it over, and I handed it to you—and I think I even managed to flirt, a little, at that time. It reminded me of you, back then—I might have even said so—talk about trite...'You remind me of a daisy'. If you had said anything, given any signal, I might have brought a whole bunch of them the next day, and the next, and for days and weeks to come. But you kind of... laughed..."

Olivia snatched her hand back at last, at that. "John—I never meant to—"

"I know," he said gently, reaching out his own hand to pat hers lightly before tucking it away again as he crossed his arms and leaned his elbows on the table. "I wasn't accusing you of anything. You had no idea so you couldn't have possibly responded the way I might have imagined you might respond—and by that stage, anyway, the pendulum had swung very far the other way..."

"What do you mean?" Ellen asked.

"In high school, I was Mayan. I chose to be. It was an act

of open rebellion and defiance—once I learned the truth, the only way I could hurt my father with it was to embrace it, totally, completely. By the time my second year of college rolled around... I was struggling to be anything *but*. I wore shirts which covered up the jaguar tatt. I cropped my hair short. Nothing I could do about my face, but every single photo I had seen of the Mayans from Central America had eyes that were dark with some kind of deep sorrow so I turned my back on that completely and became Happy Party Boy instead. I was trying very hard to forget everything that I had been or thought when I was fifteen. But that whole package included... a whole heap of self-loathing and self-rejection, even when those things weren't coming in from the side. And then you... well, you...."

"I what?" Olivia said.

John glanced from her to Simon, and back again. "You. And him. And you seemed, for a little while at least, happy—and I wasn't about to do anything against *that*. I *wanted* you to be happy. I just wished it could have, in some alternative parallel reality, have been me that you picked. But in this reality... I understood perfectly. Simon was absolutely everything that I was not, and could never be. I was not sophisticated enough, sexy enough... WASP enough... to compete."

That one caused everyone at the table to sit up as though they had been stung by the words.

"That is so not fair," Olivia said.

"It makes me feel like a total jackass," Simon muttered. "And for reasons I had very little control over."

"Did I say it was sane?" John asked, shrugging. "Besides, that phase didn't last all that long, you'll be happy to know. It was starting to wane by the time that the UNESCO woman's student assistant turned up on the scene, and then my priorities got re-focused anyway. And then everyone graduated, and then you and Simon kind of... blew up...."

Ellen winced, but John pretended not to have noticed, keeping his attention on Olivia. "And then you disappeared," he said. "Afterwards. Like a ghost. One day you were there, the next you were gone, and any chance I might have had— once I had got my act together—was gone with that. Over and done with. *Finito*. And I... just turned back to my own life, and started living that. And hoped that you, somewhere else, were living whatever you had wanted to do with yours."

"You didn't even try to look for her?" Quincey said. "I mean, by that stage, Simon and Ellen were..." She flushed, and abruptly shut her mouth.

"Yes, by that stage Simon and Ellen, as it was, *were*," John said. "And somehow it was easy enough to keep up with them and with their doings. The books helped. When there's something out there with a name on it that you recognize, it's almost an instinct to sit up and take notice. I think I even registered, somewhere along the line, the fact that you were married to a Congressman, Quincey—although that wasn't something that I was going to go anywhere with. But Olivia... seemed to vanish with a cool deliberation. As though she meant to disappear, and have none of us ever come near her again. That's a whole new ball of wax, particularly if, like me, you had cherished visions of various different kinds of shared sugarplums in your head at some point. It almost felt personal. It would have been impossible even to ask one of you if you knew where she was, never mind try to hunt her down myself. It would have felt... like stalking, almost."

"So, unless stuff falls under your feet and you literally trip over it, you wander the world looking for things or people that are completely unfamiliar and strange, and you don't look for the obvious, for your friends, for your family," Quincey said. "I don't know. That actually sounds rather a lot *like* a doctor, or at least my doctor. When my kids were very young and direct communication was still not their strong suit, it seemed to me that he would always check first for smallpox and bubonic plague before he would look for inner ear infection or the sniffles."

"Makes sense," Olivia said. "Check for the worst first, it saves time. If it turns out to be right then you can just deal with the disaster immediately rather than waffling about trying to mop up small spills and apply band aids to hold it all together."

"And I thought I was a pessimist," John said, staring at her.

"Maybe it would have done us both a world of good if you

had gone looking," Olivia said. "And found me before I had time to make my own mistakes. But then... you made a life out of it, anyway. A life in which you didn't give yourself time to miss me."

"Oh, twenty-twenty hindsight," Quincey said. "Don't do this—don't waste time looking back. It all looks so different when you're looking back, and you know so much more now than you could have possibly known at the time."

"Well," Olivia said, very faintly, "it isn't like it's the end of the world..."

John's mouth actually fell open, and then he threw back his head and laughed.

"And so what if it is," he managed at last, between guffaws. "And it's either a new world in the morning, or the old one goes on, or we all softly and silently vanish away, like the Snark. Oh, *God*, Olivia. Why didn't you at least hesitate and turn your head? We could have..."

"Who's got the salad?"

The young waitress had reappeared by their table, balancing several precarious plates on a large tray.

"Well, finally," Simon said, the relief in his voice unmistakable. "How long does it take to grill a burger?"

"Sorry, sir. The kitchen got a bit busy tonight. We're one cook short, and it had to be tonight, of course, that the place got packed out. They're doing their best back there but things are getting rather chaotic..."

"I'm sorry, that was churlish of me," Simon said apologetically. "I'm the burger, as you may have gathered. Uh—I told you hold the pickles—never mind."

"Salad," Quincey said pointing to herself. "The sandwich is for the gentleman, and the two ladies had the pasta."

"Thanks," the waitress said. "Uh, could you grab that sandwich plate, sir..."

John got to his feet and steadied her tray with one hand, dispensing food with the other. "Ellen... Olivia...be careful, the bottom of the plate's a tad warm... Quincey, salad..."

"Um, is there dressing?" Quincey said, glancing up.

"Was supposed to be on the plate," the waitress said. "Sorry, ma'am. I'll go back and get you another. Thanks, sir."

"Welcome," said John, rescuing his own sandwich and sliding back into his chair. "And, um, could you rustle up a cup of coffee while you're back there? Not the Irish stuff. Just a plain cuppa joe."

"Cream, sir?"

"Please."

"I'll be back in a tick. They probably left the dressing on the counter in the kitchen when they were putting this together. Won't be a moment. Thanks for your patience."

She sounded genuinely appreciative of the simple courtesy that she had received, and Simon stared after her thoughtfully as she retreated back toward the kitchen.

"I wonder how many times she's been yelled at tonight for things that weren't her fault," he muttered.

"If ever there was a good time to parry that with, 'Well, it's not the end of the world'—it's now," Olivia said.

Ellen rolled her eyes. "I thought you outgrew punaholism. Eventually. Like a childhood allergy to milk," she said.

"You don't outgrow *language*," Olivia said. "Or joy. Or at least I hope you don't. John... I don't remember ever seeing that tattoo of yours. Have you still got it?"

"The jaguar? Of course I do. The alternative..." John grimaced. "I would have had to go to a plastic surgeon to have the thing removed properly. That would have meant giving my father the satisfaction. I couldn't do that, not even after he died. Yeah, I still have it."

"Can I see it?" Olivia said, sitting up.

"*Now*?" John said, knitting his brows. "Right here?"

"Eh, you can stay decent," Quincey said, grinning. "It isn't as though you'd had it tattooed on your butt or something. No, come on, flash us. I want to see it too, now."

John sighed. "It isn't... I didn't do it... oh, *fine*," he snapped at last, after several abortive stabs at trying to justify the alternative of non-compliance with the request. "It's been a weird evening all around, why not round it off by showing off tattoos? But I will remind you... your food's getting cold."

Simon took a bite of his burger. "Not so," he said.

"I have a salad," Quincey said with an innocent smile. "It's supposed to be cold. And besides, I'm still waiting for the dressing."

John was wearing a blue plaid flannel shirt, and now he glanced dubiously at his cuffs. "I don't know that these'll roll up far enough..."

Ellen made a mock-provocative pose, lifting her own shoulder and laying her chin on it, looking at John sideways down her arm. "So just slip it off your shoulder, and show us, then..."

Olivia giggled.

"Can't I just describe it?" John asked, with a pleading look.

"I don't think I know anyone else with a tattoo," Olivia said. "I want to see."

"Well, but *you've* lived a sheltered life," Quincey said. "I have known people with tattoos—in fact I have one myself, and no, nobody is seeing *that* one so you can all stop looking so expectant. But John's is in a semi-public spot. I want to see too."

John rolled his eyes and began to unbutton the top buttons of his shirt. "It's not *that* spectacular," he grumbled. "You are all very strange. I'll just shrug out of..."

He was suiting action to words, but in an ill-timed maneuver he twisted sideways and lifted his shoulder just as the young waitress materialized in precisely the wrong spot with a cheerful, "Your dressing, ma'am—sorry about that..."

John's left shoulder and the waitress's right wrist connected. The little stainless steel basin of blue cheese dressing arced gracefully into the air, turned over, and landed, business side down, on John's right shoulder, spilling its contents down the front of his shirt.

There was a moment of awful silence, and then John, looking down at the mess, said conversationally, "Well, *fudge*."

"I'm so sorry!" Olivia and the waitress gasped in unison.

Quincey reached over and removed the offending container, and Olivia surged across with a napkin, trying to mop up the worst of it.

Ellen, who had just stuck her fork into her pasta, put it down again.

"You'd better go put some cold water onto that," she said practically, the mother of two, "before it sets as a permanent stain."

"It's okay, it wasn't your fault," John said to the distressed waitress. "You're right, Ellen. Excuse me for a moment, I'll go do just that. I've got a cell with me, it's got a cruddy camera—but it does take pictures—I'll snap a fuzzy snapshot of the jag for you while I'm at it, Olivia. I think we can all agree that it's a little too crowded in here for acrobatics tonight."

He scraped back his chair and nodded at the rest of them as he ambled out through the archway and back toward the restrooms.

"Someone's in that one," Ariel called out from behind his counter.

John turned. "Is the actual plumbing on in the out-of-order one?" he asked. "I just need some cold water."

"Sure," Ariel said, and picked up a folded piece of paper from the counter in front of him. "Here, take that."

John accepted the paper automatically. "What is it?"

"Instructions," Ariel said.

"For what...?"

But by the time he had glanced down at the paper in his hand and then back up again, Ariel had gone. Frowning, John turned back to the second restroom, flipping open the folded page and scanning the contents even as he pushed the door open and stepped inside.

"What the hell...?" his voice came floating out as the restroom door swung closed behind him.

And then someone else stepped up to the microphone with a guitar and began tuning it up; the swell of conversation in the café rose another notch; the minute hand on the clock on the wall skipped forward one minute. And the door to the second restroom, the one with the cheerful yellow "Out of Order" sign swinging from the doorknob, snicked shut, the small sound lost in the noise of the eve of the end of the world.

JOHN

SUMMER 1991

"*D*octor Cabot!" Olivia said, sitting on the floor of the living room with her back against the couch and her long legs stretched out before her, lifting a wine glass in a toast as John came into the room.

"Not until after graduation tomorrow, and you're tipsy, my love," John said, grinning.

"Is that a medical diagnosis?" Olivia giggled.

"Anyone who's spent any time with you could tell," John said, subsiding on the couch behind her and removing the wine glass from her hand. "That's more than enough. You don't want to be hung over at the graduation tomorrow."

"I should think plenty will be," Olivia said.

"Yes, and trust me, they will regret it. That *is* a medical opinion."

"But it's finally over—"

"Oh, Olivia, it's barely begun," John said, leaning back, letting his fingers knead her shoulder in a light massage. "The sitting around in a lecture hall might be over; the real business begins. The internship, the residency, the dealing with the real people—you know, with actual responsibility for them, without a dozen senior doctors triple-checking your every decision and the way you've spelled the word 'aspirin' on the chart... you know, the part where making a mistake doesn't mean you get a bad score in an exam, but that someone suffers, maybe dies..."

"God," Olivia said, "you really are the most sour-tempered graduate, *ever*. I'd give anything that everyone else in your class is celebrating tonight, and all you can think of is the bad stuff that's coming."

He laughed. "It isn't all bad. And you're right. It's finally over—or at the very least we're at the end of the beginning…"

"Yes Mr. Churchill," Olivia giggled.

"Actually, William Cabot. He's been giving me that little speech ever since it became clear that I would actually by some miracle graduate from the pure academic era of medical training and into actual, you know, patient contact. He seems to have no real qualms about my academics; my people skills, apparently, he is less sanguine about…"

Olivia twisted around under his hand. "Speaking of those… are you coming to bed?" she asked coquettishly.

"Far be it from me to take advantage of a maiden under the influence of alcohol," John said.

"Well, that could be arranged, but I was thinking about getting some sleep, actually," Olivia said. "It's past midnight and it'll be a long day tomorrow. You might as well get all the sleep you can while you're still allowed. Everything I've heard about medical residencies seems to point to the fact that you'll spend the next six years wide awake and exhausted."

"You watch too much TV," John said.

"Who was that on the phone? Your father?"

John, who had left the living room a few minutes earlier to answer the telephone, nodded distantly. "He's at a hotel in town. He came in earlier this afternoon. I'm… we are supposed to meet him for late breakfast… for brunch… tomorrow. Before the graduation."

"Did he want to talk to you alone?" Olivia asked. She wasn't as tipsy as John thought, having caught the slip of the tongue. "It's all right, John. I don't have to meet him *right now*. It's fraught enough, with the graduation and all—you can introduce us later, afterwards, when the pressure's off, if you want. I don't want to make this any harder for you than it has to be."

"High time he met you," John said. "You guys have tickets for the graduation and you'll be sitting next to each other. What do you mean, introduce you afterwards? Oh, hi, Dad, by the way, the young lady you've been parked next to for the last couple of hours is actually my girlfriend…?"

"Your *girlfriend*? You haven't told him that you asked me—"

"I, uh. Yeah. I kind of said that I would. Not quite that I had. It's… complicated. Look, don't take anything personally, tomorrow—he is what he is. That's partly the reason why I haven't said anything—he is hardly the huggy fluffy bunnies type. For him everything is a business deal—and it's my fault—I really should have taken you home to meet my family *months* ago. I mean, I've met yours."

"Mine are easy," Olivia said. "There's four kids for a start, and since I'm the youngest, everyone else has already done the 'hi mom hi dad here's my significant other' dance. It's part of the flow. You—only son—only *doctor* son—I'm a distraction and a possible gold digger. I suspect 'serious girlfriend' might have made him choke on his coffee tomorrow morning. Springing 'my fiancée' on him just before he sees you graduate might not be the wisest thing to do."

"You're a college graduate yourself, intelligent, witty, beautiful, and smart," John said sharply. "Don't make it sound as though I'm bringing home a raggle-taggle-gypsy-oh."

"Maybe I should go Bohemian to the graduation tomorrow," Olivia laughed, taking refuge in tipsy again.

"That," John said, getting up off the couch and hauling her to her feet, "is entirely up to you, and I confess I would actually love to see what my father would do if you offered to read his palm if he crossed yours with silver. There are times I think he would benefit immensely from being taken by the shoulders and shoved kicking and screaming into something vaguely resembling the real world… But what with him, and the graduation, and the whole day tomorrow—you're right. Bed. Let's. I'm all for it. I don't know if I could actually sleep tonight, but it's worth a shot."

"You'll be out like a light," Olivia said.

"What did you do, lace my drink?" John asked, as they padded out of the living room barefoot and with their arms around one another's waists, and he reached out to switch off the light.

She turned to lay a soft kiss on his shoulder. "No. You're exhausted. It'll catch up with you. Trust me, you'll see."

"Wake up call?"

"I'll get you up in time for facing your father in the morning," she said. "I promise. I have no idea yet if I'll have the courage to join you at breakfast. Maybe I should take the ring and wear it on a chain around my neck until he goes back home again."

"Not on your life. I put it on your finger and I will have him see it there tomorrow. I know—I handled this really badly—but you'll understand it a lot better when you meet him tomorrow. You'll forgive me, tomorrow. That, or you'll hand me back the ring and run screaming."

"That'll be the day," Olivia said softly, leaning into his side as they stepped into their bedroom.

She didn't go Bohemian to the breakfast with John's father the next morning. She wore a blue dress with handkerchief sleeves in pale blue chiffon which fluttered in the slightest breeze, bare feet thrust into slingback sandals, her only jewellery a thin gold chain around her neck and the engagement ring on her left hand, She looked cool and classy, and John had told her so twice before they left their apartment, but she was still nervous and edgy as the two of them stepped into the hotel restaurant where they were to meet Dr William Cabot.

Olivia tried to pick him out as her eyes raked the tables, but the place seemed to be full of upright and spry white-haired aristocratic gentlemen that morning. She had wanted to have a chance to look at him before he saw her, but apparently she and John had arrived early because he concluded his own sweep of the dining room with a small shake of his head.

"Not here yet," he said. "We'll get a table, over there by the window, and wait. He should be down any minute."

"We should have been late," Olivia said.

"You are *not* late for an appointment with Dr Cabot," John said. "Just not done. Come on, stop looking like I've brought you to your own execution. I already admitted I was an idiot for not dealing with this before. It'll be awkward, maybe, for the first few moments, but he's always known how to be gracious under stress. It comes with that patrician bearing of his. Noblesse oblige, and all that. He will be utterly pleasant and polite."

"If he disapproved, I'd almost rather he ranted and raved," Olivia said.

"If he disapproves, he will not neglect to have that opinion taken note of," John said. "But not here, not now, not today. Relax. If ever you've been in a protected space, it's at this moment."

They were shown to a table, and John handed her into a chair before pulling out the one next to her and settling down himself.

Less than a minute later, he indicated the entrance of the dining room with a subtle toss of his head.

"Here he comes," he murmured. "Brace yourself."

William Cabot was a tall, rangy man with a full head of silver-white hair and a closely-trimmed beard. His face was chiselled, his nose aquiline, and his eyes a disconcerting steely blue between high cheekbones and a wide smooth brow. Olivia, who always focused on hands when it came to men, could not help but admire William's—a surgeon's hands, long-fingered, steady, his smooth skin belying his seventy two years.

"John!" he said as he approached the table, where John had stood up to await him. They did not hug, but William reached out to grasp John's shoulders firmly with both hands, both offering greeting and at the same time holding his son at an arm's length for a long apprising glance. "What a day, son. Congratulations, Doctor."

"Not for a few hours yet," John said. "Dad, there's something else you can congratulate me on." He reached out and laid a hand on Olivia's shoulder. "I'd like you to meet Olivia Halloran. My... fiancée."

Olivia lifted her eyes to meet William's with an effort, but John had been right—William had not missed a beat. If anything, his smile had widened under one archly raised eyebrow. "You're a dark horse, John Cabot," he remarked easily. "It would appear that I gain not just a doctor for a son but also a bonus prize of a future daughter. Olivia, is it? Congratulations, my dear. Are you another budding doctor?"

"No, sir. Science grad. I'm chasing a post-graduate degree, but I've been working part-time over the last year or so while I get all my ducks in a row. There's a scholarship I'm in line for next year."

William appeared to take all that in with a polite and

concentrated attention, and then, with his next words, dismissed it all. "Engaged, eh. So what are the wedding plans?"

"Not for a while," John said. "It'll be a leisurely engagement. I have the internship year to get through, and that will be tough enough without bringing in caterers and florists and such. There's plenty of time—we're young, and we're together. That's all that matters right now."

"Admirable. Young lady, you're very brave," William said, in a tone which let Olivia know in no uncertain terms that he believed that, at least in this case, the line between bravery and arrant idiocy was a fine one. "A first-year intern is not someone you will see very often, over the next year. The schedules are brutal, and they will keep his feet to the fire."

"We know," Olivia said. "I'll be home when he gets there."

"Beats a cat," John said. Olivia flushed and swatted at him, but William laughed. Olivia thought it was a strange laugh, with a tinge of something that was almost triumph on the edges of it—but John didn't seem to notice. He grinned at his father, his expression one that Olivia, if she had to put a name to it, might have called smugness.

"Well, you're a grown man. You know your own mind," William said. And then, after a beat, "Welcome to the family, Olivia."

"Dad liked you," John said to Olivia later, as they drove to the Great Hall for the graduation ceremony.

"No," Olivia said. "He didn't. He didn't like me much at all. Or, more to the point, he doesn't like the idea of me. I very much get the feeling that you are supposed to inherit his kingdom, and the prospect of marriage—to someone he hasn't vetted and doesn't know—makes all his warning lights go on at once. You didn't see the way he was looking at me?"

"He's a grumpy old man," John said.

"That's not what you said before. You said he was... something much bigger. Much worse. A master manipulator. And he does a fabulous job on you."

John turned his head sharply to look at her before returning his gaze to the road. His hands had tightened on the steering wheel of the car. "And what's that supposed to mean?"

"You're competing with him," Olivia said flatly. "And this is a competition you can't possibly win. He's got too much of a head start. You want him to see you become him, but you'd need the forty years he's got on you to start out on an even playing field. And he... he wants you to be him, but not yet, not *ever* just yet, not while he's around to see you catch up with him."

John was shaking his head. "I have no idea where you're getting any of *that* from."

"Look at this morning," Olivia said. "He didn't really want you to have me. It didn't fit... some image in his head. It's as though you'd win some point that he couldn't match."

"I get it—you don't like him," John said.

"No, it isn't that. I can get on with just about anybody... and he's your father, and that's a powerful incentive. But he doesn't like *me*. And there's something else too..."

"What?"

"I don't think I like who you turn into when you're with him," Olivia said slowly. "When you're in class, or you're alone with me, you're a loving and caring human being—in that restaurant you turned cold and competitive and flippant about the things you say you love. Including me. And... and *smug*, when you thought you scored a point off him."

"Oh?" John said. He didn't want to quarrel, not now, not just before the graduation ceremony—but the things she was saying stung, and he couldn't make up his mind whether it was because she had a point or because she was spouting psychobabble.

"'Beats a cat'...?" Olivia said softly.

John flexed his hands, stretching his fingers wide and then curling them around the steering wheel again. "That was a bit crass," he said at last. "I'm sorry, love. I didn't mean it—not the way it came out. It's just that the internship... and when he..."

"I know," she said, reaching out to lay her hand briefly over his. "It's okay. So long as you revert back to yourself when Doctor Cabot Senior is not about, it's okay. I can handle occasional bouts of the two of you locking horns. I can just retreat to the kitchen and make copious amounts of lasagna—it's comfort food and I hear psychological warfare can leave one hungry in the aftermath of battle."

John threw his head back and laughed. "I love you," he said, with complete and utter sincerity, glancing at her with the broad smile that was the legacy of his laughter still on his face. "You do know that, don't you? You won't ever forget it? Even when I'm being an ass?"

"I'll try and remember it especially when you are being an ass," Olivia said with an answering grin.

She and William were seated next to one another at the ceremony; he was already there when Olivia made her way down the row, apologizing to other people as she stumbled over their feet, on her way to her own seat. William looked up as she sat down next to him.

"The future Mrs. Cabot," he said affably.

Olivia smiled. "Sir," she said. Polite, and flattering, and coolly impersonal.

William lifted an eyebrow, his lips turning up into a slight smile. He had been acknowledged, and then put in his place—*dismissed*—by this slip of a girl. It was not an experience that had often come his way.

The ceremony started on time, and was long, and intense, and steeped in stately tradition. When John Cabot received his diploma, William applauded with the dignity of a Roman Senator and Olivia with a wild and loving enthusiasm, trying to catch John's eye across the intervening rows of audience and other graduates, trying to send a silent message across that empty space—*I love you, I'm proud of you*. He might have heard, at that, because he looked out over the audience and smiled.

After that, it was just a question of waiting impatiently until the last graduate walked away with the diploma, and the ceremony was brought to its solemn conclusion. Olivia couldn't wait to push through the crowds and find John where he stood waiting for them, diploma in hand. She flung herself into his arms, laughing, and he wrapped them around her waist and lifted her off the ground for a moment in a gesture of pure triumph.

"Doctor Cabot, I presume," she said, giggling.

"Apparently so," John said.

"Congratulations," William said, coming up behind. John

transferred Olivia into the circle of just one arm, his diploma dangling from his left hand, as he extended his right to shake hands with his father.

"Now, don't get cocky," William said. "Don't let that piece of paper turn your head. This, as Churchill once said, is only the end of the beginning." John caught Olivia's eye and smothered a grin, remembering their conversation from the previous night. "All that the books could teach you, that diploma says you have learned," William continued, without giving any hint that he had caught that unspoken exchange. "Now comes the hard part. Telling the patients that you know what you know. And trust me, no medical protocol has *ever* completely survived contact with the patient... What the hell is *she* doing here?"

The little speech ended with such an explosively violent tone that Olivia actually flinched, and John's head snapped around to search the crowds in the direction his father's gimlet gaze was pointed. When he saw the thing that had set William off, he sucked in his breath sharply.

"Mother?" he said.

"Did you invite her?" William asked.

John turned back to look at his father, his expression oddly defiant. "I might have, but I haven't had a valid address for her for years. The last time I wrote to her it was a Christmas card with a letter of what I'd been doing that year, and I sent it to the last known address I had for her, and it came back to me with a stamp that said that no such person lived there. After that, she just disappeared."

"You've had no contact with her?"

"I just told you...."

"Then how did she know that the graduation was here, today?"

John sighed. "Dad. She *did* know I was in med school. And the graduations are kind of public knowledge. It isn't as though someone has let slip a state secret. It isn't inconceivable that she should find out." He turned to stare at the woman at the edge of the crowd, who had not moved. "She looks awful, actually. Has she lost weight? A lot of weight? Those clothes are hanging off her. And that hair... even from here..." He suddenly went white, and gave his father a long accusing stare. "Is she sick?" he demanded. "Did you know? Why didn't you tell me?"

"She's *always* been sick," William said. "Always something."

"Hang onto this, Olivia," John said, handing the diploma to Olivia. "I'd better go talk to her."

William reached out a hand. "John..."

"She's entitled, dammit," John said, shaking the hand off. "Whatever beef you two had with each other—and I never really knew, and I doubt I ever will, and that's just fine with me—she is still part of my family, and I never shared that beef. So you can stay here if you like, but I'm going over to talk to her. It doesn't look like she's ready to come to us any time soon. And besides, she looks like she's about to collapse where she's standing. Really, Dad, I don't like the looks of her. Is she in chemo or something...?"

He gave Olivia a reassuring glance, and stepped away from the group. William waited, stiff, until John was a couple of paces away and then swore softly under his breath and strode after him, leaving Olivia standing alone clutching the brand-new diploma in her hands.

William had caught up to his son, and they both reached the thin woman in what was a good-quality but still fairly obvious blonde wig at the same moment.

"Mom," John said, and in the same breath William spoke sharply beside him,

"Stephanie? What are you doing here?"

"The boy is graduating," Stephanie Cabot said to her ex-husband. "You still think I have no rights in this at all?" She held William's gaze with her own, defiantly, and then turned to John. "I never really wanted you to go into medicine," she said. "But I guess William had to get his money's worth."

"*Stephanie,*" William said through gritted teeth.

"What? What are you going to do to me? You'd be less of a doctor than you are not to realize that I'm dying, William. What can you possibly threaten me with?"

"I am not threatening you at all. I am reminding you of your promise."

"One gets released from stupid promises when one is on

one's deathbed," Stephanie said. "Or at least one should be."

"What are you two talking about? What promise?"

"Some day," Stephanie said, reaching out to touch John's cheek with genuine tenderness, "you are owed the truth."

John glanced over at his father, over the edge of Stephanie's hand. "Dad?"

But William was looking at his ex-wife, with an expression of such disgust and loathing on his face that John actually gasped out loud.

"It's money, isn't it?" William said. "You've run through the last lot, and now you want more."

Stephanie dropped her hand from John's face, lifted both hands to her hair.

"I could use a better wig," she said, but the tone was sarcastic, facetious. "I'm not going to waste any more money on me, William," she said after a pause, and the voice had changed—the core of bitterness was still there but she was no longer using words as weapons. "I'm done. I know that. I've had several doctors hand down a verdict and although no two of them can agree on what *precisely* will kill me not one of them gives me more than three or four months, on the outside—and this particular outing they released me on only under complete duress. It is probably the last time I'll walk anywhere, even with *that*."

She glanced to the side, and it was only now that they noticed the four-pronged cane resting against a wall which she had been using to prop herself up. "I just wanted to see you, John," she said. "This last time, perhaps. And to ask you to forgive me."

"It won't be the last time, let me know where you are, I'll come and see you," John said, casting a defiant glance at William. The two of them might be divorced but that contract did not bind John—and, as William himself had pointed out, he was a grown man now and able to make his own decisions. "And forgive you... for what?"

"You'll know," she said faintly, "when the time comes. Just remember that I asked you to forgive me. And as for seeing me... there is no reason whatsoever for you to watch an old woman die. I'll make sure I keep myself out of sight. I've got enough money left for them to stick me into some oven after it's all over and then scatter my ashes wherever it's convenient—I don't hold for mourning, it blights the living, when you hear I am dead just assume that my spirit, together with what remains of this outer shell, is out there, everywhere, and that when you look at a tree or the sky I might be looking back. Come here, kiss me—" She drew John's head down to hers and he slipped an arm around her fragile shoulders as his lips brushed her cheek. Then she released him, and all but pushed him away, even though it was with infinite gentleness. "There. Let that be the way you remember me."

"I'm getting married," John said impulsively, glancing over his shoulder to where Olivia waited, aware that there was a family drama going on and she was not—or at least not yet—family. "She's over there—I'll just call—"

"No, it's all right—if she never knew me back when I'd rather she didn't remember me at all—not like this," Stephanie said. "You love her?"

"Very much."

"Good. Don't let him wreck it for you." That was accompanied by a sharp sideways glance at William, whose brow was drawn into a black scowl.

"*Wreck* it," he echoed, his words dripping with irritation, even anger.

"Oh, it's one of those things you're very good at, William," Stephanie said calmly. "Wreckage. I have to go now, John. Will you help me to the steps there?"

"Where are you going? You can't possibly walk—"

Even as she moved away from the wall, reaching for the cane, a woman rose from where she had been perched a little way away on a lower part of the wall and stood waiting expectantly.

"I don't have to walk far," Stephanie said. "She's there to help me, and it'll be back into a cab, and I'll be fine. John... I'll be fine. Part of me had actually hoped that I might catch a glimpse of you but that you would never see me here at all—I know this isn't the easiest way to leave it, but trust me, it's for the best."

"Leave me a contact address at least."

"No, I'll be in touch with you. Congratulations, John—remember, *he* might have pushed you here, but for the rest of it... make it your own. Don't let him bully you. Now help me—she'll come get me at the steps, I told her to leave me alone until I needed her help—" She lifted one hand and gave a small wave, and the woman watching from the far end of the wall acknowledged by lifting her own hand and then strode briskly toward the bottom of the stairs.

"Who is she?"

"Nurse," Stephanie said, "of sorts. Just help me down the stairs, she can take me from there."

The woman reached out for Stephanie's elbow as she stepped unsteadily off the last step and onto the pavement.

"We'll be fine now," she said to John, in a pleasant, smoky alto. "Thank you."

"That's my son," Stephanie said, leaning on the woman's arm.

"Thank you, Mr. Cabot," the woman said, smiling.

"That's *Doctor* Cabot," Stephanie said, her lips curling into a smile of her own. "Let's go, Leanne. I'm very tired all of a sudden."

Leanne gave a brief professional nod to John and then she was at Stephanie's side as the older woman turned away and began to walk away, fishing out a cell phone out of the pocket of her tailored slacks and barking out a few short peremptory words about the taxi being needed immediately.

They left John standing with his arms hanging by his sides, his expression confused and worried. He stared after them for a moment, and then lifted his head to look back at his father, still at the top of the stair they had struggled down.

"What did she mean, the truth?" he asked.

"Stephanie is a vindictive and vengeful woman," William said. "She might have meant anything at all. And I'll look into this whole thing tomorrow, see if I can find out where she's staying. Trust me, there is only one reason she came out here today—and yes, she very much meant for you to see her—and that's to present as pathetic and noble a face on it as possible, and wait for the money to roll in."

"Dad, she really looked ill."

"As for that, your diploma still too fresh and shiny for you to be diagnosing patients on sight out on the streets," William said, a little sharply. "You need a few years' experience under your belt before you can do *that*."

"Diploma," John said. "Oh, God. Olivia."

He turned and raced back up the stairs where Olivia stood waiting, white-faced and very still, her hands folded tightly around his rolled-up, brand-new diploma.

They were meant to go out to dinner that night with several of John's colleagues and their significant others, but John pleaded out of the social engagement. He talked briefly to his father on the phone, a conversation that was oddly monosyllabic at least on John's end and did not seem to improve his mood, and then he sat brooding on his couch, flipping channels aimlessly on the TV.

"We gotta eat," Olivia said at last, having left him to his funk for a little while and hoping it would lift by itself. "How do you feel about pizza, if you don't want a fancy restaurant? I could order in..."

"I'm sorry, love," he said, tossing the remote control onto the table and reaching out for her. "I've been a bear all day. We should have gone out—it would have done us both good. It's too late now—but we can have whatever kind of pizza you want."

"Even Hawaiian?"

John made a face. "I'll never know what you find palatable about boiled pineapples," he said, "but fine. Even Hawaiian. As a sign of good faith, I'll even order it myself. And Olivia... I'm sorry. Truly. It's just that things..."

"Yes, things—and things will get worse before they get better, with internship hours and all that. And I always knew you were a moody bastard—la, sir, fie, you should have been a poet or a painter or something where dramatic temper tantrums would have served you well. Instead, you have to sit on everything, and be a nice, calm, professional doctor. It's okay, I know I'll be a sounding board every now and then. I can live with that. I just wish you'd tell me what happened back there."

"I would," John said, dialing the pizza place, "if I knew.

I have a feeling that *I* don't know what really happened back there...ah...hello. I'd like to order a large Hawaiian, please. With double boiled pineapple."

The internship started out tough, with all the difficulties that all of them had foreseen—the long hours, the sleepless nights, the complete dedication to the work while at the same time having dropped instantly from the very top of the status pyramid—young graduate MD with a fresh-minted diploma in hand—all the way back to the bottom once more, the lowest on the totem pole, being sent hither and yon by attending physicians who assumed the fresh intake of interns knew nothing at all (in which they were sometimes correct) and older residents who had moved a year ahead in the pecking order and assumed that the fresh intake of interns knew nothing at all compared to them (in which they were more than frequently wrong).

But John handled it with as much grace as he could muster under the circumstances, and Olivia tried to be everything that he needed her to be, a sympathetic ear when he wanted one, an extra pair of eyes on a problem even if she didn't know all the medical minutiae of it, a home and a haven. And it all worked, in a ponderous ramshackle fashion, until the fourth month of the internship.

When an intern dropped out of the Children's Oncology Ward rotation, and they drafted Dr. John Cabot into the vacancy.

He was given four charts on his first day on the job, and he flipped through one after another, puzzled.

"There doesn't seem to be much..." he began, and Dr. Steve Price, one of the more senior residents who had brought the charts, grimaced.

"There isn't," he said. "They might go into remission, or they might not, but once they land in here, those kids are in God's waiting room. In the rest of this hospital—in the rest of the medical Universe—in most cases you'll ever have to deal with—your job is to cure the patient and send him home. Here... you take it day by day. And you're grateful for every one that you get. Let me introduce you, they're quite a bunch of characters."

He sorted a chart to the top as they entered one of the

two-bed rooms, and smiled at a little girl who looked dwarfed by her pillows.

"Hey, Lizzie. How's things today?"

"I'm doing okay," Lizzie said. "My IV itches a little."

"We can fix that. Here, hold these." Steve handed the charts to John and bent over the frail body where the IV line entered her arm. "Lizzie Squires, this here is Doctor Cabot. He's new. Y'all just say howdy while I get this sorted."

"Howdy, Doctor Cabot," Lizzie said.

She wore a scarf wrapped around her head, hiding, presumably, a bald little head with hair taken by chemo—but she was bright-eyed, and looked alert, almost happy.

"Just call me John," John said. "Who's your friend over there?"

Lizzie looked over at the second bed, where another little girl seemed to be sound asleep.

"That's LaToya. She's new, she only got here middle of last week. So far she does a lot of sleeping."

"How long have you been here?"

"I can't tell," Lizzie said. "I go home sometimes, but it's like I visit at home and I live here, really..."

"There, better?" Steve had finished fiddling with the IV line and straightened, holding out his hand for the charts. He flipped open Lizzie's, beckoning John over. "She's on new meds, we're trying something so new that it's almost experimental—but she's responding to it really well. You need to stay on top of it, though. This needs monitoring closely." He glanced over at the other bed. "We'll leave those introductions until she's awake enough to remember your face. Let's go next door—I'll see you later, Lizzie!"

"Okay," Lizzie said. "See you later, John."

In the next room they found two boys. One of them looked on the verge of puberty, perhaps just pre-teen. The other, tiny and quite bald, couldn't have been more than seven.

"Brad Teller," Steve said, pointing with the charts to the older boy, "and Adam Wells. Guys, this is John Cabot, the new doctor on the ward. You'll be seeing quite a bit of him. How's the troops today?"

"Been better," said Brad wanly. He looked tired, wrung out, as though his body had sprung a fatal leak somewhere and all the life had leached out of him. His skin was sallow, and there were tinges of yellow in the whites of his eyes.

"Liver?" John asked softly to the resident, teasing out Brad's chart.

"Yep," said Steve. "And other stuff. I'll fill you in on the history later. Adam? What about you?"

"Mom said she'd bring me a new soldier today," Adam said.

John glanced at the shelf above the boy's bed; it was crowded with tiny figurines of painted soldiers, anything from drab khakis and camouflage to resplendent scarlet uniforms of eras gone by.

"How many have you got there?" John asked.

"I don't know. Lots. They've all got stories."

"And he'll tell you them. In detail. If he can corner you," Steve said, laughing. "Doctor Cabot will be around, Adam, save the stories for later. Perhaps after the new man comes."

"Okay," the boy said.

"When's your mom coming?"

"She said this morning."

"Come on, John—maybe we can catch her out in the hall and I'll introduce you."

They slipped out of the room and Steve shuffled through the charts one more time before wrinkling his nose in an expression of resignation and handing them over to John.

"You'll have to keep on your toes here," he said, "because those charts can change really fast. Lizzie is our osteosarcoma yo-yo, she's something of a fixture—the first time she came in she presented with a shattered femur which could not remotely be explained by any rational reason—so they did a couple of tests, and they realized that all the symptoms had been there from the start, that she had pain in her joints which somebody had misdiagnosed as Polyarticular Juvenile Rheumatoid Arthritis, but until she broke that leg bone—her second serious break in a year, by the way—nobody had really thought to test her for bone cancer. So far she's had two surgeries—we're trying to save the limbs—that original shattered femur has been all but replaced with a titanium rod, and we've had to go in and reconstruct her knee once already—the first bout of chemo she lost so much weight that we thought we would find just the empty bedclothes one morning and a small pile of bones underneath, probably crumbled to powder. She's been on that chemo IV for a week, this time—she has so little appetite that someone has to sit with her and beg her to swallow each mouthful of food at mealtimes. We've had to downgrade her from recurrent to metastatic— there are a couple of spots in her lungs that we're watching."

"How old is she?"

"Nine," Steve said, and shuffled out a second chart. "Adam. He's a brush fire we keep on putting out, and the flames just keep on popping up somewhere else. When he came in they thought he had a bad bout of some exotic flu—fever, chills, aching joints, fatigue, white as a ghost and with a bunch of swollen lymph nodes all over the place. The first doctor who saw him recommended aspirin and a week in bed. But then someone else noticed that he bruised as soon as you looked at him, and they put him through the wringer—"

"Acute myeloid leukemia with abnormal bone marrow eosinophils," John read from the chart.

"He went from being in partial remission after induction chemo—and practically symptom free, we had cautious cause for optimism—to being classified as a recurrent AML patient. Like I said, bushfires. Every time we thought we had it beat it came right back—and after induction we hit him with intensive chemo, and we turned him into that bald little wraith you see in there today. And it's been going on for quite some time. Count the toy soldiers."

"The soldiers?"

"His mother brings him in for a new bout of chemo and a new soldier comes with him," Steve said. "Then he is discharged again, and a new soldier comes for that—and is left there, on that shelf. Then he comes in again, inevitably, and a new man follows him."

"There's got to be more than fifty toy soldiers on that shelf!"

"I haven't really counted," Steve said. "Some part of me doesn't want to know."

"Marrow transplant?"

"Every time we have him strong and stable enough for one, something happens," Steve said. "He *nearly* had the procedure three times. We're looking at ALLO stem cell transplants now—but the only potential sibling donor is a younger brother, and Adam himself is only seven. I don't want to make matters worse. The parents have been informed, and we're looking to see if we can find an unrelated donor in the registry database—but that also carries all sorts of graft-versus-host issues and I don't know if he can handle that right now. And in any event it would mean even more aggressive chemo, and radiation—and God knows what else. A large percentage of leukemia kids shake the monster entirely, these days—it isn't the death sentence it once was—but Adam—I don't know. His odds have never been good. He actually has very nice hair, you know—it grows back every so often when we stop zapping him, and then he looks like any other dark-haired curly-topped little boy. And then his blood count goes for a loop, and off we go again around the mulberry bush."

"And the other two?"

"Brad has what we suspect to be an aggressive extraosseous Ewing sarcoma—and it's on his liver, and it's already practically destroyed his left kidney. Not a great prognosis. LaToya—she's a new admission—she's got a tumor the size of a tennis ball with claws deep in the CNS; inoperable without killing her. Adam and Lizzie, they're our staples—those other two beds, they rarely stay filled for long." Steve handed all the charts to John, and gave him a tired smile. "Like I said—in this bastion, you fight for every day. Cures are miracles handed down from God, and they don't come often."

"But what am I supposed to do…?"

"Keep the stats as close to normal as you can under the circumstances, keep them comfortable. And don't let them shred your heart."

LaToya was gone within a week, Brad in less than three. Adam, too, disappeared—but only briefly; he was back in his bed within two weeks for another tussle with chemo, complete with more additions to his manpower shelf, now bristling with unlikely soldiery: a Roman centurion standing side-by-side with what looked like a Hussar and a WWII aviator.

This time he was in real pain, although he bore it bravely. John found himself falling under the boy's spell, allowing himself to be detained for longer than he ought to have been while Adam told him the individual stories of his toy soldiers, checking his bedside and his chart obsessively to ensure that he was in no more pain than he needed to be.

"There you go, Kojak," he told him at one point, after the curly hair had gone again and Adam sat shiny-pated and huge-eyed in his bed, handing him a Fentanyl lollipop for the pain.

"Thanks, John. Who's Kojak?"

John laughed. "Before your time, young'un. Damn near before mine. He was a badass cop in a TV show, and had about as much hair as you, and loved his lollipops."

"Cool," Adam said, managing a smile. "I'm on television. Kojak. I must remember to tell Mom about it when she gets here."

"You do that. Gotta go, Kojak—I hear them calling my name. I'll check in with you later."

It was one of his nights off that night, and he dragged himself home, heavy-hearted and dull-eyed. Olivia waited with a meal, a hug, and tea and sympathy—but he could barely make himself eat.

"Another bad couple of days?" Olivia said. "Talk to me, John. Let it out. You're bottling up the poison."

"There's nothing I can *do*," John said, burying his hands into the hair at his temples and holding his head between his palms as though it would explode otherwise. "There just isn't anything I can do. I'm just standing there with my finger in the dike, holding back the deluge by main force of will, by refusing to countenance defeat, and knowing that what I think or feel just isn't important in the grand scheme of things. Olivia, I have to get out of this ward, soon, or I will get out of medicine. I cannot handle those children's faces for much longer. I don't know what's worse, when they're smiling at me and being all brave and bright or when they're crunched up in pain and screaming and all I can do is pass out Fentanyl lollies."

"It'll be all right," she murmured, gathering his head to her breast and rocking him like a child. "It'll be all right. You'll see."

That was the week of the roller coaster, a week that John would remember only as a blur afterwards. Adam would rally, and then slip, and then rally, and it was impossible to know which boy John would find when he stepped into the ward. Adam's roommate on the ward changed twice that week—first one small boy being brought in almost unconscious on a drip which contained a poisonous cocktail of pain meds, chemo drugs, and the Gods alone knew what else, a child who did not last the night, and then another boy, only a few years older than Adam himself, but one who came from a large boisterous family and who was a good candidate for the marrow transplant surgery with several siblings willing and able to donate the precious healthy cells.

That was also the week that John was distracted by a phone call from a lawyer, informing him that his mother had died—of cancer... of cancer, of all things, right at that moment—and that she had left a sealed box to be given to John after she was gone. It had arrived by special delivery at the house on his afternoon off, and he had signed for it, and accepted it, and then stood staring at it for a moment as though the package might suddenly lose its boxy four-square shape in his hands and metamorphose into a hot water bottle or a snapping turtle.

"Why do I have such a bad feeling about this?" he muttered.

"You don't have to look at it now," Olivia said, tugging at it.

"I keep on remembering, back at my graduation, she asked me... to forgive her. For what she was going to do. Haven't heard a squeak from her since then—until now. Until this. Is this what I am to forgive her for? Olivia, I don't have the strength for a family drama, not now, not while Adam..."

"Adam is not here. Adam is in the hospital. And this is your day *off*," Olivia said. "It might be just what you need, at that, taking a look inside that thing, thinking of yourself for a moment and letting God take care of things back at the ward."

He handed her the box. "You open it."

Olivia sliced open the packing tape with a paring knife, and then, glancing back at John for approval, broke the seal that was still on the box and peered inside.

"It's papers," she said. "Not that much of it, but it looks like... wait, there's a photo... who's this? Do you know her?"

John took the photograph Olivia handed him, and studied it—a slightly out-of-focus picture of a young dusky-skinned woman with glossy dark hair parted severely in the middle and pulled back away from her face. She was not precisely beautiful—her features were too broad and flat for that, her mouth too wide—but her eyes were extraordinary: large and dark... and wary with the caution of a deer which had caught the scent of a wolf pack.

"I have no clue," he said, flipping the picture to look at the back. "There's a name. Rosalina. Nothing more. What else is in there?"

"John... you *were* adopted? You told me that, back when we first met?"

"Yes," John said, "they could hardly pretend to get away with it, otherwise. Both William and Stephanie were blue-eyed blondes; they could not possibly have a natural child with my own dark coloring. They told me I was adopted back when I was a kid, before they divorced, even. Possibly the last joint parenting decision they took."

"I think this is your original birth certificate," Olivia said, staring at a piece of paper in her hand. "In fact...there are two. On one of them you're listed as Juan, not John. On both... John... your father is listed as your father. You weren't adopted, at least not completely. He is your natural biological father, apparently."

"That doesn't make sense—and then who is this woman, then, my biological mother? Why would my adoptive mom suddenly want me to know who my natural mother was, after all this time?"

"Maybe she asked, she wanted to know—it happens sometimes—what's this doing here?"

"What?"

"A bunch of newspaper clippings about the civil war in Guatemala... and another bunch, over here, about the women who..."

John looked up after a moment, when Olivia appeared to have stopped speaking mid-sentence. He saw her gather up the papers with a stiff, clumsy motion, shoveling them back into the box.

"This'll keep, John," she said.

"What is it?" he said, suddenly alarmed by the expression on her face. "What did you find?"

"No, not now—you don't have the..."

John tugged the box out of her hands. "Now you're scaring me. Give me that thing."

She hung on to the box for a moment, denying him possession, but she finally released it at his narrowed-eye glare, and bit her lip.

"I don't think you should look at it, not right now," she said.

John opened the box again, still staring at her. "Between her asking me to forgive her, and your face right now," he said, "I feel as though I'm about to get shoved into some abyss—"

"John..."

"She felt it was one I needed to dive into, though."

"Your father didn't."

"My father... often does things for reasons I don't wholly agree with," John said. "I have a feeling this will just fester if I leave it."

He shuffled out the papers again, and spread them out over the coffee table.

Olivia knew when he found the headline that had stricken her to the bone, by the sudden tensing of his shoulders. *Women for sale*, it said, and in the first paragraph of the article there was mention of several prominent men—including professionals like doctors and leading academics—whom the authorities had caught in a sting operation. And then the sentence that somebody had underlined heavily in black pen: *Of course, for every one of the men who has been indicted there are probably two others who have taken greater care to cover their tracks.*

The implications were obvious, and stark.

"No," John said. "No, that *can't* be right. Not even William Cabot would buy a human being to use for... no. I can't... no."

Stephanie's voice came to him, his mother's voice, the voice of the woman he had called Mom all his life, a ghostly echo from the day of his graduation. *I guess William had to get his money's worth. I came to ask you… to forgive me.*

To forgive her. For being complicit in this. For… for having known about it. For having wanted a child of her own to love badly enough to have turned a blind eye as to how William had gone about the begetting of it—rendered infertile in her twenties by polycystic ovary syndrome (those papers had been included, too, as though in expiation of her own role in the matter) Stephanie Cabot could not give her husband the son he wanted. She had pleaded to adopt, but William had not been keen on the idea. Instead… he had brought home… Rosalina.

Sixteen, scared, bought and paid for. A vessel for his seed.

They could adopt, after all. But they would adopt William's natural child, not some other man's seed. William would get his son—*his* son, the fruit of his own loins, his own genetic legacy to the world—no matter what stood in his way.

There were other clippings. News stories about human trafficking, and how almost impossible it was to find people who knew how to cover their tracks, who had the money and power to do so. There would have been few people in positions of authority who would have believed that the well-to-do plastic surgeon from the wealthy part of town was keeping a girl locked up in his basement against her will, and he would have known how to head off those who harbored any such suspicions. William Cabot, pillar of society, on the board of the local Hospital and a stalwart supporter and patron of philanthropic organizations whose purpose was to bring succor to the teeming masses of the developing world, slave-owner, and rapist.

He, John, was not the beloved heir. He was the fruit of the master with his concubine. The slave-son.

He became aware that he had not moved in some time only when Olivia laid a gentle and questioning hand on his shoulder.

"John? Are you all right?"

"I should remember," John said, "some of this."

"There's no way—you were just a baby—"

"No, later," he said. "She took me. Look. It took William nearly three years to find me. I was three when they took me from my mother, my real mother, and they brought me home to the mansion. I was three. Three is old enough to remember."

"There is no requirement that you remember."

"Yes," he said savagely. "There is. I owe her that much."

"Do you want me to make you a cup of tea..."

"Tea?" he stared at her incredulously. "You think all of this can be swept away by a nice cup of tea?"

Olivia flushed. "No, of course I don't. I just wanted to do something—something that I was able to—"

His quick anger had evaporated even as she spoke. "I'm sorry," he said dully. "No, I don't want any tea. In fact, I'd probably better get back to the hospital."

"It's your day off, you can't work..."

"I will be better off working," he said. "I'll take someone's shift in the ER for a couple of hours. I need to keep busy, Olivia. Right now, I need to keep busy."

"What do you want me to do with these?" Olivia asked, as he rose, leaving the papers strewn across the table, and stumbled toward the door.

"Leave them," he said. "Don't touch anything. I will want to go through it all later. Line by line."

Olivia stared at him, hurt, puzzled, worried. "John..."

He cut her off with a curt hand gesture. "That's not even my name," he said quietly. "Don't you understand? He took *everything* from me. I no longer... even know who I am."

"You're someone I love very much," Olivia said fiercely. "You're a goofball. You're a doctor..."

"Yes. I am that. I'd better go and be the one thing I know for a fact belongs to me. I earned that diploma myself. I'll see you later, Olivia. I'll catch forty winks at the hospital tonight—I'm on call tomorrow, anyway."

"You'll kill yourself," she said.

"Maybe," he said, at the door. "Maybe that's the only way to absolution."

Olivia stared at him, alarmed now, reduced to silence.

He turned once more, and tried to smile. The smile was a feral thing, a grimace, and his eyes were wide and too bright and the smile never touched them at all. But it was a genuine attempt, nonetheless, and he shook his head very slightly in emphasis of his words as he spoke.

"No, I won't walk under a bus," he said. "I'm still sane enough for that. I'll call you, later. If I can."

He met up with his friend Jesse Winters in the bowels of the ER, and released him for a few hours while he took over the duties of the moment; the ER was mercifully overflowing with the walking wounded from sixteen different kinds of accident, with one or two mugging victims, with a couple of women who had 'walked into a door' and sat proud and silent nursing purpling bruises in hidden places, with uninsured children gasping for breath and brought there as a last resort by terrified mothers who—ah, but this was acid into his wound right now!— barely spoke English and often tried to tell him what the matter was in incoherent strings of Spanish which he now keenly felt he should have been able to at least understand more than a few haphazard words of, if not fluently speak.

I'm from Guatemala. I'm the son of Rosalina from Guatemala. I am Juan, son of Rosalina from Guatemala.

It pounded in his brain. He could not stop thinking about it. That country. Those names. The identity that was now long lost, so thoroughly gone that there was no place for the names to settle and rest and stick. He knew the truth of them, but they fluttered in his mind like a flock of disturbed birds who could not find a secure place to come to roost, wheeling in noisy black circles, screaming out those names. That country.

Juan. Rosalina. Guatemala.

"Doctor...?" The words were soft, the hand on his wrist gentle—a concerned nurse, in fresh scrubs, peering into his face. "Your shift ended twenty minutes ago. Dr. Parker is here to relieve you. Are you okay? Can I get you some coffee?"

"No. Thank you, no. Thank you. I'll be fine."

He never did go home—he snatched something to eat in the hospital cafeteria, and then hung around the clinic area until his own shift, up in the Pediatric Oncology ward, was due to start. John went up to the ward early and pored over the charts for a while—they had a new patient in, a girl by the name of Tania Yevgroff, presenting with yet another case of leukemia, the same thing that young Kojak was battling so valiantly in the next room. John peered into the girls' ward through the glass— Tania was a pale wraith of a girl, lying back against her pillows, her eyes closed. She looked like the heroine from some tragic Russian movie.

Her blood counts were appalling. John made a few notations on her chart, then left it in the slot by the door and pushed open the door to the other ward.

"Hey, Kojak," he said. "How are you doing?"

"I'm okay," Adam said. *"Have you seen my Spartan? He's new."*

"I thought you only got new men when you came into the hospital or when you went home," John said, dutifully admiring the Spartan warrior.

"I'm supposed to be going home tomorrow," Adam said. "For a little while, at least. I had a headache for the longest time—but they fixed that, but my blood count isn't high enough for chemo this week so they're sending me home for a little bit, and then I'll catch up on everything next week. So Mom brought the Spartan this morning. They're coming to get me tonight."

"Good-oh," John said. "You take care. That's a nice Spartan."

His shift proper started, and before he quite knew how he'd got roped into it he got involved in a lengthy consult with the family of another regular patient who was due back into the hospital the next day. His colleague, Steve, the same resident who had introduced him around the ward when he first came there, had been part of the same consult, and when the parents and the grandfather of the patient had finally concluded their questions and shook the doctors' hands and departed, Steve gave John a long apprising look.

"You look like shit," he said. "When was the last time you slept?"

John gave a vague wave of his hand. "A while ago."

"I know it's your own shift, but you're grabbing a couple of hours of down time, right now. Doctor's orders. Go on, get out of here. You need to have your wits about you in this place, and right now you don't look like you'd know your own name if I asked you point blank."

That was so close to the truth that John couldn't help a snort of incredulous laughter—which only seemed to confirm the senior doctor's diagnosis. John was escorted to the on-call room and bundled into a bunk with little ceremony.

"I couldn't sleep," he protested weakly. "I have too much on my mind."

"You will so, if I have to dope you up to get you to do it," Steve said. "Close your eyes and rest your brain. Sleep comes when you least expect it. Trust me on this."

John honestly didn't think that he could have slept, but somehow Steve was completely right—he must have been unconscious as soon as he allowed his eyes to close. He woke, with a start, some time later and lay disoriented for a moment, not quite sure where he was or what was going on. But then the intercom crackled into life with the tail end of some message about someone being needed somewhere, stat, and John shook his head and brought himself back to reality.

The names had not gone.

Juan. Rosalina. Guatemala.

But he could push it into the back of his mind for now. There was work to do.

He washed his face in cold water, to wake himself up the rest of the way, and walked up to the nurses' station on the cancer ward.

"I'll just grab myself a cup of coffee, and I'll be ready to…" he began, and then glanced over into the boys' ward room, where… where…

The curtains were drawn around Adam's bed.

"Everything okay there…?" he asked the nurse, wrinkling his brow into a puzzled frown. "Kojak said he was supposed to be going home tonight…"

"His family is with him," the nurse said. "Dr Cabot… he crashed, an hour ago. Hard. He's…"

John had pushed himself off the counter, taking the few long strides necessary to reach the ward room, but he was intercepted at the door by the nurse, who had raced around from her station to skid to a halt beside him, a hand on his shoulder.

"Dr Cabot. *His family is with him.* There is nothing that you can do there right now. Let them have this time."

"Crashed? What do you mean—crashed? Give me his chart—dear God, of all the times to take a nap—what happened?"

The chart told him everything, and nothing. The facts and the figures, no more than that. No trace of the little boy with a new soldier on his shelf. The little boy who had been signed out for going home that day...

It was the Spartan that undid him, in the end—the new soldier, freshly painted, lying on the floor just on the edge of the curtain which had been drawn around the bed to give the family privacy in this hour. The new Spartan—the soldier who was to have overseen the going home—lying abandoned where someone had dropped it and then kicked it aside in the chaos of the crash.

Have you seen my Spartan? He's new...

John clutched the chart into his midriff and doubled over it, his breath coming out in a huge sobbing hiccough, his eyes suddenly so full of tears that he could barely see the ward room door in front of him. And then he was led gently away by several pairs of kindly hands, back into the relative seclusion of the on-call room, where he could not seem to stop crying, his shoulders shaking with great heaving sobs, his hands spasming into fists and then into a helpless release over and over and over again.

They made him take a pill, he didn't know what, he couldn't seem to care. After he swallowed it, with a few gulps of water from a plastic cup, they rolled him over onto a bed and he curled up like a child on his side, still crying softly until the moment that the sedative took effect and he drifted off to sleep again.

He was given two weeks' leave, after this, and told that he would not be coming back to the cancer ward when he returned to the hospital. They sent him home, and Olivia tried to nurse him through it, making sure he ate enough to survive even when he had no appetite for food whatsoever, making sure he drank enough to stay hydrated, making sure he took the sedatives that he had been given to help him sleep at night. He did as she said, without complaint, without much communication at all. She might have been just another nurse in the hospital, a new one, a stranger.

His father phoned. He knew this because he could hear Olivia talking with him on the telephone; it was hard to care enough to keep paying attention, but the old man apparently wanted to come out and Olivia was telling him in no uncertain terms that she thought that it was a terrible idea under the circumstances. If they got into the reasons for that, John could not remember the details. He just felt vaguely relieved that he would not have to face his father—he was feeling drifty enough not to really question why, although certain words, like disturbed birds, still kept fluttering in his brain.

Juan. Rosalina. Guatemala.

He felt as though he should discuss these with his father.

It didn't seem to be hugely important, right now.

It could wait. Everything could wait.

Perhaps they thought they were being kind, when they reassigned him, to give him to the Pediatrics ward. When he walked in on the first day that he returned to work, he thought his heart would burst from his chest—but this was not the terminal patients, not the children who would never leave these halls. It was different. It was *different*. And yet it was just sufficiently the same that he found himself picking up familiar patterns.

He was good with children, it turned out. He had never known that.

He also knew, with a vivid certainty, that he never wanted any of his own.

Not after the contents of that box. Not after the children on the cancer ward. He could go on to care for other people's children, to cure them, to make them smile—but he was broken, and he knew he could not give that part of himself that would be essential to making a good father.

Perhaps it was that, finally, that drove Olivia away, a little over a year later. She had stood by him, sturdily, loyally, throughout it all—throughout the multi-layered crisis that had brought him low—but even that kind of loyalty could smash against the walls that he had put up, all unwitting, all unwilling, and did not seem to know how to tear down again. She left him a note, one day, late into his Pediatrics Residency, and she was gone.

It hurt. But not as much as he had thought it would.

He was thirty five years old and a fully-qualified doctor when the names finally came to rest in a safe place in his mind where he could bear to look at them and examine them.

Juan. Rosalina. Guatemala.

William Cabot. Dead from a heart attack himself, these last couple of years. Taking what was left of the secret into the grave with him.

There are children out there. Children like me.

John Cabot was accepted into the Doctors Without Borders program with open arms when he approached them, and for the five or six years that followed he travelled the world with the organization. It was hard picking up the pieces—often literally—in places that had been devastated by the flames of war or ravaged by raging out-of-control epidemics. He learned—or re-learned, if he had known it before in his cradle and had forgotten it—fluent Spanish; he picked up bits and pieces of other exotic languages, including a smattering of Lingala and Swahili from the couple of years he spent in central and eastern parts of Africa, particularly the curse words with which he would excoriate those in charge of providing supplies or protection, if he perceived them to be falling down on the job, to his young charges in the field. He found his way into the orphanages of Romania and China; he held hands and bathed brows in Bangladesh and in the slums of India; he followed behind the line of fire where armed insurrections left death and destruction in their wake, in South-Eastern Asia, in the Middle East, in South America.

He might have been looking for a woman called Rosalina, and finding her everywhere. Or a small boy named Juan, torn from his mother's arms and given back to the man who had bought him, paid for him, owned him. Who had ensured he had everything that a boy could wish for—the toys, the indulgences, the education—everything except the truth, and his own real identity.

William had done all this in order to produce a son who would be an heir apparent for him—John had no doubts that some day William would have taken him aside, talked to him sensibly about having sowed his wild oats, and pointed out that there was a place waiting for him in the "family" firm. If everything had gone according to plan. If he had become a surgeon. If he had never found out the truth. If young Kojak had not died.

But there had been a point at which John knew nothing at all about himself except that he did not want to turn into anything that could be said to resemble his father in any way at all—and that he would have done almost anything to prevent that. Even quit medicine completely, if that had been seen to be required.

But he had worked through that, and had stuck to his guns, and was a pediatrician. A doctor for the children. For the children who suffered.

It was in the dusty remains of what had once been a village, somewhere in Somalia, that John Cabot straightened one hot and miserable morning and looked around, wiping the sweat from his forehead. There had been a new shipment of food and medicine the previous night, and they were all still under the influence of that out in the tent-city pitched in the dust, they had gone to their cots with their bellies full and it had felt like a holiday. It took so little to make them happy.

"It feels almost indecent to be happy that they're happy," he murmured, out loud, talking largely to himself because of those around him at the moment there might have been some who were perfectly capable of understanding the language there would have been very few to whom the sentiment would have been explainable.

"It's always good to be happy when someone else is happy."

He had not expected a response, and turned his head to see who had spoken. He could not put a name to the person who stood in the shadows a few paces away from him, although something about him felt naggingly familiar. Those eyes. He had seen those gray eyes before, somewhere.

"Do I know you?" he asked, tilting his head a little, frowning.

"It'll come to you," the other said. "In this place, right here, right now, I've only just arrived. Ready for a break?"

"Eh?... I—yeah, sure, I can take a break—who are you, exactly, then? Do I need to be somewhere?"

"You need to be where you want to be. Want to talk?"

"About?" John said, perplexed. This strange person seemed to have come from nowhere—the new supplies had arrived the previous night, to be sure, but John had not been aware that any new personnel had done so, particularly of the kind that would find their way straight to himself.

"This," said his companion, with a motion of his hand which encompassed the dust, the pitiless sun, the sharp black shadows. "Your work, Dr. Cabot."

John snorted. "There are days I think they don't need the title around here," he said. "Most of the problems these people have are not medical ones. Or at least they don't start out that way. One does not 'cure' malnutrition—one feeds the patient. If the lives of people are improved before the doctor is called in, then a doctor is often not even necessary. And if they are not improved then the doctor is merely the band aid on an oozing wound—there is little that he can do. Honestly—sometimes, in these godforsaken places where people cling to humanity by a thread, a doctor is merely one step ahead of a clergyman, of whatever faith prevails, who's carrying the local religion's equivalent of the book of last rites." He stared at the gray-eyed man, frowning. "Now why in the name of God do I look at you, here, in this hellhole, and think about an Irish Coffee?"

"Ariel."

"What?"

"The name is Ariel. And yeah, I do know how to make an Irish Coffee."

John shook his head, trying to clear his mind. It had fuzzed over, as though too many memories were trying to crowd in, to step on one another's toes or (if they found themselves able) to annihilate one another... until only one set was left... but in the meantime...

"Olivia," he said slowly. It was a name he had not uttered in a lot of years.

"Yes," Ariel said, nodding. "Amongst others. Are you happy?"

The question was so unexpected, so out of left field, that John stopped to stare again.

"Am I *happy*?" he echoed, baffled. "What's that got to do

with the price of hand grenades in Somalia?"

"It'll come to you," Ariel said again. And then, raking John's expression with shrewd gray eyes, nodded. "It all already is. Give it a moment."

"I'm here," John said, choosing to answer that incongruous question, much to his own astonishment. "I may not be writhing in ecstasy, but I am not discontented. In some way I do manage to make a difference. I've come to terms with the fact that my usefulness—my *medical* usefulness, at least—is of necessity limited. Where people are packed together in swamps or dustbowls, in places where fleas and flies and mosquitoes and cockroaches carry everything from typhoid and cholera to malaria and AIDS and bubonic plague—the doctor can treat the symptoms, lance the boils, hand out the aspirin. He can't—*I* can't—make things well. It's not up to me—my own meager skills are way too insignificant to heal the true patient."

"The true patient?"

"Yes—the poverty, and the hunger, and the want. Those are beyond a mere doctor's power. A doctor cannot cure ignorance or stupidity, or vaccinate against arrogance and greed."

"Poetic," Ariel said. "Is it true?"

"Metaphorically speaking, yes. Every word."

"So do you think you wasted your time?"

"Doing what?"

"All that time, spent studying. All those days of breaking your heart. All those years of slaving in the wards at others' beck and call. To become a doctor, in the end. To be a healer. Was it something that you wanted... or something you did because your father expected it of you?"

"Whatever he expected," John said sharply, "I've gone past that. You ask me if I am happy—I am, about that. I am happy I never turned into that kind of cold monster."

"That's harsh."

"And you know it's true," John said slowly, narrowing his eyes. "Olivia. Ariel. Irish Coffees. At... at... Spanish Gardens." He blinked. "Where did that come from? I haven't thought about that place for years."

He scratched absent-mindedly at a tattoo on his left shoulder, a jaguar head with open snarling jaws. He had got that in a dive in Guatemala, against his own better judgment but as a sort of both gift and promise to himself, on his thirty-eighth birthday—he had reproached himself bitterly in the cold sober light of the following morning, when his shoulder had been sore and red and inflamed, and had made sure that he took a course of antibiotics against possible infection at the site when it looked like the whole thing might go bad, but it had settled down eventually, even though the artist had been less than steady-handed and the jaguar had an odd squint that made what was meant to be the snarl look more like the delicate yawn of a bored house-cat. But it had been a sort of… brand. The place where the names could land. *Juan. Rosalina. Guatemala.* The place where his body touched his lost past.

"Did you ever find her?" Ariel asked softly.

"Find who?"

"Your mother. Your real mother."

"In every woman I looked at in Guatemala," John said evenly, meeting Ariel's eyes.

Ariel nodded. "I see. John… are you starting to remember now?"

"Choose wisely," John said, after a long pause.

Ariel nodded again. "They've both been tough," he said. "These lives."

John shook his head, baffled. "I don't understand," he said. "I remember everything. But I don't understand how it is possible to remember as a true past two entirely different sets of events that have very little in common."

"They have you," Ariel pointed out.

"Seeing as I am the one doing the remembering, yeah, sure, they both have me. That doesn't answer any of the questions. How can I hold two different lifetimes in my head…?"

"You don't. You can't. That's obvious."

John actually glared at Ariel. "You are not making any sense at all."

"Oh, but I am. See, here, this is the only point—*ever*—that you will have this particular problem. It's hard, right now, because yeah, it's damned difficult to be two people at once—and you are, you're looking down two different roads and responding to each of them as a very different person. But the moment you take the first step on either one of those roads—the moment a choice is made—there's only one you,' only one life, only one set of memories. You might remember stray thoughts from the other—life lessons, if you want to think of it that way—but you will never know where they came from, how you came by them. It's a little bit like slamming a door behind you, for good, but you know that you're still able to peer through the keyhole every so often. In everyday circumstances, that feels like instinct, or intuition, or dream. But right now—right *now*—you know it's *all* real, and every tiny piece of knowledge and experience that lies within you...you earned, and you paid for. In real currency."

"Back there—back then—I was a different me," John said slowly. "I was not a doctor. But I was doing much the same sort of work as I do now, really, wasn't I? It was because of *him* that I went into med school. Because of William. Because he wanted me to. Needed me to. And it broke me—it *broke* me—what am I now I couldn't be then. Back then... in that other life... there was no danger, not ever, not once, of turning into William Cabot Junior. But there was no Olivia either, back then, was there...?"

"There is no Olivia here," Ariel pointed out.

"I was broken. She left to find somebody whole, I guess. But not before trying her damndest to put me back together."

"She loved you. You had that. Here, you had that."

"And back there?"

"A crush. An unrequited love. That's all. Is that what you're going to base your decision on—Olivia?"

"Decision?"

"You're making one, right now," Ariel said gently. "*Right* now. Between this life, and the one that's waiting beyond the doorway right there. The choice that will transform that door—either it stays just a hole in the wall through which you can step back and forth but stay in the same reality, or a portal which will take you back—away from this, away from being...how did you put it... the Band Aid with a 'Dr.' in front of your name. Back to the Spanish Gardens. Where she is, incidentally. Only not yours—she was never yours, back there—but she's waiting at the same table at which you too were sitting. And your coffee has just, I believe, arrived."

"My coffee."

"You had," Ariel said helpfully, "just ordered a cup of coffee, back at Spanish Gardens. Not Irish—a plain cup of joe, you called it. Your waitress is being most apologetic about spilling the salad dressing on your shirt. I do believe that the coffee at least might be on the house."

John was shaking his head. "You make no sense whatsoever."

"Except when I make all the sense in the world," Ariel said. "All right, I'll give you that—just go look, take a peek."

"At what?"

"Through the door."

John, one eyebrow lifted into his hairline, stepped up to the doorway of the cottage they were in, and peered outside.

He had expected to find a dusty expanse of ground, a cloud of black flies, the distant sound of women's voices. Instead he caught a glimpse of red plush curtains, smoky lanterns on café tables, and there, in the corner, with her chin cupped in her hands and smiling at something that someone at the table had just said… Olivia.

John's breath caught unexpectedly. He suddenly remembered her—all of her—*two* of her—the one whom he had loved, and the one who had loved him.

In one sense Ariel had been right—it suddenly seemed to be all about Olivia. As if she was the symbol of everything.

She was the price that had been paid for his own shattering.

"Was *she* happier, back there? I can't remember that well…"

"That's because it's none of your business," Ariel said.

"Will she also have this…? This choice? Will she have to live through all of that, with me, all over again?"

"Again, none of your business. But I'll tell you this much— none of you get to pick which of the alternate lives gets laid out for you to live. If and when she gets her turn, she might live something else again, something completely different. Something without you in it at all. *She* was in *your* life, this time. Not vice versa. But it is not your job to make anyone else happy. Just yourself."

"Who are you?" John said, turning his head back to stare at Ariel.

"I? I am just the messenger. Or the conductor, if you like. Come for your tickets. So, which train will it be for?"

John turned to stare back into the other place, the place with music and laughter and civilization... and the presence of the woman whom some part of him still loved. It seemed to become more solid with every fraction of a second his eyes were upon it.

He felt the hand between his shoulder blades, a light touch, hardly a push at all—but he took a step forward. And another.

"You've done what you can do here," Ariel said, his voice glowing with compassion, with pity, with pride. "Go. Take it back. It's yours."

Another step and the harsh Somali sun winked out as though it had never been.

John found himself stepping out of a restroom which bore an OUT OF ORDER sign on the door, brushing down the wet patch on his shirt where he had just cleaned off the spilled salad dressing. He had a cell phone in his hand. He knew that he had just taken a photograph of a jaguar tattoo on his shoulder, to show someone back at the table.

He could not, for the life of him, remember why.

INTERMEZZO 3

Thursday, 20 December 2012

"Did you manage to get that stuff off the shirt?" Ellen asked, as John slipped back into his seat at the table. "Your young klutz came crawling back to apologize, brought your coffee, told us to tell you that it was on the house and to holler if you needed it warmed up…"

"Most of it came off, there's probably going to be traces—if the world doesn't end tomorrow the shirt is going into the laundry and if it does, well, I'm going out with dressing on top," John said. "It could be worse. Here, who wanted to see the wretched tattoo?"

Olivia snaked out a hand and grabbed the cell phone.

"Very macho," she said, grinning.

Ellen snatched the phone away and she and Quincey leaned in over it together.

"Wow," Quincey said, "that was quite an act of rebellion for a teenager. Most people go for something trite and unoriginal."

"A friend of mine had '© 1964' tattooed on the side of her foot," Ellen said, smiling. "She had *that* done when she was fourteen, in secret, in the fall, and it promptly vanished into socks and boots for months—and her mother never even saw it. It lurked away in its wraps for the next five months or so, and by the time summer rolled around again and she slipped into sandals and flip-flops, barefoot, she'd practically forgotten it was there…but even though it was so tiny and so discreet and so out of the way her parents pitched a fit when they found out. I can imagine what your father said about that cat head."

John shrugged, and then allowed himself a wolfish grin. "You had to be there."

"Does Abby have any tattoos?" Quincey asked with an innocent expression.

"I keep an eye on the Teen Skin Real Estate, as much as I can," Ellen said. "Not as far as I know."

"And you wouldn't pitch a fit," Simon said, grinning. "Oh no, not you."

"Would it matter as much if *Josh* did it?" Quincey said.

"Are we going to be sexist about it?" Olivia asked. "What a boy does is all right so long as a girl doesn't do it? Rebellion can't wear a skirt?"

"I wasn't advocating that," Quincey said. "In fact, quite the opposite."

"I... hate that it matters, but it kind of matters," Ellen mumbled. "Right or wrong, I tend to think of tattoos as 'tough', and I don't want my little girl to be classified as 'tough' by someone else who might share that mindset. She might get treated more roughly than she can handle, if she presents a tattooed shoulder to some guy somewhere. I don't care if it's all hearts and roses, it's still a statement—*I'm tough I can take it*—that I don't want her making. Josh..."

"Ellen, Josh is more of a lady than Abby is," Simon said. "If anyone would be sending fake messages with tattoos, it's your son."

Quincey laughed. "What will you give me never to tell Josh you said that about him in public?"

"Still," Ellen said, sticking to her premise, apologetic but stubborn. "It's the way I was brought up. I'm still wearing the skin my parents and my grandparents wrapped around me."

"No tattoos?" Quincey said, trying to keep her face straight.

Ellen batted at her shoulder, like a cat. "No, no tattoos! I suppose I could always shed that outer skin, now that I'm an adult and am not responsible to them for my actions and opinions, but I suspect it's grown on by now, and it would *hurt*."

"Hmm," said Olivia, leaning her elbow on the table and cupping her chin in her hand. "I keep on hearing that we're past that—the gender gap—that girls can do anything a boy can do, dammit—and yet here it all is, tripping us all up right here, right now, on the eve of the end of the *world*—there are things we carry with us as a species, it seems, even as we are about to fade away into the final darkness. Boys are better."

"I didn't say *better*," Ellen said defensively. "I said tougher."

"What would you have done differently with your life if you had been born a boy instead of an Ellen?" Olivia asked, turning to her. "Other than not marrying Simon?"

Ellen grimaced. "I was *supposed* to be a boy," she said. "First grandchild, on both sides of the family. My parents were... problematic. My father was Jewish; he was not very devout, being more of a secular and cultural Jew than a strict synagogue-going one, but his family was kosher. It was bad enough that he chose to marry my mother, who was a lapsed Catholic of Irish descent..."

"About as far away from being a nice Jewish girl as it is possible for a bride to be," Quincey murmured.

"Exactly," Ellen said. "It took a while for the families to come to terms with that, and with the knowledge that there would have to be an active competition for the soul of the first grandchild when it came. They were already, according to my mother, drawing up the battle lines for that before she even got pregnant—and my word, the war hotted up considerably when she first announced that I was on the way, still barely a handful of potential in her womb."

"I met her father's mother," Simon said. "After Ellen and I were married. Believe all this—the old lady was a grand old battleaxe. I was given to understand in no uncertain terms that it was my fault that Ellen had slipped even further from the Jewish fold. The very least that she could have done, after having had the misfortune to have been born to a shiksa, was to find a nice Jewish boy to marry and so bring the next generation, at least, back where they properly belonged."

"Even the name," Ellen said. "Oh, it's funny in retrospect, all these years later, but my name itself is a fluke. My mother wanted to name me after her own father if I had been the son everyone was expecting—he had died not long before, and she was still mourning him, and she wanted to make this gesture— but this was something that my father's family was up in arms about, because it was such a weird wussy name for a boy..."

"What?" Olivia asked, diverted.

"Allen. A-L-L-E-N. That's how I ended up with *Ellen*—because my father wasn't there at the birth, and my mother was half out of her mind with the pain, and when they finally announced that the baby was born they either failed to mention that it was a girl or she failed to hear it. When they asked her if she had a name, she said Allen—and because it was obvious to everyone else that the child was, in fact, a girl, they simply assumed she meant Ellen and that was written down...and then it stuck."

"It could have been worse," Quincey said.

"Uh, yeah," Simon said.

"Oh?" Quincey said, sitting up. "I was being rhetorical. What?"

"If I had been a boy...the paternal side of the family wanted me named after the great-grandfather, who had passed away some five years before," Ellen said.

Quincey motioned with her hand for Ellen to continue. "And that name would have been...?"

Ellen exchanged a long-suffering glance with Simon. "Isaiah," she said. "Like the prophet. I would have been straight out of the old testament."

"I still think your mother would have at least managed a middle name which would have stood up to the wear and tear of a modern playground," Simon said, grinning.

"Yes, and that would have meant a lifetime of cold-war relations, with the grandparents never invited when any of my friends were around—because they would have insisted on the full fig. And besides, I would have probably been pressured far more to conform to the cultural paradigm."

"Bar mitzvah and stuff?"

"Something of the sort. I kind of cleared the way, though, and by the time my brother arrived, the real grandson, the grandparents had run out of steam somewhat and they were able to name the poor boy Daniel—which was Hebrew enough to placate my father's parents and certainly gentile enough to work out in the secular world. And also happened to be a name of a deceased male relative on my father's side. So it was all good."

"Yes, but was it?" John said. "You were still the first

grandchild. Even if you were a girl. Did they expect you to shoulder a grandson's responsibilities despite the disadvantages of your gender or was all of that shifted onto Daniel and you were expected to do the best you could, under the circumstances...?"

"Like marry well and produce the next generation?" Olivia asked. "I mean, I also met your grandparents on your Jewish side. I didn't spend long enough in their company to pretend to know them very well, but now that we're on the subject—what *did* your grandma think of your idea to go into science?"

"I told her that I wanted to become a pharmacist, eventually, and that was almost all right," Ellen said. "If my life *had* to include a career, then a healing-related one was something she could see a woman pursuing. Although she disapproved, all of her life, of women doctors. I remember her reading a newspaper article once, about some surgical feat that had just been performed by a female surgeon, and she kept on snorting that the woman should have left it to the professionals. I told my grandmother once that a friend of mine—a *girl*—said that she wanted to be an astronaut when she grew up, and my grandmother looked at me as though *I* had suddenly turned into an alien life form for even uttering such strange words. In her world, the female of the species stuck to her own mudball and had no business off playing amongst the stars."

"Your grandmother never believed in the moon landing, either," Simon said. "That isn't sexist, that's just generational. For those of her age and era, the moon might as well have been made of green cheese. The concept of alien worlds was... just that. Alien."

"Sir? Do you need your coffee warmed up?"

The young waitress was back, hovering just out of range of flailing elbows, a pot of coffee in her hand. John reflexively glanced into his cup, looked faintly astonished to find it empty, and held it out for a refill.

"I do want to apologize again, sir," the girl said, pouring the coffee and keeping her eyes downcast.

"Don't worry about it, it's a zoo in here tonight and accidents happen," John said.

"Thank you," she said, a quick smile of relief lighting up

her features, and vanished again, back into the clamor of the crowded café.

"I never really thought about it," Olivia mused, "but there were four of us kids and I'm the youngest and I'm the only girl. I always assumed that much of the leeway that I was given was due to the older three having thrashed out a trail through the wilderness before I got to walk in their footsteps—that the parents were kind of tired of reinventing the wheel so I was more or less indulged in whatever I wanted to do—but now I wonder how much of that was really due to my being the girl-child, and petted, and pampered, and spoiled. Right until the moment I blew it all up and quit talking to any of them, when David decided to go and play the conquering hero in the Gulf, and my mother blamed my father, and I blamed them both..."

She stopped speaking, glancing over at Simon, who had thinned his lips a little and was staring down at the remnants of food on his plate. This was the thing that had shattered the two of them, so long before—the book that he had written after Olivia had showed him David's letters from the war, the way he had used those letters as inspiration when all she had wanted from him had been someone to confide in and talk to about something that she could no longer talk about with her family.

Quincey glanced from one to the other, and stepped into the breach.

"I don't know how much leeway spoiling gets you," she said. "My brother was the one who was indulged, in my family—and it didn't do him a bit of good. He grew up snotty and entitled, and he's never managed to shake that."

"I suppose we were all spoiled brats, in our own ways," Ellen said.

"I was not spoiled," John said. "I was *groomed*. Right until that all fell apart, when I found out who I really was, where I really came from. I suppose, in comparison to *that*, I was utterly spoiled—but not in the sense that you mean, Ellen."

"You were not spoiled so much as the spoils," Quincey murmured.

John shot her a startled look. "Something like that."

"I wonder how different I would have been—my family

would have been—my entire life would have been—if I had been the fourth boy," Olivia said. "Or if it would have made it worse, to be the only male in the family who did not *understand*."

Simon risked a sidelong glance. "They told you that you didn't understand?"

"My father did," Olivia said, her voice inflectionless, not looking up at Simon. "The last time we spoke face-to-face he flew into a towering rage over my 'disparaging' David and the things he had done, and he believed in. We talked once more, after that, on the phone, and I got handed that 'you will never understand' line."

"Your father was a vet," Simon said gently. "His son going into the Army was the greatest compliment that he could have given his old man. There is a lot of that."

"So a son's greatest gift to his father is to become him?" Olivia said, her fingers tapping on the table.

"Hell, no," John said. "Sometimes it's just the opposite."

His voice had been flat, expressionless; Olivia glanced over at him, and met dark eyes that were glittering obsidian. She gave him a small wan smile.

"I can understand that," she said softly.

"I can't make up my mind whether my father is proud of the things I have accomplished or is vaguely embarrassed that I'm accomplishing the wrong things," Ellen said. "There are times when just a little bit of clarity would make the world of difference."

"Actually I think there is quite a bit of clarity there," Simon said. "When your father is acting under his own impulses, he's the kindest and sweetest man in the world, and the buttons are coming off his vest when he looks at you—at you *and* your brother—he's proud of you both. But let him anywhere near his extended family, who remind him of his own inadequacies such as they perceive them to be, and he becomes a different person altogether, demanding and supercilious and dismissive of anything that he thinks won't cut the mustard with the family."

"How long have you two been married, again?" Quincey said, looking from Simon to Ellen and then back again. "That's kind of profound, for an insight about a family which is not yours by blood."

"Sometimes," Simon said, "it takes an outsider, looking in." He turned to Olivia, catching her eye and then holding her gaze. "It's like, with you—with your family—David was my friend, too, as well as your brother, and I knew him and the family he came from pretty well. But obviously there were things to which I was as blind to as I could have possibly been—Olivia, I'm truly sorry. The way you reacted to that book blindsided me completely. I thought I understood—but really, I never really gave that much thought to how you'd take it, how the family would take it..."

There was an awkward silence for a moment—Ellen was staring at her husband, trying to figure out if this had been the plan all along, that the reason that he had had the idea of bringing them all back together in this place was because he had unfinished business with Olivia which he could not square away in any other way. She wondered if he had tried—if there had been attempts to find Olivia, to contact her, to have a sort of on-going relationship with her in whatever way seemed to be possible, attempts of which she had known nothing, turned inward, bringing up two children one of whom had been conceived in the immediate aftermath of Simon's breakup with Olivia. Abby's identity, her very existence, suddenly seemed fraught with a significance that Ellen had never realized was there.

Abby was the reason Ellen was here. Abby was the reason she was married to Simon. Abby and Josh were the reason that she had made up the stories that she had told the two children when they had been very young, the stories that had got published, had got Ellen a name, a reputation, a career. A career which had been constantly and consistently—and perhaps inadvertently, because of all this other baggage—been both dismissed and resented, in equal parts, by Simon.

Olivia finally broke the stasis, lifting her shoulders in a small helpless shrug, "Hell," she said, "*I* didn't know, until it hit me. Maybe I over-reacted. I don't know. Way too late now. It seems so long ago, so far away, like it happened to someone else—and yet, if I had never shown you those letters, if you'd never used them in the book, I might have had a very different life..." She shivered, as though she were suddenly cold, and wrapped her arms around her own shoulders. "Maybe I should have been born that fourth boy. Maybe I would have been the youngest son, eager to follow in everyone else's footsteps. Maybe I would have been the one to leave everything behind, go racing off to war, and never come home."

Quincey turned sharply to stare at her. "Your brother was *killed*? I never knew that...I'm so sorry..."

"Worse," Olivia said. "He disappeared. He is just... gone. He vanished. One of his unit did get killed in action, but David... we don't have a body. We don't have a story. All we have is an unquiet ghost who will not leave the family in peace. He brought his wars home to us, he brought them to sit at our table, to live under our roof, and they drove all the rest of us out, scattered us to the four winds..." She paused, her throat suddenly tight at the memories of wrecked relationships, broken lives, silences which began as pauses in conversation in order to catch one's breath and then lengthened, into days, or months, or years. "We lost it all when we lost David," she said at last, fighting to find the words. "We might have been able to piece it back together if we could have buried him. But we will never bury him. In the worst possible way, for this family, he will never die... and you, Simon, you and that book, perhaps I knew when I first laid eyes on what you wrote, but that book makes us all remember, everything, constantly, all the time..."

Ellen suddenly stirred, shoving at Quincey to move. "Excuse me," she said. "I think I need some air."

Simon turned quickly, reaching out for her arm, but she shook him off and Quincey, after a momentary hesitation, slipped out of the booth so that Ellen could edge out from behind the table. Ellen paused briefly at the archway, holding onto it with one hand in a manner that suggested at once that she was barely touching the wall and that she was using it to help her stay upright, and glanced back at where Simon sat frozen in his seat, staring at her with haunted eyes.

"It's all right, really," she said. "Give me a couple of minutes."

She didn't know why she obeyed the impulse to do so, but she felt hot and flushed and almost feverish and it might have been the idea of cooling herself down which had appealed—but somehow she found herself pushing open the glass door with the faded gilt lettering and stepping outside into the deserted courtyard where snow drifts were beginning to pile up in the corners and large white flakes were still drifting down from the distant black sky. It took only a moment for her to start shivering, the snowflakes falling onto her hair and trembling for an instant before they melted away and then, as they cooled down the surface on which they landed, not melting at all but starting to stay, a scattering of white on her head and shoulders, glittering in yellow light of the naked light bulb hanging at the mouth of the alley.

The weight of a coat falling on her shoulders startled her, and she turned her head to look at the person who had laid it there, meeting a pair of compassionate gray eyes.

"You'll catch your death out here," Ariel said softly.

"I didn't know," Ellen said. She stared at Ariel as though she was looking straight through him, into the snowfall, into the dark.

"You didn't know what?" Ariel asked, standing beside her, close enough to share a little bit of body heat in the night, not so close as to be thought threatening—although it was doubtful if Ellen would have registered it at that moment even if he had.

"He's always been in love with Olivia," Ellen said. "He still is."

"He married you, twenty one years ago. Not Olivia."

"Only because he could no longer have her, and I was carrying Abby," Ellen said bitterly.

"You don't know that, either," Ariel said. "You are not a mind reader, or a heart reader. And even if something along those lines had been true back then it's had twenty years to solidify into something else. What, you don't believe your husband loves you, or your children?"

Ellen focused on him, properly, for the first time. "Who are you?" she asked.

"No one," Ariel said. "It is not given to me to know, either. Not all of it. Not at once."

Ellen gave him a long, considering look, and then appeared

to dismiss him, or his identity, from her mind. It did not matter who he was. Not right then. "They're all in love with Olivia," Ellen said, dropping her eyes at last to the snow at her feet. "It's true, it's always been true, she had something… something… I don't know. She had the gift of it, all she had to do was look at a guy and she'd have flowers thrown at her by the bouquet and mantles flung at her feet so that her shoes wouldn't get muddy if she stepped into puddles. She's… a chivalry magnet… and I never was. I had to work for every kind word I ever got from a man. It isn't fair."

Ariel's eyebrow lifted. "Really?" he questioned. "It isn't fair that here you are married with two lovely children and she is alone? At the end of it all—or so some would believe at least— she is alone?"

Ellen shivered. "That's not… what I meant…"

"What did you mean, then?"

"Choice," Ellen whispered. "She always had a choice."

"So did you. You still do."

"I'm cold…"

"Good," Ariel said, "that means you're back to being rational. Come on back inside. You really *will* catch your death out here if you don't."

Ellen allowed herself to be guided back into the café, which suddenly seemed almost unbearably warm when she stepped inside—but Ariel was already slipping the borrowed coat from her shoulders.

"Here," he said, thrusting a piece of folded paper into her hand.

"What is this?" Ellen asked, lifting it up to stare at it.

"Choice," Ariel said gently. "Go on, splash some warm water on your face, warm your hands. The restroom on the left is occupied, but the plumbing works well enough in the other even if it does say that it's out of order. Go on. It'll be all right."

Not quite knowing why, Ellen found herself obeying this exhortation, and drifting toward the restroom with the 'Out of Order' sign, reaching for the doorknob on which the sign had been hung.

"Hey," Ariel said, and somehow his soft voice carried

through the hubbub of the throng inside the café.

Ellen turned.

Ariel nodded at the piece of paper in her hand. "Read that first," he said.

"What?"

"Don't look at me," he said equably. "It's the rules. Go on, then. You'll be fine."

Ellen unfolded the paper with her fingers even as she dropped her eyes down to it, pushing the door open with her other hand. She skimmed the message on the paper, eyes darting over the words, barely landing on them; the door opened, she stepped inside, and an insistent whisper surrounded her in the darkness.

Choose wisely.

ELLEN

SUMMER 2004

The auditorium was finally empty—Allen had shaken the last professorial hand, accepted the last awed accolade from an earnest post-grad, smiled and nodded as the final few members of the audience trickled out of the doors at the top. He sighed, the smile drifting away from his face as he ran his hand through his prematurely (and unfairly, he thought) thinning hair, and glanced down at his scattered notes on the desk at the bottom of the curved ranks of benches rising up to the exit doors at the top of the amphitheatre. He had always been a neat man, and the papers, although loose in a folder rather than bound in a file, lay in an orderly pile as he picked them up to tap the bottom edge on the desktop and square them properly away to be replaced in the folder.

The carousel with the slides from the talk he had just given was still in the projector, on a raised platform halfway up the slope of the auditorium. Even as Allen lifted his head, preparing to climb the stairs up to the middle row to retrieve his slides, a voice from what he had thought was an empty hall startled him considerably.

"Do you need any help with those slides?"

Allen peered up into the benches, shading his eyes against the light which glared into his eyes from the top of the hall. "Who's there?"

"A friend," said the voice. A hand lifted from somewhere in the midst of the auditorium, close to the projector platform. "Over here."

"I thought everyone had gone," Allen said, rather stiffly, feeling a strange need to explain his startled reaction.

"Everyone has," the voice said in a tone of mild agreement.

"Where there's an audience of one…" Allen said

"Oh, I may be *one*, but I'm not everyone," the voice said. "I'm Ariel."

"Well, Ariel—are you a student? I think I've got it covered, thank you. Thanks for the offer..."

Bur even as he spoke, the projector whirred into life, and threw an image onto the screen which was still down in the front of the auditorium.

Allen clicked his tongue against the roof of his mouth in annoyance, and started up the stairs. "No, please leave that alone—I need to get them organized in the order in which they…"

He made the mistake of glancing back at the screen, and stopped abruptly, turning fully to blink at the image he saw there—a boy, maybe eight or nine years old, staring with an expression that was equal parts awe and covetousness at a glassed-in shelf containing a row of what looked like ancient volumes with fragile bindings.

"Wait. What…?"

"Oh, things slip in sometimes," Ariel said, from somewhere in an auditorium whose lights had suddenly and inexplicably dimmed into flickering shadows as the projector had sputtered into life. "Remember that…?"

Allen Brosch started out being a little bit afraid of his paternal grandfather—he was an irascible old man who didn't, on the face of it, like children very much at all—but Allen was the first grandchild with whom he had been presented, a boy to carry on the family name. Avram Brosch knew his responsibilities, given these facts. He had simply demanded the child's presence in his study, for at least a couple of hours a week, from the moment that Allen had been old enough to carry on a semi-coherent conversation. What the two of them did together in that study, sequestered away from everybody else, rapidly evolved into their shared secret, one which they both took care to keep—but the child certainly seemed to come to no harm there, and his parents raised no concerns so long as everyone was content with the arrangement.

But that didn't mean that Allen's mother, Serena, didn't have concerns. She had not raised any objections to these closed sessions at the time—but she had apparently had to bite her tongue to keep silent. On one occasion, aged six, Allen had paused at his parents' bedroom door, which had been ajar, and caught a little bit of what gave every impression of being an ongoing conversation.

"What could the old man possibly want with him?" Serena had demanded of her husband. Allen could see her through the crack in the door, standing at the foot of the bed, brushing her loose waist-length hair with long, angry strokes. "Allen is six years old, for Heaven's sake. That hidebound old library in your father's study hardly contains picture books, and I don't know that I want him exposed to some of the stuff that might be in there, not this young..."

"This is his grandson," Aaron Brosch said. "My father would hardly mean harm to him."

"Your father hasn't had a child in his care for fifty years," Serena retorted. "And some of the things considered acceptable in his day would very much be considered harmful today."

There was a hesitation—Allen could not see his father from where he stood—and then Aaron's voice came from somewhere behind the half-open door. "If I see anything untoward developing, I'll put a stop to it," he said. "I promise. But for now—he's Allen's grandfather. He has the right to form the kind of relationship that he feels is appropriate. Let's give him a chance."

That had not been the end of it, not by a long way. Serena was not about to give up easily. She had tried to wheedle the details of the visits from Allen, but he remained close-mouthed about it, particularly after having overheard that conversation between his parents; he had begun to harbor an irrational fear that if he said anything at all about his visits with his grandfather, his mother would find a way to stop them. But it was this very secretiveness that triggered Serena's anxieties, and she had even gone so far as to demand if his grandfather had made him promise to keep quiet because something bad was happening to him. But Allen had simply shook his head, and kept his secrets.

There was a reason for that.

If someone had asked of the young Allen what his idea of heaven was, he would have been inarticulate on the subject—but the truth was that in that book-lined study, and in his grandfather's stern and dignified presence, he had found the closest thing to heaven he knew. He was barely seven years old when he fell in love for the first time in his life—fell hard, and gave his heart completely. He fell in love with history, and with books.

Avram Brosch collected primarily Judaica, books about Jewish history and culture, but he had not confined himself to that topic alone. His library contained volumes on medieval battles, with ringing names that the young Allen loved the sound of when his grandfather would read him a passage or two aloud during their hours in the library, and books about the lore and mythology of peoples from parts of the Earth that Allen had not even known existed. There were books of poetry—something Allen had still to grow into an appreciation of—and biographies of long-dead philosophers and writers and scientists who came to life for Allen through his grandfather's books.

And there was a special shelf, kept locked, behind glass. The oldest and the most special of Avram's collection.

Allen had asked about them.

"When you are older," Avram had said solemnly. "You need to have the proper respect before you are allowed to touch those books. Some of them are very old, and very fragile."

"Tell me about them," Allen demanded.

"In good time," Avram said. "I have a new history for you today, and it's an illustrated one. Come, have a look at these plates..."

Allen's tenth birthday present from his grandfather was nothing tangible, nothing that he could hold in his hands and unwrap. It was far more precious than that. It was the day on which the key had come out for the glass-fronted cabinet, and the first of the special books had been pulled out and put into his hands with an admonition to be careful in how he dealt with it. Avram carefully turned the fragile pages to the front of the book and pointed at the year of publication.

"1798," he said. "It's a first edition—that means this is a copy of the original first printing of the 'Lyrical Ballads' This book you are holding is one hundred and eighty five years old."

"Wow," Allen breathed, deeply impressed.

"You've seen some Coleridge before," Avram said. "But this is the first time that one of his most famous poems was published. The first time the world ever saw it."

Allen could barely get his head around the book's age—it looked almost new in his hands, beautifully preserved, bound in red leather with gold lettering on the front and the spine, its pages edged in gilt so that they shimmered under the library's lights as though they were dusted with magic.

"Wow," Allen said again. "How did you find it?"

"I search for these things," Avram said. "Or, more to the point, I have a man who deals in rare books do so for me. Some of them are very valuable, indeed. That one is—it's a first edition with very little wear and tear, and I was extremely lucky to get it."

"Can I find books like these?" Allen said, looking up.

"If you mean own them, you'll have to wait until you have the means to get them—and that'll be a few years yet. But all of these—all these treasures in here—they will be yours some day, when I am gone. That, I have already arranged. That book that you are holding, that is yours—it is on loan to me, if you like, while I am still here with you and in this library. We will share it for now. We can read it together."

Allen became aware that he had frozen on the stairs of the auditorium, his head turned so that he could stare at the screen. He sighed, allowed his stiff shoulders to relax a little, turned his head away.

"That," he said, firmly but quietly, "does not exist. That picture. There was nobody there except the two of us. There was nobody to take it."

"All pictures exist," Ariel said.

Allen lifted his eyes to the shadowy form in the audience, and, aware of the look, Ariel lifted his hand to tap first his chest over his heart and then his temple. "Here, and here. All pictures exist there. Although I'll allow you that we aren't on the same carousel of slides that you put into that machine with your own hand when you prepared for the lecture."

"What have you done with my slides?" demanded Allen. "Seriously—leave that thing alone, it's a professional presentation... you're tampering with my... should I be calling Campus Security here?"

"Oh, the slides are perfectly safe, they are all right here, you'll get them back," Ariel said. "For now, I'm using them as a foundation to project... some other things. There is something interesting going on here, and it needs both of us to figure it out."

"What are you talking about?"

"In good time," Ariel said. "Look at the screen."

The image on the screen had changed, tight-focused now on the inconsolable face of a teen-aged boy whose eyes, behind a pair of smeared spectacles, looked hot and dry, as though they had been drained of tears.

"That was after his funeral," Allen said slowly, subsiding into an aisle seat in the auditorium, suddenly struck to the heart with the memory of the scene behind the image he was staring at. "I was fifteen years old. And I thought the world had ended."

"A certain world did," Ariel murmured. "What happened?"

"His will left all the books to me, as he said he would," Allen said. "But he had not taken a great many things into consideration. One important one was that he had left relatively little by way of a legacy for his widow to continue to survive on. The house was too big and too expensive to keep up, and once the decision was made that Grandmother would move, there was a question of what to do with the contents of the big old place when she moved into the smaller new one. There was certainly no room for a library there, no room for special books."

"So what did they do with them?"

"My father talked to me," Allen said. "I was made to understand that storing all these things somewhere would be far too expensive, particularly if they were to be stored in a special way, as some would have to be, in order to survive. The books were mine—and I knew many of them well, from those hours in the library with my grandfather—and I loved them all… but I was told that I had to be practical. I could keep, if I insisted, a handful of the most special. The rest… arrangements would have to be made for the rest. It was the first time I really knew what betrayal tasted like…"

Ariel leaned forward a little. "I'm sorry," he said, and his voice was totally sincere. And then, apparently because he couldn't help himself, added, "What *does* it taste like?"

"Dry, and bitter," Allen said. "I'd come across the phrase 'bitter as aloes' in those self-same books whose fate was being discussed—but I had never known what that meant, not viscerally. Not until the moment that I had to give the books up."

"What happened to them?"

Allen tossed his head, defiance that was still there so many years after the events of which he was speaking. "I refused to sell them," he said. "Absolutely refused. That's what everyone wanted because there were some valuable books in that collection, and they would have brought a good sum of money if they had been sold at market value. But they were…they were…my grandfather's spirit, his soul. I could not sell that. Not for any money. So I told them to give them to the University Library. As a collection."

"And did they?"

"They still managed to sell them," Allen said. "They did give them to the library, and I was there to witness the handover—but I only learned much later, when I was about to start college, that my choice of which college to attend was kind of limited to one—the one with the collection—because the price of that collection had been a scholarship for me, full tuition, and my parents had accepted that on my behalf without mentioning that to me at the time."

"So did you take it?"

"They wanted me to study something practical," Allen said. "Like law, or science. But I insisted on doing what my family considered a completely useless degree—my majors were history and philosophy. And then, when I graduated, I apprenticed myself for a year to a bookbinder…"

"That one?"

The picture on the screen had changed again, showing a round-faced man with prominent ears sticking out from the sides of a largely bald pate ringed by a thin ring of hair, as though he was sporting a medieval monk's tonsure.

"Mr. Wentworth," Allen said, sitting back with a small smile. "I haven't thought about him for years. I wonder if he's still alive."

"No," said Ariel regretfully.

Allen turned to stare back into the shadows, frowning again. "Who *are* you?" he murmured.

"In a minute," Ariel said. "And after you and Mr. Wentworth parted ways?"

Several pictures came and went in quick succession. Allen as a young man bent over the broken spine of an old book, his hands gentle and soft upon it as though his touch alone could heal it. Allen as a slightly older man, sitting at a desk overflowing with papers in a small room whose every available surface was stacked with books—on shelves against every available wall, in boxes on the floor, in teetering piles leaning against the side of the desk; Allen at an old-fashioned computer, the bulky monitor taking up most of his desk space, peering at the small screen with green lettering on black background.

"I made them my life," Allen said. "They took the legacy from me, but I rebuilt it—and then I reached out to other people. That man my grandfather once spoke of, the man who searched for and found rare books for him... I didn't quite set out to become that man, but that's exactly who I turned into. I remember that room, it was just a small bedroom in the townhouse I lived in—I ran the business from there, for years. I travelled..."

The picture changed again. Allen wrapped in a winter coat and carrying a black bag rather like the one old-time doctors used to carry, on a snowy street with baroque European architecture all around him; Allen in more casual wear, a leather satchel over his shoulder, standing on a piazza in what might have been Florence or Venice; Allen poring over old books with an old woman standing with folded hands and an expression of both regret and raw need written upon her face; Allen in the chaotic remains of a library damaged by the elements, holding a fragile-looking book as though it could disintegrate in his hands at any moment.

Alone—except for such company as that old woman, if she could be called company, always alone.

And then the screen threw up something unexpected. A smiling young woman with red hair falling around her face in wide, smooth waves, her eyes big and gray, a few stray freckles scattered across the bridge of her nose as if her Creator had started to set them there and then got distracted by something more important and forgot to finish the job.

"Lila," Allen said, with a slight catch in his voice. "Lila Rabinovich."

The party had barely begun—Allen was, as he always obsessively was, early, which meant that he was one of only a smattering of other guests, rattling around in the great open-plan living area of his friend Olivia's house, cleared for the party. Olivia herself, who was lending her house to a friend for a surprise party on the occasion of her friend Marjorie's's husband's forty-sixth birthday, was busy with last-minute stuff in the kitchen, talking animatedly with someone who seemed to have brought ice—although Allen, trying not to eavesdrop, was not certain if it was too little ice or too much. He lingered at a table set up for snacks, practically covered with a scarlet paper party tablecloth, but there was as yet little on it except a large bowl of salsa dip and a couple of other bowls overflowing with corn chips. Allen, a beer in one hand, dipped a succession of triangular chips into the dip and lifted them with careful fastidious motions to his lips, glancing around at others who had, like him, arrived in effect too early for the party.

There was a girl sitting by herself in an armchair by the window, nursing a half-full glass of wine. Her dark-red hair was pulled back into a chignon which was too severe for her features, throwing into prominence a strong face with a firm jaw and a nose which made for a striking, if not wholly fashionable, profile. She was gathered into a private space, self-contained like a cat, knees together and feet neatly arranged below, her shoulders rounded as though she were trying to convey an attitude of protective armor, head bent a little and looking down into her lap.

As though aware of his scrutiny, she looked up, met his eyes for a moment, looked away again.

Her entire attitude demanded that she be left alone, solitary, undisturbed… and yet there was something else there, something just underneath that thin veneer, that Allen thought he could glimpse the barest shadow of—a deeper vulnerability, perhaps, a sense that her isolation was worn as a mantle of protection rather than being a part of her true self. A sense of wearing tragedy like a cloak, trying to hide underneath its folds, shying away from the presence of any other soul.

He was here on his own; so, apparently, was she—or at least no companion approached her for the short while that Allen watched her. Other people began drifting in, in pairs, in groups, and the room began to fill; bodies began to block his view of the girl in the chair, and he found himself craning his neck this way and that to keep her in sight, unable to take his eyes from her.

Olivia skipped past him on her way to some urgent errand, and smiled impishly at him.

""Hey," he said, reaching out to grab her arm before she had a chance to quite disappear again, "that girl. Over there. Who is she?"

"Oh, Lila," Olivia said. "Go talk to her, if you want, only don't frighten her off again. She's crawled out into the world for the first time tonight after nursing a deeply broken heart—it took me and Marj two weeks of wheedling to even get her to come. So tread gently. But go on, go talk to her. You guys, actually, should get on great."

"Great, assuming she doesn't look at me and shriek, oh, a man, and run for her life?" Allen asked grumpily. "Was this party a set-up, Olivia?"

"Whatever are you talking about?" Olivia asked, her eyes wide and innocent. "It's Marj's husband's birthday party…"

He growled at her, and she laughed, and was gone.

So, when he looked back to the armchair by the window, was Lila.

His eyes darted around the room, sliding off strangers whom he did not know, until he found her again, standing by the glass doors which opened out into the garden—closed, now, because it was cool and drizzling and rapidly getting dark outside. She was wearing a dark cotton sweater over a long skirt that fell to mid-calf—the outfit effectively hid her shape but accentuated her form, tall and lanky, the legs hidden by the skirt promising long-boned elegance, the neck graceful and pale and swan-like rising from the collar of her sweater. The shoulders were still hunched over, though, and a lot of the height sank into that, as though she were trying to make herself as unobtrusive as possible. It was as though there were a red neon sign above her head, flashing DO NOT TOUCH.

The crowd thickened for an instant, and he lost her again, only to find that she had taken a seat once more—her original armchair had been co-opted so she had reluctantly gathered herself into a corner of an overstuffed couch and sat staring out into the chattering throng as though it was the people in that room who had trapped her in that spot.

Allen made his way over with cool deliberation, and caught her eye again when she looked up with a certain degree of consternation as he stopped a few paces away from her and stood there smiling gently.

"Hi," she said after a beat. "Who are you here with?"

It was an odd question, but now that Olivia had given him a heads-up he could understand where it came from.

"Nobody," he said. He indicated the empty seat next to her. "Anybody sitting there?"

She shook her head, very slightly, and he subsided onto the couch beside her. Neither of them could remember, after, who had started talking or about what, but after a while—after what seemed to be a long while, judging by the state of the party around them—they both became aware that they had been monopolizing each other in conversation to the exclusion of everyone else.

"I think I need a refill," Allen said, hefting his empty bottle of beer. "Can I get you anything?"

She shook her head. "No. Thank you. I'm fine."

By the time he came back a couple of people seemed to have taken up the rest of the couch beside Lila; he caught her eye and read there a frustration equal to his own. One of the people got up to leave at more or less that instant, but it was not the one sitting directly beside Lila—nevertheless it was the closest seat there was and Allen took it, smiling at her across the inconvenient person between them. And she, blood rushing into her cheeks, smiled back.

She fled, alone, not long after that. Allen stayed for a long time, stalking Olivia, demanding more details about Lila and her past; Olivia finally told him to come back the next day for coffee so that they could talk about Lila. When he did, Olivia showed him a sheaf of photographs which were oddly ethereal, as though someone was trying to paint with light through a camera.

"Lila did those," she said.

"She's good," Allen said, sifting through the photos, astonished at the numinous quality.

"She hasn't taken any for more than six months," Olivia said. "I told you, she's been pretty ill-used. What are your intentions, Sir Lancelot?"

"Entirely honorable," he said. "Do you have a phone number for her? An address?"

"I think she screens her calls, but here's her number," Olivia said, scribbling on the back of one of Lila's photographs as she spoke. "You might have better luck writing her a note. That's her address. Here, you can keep this one."

Allen, thirty years old, felt oddly insecure and light-headed, like a raw teenager angling for his very first real date—which, in many ways, he was, having focused his life almost exclusively on his books and his business after he had left college. But he wrote a note, as Olivia had suggested, and mailed it before he had a chance to develop second thoughts. He allowed, with increasing impatience, a week to pass before he called Lila, and when she answered the phone he almost lost the ability of coherent speech altogether, getting tongue-tied and awkward. But he did manage to ask if she wanted to join him for dinner some night that week, and after a small hesitation she said yes.

He had felt almost totally unable to communicate to her just how much that dinner date had inexplicably meant to him. Instead, he wrote her another note, And then asked her out again. And this time, brought her home, to his townhouse, so that he could cook the meal himself.

"I didn't know men could do this," Lila said, finishing off a plate of chicken Alfredo. "It's really good."

"I've been living alone for a while, and you learn stuff," Allen said, getting to his feet to start clearing the table. "No, stay there—I've got dessert."

"You bake, too?" she asked, with a small appreciative laugh.

"I would love to take credit for the profiteroles," he said, "but alas, they come from the very good bakery just down the street here whose faithful customer I've been these many years."

They ate the profiteroles—light and fluffy, with a brittle hard crust on the outside and a burst of delicious smooth cool custard on the inside that filled the mouth with vanilla-tasting sweetness as they cracked the outer shell between their teeth. And then they sat on Allen's old leather sofa, Lila curled up against him as he held her, and it felt good, natural, inevitable, as though she had always been there, always would be.

"Lila," he whispered into her hair, holding her gathered up against his chest, his voice unsteady, "I feel as though this is... this could be...if you don't want to make it permanent, walk away now."

She did not answer. She also did not move. Which was answer enough.

The fledgling relationship was tested only weeks into it, when Allen had to leave for a long-prearranged book buying trip to Europe on which it was impossible to take Lila. They spent just over a month apart, wrote letters to each other almost every day, and when he returned from Europe they fell into an easy routine. She did not move in, but she spent most of her time at his place, staying over every so often, changing a little every day, opening up that tightly closed bud that she had been when he had first met her and beginning to blossom into a flower of indescribably beauty and intoxicating scent...at which point Allen began to feel unaccountably afraid.

The last time he had fully trusted someone it had been his grandfather, fifteen years before. After that, he had closed everyone else out—since he was in his mid-teens he had fended for himself, did his own thing, been independent of mind and spirit and, as quickly as he could manage it, means... had lived alone, been enough as and of himself.

The future now... changed. There were responsibilities in it. There was a sharing of space, of mind, of existence. Lila had answered his heartfelt plea, that night, lying in his arms—and she had taken that as a sort of a pledge between them. She had become a part of his apartment, had taken it on herself to put away his laundry on occasion, wash the dishes, make the bed that they had shared.

She may not have been living with him in the flesh but it was clear that she was in spirit, and that she had begun to plan her life around a time when she would cross that divide and become a more permanent part of his life.

All of a sudden the loving woman whom he had asked into his house began to feel oddly suffocating—he could not seem to look anywhere without meeting those calm gray eyes, and reading into their expression things that Lila had not remotely wanted to put there.

He took refuge in the only way he knew how—by putting an emotional distance between them, growing cool, not being altogether with her even when she was in his arms, pleading pressure of work as an excuse. He went on at least one trip without any book-buying reason to do so, just to get away from Lila, from his own home, from the trap that he felt closing around him there.

When he was at home, and she came to touch him or lean against him as she had a habit of doing, he no longer reached out to return the touch, going on with whatever he was doing as though she was not there.

Once, sitting at his feet as he sat on the couch cleaning an old camera he had taken to pieces on the coffee table in front of him, Lila sighed.

"Your cat gets more attention from you than I do," she murmured, a rare reproach.

He continued rubbing a soft cloth over a lens. "The cat doesn't have expectations of me," he heard himself say.

He felt her stiffen where she leaned against him, and then she silently rose and padded away into the kitchen. It was clean, the dishes already done, but she found something to busy herself with—anything—so that she wouldn't have to be in his space right then.

And Allen, who had listened to his own words with an appalled clarity of perception, knew that he was about to break his own heart and hers—because he could not, would not, do this to her again. If she had expectations, it was he who had handed them to her—and if he was not going to honor them it was time to take that back.

He told her the next morning that the relationship wasn't working any more.

He held her as she cried, asking if it was something that she had done, if it was something that she could undo, and giving her no reprieve.

But then he himself pulled back and things stumbled on for another week or so, mortally wounded, leaking heart's blood. They even made love again, and when they were together like that everything seemed possible, everything seemed right— but then they would leave the bed behind and Allen would be besieged by his own feelings again, afraid, wanting something he knew that he would destroy and knowing that he was eminently capable of doing just that if he left things to coast along as they were. They circled around the unspoken things between them, and finally he brought the matter up again. This time, even, asking her—asking the woman he loved, whom he understood intimately and for whom he knew his request would be impossible—if she thought they could just stay friends.

She had recoiled from that, as he had—in retrospect—known she would, expected her to. This had been a weapon of sorts, raised against her, insurance that events would work out the way Allen was shaping them but shifting the responsibility for them, being able to say, afterwards, that he had bade a genuine offer and that it had been Lila who had turned him down, who had walked away.

She had turned away from him and cried silently, into her hands, her shoulders heaving with sobs. He had got up, then, left her curled up on her side of the bed, pulled on a t-shirt and a pair of jeans, and padded barefoot into the kitchen. He made tea with the last herbal tea bag in the house—oddly symbolic, he thought as he dunked the teabag into the hot water and stirred it around to release the tea—and brought it back to her in the bedroom.

"I'm sorry," she said, looking up as he entered, her eyes red and swollen and her face streaked with tears. "I'm such a quintessential stereotypical classic wretched female."

"You are not that. You will never be that. You're a very special person," he said, and he was wholly sincere. And then, because he saw something kindle again in those eyes, continued, "Even if it's only because you're amongst the few people I know who would use four adjectives in a single sentence and get away with it. Here. Have a cup of tea."

"Thank you," she said, sitting up, accepting the mug from his hand and setting it down gently on the bedside table. "Would you... excuse me for a moment?"

Allen gave her a twisted little half-smile, nodded, and crossed the corridor into the second bedroom that he had made into his study, his sanctuary, the place where his beloved books were. He left the door ajar, but somehow completely failed to hear Lila get dressed, pick up her handbag and coat from the entrance hall, and leave his apartment. He heard no door open, no door shut, no car start. All he found, when he peered into the bedroom about ten minutes afterwards when he suddenly became aware of the silence, was a cooling cup of herbal tea on the bedside table next to the bed where Lila had loved and laughed and slept. The bed itself, the sheets twisted and rumpled, was already cold—had already forgotten the shape of her, as though she never existed.

Allen had thought that he might cry, then. But he didn't. He made the bed, phoned his travel agent to book a ticket to Europe leaving the next day, spent the rest of the afternoon packing methodically, arranged for his neighbor to feed his cat, and left for an extended trip to France and Germany.

He returned from that trip having found a lot of treasures. He sold them for a good price. And wished he did not feel as though he had also sold his soul.

Allen lifted a hand to his face and realized, somewhat to his astonishment, that his cheek was wet with tears.

"Why do you show me this?" he whispered. "God knows I've spent enough time thinking about it, wondering what would have happened if I had been stronger..."

"Have you regretted it? Regretted her?"

"Every time I think I have managed to leave her behind, she pops up somewhere," Allen said. "I see a woman with red hair, and I remember hers on my pillow. I see a kid with freckles on his nose, and I wonder if we'd have had one of those, if one day, in the fullness of time, I might have had a chance to set it right, to leave my own collection to my own grandson just like my grandfather did to me and this time make it right, make it stick..."

"You don't get to go backwards," Ariel said.

Allen twisted sharply in his seat, narrowing his eyes and staring at Ariel. "All right—what is going on here? None of this—none of this is possible—none if it is fair..."

"If you had the choice, right now—between your books and children born to be the heirs of whatever legacy you may have to leave them—what would you pick? Really?"

"What kind of a question is that?" Allen demanded. "What are you, my conscience?"

"Nothing so complicated," Ariel said. "But I am interested in the reply."

"Why?" Allen demanded, his voice rising into shrillness. "What is my life to you?"

"Lives."

"What?"

"Lives," Ariel said. He leaned forward, and some stray shaft of light suddenly caught him as though in the spotlight, and the expression on his face was interested, intense. "I'm not really supposed to get involved this deeply—I'm supposed to explain, and then get out of the way—but this... interests me. Because, you see, you have three timelines."

"Three timelines," Allen repeated, his brow knitting in confusion.

Ariel began to count off the fingers of one hand with the other. "This life, the one you're living right now... this was a choice. There was another choice you could have made."

"You are making no sense. No sense at all," Allen said, shaking his head.

"Look on the screen."

Allen turned to stare at the screen, and the images began to change again. After a moment, he lifted a hand to point at the screen.

"That boy... that boy is me," he said. "Isn't it?"

"Kind of," Ariel said. "You might say, more accurately, he might have been you. But he lived his own life. Watch."

Images followed one on another. A boy, playing in the yard. An older boy, stepping into a school gym decked out for a dance, an awkward girl swathed in yards of pink tulle on his arm. A young man, bent over books in a library study carrel. A young man, wearing a graduation gown and cap, surrounded by parents, family, and a girl who clung to his arm. The same young man, with a young woman gowned in frothy white—not the same girl from the vision of pink tulle—on his arm, leaving a wedding reception, a crowd of smiling people blurry in the background. The young man leaning over a hospital bed where the woman who had lately been a bride lay cradling a red-faced bundle swathed in a pink blanket. A slightly older young man leaning over the same new mother, holding a different pink-swathed bundle. A picture of a family on summer vacation—pretty mother in a strappy sundress, proud father wearing a white Panama hat, and two little girls with dark hair tied up in curly pigtails. A dance recital. A high school graduation. More weddings, where the father stood with first one then the other of his daughters, dressed as a bride, on his arm.

The pictures came faster, and in them the central character, the man who was Allen Brosch, aged before the eyes of the Allen who was watching from the auditorium, holding his breath. The girls whom he had given away in marriage grew round-bellied with child, each in her turn, twice for the older, three times for the younger, and then the grandchildren started to grow up. The Allen in the pictures grew older; there was a retirement party at the office where he worked, and they waved him away from his desk with cake and applause and a small present wrapped in shiny blue paper—an engraved watch. His oldest grand-daughter's wedding; the birth of his first great-grandchild.

A family surrounding a hospital bed, crying, hiding the occupant—but Allen knew it had to be himself, the other him, the one who had lived that other life.

Then the screen dissolved into whiteness, into what almost looked like complete emptiness if it weren't for the very subtle texture that remained imprinted behind—almost like the downy wisps at the base of a feather.

"That," Ariel said, "was the other option Ellen had when she stepped out into her choice. This life, the one you're leading now, or that one, the one you've just seen. She stepped into this one. But this one—she had no way of knowing, of course—was so much briefer. Allen Brosch, in your current life, right now, you have less than three years to live. Under ordinary circumstances I would have left it until then—but you don't have the time, you won't have the mind..."

"Wait, stop, back up a minute. Ellen? Who is this Ellen? What choice? Less than three years to live...?"

Ariel sighed.

"Maybe I went about this the wrong way," he muttered. "But if I had left it to run its course you wouldn't have been able to choose at all, in just over a year. And you have to choose. You have to remember."

"Remember *what*?" said Allen sharply.

"Screen," Ariel said, pointing.

Another image had just materialized on the screen. A dimly-lit café, full of young people laughing and talking at crowded tables, and a table in the far corner. A table with five people. A tall, slim, lanky blonde woman. A stocky dark man. A woman with sad eyes. A man with distinguished silver-white hair and a proud carriage. And, in the corner...

"*That's* Ellen," Ariel said softly. "This is going to be difficult, but I need you to remember. *That* is the life you left, right there—your friends—Quincey, John, Olivia. Yes, *that* Olivia, the one who gave you Lila in this lifetime—I don't actually believe they ever met, she and Lila, in that other one that you're seeing there. And beside her, there, your husband, Simon."

"My *husband*?" Allen repeated, completely bewildered.

"Yes, husband. Back there, you… you… well, let me put it this way. It's the only life of the three alternative timelines that you have been given in which you are… a woman."

Allen let out the breath he hadn't realized he was holding, in a long, deep sigh.

"Yes," he said slowly. "I—I think—I remember—but I don't understand—"

He hadn't heard Ariel move but somehow he was sitting right behind him now, and there was a gentle hand on his shoulder.

"I am the Messenger," Ariel said softly.

"There was… snow. I was standing in snow. Cold. So cold. Why was I so unhappy? And there was… a piece of paper. You gave me…"

"Instructions, yes." The voice was even softer, deeper, full of a strange compassion. "Don't fight it. Let it come. It has to come."

Allen drew a shuddering breath. "There is something you are not telling me."

"I will tell you if I can. What is it that you wish to know?"

"You said… I will die. I will, I, this person sitting here right now, the only person I have rational reason to believe I can be, will die. Very soon. But before I die…you said I will lose my reason, my mind, my capacity to choose—and that this is why you are here right now."

"Yes," Ariel said.

Allen turned to look at him, holding the smoky gray eyes with his own. "What of? It sounds like I will die slowly, and in agony, and it will all be a waste, and I will have accomplished nothing. What will I die of?"

Ariel hesitated, and then sighed again. "I suppose I opened

that door," he said. "But hey—I'm already in deep trouble with the Big Boss. I should never, *ever*, have gotten this closely involved—all I'm supposed to do is be there at the moment of choice, give a noodge if the person caught in its clutches was vacillating. I'm certainly not supposed to hand out sensitive information just because you ask me to, and as for having extended philosophical discussions on the matter... Oh well. I suppose I will just have to take the consequences. But anyway— just as a disclaimer—this is not the kind of thing a mortal mind is given to bear; you are not meant to know how and when you will die. You buckle under that knowledge."

"Tell me. What do I die of... here, now? What did I die of, in that other life? What did...what does... *she* die of? Ellen?" He shook his head. "That's confusing. It's almost the same name, but not..."

"Long story, that, and not relevant right now," Ariel said. "You can *all* blame your mother for it, all, um, three of you. But as to your question—and I'm sorry, I will tell you, but you will forget that I have told you almost instantly, because you shouldn't know and it isn't relevant to the other choice you must make— that other Allen died because he was old and worn out and spent, and had lived a full and long life, and his count of years was 80 when he went. Ellen suffers from high blood pressure, which is a family thing, and will die of a massive stroke... some time from now, having lived a decent span of years of her own. You, too, have the high blood pressure...which you know, but have ignored for years. Your stroke won't be instantaneous, as hers is, or was, or will be. Yours will come in many small cuts, taking you slowly, one piece at a time. At the end you will be lying in a hospital bed, still aware, but unable to voluntarily move your arms or your legs—and at the very end you will have to have a machine breathing for you, for a little while. It is not a good end. I am sorry. You asked, and I have told you—now you must forget that you ever knew."

"How...how..." Allen licked his lips. There were suddenly beads of sweat on his brow, and he lifted a hand, which he noticed dispassionately was actually shaking, to wipe them off. For a moment he could hold on to the question that he had meant to ask—how would anybody be expected to make any kind of rational choice, given the scenario that Ariel had just painted? But then it seemed to dissipate, shred into streamers of mist he couldn't quite hold on to. He was left with a vague sense of unease, as though some part of his consciousness had been anaesthetized, but his hand had steadied, and he was able to look steadily at Ariel again.

"You all right?" Ariel asked, his head tilted a little. And then, giving himself an answer in the shape of a slight nod, continued, "But now we have to talk of the choice that you've got to make."

"And what is that, precisely?" asked Allen, after a beat of silence.

"Which life you will own as yours. This, which you are living, where we are speaking right now? Or that—" Ariel gestured toward the screen where the picture of the five people at a café table, the picture of Ellen, still burned.

"You said three," Allen said.

"No," Ariel said. "Not quite. I said you had three possible timelines—but when Ellen, over there, stepped through that door... *this* is the life she chose as her alternative. This, not the other. The choice is always only between two. And when you do choose—there might be a few life lessons that linger between the worlds but you will forget everything except the life that you choose to continue with. Don't knock that, it's a gift—if you were allowed full knowledge and free memory you would be paralyzed, you would never be able to take another step in any direction at all because you would be second-guessing yourself too hard..."

"Messenger," Allen said, staring at Ariel. "Whose Messenger?"

"Right now, yours," Ariel said, with a smile.

Allen allowed his gaze to drift back to the screen. "I remember," he said slowly, "being... there. Being *her*. I remember it right now."

"In the moment of choice all the memories are yours," Ariel said. "How else would you choose anything?"

"She is different from me. So different. She was always

late—I am always, *always* early. She has a family, I have none. She is…" He allowed his voice to fade into silence, staring at the screen.

"But she and you… you're the same," Ariel said. "You drove away the love of your life. She stole hers, in a way. But underneath it all it's the same thing—it's the insecurity, it's the fear, it's the need. You've both got that. You share that."

"But she made something of it," Allen murmured.

Ariel lifted his arms in an expressive gesture, indicating the auditorium around them. "So did you," he said. "Look at you. You're invited to talk at Universities. You've made a name for yourself."

"That's all I've made," Allen said. And then chuckled, glancing back at Ariel. "Schrödinger's lives," he said. "I get it."

Ariel tilted his head a little. "In what way?"

"You shove these two people into a closed box—the two of us—me and a woman called Ellen. And then you close the lid. And neither of us is alive or dead until somebody actually opens the box. Like Schrödinger's Cat."

"It isn't quite as passive as that," Ariel said. "*She* had a choice, back there—instructions in her hand—it was up to her whether to step through a certain door, or simply go back to the table and forget anything strange had ever happened. *You* have a choice here, now…"

"But if she had not made her choice then I would never have been self-aware enough to have this conversation with someone like you," Allen pointed out. "Not even in a dream. I'm not entirely sure that I won't suddenly wake up, down at that desk there, lift my head after an unexpected nap attack, and find myself barely remembering any of this, as though seen through the frustrating and concealing mists of dream and fancy—although I wouldn't have believed myself capable of such fancy, if you had asked me. I always thought of myself as fairly practical."

"Sure," Ariel said, with a grin. "Practical enough to study history and philosophy at college, and then manage to carve a sort of career in the real world with those disciplines, so grounded in the past, in what had long since happened and could not be changed."

"Maybe that's the answer," Allen said slowly.

"What did I say?" said Ariel, raising an eyebrow.

"Something's happened—at least potentially—that can't be changed," Allen said. "There has to be a reason that, if there are multiple channels that my life could have been poured down, there is only one of them that is... different. Only one in which I am a woman. Only one in which I—for whatever value of I that might stand for—am capable of actually integrating everything that's in my particular karmic load, as it were, and living a relatively balanced life while carrying it. Look what I've done, myself, *this* myself, right here, with this life... you tell me that I'll die in less than three years—tell me, who have I got right now who'll be with me when I do?"

Ariel opened his mouth, and then closed it, shaking his head minutely.

"There, then. Alone. That's what I've accomplished in this existence. Perfected the art of being alone." Allen paused, and then ran a hand through his hair. "In the other life-thread, the one you say is not an option at this time—there's family around me, but I don't get the impression that I've done anything other than... you know... just exist. Exist for long enough to reproduce. For another generation or two with my blood and my genes to step onto this earth. But I, myself... I just existed, and then I got erased. This existence, right here—you're right, here I am, speaking at Universities, with a name for myself—but when I shuffle off the mortal coil it will be unmourned except by a couple of clients who'll soon find another to serve their needs. She... Ellen... I..." He paused, rubbing his hand along his jaw in a pensive gesture. "It's hard, this," he said. "Keeping all these memories straight."

"What do you remember?"

"I told you. Everything. Ellen... I, as Ellen... Dear God, I remember being a *woman* and somehow I can handle thinking about that without falling apart... what have you done to me?"

"You have always," Ariel said, "been stronger than you have believed yourself to be."

"I can think of a few moments in that life—*her* life—that were not proud ones. But overall, it's a good life. It's the best life it would seem that I am capable of leading. And like I said... it's the only one that's different. Maybe that makes it the only real choice. All of this... everything here... I've been trying to find something in this life right here that I would regret leaving, and if there are twinges here and there at memories that I will inevitably lose... *she* never had the grandfather that I had, shared that library... there's nothing. Nothing major. If I think with her mind and her memories, I think of rubbing that life, her life, out in order to keep this one... and I can't find a single compelling reason to do it." He gave Ariel a lopsided smile. "Looks like Schrödinger is about to open the box, Messenger."

He slipped out of his seat, and started down again, toward the bottom of the auditorium, the lecturer's desk, the screen where the image of the café was beginning to fade.

"Where are you going?" Ariel called out.

Allen stopped. "Through the looking glass," he said, "of course."

Ariel chuckled. "I may be able to step across lifetimes and realities, and I certainly have the gift of walking through walls if that becomes necessary, but I'm afraid the same doesn't apply to you, my friend."

"Eh?"

"Sometimes the screen is just a screen," Ariel said. "All you would do if you tried walking through that one would be to rip it, and then hurt yourself against the very, very solid wall that lies behind it." He gestured with his right thumb, indicating the doors at the top of the auditorium. "That way. There's a perfectly good door waiting up there."

Allen gave a small accepting shrug, and began to climb the steps again. Ariel reached out and touched his arm gently as he reached his seat, and Allen paused.

"All this...?" Allen asked, his voice lifting in a question as he spread his hands to encompass the auditorium, the world at large.

"I'll clean up," Ariel said, with a smile that lit up his whole face. "Don't worry about the things you leave in my hands."

After a moment Allen gave a sharp nod, and looked away. He gently shook off Ariel's hand and continued to climb the steps to the top of the auditorium. There was a glass panel in the double doors, and ordinarily one could see the corridor outside through them—but right now Allen could see nothing, nothing but darkness. And yet for some reason he was not afraid of this at all.

"Hey," Ariel's voice came floating up to him as he reached out a hand to push open the doors.

Allen glanced over his shoulder, met a pair of soft gray eyes which might have been half-way down the auditorium amphitheatre or right beside him, it was hard to tell.

"Tell Olivia I said hello," Ariel said.

Allen pushed open the auditorium door.

The darkness flowed into the room, and swallowed him.

INTERMEZZO 4

Thursday, 20 December 2012

Simon was standing by the corner table as Ellen came back into the main room of the café.

"Are you all right? I was about to come after you," he said, reaching out to her. "Did you go *outside*?" he demanded, as his fingertips met hair cold and damp from melted snow. "Without a coat on?"

"Yes. No, I had a coat. Let me in—sit down—I'm fine, it's fine, really..." Ellen brushed his hand away with a hint of impatience, but smiled as she was doing it, drawing the ghost of an answering smile from Simon—unspoken communication between partners of long standing. He moved aside to let her sidle into the seat she had just vacated. His eyes had yet to leave her. "And outside—it's just—it's beautiful, it's exactly what an evening at the end of the world should look like," Ellen said. "Empty and quiet in the snow under a yellow street light. Like a woodcarving, an illustration from an old book..."

Quincey's eyebrow rose at that. "What, you're suddenly a poet?"

"There's poetry hiding in many a place where you least think of looking for it," John said unexpectedly. He shrugged his shoulders when everyone looked at him as he uttered those words, with expressions ranging from mild astonishment to outright incredulity. "All right, all right, yes, I admit it, I wrote some. Many years ago. A long time ago. A lifetime ago. It was all uniformly terrible, I suspect, but it was a way of getting the questions in my head sorted out so that I'd be able to figure out where to start looking for the answers."

"Did it help?" Ellen asked.

"Have you still got them?" Quincey said, in the same instant.

John gave Quincey a sardonic sideways glance. "No, ma'am, I will not be showing off any more tattoos in public," he said. "Not after the last time—God knows I might get worse than blue cheese dressing spilled on me if I'm not careful. And no, Ellen… not entirely. There are some answers that don't come until you figure out what the true questions are—and that isn't always obvious…"

"You're a damned philosopher, if not a poet," Simon said. "There's a lectureship opening at the University—should I put a word in?"

"I don't spout wisdom on demand," John retorted. "Send them to my anchorite's cave occasionally, if you insist, for extra credit."

"I used to write haiku, about people," Olivia said.

"About people? What do you mean?"

"Oh, a kind of party trick. Like a fortune cookie. I used to do it at the parties that the, um, Vanderbilts threw at the penthouse." She threw a grin in John's direction as she said the name, and he grinned back, acknowledging the barb. "It used to amuse the husband, and it annoyed the mother-in-law—it was a victory on both those counts. And it was actually kind of fun."

"I'd never have thought it of *you*," Quincey scoffed. "You're the proper and principled one. Playing with people's lives that way is hardly an honorable thing to do. And anyway, you're not supposed to *enjoy* it."

"Yes, but I hardly ever got to put one over on the mother-in-law where anything else is concerned, particularly with the full support of her own son—in a way it was a declaration of independence, the two of us as separate but equal grown-ups as opposed to her own extruded extensions doing her bidding, the two of us against the world. That was one of the only contexts where I felt as though I had his full support." She smiled, a little sadly. "And it was a parlor trick. That should have told me something, I guess."

"So what did you do, sit in a corner at a small table draped with a tablecloth printed with moons and stars and spout poetry at all comers?" John asked. The expression on his face told eloquently of his mental image of that particular situation.

"Come to think of it, the whole thing *was* rather alike a Tarot reading," Olivia said, laughing out loud. "There *would* be a quiet corner with some sort of table—sorry, no moons and stars, but there you go—and I'd sit there, and they'd all come drifting by, scoffing at the whole thing but they couldn't help themselves, they were interested and anyway the dowager hostess seemed to have endorsed the party game. So they'd come along, the cream of New York society, and I'd sit them down and ask them to tell me something about themselves... and they would, oh heavens, they would. Sometimes stuff I'd have paid money never to have heard. But the thing is, they simply turned off a sensor when they did that. I swear that half the time they weren't even aware of what came spilling out."

"Like a confessional," Ellen said. "Sitting there in plain sight."

"More like an analyst," John said. "I hear those make a good living in New York City."

"You watch too many Woody Allen movies," Simon said.

"So what did you do with all the New York Confidential stuff?" John asked, leaning forward a little, intrigued despite himself.

"Oh... I'd just listen for a bit, and then the haiku would write itself in my head, their dramas and problems distilled into those spare Oriental syllables. I'm not sure myself how I did it, most of the time—it just came to me. And yes, there were times I was way off target, and I could tell because those people kind of smirked and tossed their haiku away with a contemptuous gesture, and called you a pretentious twit behind your back while making sure that you could overhear them doing so. But often I got a real hit, and I could tell that, too—they'd read the poem and they'd go white, or red, and they'd scuttle away in silence, shoving the haiku away into some safe spot for later, wondering how much of their secrets I really knew... or if I intended to do something about it."

"Do one for me," Quincey said unexpectedly.

"What, now?" Olivia asked, caught by surprise.

"Yes, now!" Quincey said, laughing. "I suppose you could

mail it to me next week but given your track record for keeping in touch I'd rather not take the chance, thanks..."

"I haven't done it for years," Olivia protested, suddenly blushing and self-conscious, staring down at her hands on the table.

"Oh, go on," John said. "If I can flash my tattoos in public, you can write a few lines of poetry. Do me too."

"Do all of us," Quincey said.

Ellen looked up, her expression slightly panicked. "Not me..."

Simon suddenly reached over and curled his fingers around hers. "Do one for both of us."

Olivia glanced up, her expression enigmatic. And then she sat up, straightening her shoulders. "All right then," she said softly.

She allowed her eyes to rest on Quincey, and for a moment or two she sat quiet, staring at Quincey's face, holding her eyes, until Quincey stirred and gave a small self-conscious laugh.

"Should I be afraid I started this?" she murmured.

Olivia hesitated for another fraction of a second, and then said,

"Snow melts underfoot—
The winter of discontent
And troubles is over."

Quincey lifted her head sharply. "What brought *that* on?"

Olivia shrugged. "I told you. It's a party trick. That's the card I pulled from the Tarot deck. But that reaction usually comes from somebody whom the dart has hit rather squarely. And anyway, from just tonight, you've had a bunch of years which had a bunch of discontent and troubles in them..."

"And other stuff," Quincey said defensively. "Like the kids..."

"I didn't say *everything* was bad," Olivia said. "And anyway, it's all in the interpretation."

"I'm almost afraid to ask," Simon said. "But now I'm intrigued. Do mine. Do one for Ellen and me."

Olivia hesitated. And then shrugged.

"Spring and fall combine

Leaves budding and leaves falling
Balancing the year."

"Is that an observation or a curse?" Quincey asked.

Simon ran a hand through his hair, his expression both wryly amused and puzzled. "I'll take it as the former, thank you," he said. "I sincerely hope that our fate is not that it's impossible for one of us to do well unless the other is doing badly."

"And what about mine?" John said.

Olivia tilted her head, gazed at him for a long moment, and then said,

"Where have you come from?
The lands of endless summer.
Where are you going?"

John actually flinched. "Ouch," he said. "I think that if I had been at one of the Vanderbilt parties I would have been the one scurrying away with furtive looks to the side and stuffing that one out of sight."

Olivia gave him a helpless look. "Sorry," she said. "But I never knew... about all that about yourself that you just told us. And I'm probably still processing it. It's going to take a while..."

The distinctive sound of a champagne cork popping came from somewhere in the crowded café, and Simon looked up, frowning.

"I didn't know they served champagne in this place," he said. "It isn't the kind of place for a good bottle of..."

"They're not all good bottles," John pointed out. "Likely they go for the cheap and cheerful stuff."

Quincey glanced at her watch. "Oh, good God. It's getting on for a quarter to midnight. They *are* treating tonight as a sort of mega New Year's Eve, champagne and everything. I swear, if anyone starts singing Auld Lang Syne I'm out of here."

"Maybe it's time to leave it to the young'uns," Simon murmured. "Anyone want to take the party elsewhere?"

"Maybe it's having very young kids," Quincey said, "but I've kind of grown out of the habit of really late nights. I think I'm for calling it a night, myself." She smiled at Simon. "When you first proposed this," she added, "I have to confess that I had a twinge or two about whether it was a really good idea, given all the… but anyway… I'm glad it worked out like this. I honestly enjoyed seeing all of you again. Here. It just brought… a lot of memories back."

"For the record," Ellen said, her own smile a little lopsided, "my own vote was either against, or abstain…"

"It's odd," John mused, "it's been, what, twenty years…"

"Twenty one," Simon said, his eyebrow twitching. "Remember Abby? The one about to celebrate her twenty first birthday?"

"Touché," John said, laughing. "But what I was going to say is… I walked in through that door, and those years were just… gone… and I was young again. I'm not sure if I was entirely happy about that, Simon, but at any rate it was… *interesting*. Thank you for the experience."

"I was half ready to go sit in a corner somewhere and watch if anyone came, and if they did if they would actually know me," Olivia murmured.

John gave her a strange look. "I would have known you," he said. "I would have known you if you had come in wearing a Cruella de Ville wig and make-up applied with a trowel."

"Yes," Quincey said slowly, "here, in this place, yes. Anywhere else, out on the street, in a shop, in some other restaurant, on a plane, I might have walked past any of you and not turned my head. But here—here—everyone who walked into this room I knew. You might have changed your hair color or your weight class, you might have gained or lost confidence, but here, now, tonight, at the end of the world, you were all instantly recognizable as the friends I left behind here so many years ago. It's strange. This is the kind of place where you can wrap yourself in disguises, layer upon layer, but somehow it gets the truth out of you anyway."

Simon caught the eye of their young waitress across the crowded room and mimed writing in mid-air. "Check, please? Okay? Okay. I think she saw me."

"She's going to put it all on one tab?" John said. "This could take a while. Can anyone remember how many Irish Coffees you've had?"

"I'll put it all on the card," Simon said, "and we can sort it out at leisure."

"Living on credit on the eve of the end of the world? I'm not sure I approve," John said, grinning.

"Uh huh," Simon said, dismissing this with a wave of his hand. "Either the world ends and it ceases to matter much or else it doesn't and I'm good for it."

Quincey was rooting in her wallet. "I have no memory of how much the Irish Coffees were but I think I had two of them anyway—and the salad—let's see—this should take care of my tab…"

While they were all counting money and figuring out what their contribution should be, the young waitress swept by the table and dropped a long scroll of paper from the cash register onto the table.

"Everything all right?" she said in passing, and then, glancing down at John apologetically, "Aside from me flinging foodstuffs about…?"

"Everything is fine," Simon said. He fished out a Visa from his own wallet and held it out to her. "Here, start this going—put it all on the card, and bring me the slip. Leave us this copy to sort it out amongst ourselves, would you?"

"Sure thing—I'll be right back," she said, and vanished into the noisy throng.

John had hold of the bill, poring over it. "She *did* give me that coffee gratis, it seems—can't see it in here. Let's see—*this* was me, and ye Gods, *how* many Irish Coffees did we put away in total? I'll pitch in for two of 'em…"

"Give me that," Quincey said, counting out her own dollars and running a finger down the bill. "There, that should cover me and my share of the tip," she said, passing the bill to Ellen.

"Whatever's left is going on the card anyway," Ellen said, glancing at the bill in her hand.

"Give it to me, let me see how much I need to pitch in for," Olivia said, her hand out across the table.

Ellen began to hand it to her, Quincey said something to her and distracted her, she turned to her to reply, Simon said something at the same moment to John across Olivia's head, and somehow in all the confusion Olivia found herself clutching two pieces of paper. One of them was the long and by now much-handled bill for their meals. The other was a folded piece of paper which appeared to have writing on it.

"Ellen..." she began, lifting her head, and then, as the paper fell open, began reading, and did not complete her sentence.

Choose wisely. And at the end, in Ellen's own handwriting, *Say hi to Olivia.*

Olivia looked up, but for the moment she seemed to be out of the group, an outsider, watching people she did not know. She entertained a thought that it was that piece of paper that she held in her hand that had made her suddenly... invisible to them, while she considered its contents, while she made her choice, whatever the choice was supposed to be. Her hand trembled for an instant as she contemplated testing her theory and just tossing the paper on the table, letting go, breaking the connection between the page and her fingertips, and see if they all turned to include her again—but something held her back, and her fingers tightened on the page instead.

She looked up, through the archway, out where the glass display case flanked the entrance to the Spanish Gardens. And caught the solemn, serene gray gaze of the one who had introduced himself to her as Ariel when she had walked into the place.

He raised one perfect eyebrow at her, and actually winked— which startled Olivia considerably, enough to almost drop the paper in consternation. But then his eyes slid off hers for just an instant as he made a small gesture with his head seeming to indicate that she should follow his directions to somewhere— and that, together with those words on the paper she held, was, irrationally, enough.

She pushed her chair back, still clutching the paper with the instructions.

"Excuse me a minute," she murmured, not certain if anyone heard, not certain, in that moment, she cared if they did.

Quincey glanced up; John turned his head; Simon gave her a hint of a smile; Ellen stared at her for a moment with furrowed brows as though she was trying to remember something very important that she really ought to have told Olivia but which had slipped her mind—and then the thought fled, and she nodded once, barely, and turned back to Quincey.

Olivia, leaving the chair slightly askew to the table, stepped softly out behind John and sidled past a knot of laughing young men who had just turned into the main room through the archway. She lost sight of the table where her friends were sitting as this group came between them, and then she was through the archway and into the smaller room and they were out of sight.

Ariel nodded at her. "That way," he said. "You'll know what to do."

"Did they all...?" Olivia began, glancing over her shoulder, suddenly convinced that she was merely the last to stand here with this paper in her hands.

But Ariel shook his head minutely, although his eyes were glittering strangely. "That isn't important," he said.

"No," Olivia agreed, after a moment's reflection, feeling oddly calm. "It isn't."

"Go on," Ariel said. "It's waiting for you."

Olivia's fingers tightened on the paper, crumpling it slightly. "What is?"

"Everything," Ariel said cryptically.

She turned away, toward the second archway which led to the small vestibule before the restrooms, and then turned back for a moment, staring at Ariel.

"Just tell me," she said, "and don't tell me you don't know—is it true? Does the world really stop tonight—only a few minutes from now? Is that even possible?"

"Yes," he said, smiling.

"Yes, the world ends?"

"That's not quite what you asked. You qualified the question, both times you asked it. In response—yes, I do know if it is true or not. Yes, it is possible. On the main question though—I would have to answer it with another question. How would you define the end of the world—even just the end of *a* world, your own private one? What, in your own mind does it mean when you ask, 'Does the world stop?'"

Olivia was silent, her expression hard to read. And then she sighed, and turned away.

"The other door," Ariel's voice came drifting over her shoulder. "The one with the sign."

"It figures," Olivia murmured, mostly to herself, as she reached for the handle over which was hung the Out Of Order sign. "The world isn't perfect, after all."

The door gave under her gentle pressure. She stepped into the darkness without looking back.

OLIVIA

December 20, 2012

It was one of those rare, perfect winter days. The street outside was bright with brittle winter sunshine—and, from inside the coffee shop where it was nice and warm, it was almost easy to believe that the sunlight carried actual warmth instead of being the diamond light of December, unable to warm the chill in the air.

As the coffee shop door opened and then closed, Olivia looked up from the open leather journal in front of her, pen poised, a pair of spectacles framed in leopard-print plastic perched on her nose. The patron who had entered stood just inside the door, silhouetted against it, wearing a long coat open in the front and a jaunty scarf draped around his neck; his hair was shoulder-length, straight, neither luminously bright or shadow-dark but a nondescript color that didn't stand out in silhouette. Olivia could not clearly see the face, but she knew what it would look like, and knew that the man had soft gray eyes; his hands were stuffed into the pockets of his coat, but Olivia knew that they would have long and slender fingers, with short, polished nails.

She smiled.

The shadowy figure went very still for a moment, head tilted to one side, and then the shoulders squared inside the greatcoat and he took his hands from his pockets and walked toward her table, arms swinging by his sides. Olivia pushed out a chair from underneath the table with one booted foot.

"Sit down," she said. "What kept you?"

Her companion sat in the chair that had been offered to him and then leaned one elbow on the table and cupped his chin into his palm, his eyes on hers—the soft gray eyes she had known would be there.

"You were expecting me?"

Olivia glanced down at the journal, flipped it forward, and extracted a folded flyer from between a couple of pristine and as yet unwritten-on pages.

"You said we'd remember," she said. "And today... this."

She pushed the folded paper across the table at him and he picked it up with his free hand, opening it out.

"Ah," he said.

An advertisement flyer showing a sloe-eyed woman in a scarlet flamenco gown with red flowers in her hair and castanets on her graceful hands bore a slogan across the top of the page: "Spanish Night at the Gardens!"

"It came back," Olivia said. "That, and then some. I remember memories I don't think I should remember. It's like I'm standing up on a hill, and I can see *all* the roads from here."

"Not even I see them all," Ariel said.

"Of course you don't," Olivia said. "You're the Messenger. It's the one who sends you who sees them all. But you see the ones that matter... in any given moment. What do you see now?"

"Crossroads," Ariel said. "Several of them. I can see which roads you took—the ones that lead to here, that is."

"And Spanish Gardens?"

"It's just..."

"A different road. I understand."

Ariel cupped his chin in both his hands.

"You're staying," he said. It was a statement, not a question, and his eyes were sparkling.

"Staying? That is meaningless. I understand what you must have told the others—but it isn't a choice, not really. There are crossroads, yes, but right now I'm just... on a parallel road. There's no going back, not in the way you mean. These lives are both valid, right now. There are bridges between these roads. They can be crossed..."

"But when you pick one road over the other the bridges become invisible," Ariel murmured. "You see it clearly now because this is your moment of clarity. Tomorrow... you will not remember that you had to choose anything at all."

"Everyone else might not. But I will. *I* will. You might call one of the lives a dream, and one of them a reality lived while waking—but I know that it isn't true, see, and that which life is dream and which reality depends entirely in whose mind I choose to be at this moment. This one... or hers, back there in Spanish Gardens, waiting for midnight to strike. That's tonight, back then. Back there. Really, what kept you? It's getting late..."

"One in a million," Ariel murmured.

"How's that?"

"Well, it's a phrase. It's more than that, sometimes. Or less. But it's rare enough for that to work as an approximation—one in a million really understands, and really remembers, and knows what the meaning of the choice really is..."

"*What's in store for me in the direction I don't take?*" Olivia murmured.

"What was that?"

"Kerouac," Olivia said. "In that life and in this, I tend to quote from Kerouac and Tolkien. They both spoke of different worlds, of the unknown around the next bend, of lives perhaps lived differently—if only you knew, if only you knew. I wonder what Kerouac would have made of this, of your choice, of this one-life-or-the-other game—if he would have chosen a different life, a different existence, in which he never went on the road, in which nobody knows his name..."

"What makes you think he didn't?" Ariel said softly. "Perhaps this *was* the other life that he chose, whatever the consequences, instead of an existence that could have been more peaceful but less... inspired..."

"You knew him?"

"I may have," Ariel said. He was trying to keep his tone serene, calm, distanced, as befit the dignified Messenger—but he couldn't keep it up. An expression of pure delight spread across his face, irresistibly tugging his mouth into a broad exuberant grin, crinkling the corners of his sparkling eyes. "Oh, Jack Kerouac—and others—others like you—oh, you're so rare, but you're the light, you're what I am always looking for..."

He was brimming with genuine joy, but he seemed to catch

himself at this point and rein in his enthusiasm a little, aware that he was probably saying far too much. When it became apparent that he wasn't about to spill any more, Olivia leaned forward, her position unconsciously mirroring his—elbows on the table, chin cupped in her hands.

"So," she said. "What of me, then?"

Ariel reached into his pocket and retrieved, incongruously, a brand-new pack of cards, still in its box and wrapped in cellophane. He broke the wrapping, opened the box, pulled out the stack of cards and began to shuffle them slowly.

"Let's see what the cards have to say," he said.

Olivia craned her neck to get a closer look. "Are those Tarot?"

"Of sorts," he said, and, with a final shuffle, fanned the pack out, face down, and offered it to Olivia. "Pick three," he said. "Don't turn them over until I say so."

"Oh, really," she said, laughing. "Card tricks?"

"No tricks. Just cards. Come on, humor me. Pick three."

Shrugging, she did as he asked, tugging out three individual cards and laying them face down on the table. He squared away the rest of the deck and put it away to one side, then gestured at the cards in front of her with a wide, expansive wave of one long-fingered hand—a theatrical gesture, that of an entertainer, a magician about to perform a magnificent spell.

"Show and tell," he said. "You understand enough to realize that it's *all* real—in its own way, in its own time. It's all just a sandy beach, and you leave tracks behind you as you walk by the ocean's edge, but the tide always comes in… and then there's a new reality to leave your mark in. So, here, turn that first card."

Olivia's fingers hovered over the card. "What's going to happen if I do?"

Ariel grinned. "Nothing," he said. "And *everything.* That's the thing, about being you. This, here, now… it's one of the roads, a reminder of one of the roads, but it isn't anything binding—not for you. Because you can see that you're just looking through a window, and it's just another room. It's neither more or less real than this, this place you're sitting in now, the solid table on which the card lies. It's all yours, all the threads—but you're still going to have to tell me directly, eventually—make your choices overt—and the cards, well, they help."

Olivia turned over the card, and gazed at it with a small frown, staring at what looked like a photograph on the face of the card. A photograph that seemed to show… herself… her much younger self… and a bunch of friends at a café table. A café she recognized. "Wait," she said, starting to look up even as the picture blurred and became more three dimensional, reaching out to draw her in. "Wait, I remember this…"

"…You? You are just misguided."

Olivia was unprepared for how much those words stung.

The loose group of friends sitting in their customary corner in Spanish Gardens, Irish Coffees in front of everybody, some of them having only just shed the graduation gowns and still clad in the finery they had worn underneath the robes of academe, were still barely coming down off the high of the graduation celebrations. Everyone was flushed and giggly and laughing, and staring down the years into futures which were uniformly shining with promise—not necessarily anything concrete, not right then, they didn't need it. The glitter at the edge of the vision was enough, for now. The details would come.

But Simon, older than all of them, staff as opposed to just-barely-not-undergraduate, was the oracle in the corner, handing down pronouncements from on high. He had already told one girl, Katrina, that she would never leave the University and would just end up burrowing deeper and deeper into the academic heartwood until she was in danger of forgetting that a real world existed outside of that; a young man who went by the name of Smitty was informed that he would frustrate himself to drink if he persisted in pursuing a higher degree; John was told that he was the one person who could "damn well prove" that hard work and dedication really could be enough, because Simon could see him getting whatever he went after; Simon's judgment of Quincey's ambitions was that they were more theoretical than practical, and that she didn't have it in her to pursue those higher qualifications—and that if she tried she'd just get bored and despondent and become a dropout (but that she could have quite a decent working life with the current degree, so long as she didn't aim too high).

And then he had turned to Olivia, considered her for a long moment, and said what he said. *You are just misguided.*

She flushed, the bubble of her graduation euphoria irredeemably deflated. "Whatever do you mean?"

"You picked the safe thing," Simon said. "You *always* pick the safe thing. You've never done anything that would carry the smallest degree of risk. And yet... you dream. You dream big. I don't know how you do it, keeping those two incompatible things tightly clamped down together, but they're two quiescent cats in the same bag. They've got a truce, for now, if you like. But sooner or later one or the other will hiss and scratch, and then you'll be in trouble."

"That's... you're talking nonsense."

"Am I?" he said, leaning back, lifting his arms and lacing his fingers behind his head, leaning into the cradle of his linked hands to stare at her. "You're the kind that would like to write poetry about how a flower blooms or how a star is born, not play out meticulous empirical experiments to prove it. And yet, here you are, graduating with a science degree, with a life of experiments in front of you. What are you going to do with that, Olivia Halloran?"

"What, you think I can't do science?" she challenged, nettled.

"I didn't say *that*," Simon said. "I have no doubt that you are perfectly capable of it—and so do your professors else you wouldn't have that diploma in your hands. I'm just saying... that there is very little likelihood of your enjoying it, in the long run. Because, you see, you have nothing at all to prove to yourself. You're the kind who looks at that star and you *know* not only how it is born, but why, and how long it will live—and it will kill you to have to explain that over and over again to people who don't have the same understanding."

"I never said I wanted to teach," she said.

"I didn't say you did. Explaining things to people is hardly ever the same as teaching them something."

"Then if I go into research how am I misguided?"

He stared at her, and then he dropped his eyes, dismissing

the issue. "I'm sorry. It was a bad choice of words. Don't mind me, I'm just a jaded old professor, and I've probably been pontificating far more than I should. Occupational hazard, I'm afraid. Do you want another Irish Coffee?"

"Sure," she said, after a small hesitation. She had not meant to order another, but she needed to drown the sudden sharp bitterness at the back of her throat with something—and Irish whiskey would do just fine.

Olivia had secured a place in a post-graduate program at her University, on the recommendation of two of her professors— but the summer stretched out in front of her, endless and empty, and somehow she couldn't settle down to doing nothing. The sun annoyed her, she caught herself reading books she didn't like simply because it was something to do, and two weeks after graduation she found herself in the office of a professor from the Medical School, someone she had met briefly at a conference during her last undergraduate year, asking if the internship he had mentioned at their last meeting was still open and if she could take it up during the summer while she waited for her postgrad studies to start in the fall semester.

"Sure," the professor said. "You can start on Monday. I'll have Dr. Saldanha meet you in the lab and show you the ropes."

"It's the first time I'll actually have a chance to do some real work," Olivia said, her heart fluttering oddly. "Something practical."

"Exciting?"

"Oh yes. Looking forward to it."

But when Monday came, and the details of her duties were explained to her, Olivia's spirit quailed.

She had landed in a pathology lab. One that worked with animals. Part of her own duties would be to inject mice and rabbits with test substances, and the animals would then be... the word that Dr. Saldanha used was 'sacrificed'. And cut apart, to see what the stuff they'd been injected with had done to their insides.

The stuff that *she* would have injected them with.

Dr. Saldanha gave her a tour of the complex—three labs, a brace of animal rooms containing the experimental critters, and, in passing, with a wave of her hand, the 'sacrifice room'. Olivia glanced inside through the open door as they walked past in the corridor, and felt her breath catch a little as a man working inside the room happened to look up and meet her eyes. His own were very bright, glittering with something that Olivia's mind interpreted as marginally mad; in front of him, held in both hands which were upholstered in blood-streaked gloves, a white rat sat very still, its paws on its executioner's thumbs, looking somewhere into the distance.

Dr. Saldanha saw her pause, and dismissed the room with a wave of her hand.

"That's Joe Wiggan," she said, "don't mind him, he's a little odd but he's perfectly harmless to humans. You'll get used to him. He's happy with a clear set of instructions; he's not one for complex conversations."

"Uh—he—do I have to bring the animals…"

"When they're ready," Dr. Saldanha said. "We'll talk about the ongoing experiments. I'll show you your bench…"

The lab was familiar, full of the smells and sounds that Olivia had learned to recognize and work with as an undergraduate— but here, for the first time, she suddenly became very aware of what Simon had meant, on the evening of her graduation day, when he had spoken of the world of research versus the real world… and of how much of the one she would have to sacrifice if she were to keep the other.

They showed her where the syringes were, how to use them and dispose of them, how and where to inject mice and rabbits with experimental drugs or with toxins. Under supervision, she fought down the bile in the back of her throat and gave one injection to a quiescent mouse. The next time, she was handed the vial of experimental substance and pointed into the rabbit room, and she went as though she were going to a funeral.

The vial of viscous yellow liquid and the syringe on the bench beside her, Olivia reached one latex-gloved hand into the hutch which housed the supply of healthy rabbits and drew out a small gray specimen barely larger than her hand. She held it on the palm of her left hand, where it sat quite contentedly, staring up at her and wiggling its nose in a manner that made her smile as she stroked the soft fur between its ears with her right forefinger. And then she looked down on the bench. At the syringe, at the yellow poison.

Yes, it might save thousands, once the test results were in and carefully analyzed. But it was all suddenly a simple matter of an old-fashioned weighing scale—on the one side, there were all the potential benefits of the research, all the knowledge that could be gleaned; on the other, there was this small innocent animal and, somewhere above it, the mad eyes of Joe Wiggan who held a bloody cleaver in one hand.

She put the rabbit back into the hutch, left the syringe and the vial where she had laid them down, and fled into the ladies' restroom where she locked herself into a cubicle and wept into her hands.

She could not do it. There was something in her that reared up and froze her mind when she thought of giving that rabbit the injection that would mean, within a week or two or three, its death in the 'sacrifice room' where its distended liver would be examined and dissected for the effects of the substance with which it had been injected.

Simon's voice came back to her, haunting her: *You are misguided.*

It was only a rabbit.

It was only the first rabbit. The first in a long line of them.

She could not do it.

There were specializations which she could take, once she had her post-graduate qualifications under her belt. There were a thousand things she could do with her life, in this field, working in the discipline which she had worked so hard to master and labored over endless examinations to qualify for. And yet it had all come down to this—narrowed down to this— Olivia knew that there was not a single thing left that she could do in a laboratory and not see that sweet soft animal nestled into the palm of her hand. Her career was over before it had begun.

It would have been a victory of sorts to stay. To do what she had always done—to stay faithful to the career that she herself had chosen, to fight down the nausea that rose in her when she thought of the years to come—to remain steady, to remain solid, to remain safe.

And she knew, even as she thought about it, that she was already standing on the threshold, and that this was no more than a parting glance thrown over her shoulder. She would step out into the real world where the cold winds blew, any moment now, completely unable to see beyond the first bend of the road that led from the front door of this house of science. She would take a risk. She would follow the new road… wherever it led her.

Olivia blinked, and she was back to staring at a card with a photograph of a group of laughing young people around a table covered in a red checked tablecloth.

"That was *this* life," she said. "That led me directly here. I left home, moved to another city, got a loan, did another degree—in linguistics, re-learning in a more structured and academic way languages I'd already picked up colloquially while I was an Army brat being trailed around Europe by my Dad when he was posted there when I was just a kid—and then found a translator's job, and then a better one, and then one here at the UN… that was this life. The other life, the one you snatched me from to bring me here…"

"I did no such thing," Ariel said. "You chose. I did no snatching."

"Yes—but—that night, that other night, the place where I am, or will be, tonight with those friends, back at the Spanish Gardens—I didn't do any of that, back then."

"No," Ariel agreed. "You did exactly what Simon said you always did. You took the safe way, and followed the roads that others expected you to follow. In this life you certainly seem to have a more… adventurous streak."

Olivia considered the card on the table with a quizzical tilt to her head. "But it's like I said, it's the same road. I was there, in that crowd, straight after I graduated with my science degree. In *both* the versions. If the roads I walked were different, I can't tell from here."

"Perhaps merely superimposed," Ariel murmured. "In

either event, that might have been your first crossroads. Your first, as you called it, bridge. And here you are, and you actually remember what *else* happened along this path, somewhere over yonder in a direction you never went in *this* version of your lifetime. It's remarkable. You must forgive me, but it's rare—so rare—and I am grateful..."

Olivia shot him a startled look—he had allowed the unguarded joy to escape, yet again, and this time he had given her an opening. "Grateful? Whatever for?"

"For this," Ariel said, waving his hand to include the two of them and everything around them. "For the chance to sit here and talk with you, and figure it out as you figure it out. You do realize that with a great gift comes great responsibility, though, don't you?"

Olivia sat back. "What gift, and what responsibility?"

"You. The knowledge of it all, lying sleeping inside of you, and then waking to this—to full awareness, across multiple timelines, multiple lives. You know. You *remember.* And people like you... because they can't help it... wind up changing the world. Do you remember the last two words on that page of instructions I've been giving out?"

Olivia nodded. *"Choose wisely,"* she said.

"For them—for the others—for anybody else—that merely means what it says," Ariel said. "For you... it's greater. Choose wisely what you do next, because your words and your actions may carry great weight. Like I said, you are a light—and people may not be able to see this like I can right now but they can sense it and they will hang on to your words. Choose them wisely."

"Now you're scaring me," Olivia said.

"Oh, no, no, no—it's nothing to be afraid of. Like I said, it's a gift, and one given to few. No, don't be afraid of it. There's nothing to be afraid *of.* It's just that the sum of what you are has just become greater than just yourself—where you go, others will follow."

"But why...?"

"I've always wondered about that, actually—I myself have always been far more interested in the *why* than I should be. We're oddly alike in that way, you and I. My job's always been just to facilitate, not to try and understand. But this, now—this is a chance I don't get all that often. It's frowned on, actually. Upstairs."

Olivia grinned at him. "Talking out of school?"

"Yes, but you already know the stuff I'm not supposed to tell you," Ariel said. "It's not as if I've broken any rules. Well, all right, I've broken a few rules, but it isn't as if it *matters*—it's kind of hard to forbid knowledge to the one who already has an awareness of the secrets which are supposed to be protected."

"What, like these?" Olivia asked, flipping back a few pages in her journal and turning it to face Ariel across the table.

He glanced at the neat handwriting within.

Evening. You walk down a shuttered street; there are "Closed" signs in shop windows and on doors as you stroll past. Illuminated displays of things. This is not Rodeo Drive; you're likely to see cheap, workaday shoes. Maybe tools. Printed T-shirts.

Narrow alley opens between two buildings. There are no signs, nothing to indicate that it leads anywhere at all. But you turn. The passageway between a couple of blank brick walls widens abruptly into a courtyard. And across the courtyard, dimly lit, a coy sign above the door, there it is—Spanish Gardens.

It does not look very Spanish. It certainly doesn't look anything like a garden.

This is the place where you come for your celebrations—your graduations, your anniversaries. You bring your girlfriend there to propose. You go there in a rowdy crowd after the pomp and circumstance of the graduation ceremony, and you order Irish Coffees ("Keep 'em coming!") and get beautifully, headily, cathartically tipsy while some crooner weaves his way through "House of the Rising Sun" on his high chair and you bellow the lyrics with him when you can remember them.

You come here to laugh, and to cry, and to share, and to grow, and to guzzle cream pies and to linger over coffee after some sad movie show, and to be able to tell some newcomer, somewhere, sometime, "Ah, yes. I know the Spanish Gardens".

Ariel lifted his head. "You do realize that you remember it this well only because you—another you, a different you, some part of you—is headed there this very night, in that other life, is probably standing in the very street from which that alley opens—that the box is open and you can see in—but that there is a price you will have to pay for choosing to stay here, and the price is this perfect memory of a place you have loved?"

"But if I—a different I, some part of me—is truly headed there right now, then we have a paradox," Olivia said thoughtfully.

"Oh, yes," Ariel said, with a knowing smile.

"If I went there—and I did go, because I was there when you, or Ellen, or somebody, handed me that paper with the instructions on it before I walked into a dark room and found myself living another life—but if I went there then, there will be some sort of record of me being there. The others will remember conversations we have had this night, there, at Spanish Gardens. So if I went into the place through an ordinary door and was spirited away by some quite other means—what do *they* get to remember? Where do they go from here?"

"So—then—turn the second card," Ariel said.

"It's the same one as before—" Olivia began, staring at a scene from Spanish Gardens, red check tablecloths and all, and even largely the same cast.

"Not... quite," Ariel murmured. "Look closer."

The young waitress at the Spanish Gardens came back with Simon's card and a signing chit; he signed his name on her copy with a flourish worthy of autographing one of his books—and perhaps that was where the manner of it had come from—and handed it back to her with a nod of thanks.

"Thank you," she said. And then added, incongruously, "Have a nice day."

Ellen had gathered up the cash that the others had thrown on the table to cover their own part of the bill, and frowned, sorting the notes into denominations, counting them, and coming up with a number she could not reconcile with the stuff that the money was supposed to have covered.

"Wait, even with an eye-wateringly large tip there is too much money here," she said. "Somebody put in more than was strictly necessary."

"Give me the check," Simon said. She handed him the printout, and the cash, and he pored over it for a moment, and then pointed. "There's the trouble," he said. "They put in the spaghetti twice. And are we *sure* we had this many Irish Coffees? It wouldn't surprise me, but… oh, anyway. It's the end of the world, after all, and God alone knows how they're keeping it all straight out there tonight to begin with. Look at this place. Our girl could have done worse. I'll consider it part of the tip—it's on me. Anyone want to take back a couple of bucks?"

John shook his head. "If it was me that put in too much, I'll leave it in. I did get a free coffee out of it anyway."

"Oh, Merry Christmas," Quincey muttered.

"Are we done, then? Shall we? Is it still snowing? Traffic might still be murder out there tonight."

They abandoned their cozy corner table, one by one—first Quincey slipping out of her booth, then John scraping his chair back, then Simon sliding out of the booth and helping to hand Ellen out after him. They drifted through the archway, turning right to where the coat hooks were, and Quincey began to root through the piles of coats and jackets to where she had hung up her own.

"There's mine… Ellen, I think that one was yours… Simon?"

"The black and yellow is mine. The Goretex jacket. No, to your left—that one—no, the other…"

But it was somehow oddly difficult to make out color. The whole thing had faded to a strange sepia shade, an old photograph, all the colors blending into various intensities of a fading brown and ghost-like pale beige. John's self-described black and yellow jacket looked washed out, just a symphony in tones ranging from milk chocolate to wan eggshell cream.

But behind it, standing out in stark contrast to the loss of color in the rest of the image, one single coat still remained hanging on its peg. One coat, falling in graceful and elegant folds, a coat that was a blazing scarlet, bright red, a ghost of color and substance in a world of insubstantial light and shadow.

They all noticed it, stopped, frozen for a moment by its presence, feeling a strange familiarity wash over them as though they ought to have known all about that coat... but, in the end, didn't. John was the first to turn away, turn his head, back to where Ariel stood waiting, as always, behind the glass display case.

"Someone seems to have lost a coat," John said, although just why he assumed that the scarlet coat was actually lost, hanging as it did in a welter of other coats that must have belonged to the other patrons in the noisy, crowded café, was not something he had stopped to think about.

"I'll make sure it finds its way back to where it belongs," Ariel said, giving no indication that what John had said was in any way strange at all.

They paused, at the door, all four of them—John with his hand on the door, in the process of pushing it open; Quincey, both hands up in a motion to pull the hood of her coat up over her hair; Simon and Ellen, hands linked, his gloved in supple tan leather, hers in cheerful chunky knitted gloves—and looked back, one last time, at the scarlet coat burning in the pale background of the rest of the café, as though the whole meaning of Spanish Gardens had somehow become encapsulated in that one single garment and nothing else mattered in this place at all. And then they turned away, one by one, and stepped out into the snow.

"You can never see them again," Ariel said softly. "*Any* of them. You do realize that, don't you?"

"Yes," Olivia murmured, her fingers stroking the card lightly. "They remember a different past from the one I've now lived. Things could get very confusing."

"Not to mention fractured. It's given to those like you to make choices like this—in far greater and fuller awareness than any of the others had when they reached their own moments of decision—but it does carry a toll you have to pay."

"All of them?" Olivia asked, looking up. "Did you give all of them this choice? There, at the Gardens? Tonight?"

"You mean, will I," Ariel said. "For you, tonight hasn't happened yet."

She made an impatient gesture with her hand. "Yes, words, words, words. Answer the question."

"Yes," he said, suddenly serious. "All of them."

Olivia stared at the card in silence, until Ariel articulated her unspoken thoughts.

"I really shouldn't be telling you this, but...yes, all of them stepped out of their lives and their times, yes, they all tasted an alternative. Yes... they all chose to return to that table."

"Did you talk to them? Like this, like you're talking to me now?"

"I thought I told you," Ariel said. "You're a rare thing. I talked to them, sure—some more than others—with Ellen I broke more rules than I should have but the situation was... complicated.... But like this? No, Olivia. Not like this. I get to talk like this with only a handful of people, across all of time."

"I could still go back, you know," Olivia said. "Walk back in through that door. Throw this second card, and its story, away. Take the stream of time back into its accustomed bed. Let everything be exactly as it was when I walked into Spanish Gardens—when I walk into Spanish Gardens tonight... but..."

"Olivia," Ariel said, his voice gentle, "it's already done. The die is already cast."

"Did you ask the others to make a choice?"

"Yes," he said. "I did. That was my task."

"But you never asked me," Olivia said. "Not in so many words. Not directly. I never said yes or no to anything."

"That's because you gave me the answer before I could ask the question," Ariel said. "You had already made up your mind, before you ever saw me walk in here through that door—and you knew me, and spoke to me from that place where you had already chosen to stand. I didn't *need* to ask you. This sudden flutter of nostalgia... that's all it is. It's nostalgia. It'll go away, as you begin to forget."

"Everything? I'll forget everything?"

"Yes, even you," Ariel said. "*Eventually*. Sorry, some rules can't be broken that easily. You can't carry the burden of *all* of your lives, not indefinitely."

"But I will," Olivia said, softly but stubbornly. "I *will*. I will remember them."

"You might remember more than some—and certainly there is no requirement that you forget that you ever knew any of those people who came—who will come—to the Gardens tonight," Ariel conceded. "After all, in some form they've all been a part of that new past which you see stretching out behind you from where you're standing right now—it's just not quite the same one that they will recall. And the best way to stop the clash of memories is simply to make a world in which your paths do not cross again, yours and Simon's and Ellen's and Quincey's and John's. They're—well—there was a reason for that card being in sepia colors. They're gone, they're in your memories, they're alive and living and breathing and together *somewhere else*, and they will remember you, but they will not think of you much, not even in the aftermath of tonight, and after a while they will not think of you at all."

"So the world doesn't end after all?"

"What?"

"You spoke of the aftermath. That implies that there's… something… after midnight strikes tonight."

"Olivia. The world ends every midnight. A new world starts every morning. You know, the Aztecs sacrificed thousands to make sure that happened—that a sun rose every morning. I thought I'd made that clear."

Olivia actually laughed, a laugh as brittle and diamond-bright as the December sunshine outside the window. "You're mixing up your Mesoamerican tribes," she said. "It's the Mayan twilight, not the Aztec sunrise…"

"It s the same sun, setting or rising," Ariel said, "It all makes sense, in the end. You just have to think clearly about it."

"And by the way—you make nothing *clear*. You do realize this, don't you? You're a Sphinx, spinning your secrets. Are you at least going to tell me what the others turned from? I mean, if I'm supposed to forget everything anyway…"

"I can't," Ariel said. "I might be spinning secrets, but those secrets are not mine to spin for you. They're theirs. Suffice it to say that they had their reasons—be it pride, or empathy, or the potential to have it all *eventually* if one of them gave up something important *now*. But it's their secrets. Not mine to tell."

"If that card pack of yours was a real Tarot deck, I wonder what cards would come if I drew one for each of them," Olivia said thoughtfully.

"According to which interpretation?" Ariel inquired. And then picked up the card deck and weighed it in his hand. "Oh, go on, then. I think the Mesoamericans would be fascinated. Take four, from the top."

Olivia shrugged, smiling, and reached for the deck, laying out four cards face up on the table. The Emperor. The Chariot. Judgment. Death.

"Ouch," Ariel said, but his voice was complacent.

"Ah, no. Death doesn't mean death, not in Tarot. It's supposed to mean a transformation. A clearing away of the old, to make way for the new. A great change. New beginnings. Not death so much as rebirth—and not a bad card to draw at the end of the world, actually." She glared at him, the complacency finally registering properly. "But you *know* all this, don't you?"

"And which of them would that one signify?" Ariel said, refusing to rise to the bait.

Olivia hesitated. "I don't really know why, but I'd give it to Quincey," she said.

Ariel's eyebrow went up. "More apt than you realize."

"Oh?"

"Her secret," Ariel said, reproachfully.

Olivia shrugged her shoulders a fraction, acknowledging the hit, and drawing another card closer to her to contemplate it closely.

"Judgment," she said. "Atonement, rebirth, growing awareness. The need to repent... and perhaps forgive."

"Who?" Ariel asked.

"I still remember some of what was talked about around that table—even though it hasn't happened yet—even though some of it might never happen, now. But I still remember, enough. Enough of John's story." Olivia tapped the card. "I didn't know the half of it, not before the floodgates opened tonight, at the Gardens. If anyone has need to forgive... it's him."

"Again, pretty, good," Ariel said, nodding. "I think I should play cards more often. Where did you learn to do this?"

"Any more details?..." Olivia asked, and then shook her head with a small smile. "I know. I know. His secret. Which leaves two."

She drew the remaining cards together and stared at them, eyes flicking from one to the other, thinking about the things she knew, the things she had no business remembering, and finally touched the one on the left lightly with her fingertips.

"Ellen," she said. "The Chariot. I have no idea why—it's like, a life of holding tight onto the reins, control over at least two things pulling in opposite directions, struggle, but still, control, and going forward in a coherent direction after all. It kind of makes sense. If only because the last card..."

Ariel rested his chin on his laced fingers. "The Emperor," he said. "Of course—that could only be—"

"Simon." Olivia said, and grinned at Ariel across the table. "Tarot is never that obvious, actually. But in this case... yup. He's always kind of been the guy in charge. And in my own new-born personal history... he called me misguided, and I responded to that, and changed my life, and it mattered. It mattered enough for me to be right here, right now, renouncing him forever." She tapped her lower lip with a thoughtful forefinger. "We were lovers," she said. "Once upon a time. In a world below the horizon, never to be seen again. But it was because of him, in a way, after we broke up—it was because of what I knew—in that other life, when I got married, for all the wrong reasons—"

Ariel swept away the four Major Arcana cards into a small pile on the side of the table. "There's still one of the original cards which you haven't turned over," he said.

"Now?" Olivia asked, hand hovering over the face-down card.

"Now," Ariel agreed.

Olivia sighed, and flipped the card over with a small sharp motion.

Olivia paused for a moment outside the coffee shop door,

weighing in her mind whether she had time to stop for a coffee or not—she peered inside, and if she had noticed anyone else waiting at the counter, anyone in a queue, that would have done the trick and she would have hurried on. She was already late as it was. But she really wanted a shot of caffeine to both warm her up and to kick-start her brain, and the coast seemed clear— and she made her decision, pushed open the door, and hurried inside while drawing off her gloves so that she didn't have to fumble for her money.

Perhaps it was that, walking in with her head down and her attention on her own hands, that precipitated the inevitable— she had been eyeing the counter where one placed orders, not the counter where one picked them up, and the young man who turned from the latter in something of a hurry barrelled straight into Olivia, still fixing the plastic to-go lid securely onto his cup.

The cup went one way, the lid another, and the milky coffee in the cup poured down the sleeve of Olivia's sky-blue padded jacket in a scalding stream.

She yelped when it hit her hand, newly bared from its glove, and barely had time to look up before she found her hand snatched up and hastily mopped by a sweater.

"I'm sorry—I'm *so* sorry—I was thinking about something else entirely—it's completely my fault, I'm so sorry, are you hurt?"

"Just surprised," Olivia said, taking her hand back and casting a doleful glance at her sleeve where coffee still dripped down the seams.

The sweater found its way to the spot where her eyes rested, mopping up the coffee stream.

"I'm so, so sorry—I'll pay for the cleaning, if it stains—are you sure I didn't burn your hand?"

"You're ruining your sweater," Olivia protested, finally looking up to meet the eyes of the young man with whom she had collided.

"It doesn't matter," he said earnestly.

Olivia's mouth quirked. The thing had almost rhymed. After a moment he realized this, too, and his own mouth curved into a smile.

"Did you come in for a coffee?" he asked, and then tossed his head impatiently. "I'm an imbecile, it's a coffee shop, what else would you have come in here for, performing seals? Tell you what, it's on me—go ahead, place your order—anything you want—" He signaled the grinning barista. "Whatever the lady wants. I'm paying."

"It isn't necessary..." Olivia began, but he waved a hand in a gesture of dismissal.

"I absolutely insist," he said. "It's the least I can do. Are you sure your hand is okay?"

"It's fine," Olivia said. "Okay, just a plain and perfectly ordinary latte. Thank you."

"What she said," the young man said to the barista. "And I'll have another, to replace the one I just threw all over your floor."

"Excuse me," said one of the other baristas, who had just arrived with a mop. "Speaking of the floor. Can I get at that? Thank you."

They stepped to one side while the spilled coffee was efficiently mopped up off the floor and the coffee machine hissed and spat behind the counter as Olivia's latte was being made.

"I'm Brandon Boyes," said the young man, sticking his hand out. "Brand."

Olivia actually laughed. "Brand? As in, 'burning'? How appropriate..."

He flushed, but then could not help a self-conscious chuckle of his own at the absurdity of the juxtaposition of the name with the circumstances.

"Again, my deepest apologies. My mother taught me better than to be this careless—and I certainly don't think that she named me with that in mind." He looked up, his expression expectant, and Olivia answered the unspoken question.

"I'm Olivia Halloran," she said.

"Pleased to meet you. I wish I had done so in a more suave and sophisticated manner, and without inflicting bodily harm, but I hope..."

"Latte," the barista called out, setting a cup on the counter. Olivia turned to pick it up, nodding her thanks at Brand.

"Thanks, I appreciate it—I have to run, though, I'm late—"

"Wait—the jacket—can I…"

"No, it's fine. Really. It's fine. I don't…"

But he had whipped out a pen and was scribbling something furiously on the back of one of those cardboard sleeves that were set out at the counter to mitigate the scorch of the hot coffee through the paper cups, and even as she finished speaking he was holding it out to her.

"My phone number," he said. "Please, call me—let me know—if I can—"

Olivia took the cardboard reflexively. "Thank you," she said, not entirely certain for what.

She stuck the cardboard in the deep pocket of her coat, nodded an awkward goodbye, and walked out, gloveless, warming her hands on the sides of her coffee cup.

She contemplated calling him, briefly, as she took her jacket off some ten minutes later and realized that the coffee had not entirely left the jacket unmarked—and then she got immersed into the business of the day, and put it out of her mind. She was actually startled when her phone rang about a week later, while she was sitting in front of her TV with a slice of pizza which was supper.

"Olivia? Olivia Halloran?"

She had the feeling that she should have recognized the voice, but for a moment it was wholly unfamiliar. "Yes?" she said, frowning.

"It's Brand Boyes. Brand. As in, 'burning'. I poured coffee down your arm a couple of days ago, the coffee shop…"

Memory returned, and the skin on the back of her hand prickled a little where the hot coffee had scalded her a week before. "Oh, yes. Hi, Brand." She frowned a little as she recalled that she had not given him her phone number—he had handed her his, rather—but on the whole she was probably not that difficult to find, if he had been interested. And apparently he had.

"I just wanted to… I mean…" There was a silence, during which she could all but picture him holding the receiver of the telephone away from him while he rolled his eyes at his inarticulate stabs at starting a conversation, which made laughter start to bubble in the back of her throat. She succeeded in controlling it, and waited. After a pause, she could hear Brand heave a deep sigh, and then he started again. "I'm not very good at this," he said. "What I wanted to ask, really, is, well, can I buy you another coffee—to drink, this time, instead of pouring it— that is—can I just buy you a *proper* coffee sometime? Soon? Or maybe dinner? What kind of movies do you like?"

This time she let the laugh out. He sounded delightfully bemused, and while she had not thought that her appearance had ever turned men's heads something had certainly caught Brand's eye.

"Coffee," she said, surprising herself by looking forward to the potential date even as she found herself accepting it. "And then we'll see."

"Same time, same place?" he said, and then paused. "Uh. I mean, same coffee shop—or maybe not, given our track record there..."

"The coffee shop's fine. See you there. Tomorrow night?"

"Sure," he said. "Thanks."

They had the coffee. They had another, a couple of days later. They had the dinner, and the movie, and more dinners. She found out things about him—that he liked big dogs but had never been in a position to really own one, that he dabbled in watercolors, that he had travelled almost as much as she had during the days that her father had been in the service (although for different reasons—she had been the quintessential army brat, but he had been taken to Europe to educate him and broaden his mind). He came from old money; he was an endearingly awkward only child who had been raised under a family microscope, by a mother whom he idolized. She had been widowed early but she had never remarried or given Brand a stepfather; instead, she had concentrated on making her only son's life as extraordinary as money could buy.

He was twenty five years old when Olivia met him, but the chronological age, baldly stated, was deceptive—Brand was a kid in an adult's body, never having had either the need or the opportunity to grow up. Initially Olivia found his very boyishness appealing, and she allowed herself to be swept up, in the beginning of it all, by his ability to make extraordinary things happen. He took her to exclusive places which she had never even known existed before she met him, and he was often original and surprisingly perceptive in the things he planned— which went hand in hand with that childlike sense of wonder which he had never quite shed, and had had the means to indulge.

On her own birthday, Brand had told Olivia to be ready by mid-morning when he'd swing by to pick her up—and to wear comfortable clothes suitable for potential rough-housing. He would not tell her any more than that, even after the pick-up turned out to be in a limousine and she redoubled her questions, her curiosity piqued by the incongruity of her attire with her conveyance. She was even more mystified when the limo swung into what she realized was the parking lot to the zoo, and came to a halt a little away from the main lot.

"Where...?" Olivia began again, but Brand put a finger to his lips.

"Quiet," he said. "You'll wake the babies."

"The *babies*?"

Someone was waiting for them as they climbed out of the limo, a woman dressed in practical zoo-keeper garb who greeted Brand by name and told him that Mr. Sand was waiting for him inside.

"Who's Mr. Sand?" Olivia whispered as they passed into the zoo via a discreet side gate.

"He's part owner of the zoo. Mother knows him quite well, his wife's a regular at the soirées—and when I heard the latest news I knew I had to get you here before the crowds came. Fortunately he was quite amenable to it."

"Brand, what are you up to?"

"Left, over there. There's a private enclosure back there, the back of the tigers' habitat. Look carefully. What do you see?"

Olivia peered into the pen. "A tiger," she said practically, and then, as something shifted between the dozing tiger's paws, squealed with delight. "Oh! It's a cub! It's *two* cubs!"

"Twins," Brand said. "They won't be shown to the public

for a couple of weeks yet, just to make sure they're both doing okay. But the littler one's eyes opened only this week, and they're *kittens*, Olivia, large cute growly kittens—and I figured you might want to meet them."

"What are their names?"

"They haven't been named yet. There's supposed to be a competition, when they're released into the public pen. Until then, you can call them anything you like."

One of the tiger cubs got up and stretched, and then waddled with an endearing kittenish flat-footed enthusiasm out into the middle of the enclosure where something had caught its attention. It batted at whatever it had come there to investigate, with one outsize paw.

Olivia heard a whirr and click, and glanced to where Brand had extracted a camera from the bag he had been carrying over his shoulder.

"Come on," he said with a grin, "they're going to go in and get them—time for their weigh-in. Come say hello."

He took dozens of photographs, including one of Olivia, clad in one of the zoo workers' smocks so that her own stranger's scent didn't rub off on the babies, holding both of them in her lap, laughing as one of them appeared to be getting ready for a nice comfortable nap and the other had risen up on its hind feet, one preposterous paw on Olivia's chest and the other reaching for the enticing glitter of an earring half hidden by the loose long hair falling over her shoulders.

She kept that photograph beside her bed, framed. Whatever her mood when she woke up on any given morning, she would look over at the photo of herself with her arms full of tiger babies, and she could feel the smile she had worn on that day coming back to her face. Very little could ruin her days, after that beginning.

But Brand was full of these adventures. On another occasion he called her up unexpectedly and told her to get ready to go sailing—or he would take her riding on a beach, or up in a hot-air balloon or a private helicopter ride, somehow getting permission for impossible flight plans, both soaring high and swooping low and changing her perspective on the world.

But all that energy and enthusiasm was rationed, held in severe check, as though he did everything by permission, or by royal decree—and when Olivia finally met his mother, she understood why.

Mrs. Helen Boyes was a stern matriarch of the old school. Her silver-white hair was coaxed into a neat braided chignon at the nape of her neck, and she wore elegant black from head to toe, setting off to perfection a triple strand of pearls that was her only jewelry aside from a set of rings on her wedding finger, when Olivia came to tea. The smile was flawless... and cold. Olivia was treated with the utmost civility and affability, but it was clear that she was auditioning for a part, and that it was Mrs. Boyes, rather than Brand, who would be the director of the show.

"And what do you do?" Olivia was asked, over tea served in a porcelain cup with a pattern of pale blue roses and a gilded rim.

"I'm a translator," Olivia said. "I've done literary work, on occasion—but I'm working in the diplomatic corps right now. With the UN."

"Ah. How *interesting* that must be," Helen said, with a glitter of ice in her smile. She seemed to be given to a certain penchant for putting a slight but pointed emphasis into her sentences, which had evolved into something of a sardonic and dismissive tone, as though the very thing she had emphasized was somehow... questionable. "You must be *good* with words."

"I write poetry," Olivia said, not quite certain why she had volunteered this.

"Modern?" Helen inquired, allowing a hint of distaste to slip through.

"Classical," Olivia said, almost unwillingly, rather less than eager to elaborate but feeling as though she was being interrogated and an answer was required. "Sonnets, sometimes. Or haiku."

"An *interesting* talent," Helen said. "Do you publish?"

"One or two, back when I was a student," Olivia said, hearing a defensive tone find its way into her voice. "Nothing since."

"A hobby, then," Helen said, dismissing it.

And Olivia with it.

"She's gorgeous," Olivia told Brand, afterwards. "She looks like a Queen in one of those old-fashioned movies about Ruritanian royalty. But you don't have her eyes, or her cheekbones—you must take after your father."

"You saying I'm not fit to be the Ruritanian Prince?" Brand said, laughing.

"Sweetie, you couldn't *not* be a Prince if you tried," Olivia said, smiling—and then realized that she had just pulled Brand's mother's trick, using emphasis to make a point, and actually winced.

Brand missed it. "She liked you," he said. "I could tell?"

"How?' Olivia muttered to herself in an undertone.

Brand turned. "What?"

"Nothing—I just thought...she was rather cool..."

"It's her way," Brand said.

"How come she never re-married? Gave you a step-dad?"

"Never needed to. She was enough to make sure I had everything I needed, and after I grew up a little, she had me for the man of the house."

"But was she..."

"Hey, I have plans for this weekend," Brand said. "Make sure you're ready—I'll be picking you up early..."

To Brand, his mother ranked far higher than just Ruritanian royalty—she was a sort of goddess, even if Olivia, after another couple of encounters, decided that if Helen Boyes was a goddess it was an unholy cross between Kali and something from the imagination of Clive Barker, with the pearl necklace, if scrutinized carefully, probably turning out to consist of immaculately strung-together skulls of the shrunken heads of her enemies.

Olivia tried speaking to Brand about all of this—but she quickly discovered that he had a talent for not hearing her when she broached the subject, for not talking about his mother if there was the faintest chance that he might hear something that he did not wish to.

And with that understanding in place, she suddenly found

herself far less attracted to him than she thought she had been. She had had to learn the hard way how to stand up for herself in her own busy boisterous family, with her own authoritative Army-officer father; adding Brand's mother into that mix was not something that she found herself willing to do, and it was becoming increasingly clear that Brand and Helen Boyes came as a package deal. The bower would be romantic, and tastefully decorated, and plush, and even loving—but it would still be a gilded cage... and the one trapped within, a pretty bird of paradise for the two of them to put on display.

Brand was surprisingly good at not hearing anything that might threaten his world. He was, after all and in spite of all evidence to the contrary, still a child... and would not hear her when she tried to bring up the subject of his mother in the context of any kind of future that she, Olivia, might have been expected to share with him. In the end, she simply took a leave of absence from her job, and walked away from everything.

She didn't want to have the sort of conversation that would undoubtedly unfold if she tried to explain herself. So she wrote him a letter—a short one, telling him no more than, essentially, *I quit*—packed a bag that could take her anywhere, and drove to the airport. She had no particular destination in mind; she let her eyes slide down the Departures board until they snagged on a name that held her attention—Albuquerque. New Mexico. That sounded interesting, and it was a place she had never been. She tracked down the check-in counter of the relevant airline, and bought a ticket on the spot.

No doubt he would look for her, at first. If she returned too soon—perhaps even if she returned at all—he could probably find her again, if he wished. But Olivia had chosen liberty over security, the open skies over the protective cage.

Part of her hurt. Part of her thought that her heart might be just a little bit broken.

But the rest of her was whole, and she would keep it that way. A marginally broken heart would heal faster than a broken spirit and wings clipped by expectations, and propriety, and the demands of a society which, if it would allow her in at all, would ask a higher price of admission than she found herself willing to pay.

The sun was setting as she settled back into the plane seat, on her way... somewhere else, somewhere new, if only for a little while. It seemed fitting—a sun setting, an old life slipping away behind the dark horizon. She closed her eyes, allowing herself to drowse, and then to sleep. Her dreams were of eagles, and of sacrifice, and of a bright sun rising over the ocean on a brand new morning.

Olivia blinked several times, rapidly, as though she were really waking up from a dream.

"That's...freaky," she said at last. "How do you do that?"

"Leave the Sphinx some secrets," Ariel said. "I use what I am given. Although I can see that I'll have to read up on the Tarot. It would seem that it could be useful, in my line of work. Why Albuquerque?"

"What?"

"Why not London? Or Kyoto? Or the Mexican Riviera? Why Albuquerque? You obviously didn't *stay* there, or at least not very long, else I wouldn't be talking to you in *this* coffee shop, back in the city from where you left—"

"Why not Albuquerque?" Olivia said. "It was... interesting, but it was just a place, and any place would have done for me, back then. After all, all of life is a foreign country anyway..."

"That sounds familiar."

"Kerouac," Olivia said with a limpid smile. "Again. I told you I quote Kerouac a lot. He seems to have said a lot of things that make sense."

Ariel acknowledged that with a nod and a wry smile. "But back to the business at hand," he said. "I need you to tell me..."

"So—what would I be?" Olivia interrupted, eyeing Ariel's remaining cards.

He followed her gaze, and then his eyes came back to meet hers. "Be?" he asked.

"In your Tarot."

Ariel laughed. "Even without knowing everything about it, that would be an easy question," he said. He flipped the pack over so it was face-up, and fanned it across the width of the table—and the cards were all identical.

The Fool.

"The traveler who is off to see the world, but knows not where or how," Olivia said, choking back something that was almost a sob.

"Someone free to make their own choices," Ariel said, correcting her very subtly. And tapped the bundle slung over the shoulder of the figure clad in motley, dancing out of the frame of the card. "Carrying all of life's experiences in a bundle on a stick."

"All right," Olivia said, "I'll take it. I can see how it might fit."

"You might seem alone, on the card, but that's deceptive—I think that where the Fool leads, the path opens up, and others follow. In time."

Olivia laughed. "I'm a *dingledoody*."

"Kerouac again?"

"I always kind of thought of myself as the one who shambled after, as the quote has it. Not one of the dingledoodies, the ones who were dancing down the street, the ones who were mad to live, the ones who burned like roman candles…" She blinked, and tilted her head thoughtfully. "I kind of *was* the one who shambled after, back in that other world—I followed everybody, staying behind the lines, watching the shining people and wishing I could be like them and never having the courage to try…Ariel…?"

But he was gone, as though he had never been there. So were the cards—all except one, lying in the middle of the table, face down. There was something written on the back of it, and Olivia picked it up, squinting at the slanted writing.

You've already told me. The world has settled into a new place. We won't meet again—but thank you for helping me understand.

She started to turn the card over, but a hand dropping gently on her shoulder made her turn and look up, and smile.

"Hey," she said, tucking the card away into her journal without looking at it and closing the notebook around it. "You're early—I wasn't expecting you for at least another hour—the restaurant..."

"I kind of turned over the kitchen to René, and told him he had a free hand," Jack Kelly, her partner of almost a year's standing, said, grinning at the memory of the expression of his fellow chef in the restaurant the two of them owned jointly. "He never could resist that. I left him muttering about braised duck and shallots and hazelnuts and a number of other things that I'd have had to think hard about putting in with duck—but he'll carry it off. He has a gift. He transmutes food into something quite different than what you might expect from just the sum of its parts. You done?"

"I was just..." Olivia began, looking around, but Ariel was gone—and already starting to fade, just a little, from her memory, despite her sturdy protestations that she would remember every detail of everything that she had learned. She remembered the gray eyes, and the strange nature of their conversation, and even whole portions of what was said, almost verbatim—she remembered there were odd cards with pictures on them—but the details were starting to fuzz around the edges. And there would be no explaining any of it to Jack.

She sighed, and gathered up her notebook, stuffing it into her purse. Jack swept her coat off the back of her chair where she had draped it, and was holding it out for her when she stood.

"Come on," he said, "we can stop at that pizza place you like and you can pick one of your strange pizzas for tonight."

"You? Eating pizza? Voluntarily? It *must* be the end of the world," Olivia said, giggling, shrugging her arms into the coat's sleeves.

"It won't kill me," Jack said philosophically. He was still holding onto the shoulders of the coat as she closed it up around the front, and now his arms slipped down and forward until he was holding her against him in a loose embrace, cupping each of his elbows in the opposite hand as he held her shoulders encircled, and his lips barely touching her ear, nuzzling at the lobe. "Livy," he said, "if any of this claptrap is right and we're about to spin off into eternity, in theory it would be good if I could sit under an open sky in Tibet somewhere and watch the stars going out overhead. But in the absence of a Tibetan monastery—and, probably, the necessary clear skies, they say it's supposed to cloud over by tonight, possibly even snow—I could probably do worse than pulling the curtains closed and curling up on my sofa with a glass of wine and thou—and a piece of pizza, if that's what it takes. Let's go home."

Olivia closed her eyes, clearing her mind of everything but this moment, being held close and cherished, having lived a life she would not be ashamed to own, being accepted, being respected, being loved…being happy. Even at the end of the world, she could not ask for more than that.

CODA

Thursday, 20 December 2012

Midnight

The snow seemed to have been falling steadily for hours, piled into drifts in windswept corners of the empty little courtyard outside the café's entrance. The path from the door to the mouth of the alley, and then into the alley itself, looked like it might have been walked—a distinct trail was visible under the yellow streetlight—but not very recently, and any dirty footprints were already covered with a fresh layer of powdery snow. The flakes danced in the air, catching the light, vanishing into darkness, landing on the ground or on shoulders or hats or hair. The air smelled crisp, clean, new.

The four who had stepped into the snowy evening did not speak, as though none of them was willing to break the white silence of the winter evening. The alley was barely wide enough for them all to go abreast even if there had been no impediments, but with the drifts the only path that seemed to be left was that narrow ghost of a trail down the middle and so they split up, Simon and Ellen leading the way, John and Quincey bringing up the rear. They trudged through the alley and out into the street—and the street itself seemed oddly empty, deserted, with only one other huddled figure hurrying past on the far side with hands tucked into pockets and head hunched deep into the nest of a voluminous scarf wound about the neck, intent on some personal agenda, not even pausing to notice the quartet who stopped at the street-side mouth of the alley, turning to look at one another.

"Well," Simon said, "I'm parked way over there, a couple of blocks away."

"I'm thataway," John said, indicating the opposite direction with one gloved thumb.

"Me too," Quincey said.

They hesitated, feeling as though something needed to be said, but not quite sure what. Ellen finally broke the stasis, dropping Simon's hand and taking the short step necessary to give first John, and then Quincey, a quick hug. Simon and John shook hands as Quincey and Ellen were disentangling from one another.

"Thanks for coming, you guys," Simon said. "I enjoyed this. Not quite what I was expecting—but it was good to see you all again."

"Indeed," John said. "Say happy birthday to Abby for me."

"And me," Quincey said. "I'm kind of looking forward to going back to my own lot, tomorrow. There's stuff… I need to talk to my kids more."

John peeled back his glove a little to look at his watch. "It's past midnight," he said. "We're still here. The world is still turning. Merry Christmas, everyone. Maybe we should get together again sometime next year—not because of anyone's birthday, or any actual excuse—just because."

"That might be nice," Ellen said. "Have a good Christmas. Happy New Year."

"Okay, we'd better get going," Simon said, his tone almost apologetic. "It's a walk to the car, and the sidewalks are probably all ice underneath all this pretty…"

"I'll walk you to your car, Quincey," John said.

All of them looked as though they might indulge in another hug, as though they were saying farewell forever and not just bidding one another goodbye after a nice night out, but in the end refrained. They parted in silence, the same silence that had come with them from Spanish Gardens, vaguely haunted by something that none of them could quite put a finger on, as though there was a ghost standing there in the snow beside them—invisible, silent, but something or someone to whom they should be saying goodbye as well as to one another. John met Simon's eyes, nodded; Quincey lifted her hand in a small wave, smiling at Simon, smiling and nodding at Ellen.

And then they turned away from one another, Simon and Ellen taking a left up the street past a store window decked out in tinsel and lights, Quincey and John going right, underneath the streetlight, past a storefront dark and empty with a 'To Let' sign ghostly behind the snowdrifts piling up against the glass.

Ellen turned, once. It seemed to her that she could no longer actually tell where the alley opened into the street—that she could not remember at all, any more, what the stores were on the corners of the alley entrance, that she would never be able to find the place again, that Spanish Gardens was as vanished as though it had never been, remembered only in the taste of Irish Coffee still on her tongue.

Simon walked in silence, feeling strangely bereft, as though he had lost something precious that night and could not quite remember what—but aware that he would be extremely sorry if and when he remembered the details of that loss. But then Ellen's foot slid on a concealed patch of ice, and she staggered; his hand tightened on her own, to steady her, and then he dropped it and tucked it between his arm and his side, drawing her closer to him.

"I got you," he said.

And for some reason they looked at one another and smiled.

In the other direction, Quincey walked with small careful steps, forcing John to adjust his long stride in order to keep pace with her.

"Sorry," she said, aware of this. "I think I wore the wrong shoes for this—slick soles—I didn't realize it was going to get this messy..."

"It's all right," John said, with a smile. He was hatless, and the snow was starting to stick, white crystals, on his dark hair. "We have all the time in the world, now."

"I wonder," Quincey said, keeping her eyes down where she was picking her way on the sidewalk, "if anyone out there believed that something cataclysmic would actually, you know, *happen* tonight—like, the Earth would split like an apple..."

"You watch too many disaster movies," John said.

"Or if anyone was disappointed," Quincey said softly.

"I think we'll probably be hearing in the news tomorrow that there have been suicides," John said. "You know the mindset. It'll all come down in ruins around me anyway, so I'll just off myself first. But when the ruins don't come… it's always too late to take it all back…"

"That's me," Quincey said unexpectedly, breaking into his sentence. And then shrugged apologetically. "I mean, that's my car. Right there under the light."

They paused beside the car while Quincey fumbled out her car keys. John waited, hands in pockets, lifting his head up into the snow, closing his eyes briefly to let the flakes fall on his eyelids.

"Looks like it's going to be a white Christmas," Quincey said, and John opened his eyes, looking back at her, his expression thoughtful.

"Maybe not," he murmured. "Maybe it's time I went south of the border. Maybe it's time I found out where I really come from. The odds are against my ever finding my real mother, even if she's still alive—but perhaps I can help. Perhaps I can help someone else's mother. I have a debt."

Quincey stood on tiptoe, and kissed him on the cheek. "Send me a postcard," she said.

"What about you? Christmas with the kids?"

Quincey turned her head, staring into the falling snow, her eyes soft and distant.

"Of course," she said. "I've packages stashed in the back of every closet in the house. But afterwards…"

She tailed off and stood there, keys in hand, arms at her sides, looking as though she were looking down a tunnel of days into the future. And a small smile was playing around the corners of her mouth.

"Afterwards?" John prompted, curious.

"I might go south, too," Quincey said. "Arizona."

"What's in Arizona?"

"I think… there's a woman I need to see about a poetry book."

"A poetry book?" John echoed, puzzled.

"Yes—I seem to have been looking for it for ages, and there's this bookshop…"

John waited, but she didn't seem inclined to offer any further information. He didn't push it. Instead, he just smiled, leaned over to steady her as she stepped down off the curb, and then watched her make her careful way around the front of the car until she reached the driver's door and climbed inside. The engine complained a little as she turned the key, but caught; the car came alive, the lights flickered on, and John could not see her face clearly any more. He saw her raise her hand in a gesture of farewell, a silhouette against the snow, as she drove away into the night.

Friday, 22 December 2012

3:00 AM

Olivia woke with a start and lay with her eyes open, listening, wondering what had awakened her. Her dreams had shredded at the sudden awakening and she couldn't remember any details other than a conviction that they had been as elaborate and complex and coherent as she could ever remember them having been before.

The apartment was quiet, and dark except for the bedside clock beside her that showed it to be 3:01 AM and the jewel-toned fractured glow of the butterfly night light in the corridor outside the bedroom. Not even the cat seemed to be stirring—Olivia knew the soft patter of those padded paws on the wooden floors, and that had not been the thing that had woken her.

No. It was the silence.

It was a moment of silence that was rare in the city.

That was *impossible* in the city.

There were always voices somewhere. Traffic noises. Sirens. The sound of car doors opening of slamming, the sound of remote entry keys chirping, the sound of ignored car alarms patiently whooping away into the night. But there was nothing of any of that—nothing—not a sound. She could clearly hear the ticking of a clock in the next room.

She glanced down at Jack, peacefully asleep on the other side of the bed, his hand tucked under his pillow in an endearingly child-like gesture. Then she flung the covers back and slipped out of bed, feeling around for her slippers with her bare feet and slipping them on against the cold, pulling a sweatshirt, left draped on the end of the bed, over the t-shirt she slept in, for warmth. The curtains were almost drawn; there was a chink in the middle where they met, just enough to allow a little bit of light to come into the room from the outside—but the window of the bedroom looked out over the back, into the alley between Olivia's building and the next brownstone.

She wanted the street.

The curtains in the living room had been left open, and the streetlights outside made the room quite bright. Olivia padded to the window, leaning on the frame, peering outside.

The first thing that she noticed was that it was snowing, and that it had been doing so, apparently, for some time. The street outside was empty and quiet; for a moment she thought she could see four people standing on the sidewalk, right outside of where the alley opened onto the street, but then she yawned mightily and wiped away the tears that the yawn brought to her eyes and when she looked again there were just empty shadows. Nobody there.

Except... except that she knew the faces of those shadows, she knew their names. Simon, Ellen, Quincey, John. The people she had... left behind, somehow. They were—or had been, in another lifetime—friends. They might even have looked up at her in the last moment before she had blinked, as though they had felt her eyes upon them, before they faded and vanished into the snow and the night.

"Goodbye," she whispered, alone in her room, sending the word out to the empty street... to nobody in particular, or, perhaps, to the people who needed to hear it. People far away, in space and in time. It just seemed to be necessary.

She turned away from the window and realized that the nifty little backpack she used as a handbag was on the table, tossed carelessly and half-open with its contents spilling out. It was a gesture of pure instinct to reach out and begin to stuff the things that had escaped back into the bag—but something more made her hesitate as she folded her fingers around her journal. The one she had been writing in that afternoon in the coffee shop.

She had written something in there today. Something that

was... important. Something that perhaps had to do with the silence outside. She had written down words that had silenced a city, perhaps for just a moment, but here she was, in the heart of that silence, listening to it, being a part of it.

She knew what they were—they practically danced in front of her eyes, like they had been written on some interior computer screen in her mind's eye, and the cursor blinked with patient monotony in the space after the last period. *Ah yes. I know the Spanish Gardens.*

She didn't know if she had the nerve to open the journal and read the hard copy—not right then, not in that silence—if she did, the silence might never go away again. But as she started to lay the journal back down on the table something else fell out of it from where it had been tucked between the pages and fluttered down to the floor at her feet.

She reached down for it, and came up with a playing card. There was something written on the back of it—she seemed to recall that there had been more written there before, something longer—she had not seen the man who had called himself Ariel writing it but she could clearly see him holding the pack of cards from which this one had been taken, and she remembered the moment in which Ariel had been gone and only the card remained on the table, and the message he had left for her. But all that she could see on the back of the card now were two words—in Ariel's florid handwriting that took up most of the space on the card.

Good Luck.

She frowned, turning the card over in her hands. It was hard to make out detail in the pale light that filtered through from the outside and she brought it closer to the window, squinting at it. There seemed to be two darker shapes—a pair of arms, maybe?—reaching out from the card, as though from the person who held it; arms that might have been trying to hold something back, or letting go in blessing. The vista that opened up between the two outstretched hands was a beach, with a little girl running barefoot across the wet sand at the boundary of land and sea. She had her head turned halfway around, looking back with a wide joyous grin and a coquettish glance that were born of pure delight, and a long trail of dark footprints stretched out behind her on the sand… except for a short stretch right up close to the front of the card where a wave had come in, and broken, and a frothy lace of foam lay across the sands as the water pulled back into the ocean. Beneath it, the little girl's tracks had been erased as though they had never existed, the physical link that tied the child to the person observing from just this side of the card broken.

She heard a voice, as though from very far away.

It's all just a sandy beach, and you leave tracks behind you as you walk by the ocean's edge, but the tide always comes in and then there's a new reality to leave your mark in, after.

Ariel's voice, that afternoon, in the coffee shop.

You are a light…with a great gift comes a great responsibility…

"Honey…?"

Jack's arms came around her, holding her against him. "I woke, and you were gone—is everything all right?"

"Listen," she began, and then realized that the silence was already gone. Somewhere far away a siren wailed, dopplering away into the night. A couple passed by in the street below, arguing. A raised voice, a little further away down the street, as a car door slammed. A dolorous wail from an invisible cat, lost somewhere on the fire escape stairwells.

"Yes?" Jack said, cocking his head obediently, listening for something out of the ordinary, something strange, something that might have woken Olivia up.

She sighed.

"Nothing," she said. "It must have been the snow. It's a shame—there's too much light here, but even if there weren't—the snow—you couldn't have watched your stars winking out one by one as the world ended…"

"Well," Jack said practically, "I stubbed my toe against the bed as I got up, and you feel pretty solid, and unless René burned down the restaurant while he was putting together the Duck Surprise there's going to be work to go back to tomorrow. Come back to bed. It's *cold* out here."

Olivia's arms crept up and over Jack's. *Something* had changed for her, something had shifted, and she had a suspicion that she still had a lot of jumbled thoughts in her mind to sort out—but it could all wait until the morning. She felt vivid, and alive, and awake, as aware of herself and every detail in the world around her—the quality of the light that surrounded her, the warmth of Jack's skin against hers, the distant sounds of the city, the silence of the muffling snowfall—as she had ever been, but also, oddly, she felt clean and tired and ready to sleep.

She half-turned in his embrace, letting one of her hands slide down his arm until their fingers twined together, and reaching out for the journal on the table with the other.

The words were clear, vivid; the memory as bright and detailed as though she were looking through the walls of the world and seeing it all before her eyes.

Evening. You walk down a shuttered street; turn into a narrow alley you should never have known was there. At the end of the alley, there's a courtyard. And at the far end of the courtyard...there's Spanish Gardens.

It does not look very Spanish. It certainly doesn't look anything like a garden.

This place serves up your past like one of its fabled Irish Coffees— all froth and innocence on top and the dark, bittersweet mystery below—and watches you drain it, and then try to scry for your future in the patterns left behind on the walls of your glass.

You come here to laugh, to cry, to mourn, to celebrate—the place where only truth can be spoken, where you are forced to look all your most cherished illusions in the eye and watch them look down first and slink away, like ghosts into the shadows, leaving only the shining core of your own true self behind.

This is where you come to learn who and what you were, and are, and may become. You leave the ivied and hallowed walls of the edifices of higher education, and your textbooks, and your professors, and your exams; you come here for the love and the laughter and the understanding. You abandon education, and come seeking wisdom.

Everyone has a place like this, a stop along the way on their life's journey. Yours might be called Café Adagio, or Mama Rosa's, or Ming's Dim Sum—the name and the style and the ambience may be quite different—but if you start to tell me about that place it will not take me long to sigh, and smile, and murmur,"Ah, yes. I know the Spanish Gardens".

It was not the thing she had written that afternoon in the coffee shop. It was not the same thing she had written before, in earlier incarnations. In fact, it suddenly occurred to Olivia that she had been writing this same essay over and over again, changing it a little bit at a time, honing it over the years until she reached this particular distillation of it, clear as truth, potent as love.

"Have I ever," she murmured, folding her arm so that the journal was cradled against her breast, "told you about Spanish Gardens?"

"Some," Jack said, mystified, but willing to play along. "The café you used to go to when you were a student, yes? Why?"

"Come back to bed," Olivia said. "There's something here I want to read to you."

It had to be passed on. The memory. The recognition. Perhaps the gift that Ariel had spoken of, the responsibility, was no more than that—to keep it alive, the memory of a place where magic walked and a different world was a step and a breath away for those who dared to reach for it. And something inside her knew, despite Ariel's words, that this was something that she would not, could not, forget. This was the pivot around which the world turned. This was the place where all secrets returned, and stayed, and knew the perfect truth of themselves. This was the memory that she had been given like a treasure, the memory that she was going to spend her life nurturing and guarding and passing out to those who looked like they needed to find their way there. Ariel had called himself the Messenger—well, so was she, in her own way. Everybody needed to visit a place like Spanish Gardens in their lifetime, and Olivia Halloran would hold the candle that would light their path.

The world had ended. A certain world, at least, had ended.

A new world was about to begin.

As it did, after all, every day.

About the Author

Alma Alexander's life so far has prepared her very well for her chosen career. She was born in a country which no longer exists on the maps, has lived and worked in seven countries on four continents (and in cyberspace!), has climbed mountains, dived in coral reefs, flown small planes, swum with dolphins, touched two-thousand-year-old tiles in a gate out of Babylon. She is a novelist, anthologist and short story writer who currently shares her life between the Pacific Northwest of the USA (where she lives with her husband and two cats) and the wonderful fantasy worlds of her own imagination. You can find out more about Alma on her website (www.AlmaAlexander.org), her Facebook page (https://www.facebook.com/AuthorAlmaAlexander/) or on Twitter (https://twitter.com/AlmaAlexander). You can also support her on Patreon (https://www.patreon.com/AlmaAlexander)

Curious about other Crossroad Press books?
Stop by our site:
http://store.crossroadpress.com
We offer quality writing
in digital, audio, and print formats.

Enter the code FIRSTBOOK
to get 20% off your first order from our store!
Stop by today!